"If you love Elin Hilderbrand novels and Mackinac Island, you'll love *When the Season Ends*. The story and characters are compelling, and you'll find yourself caring for each one. When the story—and the season—ended, I wanted more!"
—Tamara Tomac, manager, Island Bookstore, Mackinac Island

"Through crystal clear prose sprinkled with quietly sharp observations about modern womanhood, Windahl tells an instantly relatable story, lovingly set on the shores of Mackinac Island's lush blue water. I loved discovering Olivia's journey right alongside her."
—Jeff Graham, award-winning writer/director of *Always, Lola*

"*When the Season Ends* touches on so many thoughts, feelings, and situations that arise as mothers move into new stages of life. The characters may be fictional, but the landscape is as real as it gets."
—Jodi Bird, literary destination influencer, Bountiful Blessings Travel

"Mackinac Island comes to life in a vivid novel that draws us in and takes us on a journey through a season that you don't want to miss. Stacy has given us a splendid story with complex characters and a strong sense of place. *When the Season Ends* is a read that is both captivating and as inviting as a warm summer's day!"
—Jody Jean Dreyer, 30-year Disney veteran and former senior corporate staff member, author of *Beyond the Castle, A Guide to Discovering Your Happily Ever After*

"A wonderful, engaging story about a woman finding her way back to herself, set against the backdrop of beautiful Mackinac Island. I was deeply connected to the main character and am hoping for another book to find out what happens next! If you love Mackinac Island and just a good story, I highly recommend!"
—Sharon Hegarty, Mackinac Island summer resident

When the Season Ends

A Mackinac Island Novel

STACY WINDAHL

M·P·P
www.MissionPointPress.com

Mission Point Press

Published by Mission Point Press
www.MissionPointPress.com

Cover illustration: Noel Skiba
Book design: Deirdre Wait

Hardcover ISBN 13: 978-1-965278-68-0
Paperback ISBN 13: 978-1-965278-69-7

LCCN: Available upon request.

Printed in the United States of America

For Jeff

Whatever a house is to the heart and body of man—
refuge, comfort, luxury—
surely it is as much or more to the spirit.
Think how often our dreams take place inside
the houses of our imaginations!
—Mary Oliver

Chapter 1

"Where are we?" Luke raised his seatback, resuming the copilot position. Shaking off a ninety-minute nap, he took a look at their surroundings. "We're definitely nowhere."

"Actually," his mom, Olivia, replied, "we're thirty miles from the biggest jerky outlet this side of Canada. Beef jerky, venison jerky, turkey jerky. Who needs cookies when you can gnaw on jerky?"

"Where are those cookies anyway? I'm starving." Luke turned and rooted through the cooler in the back seat. "Are we almost there?"

"The GPS says we should arrive at 5:51. Nine minutes early. Dad would approve."

By the time Olivia and Luke neared the gates of Lake Michindoah they'd traveled 430 miles in eight hours. They'd dropped $12.25 in tolls and another $31 in four fast food emporiums. (Sea salt on fries? Pure genius.) They'd cruised south, to start, by the sophisticated Chicago skyline; east, past the shuttered mills of Gary, Indiana; and then north by the unpretentious (deservedly so) Paw Paw Lake, Michigan. They'd driven by everything that was familiar in the city they called home into unknown places that were less urbane and far more interesting. By the time their SUV had left Gaylord and wandered north to the camp, Olivia wondered how she could turn her car around and go back home to the relic of a life that had promised permanence—or at least, routine. Better to wander Michigan than to be lost in the empty space that used to be the hub of their interconnected lives. They passed by a sign that read Mackinaw City – 50 Miles.

"Hey, Dad just texted me. Wants to know where we are."

"Tell him we're right where we're supposed to be. Early even. Tell him I'll call him tonight, okay?"

"K. I just sent it. I'm not getting great reception here. One bar."

"Hmm. We may have to stay in touch the old-fashioned way—maybe a pay phone for you." As soon as she'd said the words, Olivia knew Luke didn't know what a pay phone was. His face said as much. She continued, "I wonder when we'll be able to talk? What do you think?"

"I dunno. It's going to be crazy. Like eighteen-hour days. And we take campers' phones so I won't have mine much and not in front of them. Maybe I should call *you*, or maybe I'll text. Is that okay?"

"Oh sure. No worries. I'll be excited to hear your news whenever you can share it." Luke's phone broke out in song: *"Who can it be now?"*

"It's Dad." Luke brought the phone to his ear.

"Hey… yup… good… soon… fine… yeah… K… me too… will do… bye." Luke finished his conversation and relayed to Olivia that Nate had just arrived at his hotel in Montreal. He was going for a run and would unpack later. "He said to tell you not to wait up to talk to him. He's got some sort of late dinner thing. He'll call you tomorrow."

"Right. I'm glad he's there safe and sound."

"Oh yeah. He said he loves you and that London says hi."

"You mean Landon?"

"Yeah her. The lady with the boots and the hair. Her, right? I liked her. She smelled good."

"Yeah, Luke, her." She smelled good. Really? Even you?

Maybe she wouldn't go back so soon. Not tonight anyway. What was the hurry? She'd packed a small overnight bag—and her laptop— just the essentials until she figured out a plan. No one would be any the wiser. She'd discovered—to her surprise (or was it relief?)—that lying about her summer plans was easy. Easy because she wasn't lying. Not technically. She was untruthful, never. But vague? Almost entirely. And no one seemed to care. For all her adult life, Olivia had shared openly about her current activities and future plans. She'd answered every question—via text, email, or face-to-face in detail. Full-color, 3D responses. She assumed that's what people wanted. Turns out, people are satisfied with gray scale. No high-res, dimensional answers required.

To Nate who'd asked if she'd return to Lake Ellyn immediately or if she'd spend a little time at her sister's first, she answered, "Not sure."

"That sounds good," was his reply. "Are we out of ketchup or is there more in the pantry?"

To Luke who'd asked if she'd be going to Montreal with Dad, she answered, "Eventually." Satisfied, he asked if she had packed him some of that no-itch cream to rub on bug bites.

Olivia had told her friends Abby and Nina she'd be in Montreal for the summer but that she might also spend some time in Detroit, at Ceci's. (Which could have been and still might be true. And Nate thought it was a definite possibility.) Ceci asked if she'd be celebrating the Fourth in Montreal. "Ceece, you know Montreal's in Canada, right? They don't celebrate our Independence Day."

"I *knew* that. Duh." No further questioning.

Were they alive, her parents might have been the only people who would care where she'd be on July Fourth or if she'd be home this night or any other by midnight. "Nothing good happens after midnight," her dad used to say. But really, who's watching the clock now?

If only Olivia had known sooner that ambiguity fits the bill nine out of ten times, making out-and-out prevarication unnecessary. All the freedom. None of the guilt. Well, less of the guilt. But technically, she hadn't lied to anyone.

"Luke, you know that sign we passed a while back, the one to Mackinaw City?"

"What about it?"

"Well, the camp is close to Mackinac Island. You know, where I worked after college, the summer I graduated. No cars allowed. Just horses, bikes, and fudge. And tourists. I can't believe I've never taken you or Dad. Just too long a drive I guess, and so…" Olivia left her sentence and Luke hanging while she conjured memories of the island and that summer from her past.

"Mom. Mom!! Right turn. Back there. You missed it. Didn't you see the sign?" Luke pointed out a small sign now in the rearview mirror that he said directed them to Chippewa Road and Lake Michindoah.

"That's hardly a sign. More like a hint." Olivia turned their car around in the gravel driveway of a property marked by a wood sign, carved to read: Piechota's Paradise. Beware of Dog. Back again at the other sign they took the hint and turned left, climbing a hill for the next four miles. Olivia flipped on the SUV's four-wheel drive, usually a decorative option considering Chicago's flat terrain. She sat up straight in her seat and put a death grip on the steering wheel. They crept along the pitted road in the shade of a tree canopy that became more like a tunnel with every mile.

Olivia exhaled, "This is treacherous. I hope you won't be out on this road much."

"I won't have a car. Remember?"

"Good. As it should be. How do they get buses through here without shearing branches off trees?" But just ahead, the tree canopy lifted and their view expanded to a panorama of Lake Michindoah below them. This side of the lake, in the center, was a sprawling building with a large front porch. Either side of it were smaller variations on the theme. The buildings were evenly spaced off the center and circled the lake like a beaded necklace. Olivia slowed the car to a stop.

"The photos don't do it justice, Luke. It's breathtaking. Pristine. Where's the ropes course?" Luke would be responsible for getting campers safely through an obstacle course constructed of cables, rope bridges, wooden platforms, and a zip line suspended twenty feet above a pine needle carpet.

"It's on the other side of the lake. Hard to see it from here. I'll show you before you leave. But the zip line tower is over there, behind us."

"So cool. Let's go. Let's get you started on this summer of adventure."

"Yup. You'll be all right, Mom. Right?" He studied her profile for a moment and just as quickly returned his gaze to the camp below them.

"If you mean will I make a scene saying goodbye, get all teary-eyed and embarrass you in front of the other staff as though we've never done this before? If you mean would I do that?" Olivia took her foot off the brake to let the car roll down the hill toward camp. "I might. I just might."

"Yeah. I wanted to be prepared."

She knew he didn't mind too much. His freshman year at Michigan State, after unpacking his belongings into an eight-by-ten room and transforming the cinder block cell into a black and taupe, carpeted, electronically equipped, ambient-lighted, nearly comfortable cinder block suite, she'd held it together for his sake. When they'd finished with the room and Nate had gone to pull the car around, she locked Luke in a final hug and silently pleaded for his safety and happiness. Then she pressed his shoulders away from hers. Looking him in the eye she said, "You are going to be great. I love you like crazy."

"And you'll be great too, right?" And she was—for about an hour until her phone buzzed signaling a text message. It was from Luke. Doing okay, Bud?

Chapter 2

It was seven-thirty before Olivia was back in the car and safely on two-wheel drive surfaces again. She'd resigned herself to returning home to Lake Ellyn by way of her sister's. She'd surprise Ceci with her arrival and then face the music. "No, I'm not going to Montreal with Nate. It wasn't such a great idea after all. Long hours. I'd be on my own. He'd worry. Blah. Better for me to be at home. Blah. Blah. So here I am. A summer to myself? Sleeping in? Every day, my agenda only? Come on. That's a dream." How'd that sound? She recited the lines one more time. Hearing the story in her voice, hearing it break with emotion, she recognized she needed to work on the delivery. *I'll have it down by the time I get to Detroit.*

She could have stayed a night or two at Luke's camp. The camp manager had invited her to stay in the adult guest lodge, but she declined. It was better for Luke to jump into the awaiting adventure of Lake Michindoah without feeling responsible for his mom watching him from the shore. His sense of responsibility for her was too great anyway. Too much so for a twenty-year-old. That was her fault. Or was it his nature? Hard to say.

She drove on awhile and let her mind revisit that afternoon when Luke was six. Just a little guy, he carried an overdeveloped sense of responsibility like a tool in the backpack he toted from home to daycare, to school, back to daycare, and home again at the end of the day. The day she didn't arrive to pick him up at daycare and Aunt Ceci showed up instead was the start of it. Days later, they gave him the sparest details when he asked where they had been, why they hadn't told him they were going, and why his little sister wasn't coming after all. They said something had gone wrong, something no one expected, that everyone would be fine and there'd be another sister or brother one day. That seemed to satisfy him. He was just a kid, and even if he had been sixteen, Olivia couldn't have said more anyway. The shock and pain of her loss left her unable to speak of it. And Nate? Nate wouldn't give anything away. Nate never opened those doors. Everything was fine. It was always fine.

And so it was, even then. Everything was fine in their house. Fine. Luke believed it. He said he liked being home with her, instead of at daycare. He was happy she quit her job. That's when they started calling each other "Bud."

"Hey Bud, you okay? Hungry?" she'd call into the family room.

Luke would yell back, "Yeah, Bud. Can I have something to eat?"

They'd established a comfortable routine. He was out the door to the bus stop at the end of the driveway by eight. He was through the door again by three-thirty. Their new life was fine. Right? Bud?

So fuzzy, her recollection of those early days after it happened. Those weeks. Olivia scanned her memory for markers to anchor her thoughts. She remembered getting Luke out the door every morning and meeting him again in the afternoon, but little else. She slept a lot during that time. Showering was the first and only item on her to-do list back then. She couldn't recall much about that one day in particular, what made it different. To this day, she didn't know how many hours she'd been there, on the floor in the empty room that would have been Catherine's, but she remembered with absolute clarity Luke crouched beside her, his hand patting her back. "Bud, don't cry. Don't cry." He laid down beside her, trying to look her in the eyes. "I think we need Dad, don't you?" She could hear him even now. She could feel his small cupped hand tapping her back. "Bud, you're fine. Right? Bud? Please stop crying." Olivia shook her head to blur the sharp lines of that memory, wishing it would dissolve like an Etch A Sketch drawing.

And now what? What was she to do? She'd given up her career after the heartache of her miscarriage. She had thought Nate wanted that. Maybe it was her penance. Maybe it made life easier for him. It worked for her—for the most part. Now, though, with Luke gone and Nate off to conquer the merger, was she supposed to stay home, cut the grass, and water the lawn? Cancel the lawn service? Really? Like she had nothing better to do?

Did she? Have something better to do? Get a part-time job? Had he really said that? To her? *Damn it, Nate. I've given all that I am to you and our son and now I'm just supposed to land a part-time job. That's your answer?*

But what else would she do? Oh Ceci would tell her. No doubt. She'd say, "What the hell do you want to do? Just you. You don't take orders from anyone, Liv, not even my brother-in-law. Love him, though. But, Liv, you have to decide. What is it you want? Then go get it, Girl. Go get it."

I need a sign, she thought. Not a burning bush, or a signal flare. Just a wave. A hint.

A blowing horn from a passing truck startled her. She inhaled sharply, fully alert now, and looked around her. Oh no. Where was she? She really was lost. In Michigan. There was no sign to tell her where she was going, but the speedometer showed she was getting there fast. Olivia lifted her foot off the gas pedal to focus on the highway sign coming into view. "Ah good. Only 10 miles to Onaway. Wherever that is." Because she'd not set her destination on her navigation system before leaving Lake Michindoah, her know-it-all guide was mute. Olivia looked at the car's compass and noticed the car's shadow on the road in front of her. *Uh oh. I'm heading east. I missed the turn to I-75.*

She smacked the steering wheel with her right hand. She smacked it again. "Shit, shit, and double shit." Olivia was a closet cusser, and not an especially good one. The f-word was off-limits. She took shallow satisfaction in the fact that no one had ever heard her utter the word. But shit? That rolled off the tongue nicely. "Shit. Where the hell am I?"

(Hell seemed a reasonable choice too.) Olivia pulled off at the first gas station to consider her whereabouts and her next move. This called for a Coke. "Clearly, I've got to wake up."

Once inside the station building, she got a Coke bottle out of the refrigerator case and took it to the counter. She waited. She looked around and up to discover six glass eyes of antlered bucks watching her from the wall behind the counter. Bet there's a security camera in one of those stuffed heads. Or maybe an air freshener dispenser, eau deer. She smiled at her joke, sorry there was no one to share it with. At the same time, she forgave herself for getting lost.

Eventually a man came through the door from the service bays. On his way toward the counter, shuffling, he stopped in the aisle to replace a few packages of Funyuns that had fallen from the shelf. As he neared, Olivia could make out the name "Mitchell" embroidered over the breast pocket of the well-worn, pinstripe shirt. Mitchell appeared to be the owner/mechanic/stockboy/cashier. And deer hunter.

"Evening," Olivia said as he assumed his position at the register. "I was wondering if you could tell me where I am exactly. I somehow missed my turnoff to I-75. Am I far from it?"

"So you're not planning on staying here?" He grinned, revealing a couple of gold teeth in the corners of his smile.

"Well, no. I hadn't planned on it."

"Yup, that's the thing about our town. No one stays. Most folks are just Onaway somewhere else." He winked at her, inviting her to appreciate his pun.

Olivia tilted her head and wrinkled her nose, "Onaway— somewhere… oh, Onaway, Michigan. I get it." She laughed. "I like that. Really." Mitchell nodded, seeming pleased with himself.

She looked down at the map of Michigan preserved under the countertop glass. "So if I were 'Onaway'," she winked at him, "to Detroit, which way would I go?"

Mitchell pulled a rag out of his back pocket, moved the sweating pop bottle, and wiped the grime and water ring off the glass. With a grubby finger, he put a smudge over Onaway and traced the way west back to I-75. "Take you less than an hour to get to Mackinaw City going that way." His finger retraced that route and he poked Onaway again and then sketched an eastern route to I-23. "Now, it'll take you about an hour and ten to get to Mackinaw City this route, but you travel by Lake Huron the whole way. It's a real nice drive."

"Okay. Great. But I'm not going to Mackinaw City. I'd like to go to Detroit." She looked him in the eyes. "How would I get there?"

Now it was his turn to observe her, tilt his head, and wrinkle his nose. "Well, I could tell you how to get to Detroit all right, but the real question is," he paused, "why do you want to?"

She shrugged her shoulders. "My sister lives there."

"Well, young lady, from here you're about four hours to Detroit. But as you stand in front of me and these witnesses," he angled his head toward the taxidermy behind him, "you are smack dab in the middle of God's country."

He looked again at the map and then at Olivia. "You'd like Mackinaw City. All the tourists do. Most go on and visit Mackinac Island. You know—fudge, what-not shops, horses, and the like." Mitchell drew his right hand over his mouth and stubbled chin. He slowly rubbed his neck. "Darnedest thing. There's a state highway circling that island, but no cars. Never have been allowed. Heard of it?"

"Oh. I know it—really well. I worked there for a season. Stayed on straight through October. I've never been back."

"Never been back? That's a real shame." Mitchell shook his head in a silent tsk, tsk. "Sounds like you're 'Onaway' to Mackinac Island." He wiped the rag over the glass-topped map again. He pointed to I-75. "You're fifteen miles from the interstate. I suggest you head north and catch the last ferry. You don't want to go to Detroit."

That much decided, Mitchell stuffed the dirty rag back into his pocket and walked around the counter toward the service bays. Without turning his head he said, "Coke's on me. Welcome back to God's country. Drive safe now."

So this is my sign? My burning bush? A guy, a sweet one, with grease-stained fingers telling me to go to Mackinac Island? This is all I get? And yet, she figured, it wasn't a terrible idea. What could it hurt? Maybe the answer was there. With no other options seeming any better, she spent the next hour following Mitchell's recommended route, trying to rationalize how this seemed a good idea. It couldn't be. On the other hand. Really, this was Nate's doing. It started that morning with her mom's journal, and the message her mom had penned. The one Nate had dismissed as nonsense. It got worse in the days that followed.

"Listen to this, Nate." Olivia took a sip of coffee and leaned against the sink, waiting for him to acknowledge her. "Nate? Hel—lo?"

"Sorry, are you talking to me?" he asked without looking up from his phone.

She looked around. "Yup. Just you and me here. So, yeah. I was. Talking to you." She tossed the towel that had been over her shoulder at Nate. "Listen to this. Really." Nate caught the towel and slipped his phone in his pocket. He moved toward Olivia as she opened the small, spiral-bound notebook. The pages made a noise as she unstuck the one from the others.

"I found this in a box of Mom's stuff. She was only thirty-six. It says: 'My greatest frustration is a feeling that time is short and there's something I must do, but I don't know what it is.' Then she writes a paragraph about us going to the Ice Follies at the arena. She finishes with 'Maybe tomorrow?' and that's it. Nothing more. It ends there." She raised her head and her eyebrows.

"So what's the problem?" He handed her the towel and dropped his mug in the sink.

"Don't you find that odd? Or a little sad?"

"Nope. Sounds to me like she figured out what she was supposed to do and she did it for the next forty years. Either that, or she wrote it after too much candy." Olivia smiled at that.

When Luke was about ten, he had told them a story he'd heard at school. Some boy's parents had hosted a party and later in the night "when this kid was just going downstairs to get something to eat," a couple climbed onto the kitchen island and started dancing. They finished the performance by mooning the onlookers. The hosts' son shared every detail at the lunch table that Monday. Luke recounted the story. Thoroughly disgusted he added, "and all he wanted was more buffalo chicken dip."

Nate had seen this as a teachable moment. Hardly a surprise. "Luke, what do you suppose would make adults do something like that?" Alcohol, obviously.

"I know," Luke had nodded solemnly. "Too much candy." She smiled remembering.

"Okay, gotta go." Nate reached for Olivia's shoulders and skimmed her lips with a kiss. When he let go, she noticed something out of place.

"Hey, where's your ring. Have you lost it?"

"No. But I have lost some more weight. Enough that I can work it off my finger again. Finally. I kind of panicked when I couldn't get the thing off. Can you get it resized? Whenever." He turned for the back door.

"Well, sure. But I'll need the ring and you, or your finger, for that."

"No big deal. I won't need it in Montreal. See you tonight!"

No big deal? You won't need it? she thought.

As the back door slammed, the phone rang. It could only be her sister Cecilia this early in the morning. Ceci would think their mom's journal entry was odd, too, but for completely different reasons. She'd marvel that Jane had written anything at all. Their mom was more about the spoken word. Usually a listener, which had won her many friends, and a tight-lipped confidante, which kept them. But Jane was also prone to stir the pot once she'd had a drink or three. She loved to debate, or maybe she savored the emotions that a good argument surfaced. But, again, that was only after hours. Like Nate, Ceci would think the journal was candy talk.

"Liv. Is this a good time?"

"Yeah, Nate just left. It's his last week in the office before he heads to Montreal."

"Right. Remind me to ask you about that." She clearly had more important items on her agenda. "So did you hear about that chimp? Trevor?"

"Huh?" It was either a joke or another out-there commentary on life that made Ceci endearing and outrageous. A great dinner party guest, especially so if you were a little nervous about guest chemistry. Ceci could warm up a crowd and have them eating out of her hand in minutes. Dinners always seemed more exotic when Ceci was at the table, even if she made Nate's palms sweat.

"So this chimp, or really the chimp's owner, dressed him in pullover sweaters and had wine with him at dinner every night. She bathed with him, Liv, which makes no sense, because chimps are bug pickers as far as I know, not fond of bubble baths. Anyway, this chimp, Trevor, turned on his owner. She changed her hair style and he went bananas."

"Funny, Ceece."

"No, no. Bad pun not intended. Wish I'd meant it. He went ape. Shit. Sorry. I mean, he lost it. He tore her apart. The woman's alive, but barely. And the chimp, well, he'll be euthanized for sure."

"Weird. And your point is…?"

"The point is… the chimp is going to die because some stupid woman tried to make him into something he's not. That he'd never be. Come on. Who has cocktails with primates? Well, besides me. On occasion. But they were all blind dates. Technically, I'm not responsible. Why do we do that?"

"Blind dates, or drinking wine with monkeys?" Olivia asked.

"So it's your turn to be funny? I'm serious. Isn't this just another case of a woman trying to force a man to be something he's not? Why do we do that? I mean, really."

"I don't know. Maybe because we expect the men we love to be capable of great things?"

"Oh geez, there you go. You're such an optimist."

"Or," Olivia continued, "maybe we think if we give it enough time, eventually, every chimp will become a prince."

"Hmm…" Ceci paused at this. "Darwinism? From you? So men are actually chimps and not pigs? That's a bridge too far for me, Liv."

Olivia's sister had been quick to conclude that most of her dates, and therefore men in general, were pigs, or tended that way. But she was willing to accept dinner invitations from men—pigs—chimps, whatever, in the event she was wrong. She did seem to love Nate, though. She just found him a little uptight, but perfect for her "church-lady" sister.

"Seriously. This is a legitimate thought and possibly profound, even if it is mine. You can't turn a chimp into a man. So back to Montreal. When are you going?"

Ceci was referring to Nate's assignment in Montreal. SpiraVecta Bio, where he'd spent his twenty-five-year career, had purchased a pharmaceutical competitor headquartered in Canada. Nate had been appointed to lead the US integration team. The appointment was a feather in his cap and a weight on his shoulders since so much was at stake. Hundreds, possibly thousands of jobs were on the line. Including his.

"Actually, I've been working out the details. I think I can swing it. With Luke working at camp all summer and if I drop some other commitments, I might be free to go—or find myself alone all summer if I stay here."

"So, what's the living situation? Not some cheap extended-stay hotel is it? If I were you, I'd go online right now and land a great condo in the city. Check the apps. It'd be easy. You could do your thing, Liv. Markets during the day, fabulous gourmet dinners at night. By candlelight. Wine. A café table with water views." Disappointed by love thus far, Ceci could still imagine romance as she'd like it to be.

"Well, actually, Ceece, I was thinking I might even…"

"Oh definitely. You know if you could get the appropriate work permit you could maybe get a side hustle in some fabulous gallery or home décor shop. You could finally get back in there, Liv. Really, you deserve it after all these years. I forgot. Do you speak any French?"

"*Un peu,*" said Olivia.

"In what? So, you take a class or two. I hear it's like Canada's Paris—which I think is a good thing. Could be cold, but still, lucky you."

Olivia agreed with most of what Ceci suggested. "I think it could be fun for me and I could be a sounding board for Nate at night. You know, a voice of encouragement," she reasoned. She knew this summer could be a carefree one for her and, likely, a worry for Nate. But her being there might be some measure of support and comfort. Hopefully. Maybe. And being away with Nate could ease some of the uncertainty she had about her next chapter, her purpose. And theirs as a couple. Maybe they could discover that together.

"Absolutely. And if it doesn't work out, come stay with me. I've always said what I need is a good wife. They're more useful than husbands. Uh-oh. Got to go." Click.

Olivia had learned not to worry when Ceci signed off abruptly. Usually it meant she'd seen a police car in her rearview mirror, or dropped her mascara wand. Ceci applied her makeup only when she was buckled in her car. "The lighting is so much better in my Audi," she'd say. "Besides, that's where I keep my makeup."

Olivia took the phone from her ear, realizing she hadn't told Ceci about the journal she'd found in the box of their mother's belongings. *Maybe it's just as well*, she thought. *Maybe the message was for me.*

Chapter 3

Later that afternoon, Nate's request came to Olivia by text.

Nate: Landon McCall coming to town—marketing integration team lead. From Birmingham office. I should host dinner. Take us out? Or wow with a dinner? Don't feel overrated.

Olivia: U mean obligated? Can do. tenderloin, rosemary potatoes, asparagus, salad? Cobbler? Just one? Home?? 6:30ish? XO

Nate: Yup. Just Landon. Thx! Will pick up wine on way.

Hours later, Luke blew through the dining room and into the kitchen, basketball in one hand, size eleven high-tops in the other. "Mom, what's going on? Why's everything all… shiny? I hope you're not making some really big dinner, cause we just got ten guys to play and they're counting on me. Are you?"

"Counting on you?" asked Olivia. "No. But I *do* have a place for you at the table. And it is shiny, thank you for noticing, because your dad is bringing a new coworker home to dinner—Landon McCall. You might be bored by the business talk anyway."

"Yeah. Landon? What kind of name is that?" Luke grabbed a handful of blueberries from the colander before Olivia could move it out of the force field of his stomach.

"An important one. So, when you come home, please wash the court off your hands and introduce yourself to Mr. McCall, okay?"

"Oh, yeah sure. Home by eight. Mom?"

"Yes?"

"Mom, in case we go to Chipotle, could I have five bucks? I'm down to, like, four."

"Okay. I have a fabulous dinner nearly ready and you're going to Chipotle. Again. Nice," she sighed. Her aggravation was short of believable. "Take a ten from my wallet." Luke had already left the kitchen for the mudroom, and she figured his hands were already on her purse expecting the response he got.

"Mom?"

"Luke! I'm busy here securing your dad's future. If I poison this Landon guy, it's over for us."

Luke stuck his head around the corner and she saw his face in her peripheral vision. Messy brown hair, straight but for the last inch or so that curled over his ears and waved across his forehead, framing his hazel eyes.

"Love you, Bud." He said it in that voice. He loved her. Maybe more, he loved playing her.

Olivia heard Nate pull into the garage at six-thirty. Of course. When they'd dated, he'd tell her to be ready *between* seven-thirty. And he would arrive not a minute before or after seven-thirty. The doorbell chimed. Olivia figured Nate hadn't wanted their guest to enter through the mudroom. He must have dropped Landon at the walk to the front door.

Olivia glanced at her reflection in the microwave door. She pulled the towel off her shoulder and smoothed her hair. She stepped back and saw a smoky silhouette of a woman who, although in her forties, looked younger. In her V-neck cashmere sweater and simple necklace, she looked appropriate. "Hmm..." She was neither satisfied nor distraught. Tasteful if unremarkable. "Good enough," she said as she rushed to the foyer.

Olivia opened the oak door to greet Mr. Landon McCall. Instead, she found herself greeting a symphony of texture, scent, and color.

"Well, hey. You must be Olivia. I'm Landon and I am *so thrilled* to meet you." Landon walked through the door, forcing Olivia back on her heels. She handed Olivia a burlap bag that clinked with the sound of glass bottles inside, and a gift bag stuffed with orchid tissue paper, all the while surveying the rooms beyond the foyer. Then Landon took the leather bag from her shoulder and set it at her feet. She slipped out of her camel cashmere coat and coordinating Burberry scarf and draped them over Olivia's already-laden arms where they released a spicy patchouli scent, the aroma of woodlands and money.

"So this is May in Chicagoland? I've learned never to come north without my coat or boots." Her gaze shifted from her surroundings back to Olivia. "What a darlin' home ya'll have." She looked again from left to right, taking in the dining and living rooms in one visual sweep. "Perfectly sweet—just like my grandparents'. Like a charm on a charm bracelet."

Arms overwhelmed and head spinning, Olivia held back a sneeze, then beheld her guest. Wavy amber hair in loose curls over her shoulders, slate eyes with heavy lashes, Chiclet teeth framed by glossy lips. Below Landon's silky hair and sophisticated black wrap dress were knee-high, leather boots with three-inch heels. She dwarfed Olivia's five-foot-five frame and her confidence simultaneously.

"Ah," said Nate as he walked from the kitchen through the dining room and into the foyer. "You've met."

"Well, not officially. Landon, I'm Olivia. So glad you could join us."

"Well, it is such a pleasure, Olivia. You're just as Nathan described you."

"Really. I hope I should be flattered." She turned her gaze to Nate.

"Oh, my—yes," Landon continued. "A bundle of hospitality and competence. The barefoot princess in the flesh."

Olivia stood motionless. What would be the appropriate response? Then she understood. "You mean the Barefoot *Contessa*, Ina Garten, of the cookbooks and cooking shows?"

"Well yes, that's exactly who I mean. The accomplished housewife."

"That's me all right. A standout in housewifery. Barefoot and everything. To think of the years I spent getting that useless master's degree." She smiled with more amusement than malice.

Looking relieved that Olivia's bundle of hospitality and competence was complemented by her usual good humor, Nate jumped in.

"Liv, we got a call on the way here. Something Landon and I should deal with now, if that won't interfere with dinner too much. Should take about twenty minutes."

"That's fine. Have a drink while I finish dinner. Landon?"

"Scotch on the rocks. Thank you ever so much, Olivia."

"And make that light on the rocks," added Nate. "And a glass of water. Right?" He looked to Landon for confirmation.

"You remembered." The Chiclet smile radiated in Nate's direction. "That would be heaven. Nathan, you are too good to me."

"Nathan," mimicking the name Olivia never used casually, "since you know how Landon prefers her cocktail, would you make it?" Olivia, looking more like a coat rack than a hostess, turned to their guest. "Landon," she gestured with a tilt of her head to the chairs either side of the fireplace, "make yourself comfortable in front of the fire. I'll send Nate out with your drink and some hors d'oeuvres."

"But first, *Nathan*," said Olivia, this time with conviction, "would you be a love and tend to Landon's things?" Olivia off-loaded the coat, the scarf, her hostess gift, and the bottles, bestowing each upon her husband's unsuspecting arms. With a smile, she turned for the kitchen.

By the time Nate slunk into the kitchen to pour the drinks, Olivia's annoyance had dissipated. Nearly.

"Glass of wine, Liv?"

"You remembered. You are *too good to me*, Nathan."

"Liv, come on. We had to share our favorite drink in one of those team-building, icebreaker activities that are a complete waste of time. So I remembered." He shrugged.

"Hmm," Olivia said over her shoulder to him as she tended the tenderloin in the oven below. "But you somehow forgot to tell me that Landon was a woman? Or did I miss that?" She stood, closed the oven door, and turned to look at him.

"I didn't say? Never thought of it, I suppose," he replied evenly while meting out the single-malt scotch they kept stocked to please his father but rarely drank themselves.

"Never thought of it? Six feet of sensuality? Thigh-high boots? And you never noticed?"

"Thigh-high? Really?" With drinks in hand, he moved toward Olivia. "With the barefoot princess waiting for me at home every night? Why would I notice?" Standing toe to toe with her, Nate deposited a kiss on Olivia's lips, looked into her eyes, and smiled. Then he turned, crossed the kitchen, and moved through the swinging door that separated the kitchen and dining room.

Olivia sighed. It was worth the wait. Between periods of preoccupation and his managerial default—the moments making her feel more like an employee than wife—the Nate she'd fallen for as a college sophomore would return. And with him, that smile. The one that traveled from his mouth to his eyes. It told her what she needed to know.

"I'll just pour my own glass of wine, thanks," she said to no one listening.

Chapter 4

Olivia had distracted herself the days that followed her introduction to Landon with her usual routine. Paperwork: cards, calls, a Bible study, grocery store, random errands for Luke. She did the laundry and paid the bills. She neatly handled the dozens of tasks that made it appear as though nothing had happened in the house that day, or any day. Every morning she prioritized the miscellany on a to-do list, not because she'd forget what had to be done, but so that she could look at the list and feel that she'd accomplished something. Anything. She added unexpected accomplishments just so she could cross them off the list.

On that Friday she met the girls for coffee. (And later crossed it off her list.) The girls were two of her friends from middle school: one who'd never left their hometown of Lake Ellyn, and one who'd moved back home to raise their family. Lake Ellyn was a postcard community: a train ride to the city for professionals, Lake Michigan close enough to look at every day, traditional homes, great schools, quaint retail. It was a place where people set roots. Your children's friends were your friends' children. It was idyllic in an incestuous sort of way.

"I'm so jealous," groaned Abby. "If only we'd have started or *stopped* having kids sooner, I'd be going on an adventure. Instead, I'll be refereeing a pack of hyper and hungry boys all summer. They are always hungry." She inhaled deeply and sighed to evoke some sympathy.

"Yeah, but look what that's done for you. We should all look so good," said Nina, referring to Abby's build. Her kids were responsible for her rock-hard runner's body. Abby ran every day at the crack of dawn "for a cause" she'd say. Because otherwise, she'd have a breakdown. Nina, her other friend, managed a small but growing catering business. Olivia had helped her when she could because everyone wanted to help Nina. She was pure sunshine.

"Wait, wait. Back up," Nina continued. "Before we get to your summer in Montreal, tell us more about Nate's annoyingly gorgeous work buddy. So what did this woman—Lorraine—say?"

"Landon," Olivia corrected Nina.

"So what did this woman say about your *talents*?"

"Hilarious. She asked what I'd be doing this summer and since I hadn't told Nate about my idea to join him in Montreal, I told her I was thinking of painting, which is true technically. As soon as I mentioned it, she launched into Nate." Olivia closed her eyes and took a breath to summon her best southern accent.

"'Nathan, you never mentioned that Olivia paints. Lawd, is there anything you *don't* do? My mama's a painter and I tried it once myself, but, really, you need *oodles* of time to create anything that's worth a public viewin' and certainly I don't have time like that, though I wish I did. I so envy your life, Olivia. I do. I could pass on the travel and the meetings and the pressure and spend my days in front of a canvas, just ponderin' the lake and the landscape. Mmm. Oh, I could.'" Olivia paused long enough for drama and an even more clichéd southern drawl, "'Really, some days, I could. Tell me, Olivia, what's your medium? Watahcolah, acrylics, pencil…?'"

"So I told her." She took another sip of coffee and then continued. "Latex. I work in Benjamin Moore almost exclusively. Eggshell for the walls. Satin Impervo on the trim."

Nina leaned closer and whispered, "You did?"

"I did. I wasn't rude. Not as rude as she was. Landon went on to say that painting the house would be a wonderful thing. Refreshing the interiors. Nothing like 'injecting a little life and color into a home with such potential.' She squirmed a little when I told her I was re-painting the entire first floor—in the same color. Ancient ivory. I was glad, really, that Nate heard her suggest that I paint with something other than the same, boring colors that have covered those walls for decades."

Nate was so stubborn about that house, the one they'd bought when his parents moved to Florida years ago. Though she'd wanted to bust through walls, paint those that remained in a brighter palette, and rid the rooms of their creaky, uncomfortable antiques, Nate resisted. Nate would not, could not, bring himself to change it. Not while his dad was still living. Was it fear? Maybe. His fear kept them in a monochromatic prison, circa 1976. Except, of course, in the kitchen. She had prevailed there and won him over with painted cabinets, open shelves, subway tile backsplashes, and marble countertops that had the appearance of times past with the functionality of a new century.

"Well, interior design aside," said Nina, "I'd watch that one. Nothing more attractive than a happily married man."

"She'll be trouble, Liv," echoed Abby.

"All right, you two. Landon's okay. I sort of like her. She doesn't threaten me. Much."

"Sure you like her. That's what makes chocolate-covered spiders like her so dangerous." Abby bit into a carb-loaded, cream cheese–topped bagel.

"Chocolate-covered spider?"

"Sweet on the outside, venomous within," she said through a mouthful of bagel. Nina and Olivia laughed.

"I'm not kidding, Liv." Abby continued. "You better get yourself to Montreal. If you don't, she'll have Nathan Nash in her web by Labor Day."

"Agh. Abby, you sound like my sister. Ceci has too little faith in Nate—*and* me, I might add. I'm the barefoot princess for God's sake." A high-pitched series of pings punctuated her comment. Abby grabbed her phone off the table.

"Uh-oh," she sighed, reading the message. "I gotta go. It's blood. I told Max not to bother me unless someone was unconscious or bleeding. Henry's bleeding. Not a lot." She stood and tossed her satchel over her sculpted shoulder to make her way home to her four boys. "Liv—call me before you head off on your adventure. Coffee one last time before you leave, okay?" Then she pointed two fingers to her own eyes and then turned them toward Olivia's. "And keep your eyes on that chocolate-covered spider."

Eventually, Olivia and Nina parted. Was it the caffeine or their concern that moved her to action? Tonight. *Friday night is perfect*, she thought. *I'll make a nice dinner—something grilled, baked potatoes, and a nice cab—then I'll paint the picture for him. Three, maybe the full five months together in Montreal. Luke would be off at camp and then back to college. This would be something new for us to share, to explore. The timing couldn't be better.*

Chapter 5

"But, Liv, you don't understand." Nate took a breath and loosened the knot of his tie like a prizefighter would pull off a robe before engaging. "I won't *have* any time. I'll be working twelve-hour days and Saturdays, too. I won't be around to explore with you. You'll be on your own for the most part and this home of ours that you're picturing will be a lousy corporate apartment or, worse, a hotel room. You can't be excited about that."

"I was, until you put it that way." Her perfectly planned dinner had gone perfectly awry. Nate arrived home late. Gotta take co-wkers from Canda for drnks, his text message read when she had discovered it at seven-thirty. By that time, she was already annoyed. And worried. Well, more annoyed than worried. Grilled salmon and a baked potato were waiting for him, but the cabernet and Olivia were just about exhausted.

"You know," her chin dropped to her chest, her hand sweeping the marble countertop to gather outlier crumbs. "I just hoped this could be an adventure for us. Just for us. You know, a new chapter in our lives."

"It'll be an adventure, but not the kind you're looking for. This is a big deal for me. New people, policies, regulators up my ass… an impossible deadline. I'm on the hook to get it done—without losing investor confidence or earnings. I can't be worried about entertaining you."

"Entertaining me?" She lifted her head and looked Nate in the eye. "Really? That must explain the raucous fun I've had all these years. You've been entertaining me. I'm sure I haven't thanked you properly for that."

"Liv, come on. What's with you?"

She took a deep breath and then let the cabernet spill her confession. "It's just—I don't know—so typical. Textbook. I know it, but I can't help it. I think I'm having a career crisis or something like that. Without Luke around here, who am I? What do I do? I don't really *do* anything."

"That's ridiculous. Of course you do. You do all kinds of vitally important things for this family and everyone else, too."

"Like what?" Nate paused a little too long. Olivia poured some wine into the empty goblet that had waited hours for him and slid it across the island. "Need this?" He took the goblet and gulped from it like it was a ballpark beer.

"You… you… make casseroles. And you remember birthdays." He sounded proud of himself. "That's right! And you buy Christmas gifts. So many. And, and…"

She flinched.

"Stop." Olivia raised her hand to make the litany stop. She shook her head. "Am I that lame? Really? My life is more pitiful than I thought. And that's pretty pitiful."

"Damn it, Liv. I'm sorry. So I can't list all the things you do all day. All I know is this—Luke and I can do everything we do because of you. You make it work. You make *us* work."

Her lips formed a smile that faded when she said, "But you'll work better in Montreal without me."

She wasn't expecting a response. And she didn't get one.

Nate's phone lit up where he'd placed it, between them. It was Landon. As Nate took the phone off the island and stepped toward the dining room, he glanced over his shoulder. "Maybe what you need is a part-time job."

Chapter 6

Olivia stayed in the kitchen cleaning up and processing their conversation. For more than an hour she fussed—restoring the cooktop to its unspoiled, reflective surface, grateful that she'd ignored the experts and had chosen electric over gas. She polished the stainless steel sink to a sparkle and set up the coffee maker for the morning. She loved her kitchen. It was her refuge and her workplace.

"So nice to meet you. I am Olivia Nash, Nate's wife. I'm a casserole-maker," she said to her reflection in the kitchen window. Sounded like an AA introduction. No wonder Nate didn't want her in Montreal. She turned to address the bar stools arranged around the enormous marble-topped island. The island was designed to allow Nate and Luke a place to hang out, munch on a few goodies, and keep her company while she cooked.

"Yes, that's right. My life's work is making casseroles. That is, when I am not buying birthday cards—oh, and gifts. I'm indispensable. Truly."

The bar stools were indifferent.

Years ago, before the kitchen was so smartly designed, Nate and Luke would trip her up, slow her down, and instinctively position themselves in front of the cabinet holding the sauté pan, spatula, or spice she needed next. They had waltzed around the kitchen like this for most of Luke's adolescence. Now that the stage was set for a flawless performance, the dancers had gone. In her wish to make it better, she had dismissed what had been perfect just as it was.

She willed them to their positions, waiting. Waiting. When no one appeared she said, "I think my work here is done."

She turned back to the sink and darkened the kitchen with a flip of a switch. That's when she noticed, or realized what she had failed to notice, at the Lowes' house. Dick and Betsy Lowe lived in the elegant Victorian next door, a sizable distance between them. Olivia strained to look into their brick patio. Every night around eleven the Lowes put their dog, Dexter, outside for his last break of the night. She hadn't seen Dex in days, maybe longer. Or Betsy, for that matter. How did she miss that? They hadn't mentioned that they'd be away.

In a moment, she planned her Saturday. After running a mental inventory of pantry and fridge, she settled on pasta e fagioli soup and her roasted butternut squash soup. Maybe a quiche. Soups can mend whatever ails you. She'd call first, of course, but something was wrong. You just know these things, in the same way she knew that no one raises a banner when trouble comes. Few suffer out loud. Most do it quietly and in private, windows shut, shades lowered. That much she knew.

The next morning when Nate returned from his Saturday run—six miles, and not the weekday three—Olivia was ensconced. Apron knotted around her waist, coffee cup in hand, reading glasses atop her head, useless, as she scanned her stained and spotted recipe. He came from behind her and turned her just enough to kiss her forehead lightly without dripping his sweat on her.

"So early?"

"Hmm," she replied, thinking the soup needed a touch of nutmeg and, at the same time, registering the salty smell of him. She still loved that smell and how he looked in the shower when he washed the salt away. Her thoughts lingered there until she scolded herself. *Snap out of it, Liv.* She couldn't stay angry at him when she let her mind wander like that. On the other hand, being angry required so much energy. Forgetting was easier.

"I called Gordon this morning. After you went to bed, when I was finishing up in here it occurred to me that I hadn't seen Dex in days, maybe weeks."

"Is it too much to hope for? Did Dex finally die?" He took a swig of water. "This could make my day. Maybe my week."

"You're heartless." Dex had a habit of howling at sirens, thunder, Amazon drivers, lawn mowers, and leaf blowers. For about six years, Dex's howling had been the soundtrack to Nate's weekend yard work. "Dex is alive and well. Besides, he hasn't howled at you in years."

"That's only because we've spent a small fortune on landscapers. I should've sent Dick and Betsy the bills years ago."

"Nice. Nate, listen. Betsy's had a stroke, a week ago. She's rehabbing in an assisted-care facility. Dex is living with their daughter for now, and Dick said he's getting the house ready to sell. It's just too much for them."

"Wow," he looked at Olivia. "I'm sorry to hear that. Besty is quite a lady. Quite a lady." Nate took a piece of buttered toast with him as he left the kitchen.

"Let's cancel the lawn service. Will you do that?" he shouted over his shoulder as he took the back stairs, two at a time, to go shower.

"No I won't do that," she said to the soup. *Who will cut the grass? What if no one's here this summer*, she thought. And maybe it was then she later reflected, with so little thought at the time, she was one step closer to leaving.

Chapter 7

At the usual time on Monday morning, Olivia's phone rang.

"Hi, Ceece," she said into the receiver. "Do me a favor. Hang up and call me when you're parked somewhere. I don't like picturing you in traffic, steering with your knees. Call me old-fashioned, but I worry about you."

"No worries. I'm in my new car. It's got a screen the size of a small TV. And it's electric. So quiet. One day it'll be self-driving. Luuuuvvv it," she sang. "With both hands free, I can use eyeliner again. I may try false eyelashes."

"Ceci," Olivia said in her most maternal tone.

"Kidding, Livy. Kidding. You have got to lighten up. So when do you leave?"

"Luke and I?"

"You and Luke? No—you and Nate the great. When do you leave for Montreal?"

"Nate's leaving Friday. He's driving so he can take more clothes and some creature comforts and so that he'll—we'll, have a car on the weekends."

"Good. Sounds like a plan. So what about my handsome nephew? When do you drop him off? And how soon after you leave can I drive up and rescue him from slave labor at that cult camp?"

"Ceci, honestly. There's nothing cultish about it. It's simply a place for kids to unplug and give some thought to God. Besides, he says it's more of a resort than a camp. You really ought to visit." From Detroit, Ceci's drive to Lake Michindoah would be about four hours. "Bet it'd blow you away, Ceci. Really."

"So they've gotten to you, too."

Ignoring her, Olivia continued, "We leave next weekend."

"And then you'll be off to Montreal? Hey, I'm here at my first appointment. Gotta fly. Email me your address. Aw, who am I kidding? It's not like I'll write. Who writes anymore? Not me. Call me when you're in Montreal. I'll want to hear all about it."

"Okay. Will do. Love you, Ceece."

"Yeah. Love you, too. One last thing—promise me you'll cut loose a little. Do something completely out of character. You know something I would do. Just once. And then tell me every juicy detail." Click.

Before Olivia could take the phone from her ear, it rang again.

"Hi Liv! It's Abby. Can you believe it? Are you packed? Excited? I'm so jealous. So jealous."

"Oh yeah. Thrilled."

"Oh? You sound like a woman on her way to a mammogram."

"Yes. Yes. I *am* excited. Sorry, Abby, I'm just preoccupied with all the details of the summer. Which reminds me, I've stopped the paper and mail. I've gone to paperless bills, all of them. Our junk mail can wait for us at the post office. I've got the lawn taken care of. I won't need you to stop and check on anything here after all, as much as I appreciate your offer. I'm all set."

Except that she wasn't. She wasn't accompanying Nate to Montreal and she couldn't admit that to her sister or her best friend. It was hard enough to admit it to herself. Nate thought she'd be spending the summer at home. Her friends and sister thought she'd be in Montreal. Luke thought she'd be splitting her time here and there. Cell phones and email made her physical address superfluous. She could be anywhere she wanted to be—anywhere but Lake Ellyn.

Chapter 8

The morning that Nate left for Montreal, Olivia stood in the dark on the walk between the house and driveway. The car had been packed the night before with business attire, casual wear, and workout clothes. She'd packed him some food, a throw, and a few other creature comforts that Nate swore he didn't need but would take to please Olivia. She had nearly suggested he take the framed photo of her and Luke from last summer at the beach, the one that sat on Nate's dresser. He hadn't taken it and she couldn't bring herself to put it in his packed belongings. Her pride had stopped her.

"Hey," Nate approached from behind her, putting a hand on her shoulder. He spoke softly in the predawn quiet. "I'm set. I said goodbye to Luke. He won't remember. He was zonked."

She turned to face him. "Okay, I'll make sure he knows you tried." She pulled his collar to straighten it, a habit of so many years. "You're off. You're going to do great things, Nathan Nash. I know it. That's who you are." She was always able to summon her better self when the moment called for it. "I'll be praying for you. And I'll miss you. A lot."

"Liv, so serious. I'm not leaving forever. Just a summer. It's a season, right? We talked about that. And we'll text or talk every day. More if you want." He gave her a hug and he brushed a kiss across her lips. Then he walked around the back of the car, already directed toward the street for a smooth exit. He opened the driver's side door and turned toward Olivia. "We'll work out a visit here or there." He said a little more loudly, "Remember, this is your chance for a carefree summer without worrying about me and Luke. It'll be good for you. Oh, and you drive safely, too. Text me once you get Luke to camp." Nate settled in the seat and pulled the seat belt over his chest. Before the car door closed, she heard the sound of his phone pinging. Without a wave or a look back, Nate drove down the driveway, onto their street, and out of view.

Olivia walked the few steps to their front door and dropped to the limestone stoop, flanked by planters that hid her form. So he didn't look back. That's not a big deal. How juvenile to expect that he might have stopped the car and gotten out for one last, long hug. And a kiss that wasn't perfunctory. That stuff's for movies. She wasn't a teenager anymore. She knew that. But still.

She tried, but the tears paid no attention to her will. They wouldn't be stopped. The sadness, the feeling of loss. Her shoulders shook. She tried to slow her breathing. Regroup. *Come on, Olivia. Don't be foolish. Don't confuse feelings with facts. This is a moment in time. A snapshot. You know marriage isn't a snapshot; it's an unfolding story. You know better.* Her adult ego consoled her inner child with little success. Her shoulders stopped heaving, but her tears, fewer now, still fell.

When the door opened behind her, she hadn't heard it. "Mom?" Luke sank onto the stoop beside her. He put his arm around her back. "Are you okay? Did Dad leave?"

Olivia straightened and wiped away her tears with the heels of her hands. "Lukers, hi. I'm fine," she lied. She fished a tissue from her pocket and blew her nose. "You know I'm a sap. Goodbyes get me. Especially when it's you or your dad."

"But, mom, you're gonna visit, right? And you'll hang with Aunt C? And doesn't Mrs. Gregory have some catering gigs for you?" Luke was a fixer. He wanted everything to be right in everyone's world. All the time.

"Sure. Yes, of course. Luke, honey, I'm a little sad, but as you and your dad have said, I'm a free woman this summer. Right? My agenda only. What could be better?" She forced a smile and smacked her hands on her knees as if to settle the matter and move on. "Let's scramble some eggs and get us ready for your travels. What do you say?"

Not long after, they were on their way to Luke's summer assignment. And ten hours after that, she'd left a gas station in Onaway, Michigan, chasing down the last ferry of the day to Mackinac Island.

She'd asked for a sign. *What do I want? Where do I go next?* Her sign came in the form of a gas station owner. Mitchell had decided for her what she couldn't for herself. With the destination settled, she pressed the speed limit to get to Mackinaw City in time. That she had no idea where she'd stay or for how long was unimportant. Irrelevant. For now, anyway. She just needed to get there before the last ferry pulled away from the dock.

About an hour later, as Mitchell had advised, Olivia was in Mackinaw City, doing the unthinkable, or, at least, the infrequently imagined. As the car neared the docks of the three ferry lines along Huron Street, she vaguely remembered traveling on Shepler's many years ago. A lifetime ago. This time she elected to turn right into the Star Line docks since their billboard promised a hydro-jet ride, with a big boat and an arc of water streaming behind it. It would get visitors to Mackinac Island in only sixteen minutes as you "High Tail It" to Mackinac Island.

Works for me, Olivia thought as she pulled into the Star Line gates and stopped beside the ticketing chalet. *If I'm going to run away, I'd better do it fast. Before I lose my nerve.* Just as quickly she shot up a prayer asking forgiveness. The time to seek permission had expired.

"Ma'am, ma'am," she read the lips of the employee in his official Star Line polo after he tapped on her window, which had startled her to attention. Olivia lowered her window.

"Welcome to the Star Line, ma'am. Our last ferry is leaving in thirty minutes. You can buy your ticket just inside the building behind me." He pulled tags of different colors out of his pocket. "While you buy your ticket, I can tag your bags and get your car parked for the duration of your stay. Just leave the keys in the ignition." The well-built dock porter, sunburned from too many hours in the early June sun, opened her door.

Olivia reached for her purse, tote, and overnight bag, and stepped out onto the pavement of the receiving area. "Where will you be staying on Mackinac Island?" She had no idea but figured this was a good time to sound decisive.

"The Iroquois Hotel." She hoped.

"Nice hotel. The owners used to own the Star Line. So, what about your car? We can keep it in a secured lot for up to three nights," he pressed the top of his pen. "How long will you be staying at the Iroquois?"

"I may be on the island for an extended visit. What's the rate to stow my car for a month? Or two?" Olivia wasn't sure who asked those questions, but she thought the voice sounded like hers.

"For a hundred dollars a month we'll keep it secure in a covered garage and provide valet service if you need to come back to the mainland."

"Done. Let's plan on two months," that familiar voice answered.

"Very good. If you'll pop the trunk, I'll get your bags and tag them. Once you arrive on the island, a dock porter will take your bags to the Iroquois. You can just walk to the hotel and leave your bags to us." Olivia gave him a blank smile. He repeated himself after an awkward pause, "Your trunk? Your suitcases?"

Olivia glanced at the purse, tote, and overnight bag, all hanging from her right shoulder and shrugged, "This is it. In fact, I wonder if I have time to go across the street to a store. I need a toothbrush. Oh, and a bike."

The dock porter's expression shifted, eventually settling on a look of unfazed composure. "Well, ma'am. You travel light. Our dock porters will appreciate that. As for a toothbrush, you can buy one at Doud's on the island. And the bike? It's a little late tonight to get that." Olivia nodded in agreement while thinking she could have really flummoxed him if she'd asked where to get a few more pairs of panties. Three pairs wouldn't take her through August. She thought better of asking. Poor kid. No older than Luke.

"The best way to come up with a bike," he continued, "is to go to the police station early tomorrow. They sell bikes that employees leave there when the season ends. You wouldn't believe how many are left. Guess everyone just wants off the rock as soon as they've done their time." She remembered the reference—Mackinac, not Alcatraz. Olivia handed him her keys and thanked him for his helpfulness. *I'd better buy a round-trip ticket or they'll think I'm a security risk.*

She bought her ticket and grabbed a handful of brochures inside the red-roofed ticketing chalet. She waited only fifteen minutes before their scant group of passengers boarded the hydro-jet named Davey for the short trip across the Straits of Mackinac that separated Michigan's Lower and Upper Peninsulas. Olivia climbed to the top deck and took a seat with six other passengers. Few traveled this direction on a Saturday night, but the Davey would be filled with day-trippers, or fudgies, on the return leg.

Olivia studied her fellow travelers. Honeymooners, she guessed of one couple cooing at each other. A full-time resident, she figured of another who looked like one of the Native Americans who lived in a small community toward the center of the island, Harrisonville, "the Village." Unusual, residents don't generally sit up top with the uninitiated. The others looked young. Maybe summer workers returning from a day spent off island. Hope you enjoyed it, she thought. There'd be none of those—not on a weekend anyway—as the island geared up for July race weekends. They'd really want off the island by the time the race weekends were past.

The captain coaxed the boat away from the dock. He maneuvered a three-point turn to take the boat into some open water. Over the upper deck rails, Olivia could see the Shepler and Arnold ferry docks. Before she could place a mental bet on which ferry line was fastest, the captain pulled back the throttle, the propulsion lifting the boat and sliding Olivia back into her seat. The Davey skimmed the water as it sped toward the island, spouting a watery plume behind her. Olivia's eyes blurred and a cold spray stung her already wet cheeks. She couldn't turn back. Not tonight anyway.

Chapter 9

About twelve minutes into the trip, the island's structures came into view. From a few miles out, it looked like a scene in miniature from a vintage train set. Bottlebrush trees on a felt-covered hillside spiked the sky. Nestled among them were Victorian cottages, all of them looking diminutive from that distance—except for the Grand Hotel. "You never change," she whispered. Looking like a crown perched among the West Bluff cedars, the Grand was the island's landmark and hospitality sovereign. Only a hotel with a guest list that had included presidents and B-list celebrities, a coat and tie requirement, and a fee extracted from unregistered guests for the pleasure of walking the porch could claim royalty. She continued to study the Grand, remembering the hotel and island trivia she could once recite to any curious tourist. But just then the Grand's equally elegant and less pretentious cousin caught her eye. As the ferry continued east, threading the needle between the old lighthouse at Round Island and the breakwall light, Olivia saw the Iroquois Hotel.

The white clapboard structure with its dormers and fanlight windows looked freshly painted. It had always looked freshly painted, even back then. The Iroquois was like an elegant woman whose beauty was undiminished by the years. Evidence of her advancing age was her grace—the kind that comes only with age. The ferry moved closer to the harbor, and she saw the glow from the candlelit tables in the hotel's dining room and still other tables on the dock. It was the best spot on the island for a romantic dinner. She should have been there with Nate, savoring a bottle of wine and each other's company. But instead. Instead.

"Thank you for choosing the Star Line for your travel to Mackinac Island," interrupted the captain's voice over the loudspeaker. "Folks headed to the Grand Hotel, please look for the Grand's horse-drawn carriage awaiting your arrival. For everyone else, taxis, the kind that move by wheel and hoof, will be on Main Street. If you're staying in one of the island's hotels and you've checked your bags, you have no need to retrieve them. Your hotel's dock porter will deliver them to the lobby." The captain continued his greeting as the deckhands tethered the boat to the dock. "If you're walking to your hotel, stay on the sidewalk, or if you venture onto the streets, watch your step. Taxi backfire can be a little messy. We at the Star Line wish you a pleasant stay on Mackinac Island."

Everyone but Olivia hurried off the top deck. *What am I doing here?* Instead of answering the question, she made her way off the ferry and down the dock to Main Street. She turned right when she should have turned left to go to the Iroquois. Better check on availability of toothbrushes at Doud's and rooms at the Chip. *I don't want to seem desperate*, said her rational self. *Even if you are*, she imagined the tactless if truthful voice of her sister Ceci.

A short walk and two stops later (toothbrush in hand), Olivia determined there actually were vacancies elsewhere, but why would that matter? Her reconnaissance only confirmed what she already knew. She had to stay at the Iroquois. For her, there were no other choices.

Olivia approached the hotel. She nearly wandered down the brick path and through the gate to the employee entrance. Old habits die hard. Instead, she climbed the five steps to the porch and passed under the hotel's discreet sign. The Iroquois barely breathed its identity as an island hotel. Promotion was unnecessary and, frankly, unbecoming. People in the know, knew. Condé Nast knew. Olivia took a breath, straightened her shoulders, and entered the lobby, trying to look like she belonged.

It was quiet, of course, at ten o'clock in early June. Behind the leaded glass window separating the hotel office from the intimate lobby, Olivia could see the blurred image of someone seated at a desk, likely the manager on duty—a woman. It looked like she was in conversation with someone who must have been standing just inside the open office door. Olivia closed the large front door which gave a whoosh, and she approached the oak registration counter. She stood off to the side, hidden from view, not wanting to interrupt a conversation that sounded tense. From her vantage point, she could make out an imposing figure in a white jacket and black cap.

"You'll have to tell her later. Mrs. B is checking on the coffee service for tomorrow morning. Can I take a note and have her…?" Just then a small figure, with rounded shoulders and silver hair, entered the office area.

She's still here, thought Olivia. Mrs. Branagan was the small but fierce matriarch of the Iroquois. *She must be seventy-five years old, maybe older.* Olivia remembered Mrs. B's green cat eyes. They were sparkling emeralds when she smiled, but when she set her lips in a thin, grim line, her eyes were piercing. She could strike terror into the hearts of larger men than the one who stood before her. *She used to scare the heck out of me, that's for sure.*

"You might as well hear it from me first. I fired someone. A waitress," said the man in the chef's coat. That voice was familiar. Couldn't be.

"What? I left the dining room a half an hour ago. Everything was fine. Peaceful."

"Yeah, well, not in the kitchen. Where are you finding these servers? What's with them? Like they've been raised on chicken fingers and Pop-Tarts. They think béarnaise is a dipping sauce, for Chrissake." Could be him, she supposed.

The small figure didn't move. She must be staring him down. Or actually, staring him up. Olivia winced in sympathy. Mrs. B was a small woman, but she seemed to consider herself a dime among nickels. Half the size and worth twice as much.

The chef shrugged. "Sorry. But what the hell? What's with them?

I'm running a four-star restaurant here, not a deli."

"Sean, whom did you fire?" She called him Sean. It was him. The same insufferable, egotistical, culinary boy wonder she remembered from years ago.

"Not who. What."

"Sean…" As Mrs. B seemed to brace herself for what he was about to say, it occurred to Olivia that the manager had gone silent and motionless during their exchange. Smart woman.

"So it slows down enough for me to give Danny a break. I stop plating out front and go back on the line. This waitress… Kelley or Kenzell. Kenzie? Whatever. Some K girl. So she comes in for table three's dinners. I'm giving her the plates and she's standing there… doing… I don't know. Nothing. Not moving. Nothing."

"I lean under the rack to get a closer look. She's on her phone. Texting while the whitefish goes cold. What's with these girls? So I tell her, 'Wake up. Pull your head out of your…'" He paused.

Thank God, Olivia thought.

"You know, words to that effect."

"I can imagine," Mrs. B murmured.

"And then she says to me, 'Danny, fuck you.' Just like that, 'Danny, fuck you.'"

Honestly? He had to repeat that? To Mrs. B? It had to be Sean. Only someone like him, a boy wonder *and* nephew could pull that off. Olivia leaned over the desk a little further to hear where this was going to land.

"She obviously didn't recognize that it was me working the line. She didn't know who she was talking to, that's for sure. No one talks to me or anyone who works for me that way. So I grabbed her phone and threw it."

"Of course." Mrs. B sounded more resigned than surprised. "Threw it where?"

"In the broiler."

"Ooh," Olivia mouthed from her hiding place.

"Sean, you didn't." This time Mrs. B sounded a little surprised.

"Just for a few seconds."

"How is it?"

"The phone?"

"No. The broiler." Mrs. B always had her priorities straight.

"It's fine. Kitchen smells a little, though. Melted plastic and all. It already burned off."

"Yes. Well, all right. We'll give Kendall a week's pay, a new phone, and we'll help her off the island. You know she's the Howells' granddaughter, right?"

"Yeah. A princess. They're the worst."

"Regardless." She ignored the comment and continued, "We have another group coming in for training on Monday. We'll have a few days to get them up to speed before the festival." She was referring to the annual Lilac Festival and the official start of the summer season. "We'll review phone policy again on Monday. Meanwhile, the remaining waitstaff got your message, I'm sure. Sean, you can't go through these waitresses like you do Diet Cokes. We have a small applicant pool and we'll need a full staff for race weeks."

"Fine. Just get me some real servers. I don't need any more princesses working for me."

"Sean." The woman paused. "They don't work for you." With that dismissal, the man turned and left the office.

Olivia stepped back from the counter and cleared her throat. Thankfully Mrs. B had left the office as the manager moved through the open doorway to greet Olivia. "Cindy," her name tag read.

"I'm so sorry, I didn't hear anyone come in. Have you been waiting long?"

"Oh, no," she lied. "I just slipped in. I was hoping you might have a vacancy for this evening." Olivia smiled apologetically. "I know this is a busy time and I don't have a reservation."

"That's no problem. We actually have three rooms available, but it is June. We require a minimum two-night stay after June first."

"Of course. That's just fine." The manager handed her a registration form and Olivia extended her credit card in return. Cindy excused herself "for a moment, to run the card." Meanwhile, Olivia looked at the paperwork that Cindy had left on the counter. Employment applications. Not many of them. And the one on top was completed in ink with little purple circles dotting each "i."

"Here we are," the manager said as she handed Olivia her credit card. Cindy asked her to sign and initial the registration form. "Now, Mrs. Nash, did the dock porter bring your bags?" She leaned over the counter to scan the lobby, an enclosed porch actually, that wrapped the hotel's face and flank. Antique wicker furnishings with brilliant floral cushions and needlepointed pillows created cozy sitting areas. Crisp, chintz fabrics framed the windows with their many glass panes. Peony and lilac blooms in ceramic pots and transferware pitchers dotted the room's nooks. Everything was placed just so, to look unintentionally perfect. And not a suitcase in sight.

"Uh, well. No." Olivia smiled and pulled her bag from beneath the counter to her shoulder. "Just this. I came to shop." How stupid. Who comes to Mackinac Island for the shopping? Unless you are hoping to build a wardrobe of hoodies and T-shirts.

"Lovely. If you haven't visited in a while, you'll enjoy some of the boutiques that have opened in recent years." Olivia must have looked like a woman who aspired to more than a T-shirt that read, "Mackinac Island WTF: What the Fudge." Small comfort.

Before Cindy handed Olivia her key, Olivia asked about Wi-Fi and a business center. Was there somewhere she could access a printer? The manager gave Olivia the Wi-Fi code and pointed out a doorway just down the hall. The office had a computer, printer, and coffee maker. Free of charge for guests and open all night.

Perfect. She needed ten minutes, tops. How long could it take to print an application?

Chapter 10

An hour later, after Olivia had looked over her room and read everything there was to read about her accommodations in the hotel's welcome folder, she descended the staircase marked with a painted sign: Service Only. The hotel map showed that the service stairs would drop her on the first floor behind the lobby and manager's office. Such a small infraction to use stairs meant only for the help. And this staircase was the service she needed, thank you very much. Once she descended them, she found her way to the business center. She saw a computer sitting atop an old library table.

"Iroquois Hotel Mackinac Island" she typed into the search bar. Moments later, she'd navigated her way through the site to the application download. It printed in a flash and she began completing it—using a precise, architect's print. No sweat: *Address, cell phone number, email.* She continued to fill in the application's blanks: *College*: yes; *Degree*: graphic arts and design. And a master's degree, she could add, but decided not to. *Restaurant experience*: check, check. "Experience here, at the Iroquois," she wrote.

Then came the stumper. *Years employed.* There were spaces for the years: 20__ to 20__. *Crud. I have to lie. Or not.* She drew a line through the text and under it printed, "One year. Until the season ended." That put her in a different category altogether.

The Iroquois, like most of the island's hotels, coveted employees who could serve through mid-October. Back in the day, the Iroquois paid a thousand-dollar bonus if you worked until the season closed. Olivia had persisted and collected the bonus. Funny thing was, once the Labor Day crowd had checked out, she would have paid someone for the experience of living on Mackinac Island. When the hot hustle of summer ended, the island exhaled. People she'd pass in the street started looking familiar. Shop proprietors took time to visit with each other. Restaurant owners hosted each other in their dining rooms and lingered over coffee and after-dinner drinks. There were tables to spare and no one seemed concerned about competing for business. By September's end, the season was in the books.

And since the Iroquois offered only dinner service in September and October, Olivia had all day to explore the island. As one of her coworkers had said, "When fall comes, the employees own the island." And on weekdays, at least, it felt every bit their private paradise.

Chapter 11

Montreal, Quebec

With the confidence of a tour guide, Landon led her colleague, Olivia's husband, Nate, to Rue Saint-Paul, the oldest street in the most historic part of Montreal. The heat of midday had retreated with the sun, and June's humidity pressed a chilling dampness on Old Montreal. Landon shivered and pulled her cream-colored wrap closer. "Here we are. At last." She stood aside while Nate opened the carved door to allow entry into a bistro that looked like the wine cellar of a manor house. The floor was cobblestones set in mortar, while the planked ceiling above rested on thick wooden beams. Candlelight blurred the faces of patrons sequestered in booths or seated at tables topped with starched white linens. Meanwhile, halogen lighting high above called attention to pocks in limestone walls that with time had come to be regarded as beauty marks instead of blemishes. Lightly tarnished silver serving pieces on the walnut bar, on tables, and in the hands of waiters reflected the movement within and cast the scene in an antiqued patina.

As the maître d' led them to a table in the back corner, Landon gave Nate a foodie's commentary. "Centuries old with a modern soul, appealing to seekers of romance or back-room business dealings." He didn't reply but gestured for her to take the seat against the bookshelf behind, allowing her a view of the restaurant.

"You'll be better able to read lips and concoct outlandish stories about our fellow diners from this seat." He helped settle her into the upholstered wing chair. "Olivia does it all the time."

"Really?" Landon loosened her shawl and let it drop to the chair to reveal an ivory chiffon blouse with a wide ruffle along its neckline that obscured the skin beneath. "Is she accurate?"

"We'll never know. But she swears she's dead on. She developed this talent in college waiting tables at a resort island in northern Michigan. By the end of the summer, she said she could report on profession, occasion, and the nature of her diners' relationship before they'd ordered dessert."

"Interesting. What would she say about us?" Landon looked him in the eye and tilted her head. "What would our story be?"

Nate met her gaze and bent the corners of his mouth into a noncommittal smile. "She would say," he paused, "that you are in a witness protection program, and I am the G-man here to give you the news that you're about to be relocated to Sitka, Alaska—to reestablish a life on the edge of the tundra."

"Oh sir, this southern belle would not survive the tundra. That would be a failed protection program. And you didn't answer my question. What would Olivia think if she saw us here?"

Nate's eyes did not leave hers. His voice was steady. "She would think we were colleagues, talking business over dinner. Which is true." Just then the waiter approached their table. Landon accepted the menu he handed her and looked at his name tag.

"*Bonsoir,* Jean Marc." Landon graced him with a captivating smile.

"*Bonsoir, Madame. Bienvenue,*" the waiter responded and paused for a moment, appreciatively. "*Parlez-vous Francais, oui?*"

"Hmm," Landon nodded. "*Un peu,* but for the benefit of my companion—my colleague," she emphasized, "let's continue in English. *Et vous? Parlez Anglais?*" She beamed once more in Jean Marc's direction.

"Of course. Serving you and speaking in English will be an honor and a relief. I'm an ex-pat. Originally from New York."

"Well, we'll get along just fine." She leaned toward him and whispered, "You know how inconvenienced the true Québecois become when forced to speak our vulgar language."

"Indeed, Madame," he said conspiratorially.

"And we'll get along ever so much better if you'll refrain from calling me 'madame.' I am a mademoiselle."

Jean Marc looked a little flustered, and his eyes shifted to the emerald-cut diamond blinking on her ring finger.

Landon acknowledged his unspoken question and held up her hand. Nate's left hand, no ring on it, dropped to his lap like an anchor. "Since when has a girl needed a husband to enjoy her best friends?"

Jean Marc laughed. "With that approach to life, I expect nothing less than a vodka martini for the lady, I mean—Miss. Am I right?"

"Of course. With an olive and a twist."

Nate ordered a beer and Jean Marc left, promising to return quickly.

"Bet you do that everywhere you go." Nate looked at her and slowly shook his head.

"Whatever do you mean, Mr. Nash?" She dropped her chin and looked at him through the black fringe of her lashes.

"Flirt," Nate accused her. "You're a scotch on the rocks girl. Last I knew, anyway."

"Well, he was so proud of himself for thinking he knew my preference, how could I tell him he was wrong? That would be unladylike. Men like to be right. And there's nothing wrong with a little vodka then and again. Don't you agree?"

"Yeah. I like vodka."

She laughed. "I wasn't referring to vodka. Men. I was speaking of them."

"Liking to be right?" He raised his hand to his chin. "I suppose so, but I'm not sure we like to be manipulated. Now *that's* unladylike." Nate opened his menu.

"Really?" she purred. "In my small, unscientific survey of, oh, hundreds of men, ninety-nine percent will go to any length to be right. Strike that— to be *thought* right. Whether they are or not is largely irrelevant."

Nate continued to peruse the menu and without looking up said, "That's a damning statistic. Of those hundreds you've surveyed, and the dozens of those who have, no doubt, vied for your attention," he looked up at Landon, "you haven't found one who's big enough to admit he can be wrong?"

She looked at Nate with an unblinking gaze. "Not one. But to be fair, sometimes they just don't recognize the truth. Not even when it's right in front of them," she answered softly and parted her lips to form a practiced smile.

"Well, I recognize that you don't seem to have a very high opinion of men. We might recognize more than you think. We just don't feel the need to talk about it." Nate looked again at the menu. "So, what looks good to you?"

Chapter 12

Olivia walked from the hotel's business center toward the front desk, employment application in her shaking hand. She thought it a stroke of luck, and maybe a sign, when she discovered the post unattended. On top of the counter lay the same pile of applications she'd seen when she checked in. Hoping it wasn't destined for the recycling bin, she slipped her application underneath the others. She noticed the sticky note on the desk beside them. "Sunday: Waitstaff Orientation. 9 a.m."

"It's a date. I'll be there," she whispered before heading to the stairs. She took the guest staircase this time and went to bed. Early the next morning, she slipped out of the Iroquois to grab a coffee and bagel next door. She didn't mingle with the Iroquois guests, who were breakfasting on the hotel's signature sugar-topped, blueberry muffins in the enclosed porch. Olivia didn't want to draw attention to herself or cause Cindy or Mrs. B to discover a connection between one of their newest applicants (hopefully hires) and the guest in room 28.

"All right. All right. So," Chef scanned the group of eight before him, "is everybody here?" *Yup*, thought Olivia. *That's Sean. Same rumpled, unshaven jock look. Same gravelly voice. Same sort of inane question, even after all these years. How are we supposed to know if everyone's*

here? But Olivia was grateful for something to make her forget her nervousness.

"Let's move into the new dining room. Everybody gather up some chairs." They walked from the original dining room to the new dining room—one that had been called "new" since it was added to the hotel over 20 years ago. Olivia scanned the dining rooms, old and new. Both looked unchanged and yet completely fresh. She admired the designer's talent in updating these rooms. Like the result of skillful plastic surgery, the client looked completely herself, just well rested.

"Okay, everyone. Welcome to the Carriage House, the best restaurant on the island, serving haute cuisine since 1954." A hand shot up. "Yeah, you," Chef motioned to the young man with the raised hand.

"What do you mean by hot cuisine?" To be fair, Chef's pronunciation wasn't entirely on point. And years ago, Olivia recalled, Chef could well have thought that fine dining and "hot" cuisine were synonymous, and he said as much. The new hire had a reason to ask. The summer she'd worked here, Chef referred to the Monterey Jack cheese on a lunchtime offering as "monetary jack" cheese. She had often referred to him as Monetary Jack. But only in her head.

Olivia bit her cheeks and looked around. Only the girl with dark hair and brown complexion beside her snickered at the exchange.

"The Carriage House has earned this reputation because we care about every detail. Every detail. And what happens in the front of the house matters just as much—well almost as much—as what happens in the kitchen." He paused to lift the Tigers cap from his head, push the escaping dark hair off his forehead, and replace his cap. "I got a little ahead of myself. Mrs. B usually does these meetings, but she's tied up. She'll be here in a few minutes. Mrs. B and Tricia, the manager, will tell you how the dining room runs. How to work the POS system, what the stations are, what you wear, how to give our guests the fine dining experience they expect from a restaurant like ours."

Just then, the same guy in the group of waitstaff raised his hand. "So do we get to sample the meals here so we can describe them to the customers?"

"No. And we don't call 'em customers. They're guests. And don't ever let Mrs. B or Tricia catch you calling our dishes 'meals.' Meal is for horses and chickens. Not customers. Other questions?" The girl next to Olivia dropped her head and giggled quietly.

Out of the corner of her eye, Olivia saw Mrs. B approach from the kitchen and walk into the back of the dining room. At the same time she noticed color on the neck of the girl seated next to her. She shifted slightly to take a closer (and stealthy) look. *Was that a wing tip? And the head of a bird emerging from the neckline of the girl's T-shirt? It must have been an expensive tattoo.* Mrs. B continued toward the orientation group. Instinctively, Olivia pulled the paisley scarf from her neck and draped it over the neck of the girl seated beside her. Olivia leaned toward her and said, "You're welcome. I'd be chilly in here too without the sweater I'm wearing."

The girl looked at her, surprised, just as Mrs. B came to stand behind them. "Later," Olivia whispered and winked, turning her attention back to Chef.

"Mrs. B is here now," looking over everyone's heads to the back of the room. "Good thing. I don't do these things too well. Do I?"

"Don't sell yourself short, Sean. I am quite sure you were splendid."

"I'll leave you with this thought," he continued, drawing everyone's attention. "When you come into my kitchen it'll be noisy and fast-paced. Insane," he added for emphasis. "But I tell you, what we do here is special. When we work as a team and do it right, it's like combining some kind of dance choreography with the precision of landing planes on an aircraft carrier. Nothing like it. It's magic. And we serve some magic every night. You're lucky to be a part of it. Let alone get paid for it." He seemed to have surprised his listeners with this slip into poetic prose. Having done so, Chef smiled, nodded, and turned for the kitchen.

Where'd that come from? wondered Olivia. That didn't sound like the monosyllabic chef she remembered.

Mrs. B made her way to the front of the group. "I apologize for being late, but I am delighted you've met our executive chef. He's been here since he was quite young. At the time, the youngest chef ever to receive Condé Nast's commendation. No one cares about the Carriage House, our cuisine, and our reputation more than he does. His name is Sean. You may call him 'Chef.'"

Mrs. B moved her reading glasses from atop her head to the bridge of her nose. She studied the clipboard resting on her left arm. "Yes, yes. A number of you with restaurant experience. Good. We're lacking that. And one of you who has worked with us here before. But first, do we have any parents with us this morning?" Mrs. B looked toward the back of the group where Olivia sat. Olivia looked around, wondering where the parents were. Not seeing any, she looked back at Mrs. B and found herself caught in the penetrating stare of those green cat eyes. She was being summoned with the stare.

"Oh me?" she asked. "Well, uh, yes. I am a parent. But I am not the mother of any of these kids here."

"Are you a guest?" continued Mrs. B.

"Yes, as a matter of fact I am and I have had such a restful night. The linens here… exquisite. Truly."

Mrs. B pulled back the corners of her closed lips to form a smile. It looked more like a grimace. "I am so glad. Perhaps you'd like to join the other guests upstairs for coffee and muffins on the porch?"

"Actually, no. I'm here for orientation. I believe you've received my application. Olivia is my name. Olivia Nash."

Mrs. B glanced at her list and then released the clip to free the applications underneath. "Yes, here you are. You're the one who's worked here before." She raised her glasses back to her head. "It appears you have experience." She let the understatement hang in the air between them.

"Oh yes." Olivia plunged into the gap. "I've developed some skill in the kitchen myself and my high regard for gracious hospitality and, really, the way I serve guests in our home owes primarily to the summer I spent working under your direction at the Carriage House." She paused, "I've returned. Just trying to hone my skills." Olivia lifted and dropped her shoulders in an "aw shucks" move.

Mrs. B was too much of a lady not to acknowledge the compliment.

"Hmm. Lovely. All the same, this is unusual. As a former waitress, you must remember that we typically hire college students for seasonal positions."

"I do understand. Completely. And if it makes any difference, I am paying college tuition right now and a summer job would be a great help. Do you know what a year of tuition costs these days?" Olivia looked around her and realized her fellow servers-in-training were wide-eyed.

"I thought my experience might be valuable," she rambled on. "You said yourself that the Carriage House is in need of experienced waitstaff." Up to full speed, Olivia charged on. "And I read on the hotel's website your notice about equal opportunity hiring. You know, without regard to sex, religion, ethnicity, or, well I suppose, age. I assume that policy applies in this situation? It seems only fitting for an establishment like the Iroquois."

"Touché," mouthed the dark-haired girl next to her—the one now wearing Olivia's scarf. Mrs. B took a deep breath and exhaled. "And we are pleased to have you join us again, Olivia." She fixed her mouth into that same tight smile. "I hope you don't find the pace of service too," she paused, "tiring."

The orientation continued for the next three hours. Olivia was light on her feet, trying to show the energy of a college student on Red Bull. She remembered how to balance on her left shoulder a tray stacked high with dinner plates and silver covers. Paper doilies were still placed under soup bowls and creamers. Except for the introduction of a touchscreen order system, new uniforms, and special procedures for serving gluten-frees (and learning that Chef thought vegans were freaks of nature), not a lot had changed. The floral-patterned china in brights of blues, reds, and golds was the same. So were the napkin folds, the whitefish, and the Mackinac Island hot fudge ice cream puff.

By noon they'd finished their training for the day. They received their Iroquois-issued button-downs and their shadowing assignments for later that evening. Olivia was exhausted but not about to show it.

Glad she had reserved her room for several nights, she left the dining room, heading for the service stairs which now were legitimately hers to ascend.

"Olivia, may I have a moment please?" Olivia turned to discover Mrs. B two feet behind her. Her catlike stealth matched those cat eyes.

"Oh, hello, Mrs. Branagan." Not sure whether to thank her or to comment on just how great the morning was, honestly, not tiring at all, she said nothing.

"Do you remember the housing accommodations we provided for staff when you worked here? The apartments?"

"Oh, sure. We had a blast. Six of us over the Tap Room. And family dinners in the EDR. Great memories. All of them. Well, except for race weekends." Mrs. B had this way of making her talk. Too much. And too much like the college student she once was.

"Yes. Race weekends." Mrs. B nodded knowingly. "Well, we still serve the staff dinner in the employee dining room, but we've since built our own housing for employees farther inland. Had you considered where you might live while you are with us?"

Olivia's face showed her surprise and her realization. "Honestly, I hadn't gotten that far. I don't suppose I could be both a hotel guest *and* a Carriage House waitress?"

"That would be unprofitable for both of us." Mrs. B stated the obvious. "I am not certain you'll be comfortable living with waitstaff half your age. I can't imagine it."

"No," Olivia conjured a mental picture of her sharing a bathroom with five, twenty-year-old women. "No, but if that's all that's available to me, I'll make it work."

Mrs. B looked around her, left and right, as if she might find someone listening to their conversation. "Follow me." And Olivia followed her down the hall and into an office that smelled like lilacs.

"I am aware of someone, an island homeowner, who is unable to occupy her cottage this summer. She is looking for a tenant, but not just a tenant. Someone more like a caretaker."

Olivia's eyebrows lifted and Mrs. B shook her head to dampen

Olivia's eagerness. "It's not glamorous. It's not even quaint. It's an old place in need of renovation—in my opinion. Renovations began and then stalled. Messy. A large undertaking."

"And what would I be expected to do? I can paint pretty well if I do say so myself, but I can't drywall or work with electrical."

"Of course not. This woman is simply looking for someone to shake the dust from the place. Get the water flowing. You understand, use it so it doesn't atrophy in place. You might be just the person. She's been talking of selling the place. For years. Maybe decades. You might need to open its doors to realtors and prospective buyers. *If* she decides to sell."

"I could do that. I'd be happy to do that. How much would I pay for rent and how might I get in touch with the owner?"

"That's between you and her. But I suspect she'll offer you the place rent-free in exchange for your care of it."

"Should I call the owner? Would you be in touch with her first?" Mrs. B looked past Olivia's shoulder, fixing her gaze on the wall behind her.

"Yes, I'll propose the idea at once." She shook her stare and looked again at Olivia. "One thing, though. This might matter to her."

"Yes?"

"Will you be here, through mid-October? When the season ends?"

"Um, again, and this is so unlike me. Truly it is. I haven't planned that far ahead. I can promise you I will be here through the end of August, until I, I mean we, take our son back to college. I might be able to stay on after that. It all depends."

"Depends on?"

"My husband. Whether he returns from his assignment. In Montreal. He has a role, a big one actually, in the merger of SpiraVecta with another big drug company. It's supposed to close sometime after Labor Day. If all goes well."

"And until that time, you are working a summer job on Mackinac Island? As a server?" Hearing Mrs. B say the words, Olivia realized how ludicrous the idea was. But she had nothing else.

"Yes. Sounds strange, doesn't it? A summer job for a woman in her forties, with a college-age son. All the same, it is an adventure and Mackinac Island is one of the most beautiful places on earth to spend a summer. You must think so too."

"I do," Mrs. B agreed. "He'll miss you, though."

"Luke? Oh gosh no. He's working not too far from here, all summer long at a camp. He's having a ball."

"No, your husband. I meant him. He'll miss you." She stated it as a fact rather than a question.

"Oh, sure. I suppose so. I mean, yes, of course. But he's so wrapped up in the merger right now. It's all-consuming. For him, it'll be no different than if I was back home in Chicago. No different at all. In many ways, better."

Mrs. B studied her for a moment, saying nothing. When the moment stretched to an uncomfortable length, Olivia excused herself and started for the office door.

"Olivia," Mrs. B called after her.

"Yes?" She looked over her shoulder.

"Frankie. Expect to hear from Frankie.

Chapter 13

"Hello, this is Nathan Nash of SpiraVecta US." He sounded harried.

"Hey, Nathan Na…" She was interrupted.

"I can't take your call just now. Please leave a message and I'll return your call promptly. Thank you."

"I thought I had you in the flesh, so to speak, but I guess not. It's just me, just checking in." She scanned the room, feeling guilty for being in a place unknown to him. "Um, let's see." Be succinct, she coached herself. Don't yammer. "I heard from Luke. By text, of course. He's doing great. I'm fine." In case you wondered. "Busy." Or I hope to be. "I won't be home tonight. Trying a new restaurant." That was mostly true. "So maybe text or email a good time to catch up. Oh, that reminds…" A quiet knock at her hotel room door stopped her mid-sentence. "Oh wait, there's someone at my door. I mean, *our* door. I mean the front door. At home. In Lake Ellyn." Brilliant. She was a such clumsy liar. "Text me. Love you. Bye."

She hung up and opened the door to find the girl from this morning on the other side. In her outstretched hand was Olivia's scarf. "Thanks for this," she said. "I wasn't cold, but I don't think that's why you put this on me."

Olivia smiled at the girl and asked her to come in. "Have you seen one of the harbor-view rooms here?" She tilted her head. "It's like sleeping in a botanical garden with this floral wallpaper and matching drapery and bedding. I woke up with allergies."

The girl smiled, stepped in, and looked around. "Yeah, it looks pretty pollinated. They have something against paint in this place?" She was tall, this girl. Maybe because she was thin, she looked even taller. Or maybe it was the thick-soled boots that gave her such height. "My name's Amanda, by the way."

"I thought that's what I heard. My name's Olivia."

"Yeah, I know." Amanda smiled a little. "We all do."

Olivia shook her head. "I suppose I did introduce myself to everyone with some fanfare this morning."

"It's cool. You were cool."

"Well, without intending to be. Thanks. Speaking of which, I threw my scarf over you because Mrs. B was creeping up on us and I had a feeling there might be a policy, or predisposition, against tattoos. I thought I saw a bird beak on your neck."

"It's a phoenix. It kind of matches the china. Weird, huh?"

Olivia shook her head yes.

"I shouldn't have worn my hair up with this shirt. Stupid. Do you think she saw it?"

"I don't. And the collar on our button-down shirt will cover it completely. There may not be any issue at all, but the Iroquois has some exacting standards. Or they did. Until this morning when they hired me." Olivia smiled.

"I thought it was hilarious. You really showed her." Amanda turned toward the door. "I should probably go." She turned back. "Actually," she put a hand down for the chair beside the door. "Could I have a glass of water and maybe sit down?" She slid into the chair while Olivia grabbed a glass off the dresser and went to the bathroom to fill it.

"Are you all right?" Olivia asked as she approached her, handing her the glass.

Amanda took a gulp and nodded. "Oh yeah. Just the heat. I ran around the island before orientation. Too much too soon, I think."

"Around the island? Eight miles? I'd say that's about six, or eight, miles too much." She took the glass from her to refill it. "So you're a runner. Do you run at school? On a team?"

"Oh no. I just do it for me. I prefer jay jay, but I doubt Mackinac has a gym for that."

"Jay jay?"

"Jiu-jitsu, a martial art. Like fighting without weapons. Choke holds, joint locks, and such." She watched for Olivia's reaction. "Like self-defense stuff." She took another drink. "It requires more discipline than people would guess. And I don't actually compete. I just train."

"I don't know anything about it, to be honest. Bet my son does. I'm a half-hearted runner myself. It's a love-hate thing. I love it when I stop, and sometimes only then. I'm hoping to do some yoga while I'm here. To calm me."

"You seem pretty calm to me." Amanda put the glass on the dresser next to her.

"Yeah. Wait til race weeks. So where do you go to school?"

"I'm at Knox College," Amanda replied. "You've probably never heard of it. Small, really small college."

"Sure I know it. Outside Grand Rapids, right?"

Amanda brightened a little. "Yup, that's the one."

"I hear wonderful things about it."

"It's a good place. I'm lucky to be there. On scholarship for a lot of it." Amanda looked at her hands and played with the thick silver band around her index finger.

"That's great. Your parents must be so proud of you."

Amanda looked at Olivia. "Only my dad. It's only him and me. I guess he's proud I got in. I don't think he expects me to graduate."

"Why's that?"

"Destiny. Or maybe genetics," she answered half-heartedly. "My mom—she was messed up. I guess I look like her." She shrugged her shoulders and stood up. "I wouldn't know. Anyway, he thinks I'll screw up. Or maybe he's afraid I won't. And then he'd be wrong about me."

Olivia studied Amanda's face. She put some pieces of her story together. "So, you and the phoenix. Both of you out of the ashes?"

Amanda nodded and turned to leave, the head and wing tips of her tattooed phoenix again visible. She looked back and said, "What he doesn't know is that I'd rather die than fail. I'm not going back there. Not to him. Not ever."

Chapter 14

Fortunately, Monday nights are quiet in the restaurant business. Even on a vacation island like Mackinac, Mondays were often light. It could be blissful or mind-numbing, depending on your assigned station. Olivia had been assigned to the old dining room, charged with three two-tops along the windows, and two four-tops just beyond. Mrs. B must have decided she remembered enough to manage five tables without having to shadow a more experienced server. Olivia remembered Amanda's comment. *I know how you feel. I will not fail either.*

She didn't. Some combination of her earlier experience, years serving nightly dinners for the three of them, and frequent dinner parties for eight or more equipped her. It was and always will be about timing. She simply had to coordinate the timing of orders in, salads out, main courses served. By the time she discreetly delivered the check, no one believed they were anything less than her favorite table of the evening. One couple asked her if they were light-staffed that night. Another asked if she was a family member of the Branagans. Olivia figured they had no other way to explain her age. Or, she just looked like she owned the place. Doubtful.

Olivia served four couples and a party of four that evening and made a tidy $122.00—and a quarter—in tips. She smiled when she looked at the total. She and Nate loved and often retold his dad's signature joke. The one about a homemaker trying to help with the household budget by entertaining men in the afternoons while her husband was at the office. When her husband discovered her illicit work-at-home business, she confessed everything. "But, honey, I was only trying to contribute something to the budget. I know how you worry. At least look at what I've earned." With tears in her eyes, she showed him her ledger, the accounting of money she'd kept in a metal box. The sum was $550.25. Her husband looked at it and said, "This is a fair amount of money. But who was the cheap bastard who gave you the quarter?" The wife replied, "What do you mean?" She took the ledger from him. "They all did."

When Olivia returned to her room that night, she discovered an envelope with her name on it propped on a bed pillow. Next to it was a chocolate mint and a breakfast menu. Turn down service. How nice. Almost makes me forget I'm hired help. Almost.

Olivia loosened the silk necktie around her neck with one hand as she reached for the envelope. *Shoot. Was I supposed to leave this in the uniform room? Oh well, add it to my tab. Maybe they have already and this is my bill. Honestly, the walls have eyes around here.* She sat on the bed and slipped a sheet of white paper out of the envelope. It was a printed copy of an email, sent to the Iroquois reservations office. On the subject line she read her name and the words "Prospective Caretaker."

Dear Ms. Nash—though I hope I shall soon have permission and reason to call you Olivia.

Very sweet if a little stilted. It continued:

I have been told that you may have need of a home during your summer stay on our island. I am unable to stay in our Lilac Cottage this year, and yet, this may be a most important year for someone to awaken our little cottage from its winter slumber. Regrettably, I am expecting to sell our treasure this summer. It's of no interest to my children for whom the descriptor "quaint" is synonymous with decrepit, and "charm," a euphemism for "total teardown." And its location—inland—doesn't satisfy their requirements for an unobstructed water view. Perhaps you can tell that I don't share their point of view. (But the breeze up the hill is lovely. Especially during lilac season. They have forgotten that.) Well, I will not bequeath it to them so that it can be promptly dismantled into some pile of rubbish to be transformed into a wonder of modern architecture. Not on my watch. Why is it that more privileged generations are apt to miss the hidden gifts of something far simpler?

Olivia reread the first paragraph of the email. It seemed anachronistic to read this sentiment in a printed copy of an email. She suspected the writer preferred longhand script to typed correspondence.

But I go on. Forgive me. I expect I may yet sell our cottage to a suitable buyer. Until such time, I have need of a renter, more appropriately, a caretaker, who will be willing to polish our forgotten gem and show it off from time to time to prospective buyers who meet with my approval.

Now, Olivia (I hope I have already earned the privilege of referring to you as such), I understand you may have the, how shall I put it... the maturity and appreciation for the gracious living that I believe embodies the spirit of our cottage. College students who roam Mackinac Island during the summer have an underdeveloped appreciation for the art of hospitality and homemaking. For this, they cannot be blamed. After a season of extending hospitality for the sakes of their paychecks and tuition obligations, some seem to gain an understanding of what their mothers have spent a lifetime providing for them—even those mothers who spend their days away from those very same, welcoming homes.

It's as though I am having coffee with this woman, Olivia thought. *She can really chat. But her language is captivating.* Olivia's eyes dropped to the bottom of the page to read the name of the letter's writer. The email address at top revealed little. Just "lilaccottage@gmail.com." Another anachronism. Bet in the day, this woman had scented stationery embossed with the words "Lilac Cottage."

Yup. It read, "Frankie." Just as Mrs. B had said. Frankie could be a man or a woman, she supposed. But this writer is definitely a woman—a throwback, and a woman. Olivia scanned the rest of the letter. She found the address. Mrs. B would get a set of keys to her. She would not be asked to remit a rental payment, but she would, instead, be offered a stipend for opening up and maintaining the house. And she would have a fund, amount to be determined, should she feel inspired to spruce up the place.

What? A decorating allowance too? This is too good to be true. There has to be a downside. But the only one she could discover was Frankie's apology for the dust and dust covers that would welcome her. And Frankie provided the name of her exterminator, Lady Bug Exterminating, "should the mice have forced entry and set up shop."

Two days later, while Olivia was entranced folding the limitless pile of napkins for dinner service, she was startled by the sound of keys dropping into the center of the pile.

"I would suggest you visit in the morning," Mrs. B said, cat eyes penetrating Olivia's fog. "It'll be too dark to visit after your shift ends. You might change your mind about staying there. Better to see it in the light of day."

"Oh no, I can't imagine anything would change my mind. Do you know, Frankie has provided me an allowance in case I want to have a little decorating fun?"

Mrs. B arched an eyebrow. "Fun? Perhaps you should start by unearthing the cottage contents from months and months of accumulated dust. Perhaps you won't have quite the same enthusiasm for decorating once you've accomplished that."

She is such a downer for a woman surrounded by beauty and lovely things, living the good life as she does, Olivia thought. "I have no dust allergies, thankfully, and housecleaning is far more enjoyable when it isn't your home that you're cleaning, don't you think?"

"I wouldn't know."

Of course. She hadn't cleaned her own home or anyone else's in years, if ever. She does white-glove tests, not rubber-glove work.

"Olivia," she stopped in the doorway which only made her look more diminutive. "You have my permission to take some of our rags and cleaning supplies with you to Lilac Cottage. You may know we make our own cleanser and wood polish?" Olivia shook her head no. "I'll have a bag of supplies gathered for you."

"Thank you so…" Mrs. B hadn't lingered to accept Olivia's thanks.

Chapter 15

As had been suggested, it was midday when Olivia climbed the four steps of the cottage's walk to its porch. Affixed to the siding was a faded historical marker. "1883?" she said aloud. "That's practically Civil War." She imagined the sagging floors, drafty rooms, and forlorn windows that awaited her inside. But just as quickly she noticed the porch she was standing on. It wrapped around two sides of the cottage's white clapboard frame. The porch had a view of a neglected garden offset by a neatly trimmed lawn that fell away from it. The narrow planks of the porch floor could use a fresh coat of gray paint, she thought. But overall, it seemed sound, at least structurally so. She looked up and saw four hooks placed in position and wanting for a swing. Oh, the summer breezes to catch here. "Hold that thought," she whispered to the hooks. "I'll find your missing swing and you'll be back in business in no time."

She juggled the key into the dead bolt, recognizing that she was opening a Dutch door. Of course, so quaint. It had to be. With a good shove, the door gave way and Olivia stumbled into the darkened room. She made her way to the east-facing windows and folded the shutters back on themselves. The sunlight rushed in as if finally released.

"Oh, this." She looked around the room. "You little jewel. You're not nearly as decrepit as advertised. You were done wrong, little cottage." Olivia wandered the rooms on the first floor, pulling sheets and threadbare comforters from upholstered pieces, end and coffee tables, and a piano. "A piano?" To the left of the entry was a sizable bedroom with an en suite bath. "Surprising. On the first floor?" she said aloud. The bath was small but charmingly outfitted in white porcelain, brass fixtures, and a penny tile floor. It offered a walk-in shower. "This is convenient but somehow out of place. Bet there was a claw-footed tub here at one time. Too bad."

She reentered the living room which adjoined the dining room. There, pine paneling covered the lower walls. A faded floral print papered the walls above. That paper was met by a far more masculine, patriotic-looking wallpaper in the dining room. There'd been a debate here, she guessed, and a suitable compromise. Floral meets bicentennial eagles. Floral, or at least white paint, was going to win the next skirmish if Olivia exercised her option to refresh this little pine palace.

Up a steep staircase, Olivia found two more bedrooms and another bathroom. This bathroom was outfitted with a claw-foot tub and, just beyond, a hinged window draped with white café curtains. "Oh, you're mine." A long soak, a good book, a glass of wine, and quiet. That would be reward enough for helping Lilac Cottage breathe again. She broke from that scene and wandered into the nearby bedrooms to discover more tongue-and-groove paneling. Maybe drywall was expensive? Or hard to get here? In someone's flight of fancy, the paneling had been painted in pastels. One room in mint-chip green and one in cotton-candy pink. These have to go. Mint green reminded her of her dentist's office, circa 1951, antiseptic in color and scent. "We're going to need a lot of paint, Frankie," and she made a mental note to calculate what that growing cost might be.

Down a nearly hidden, even narrower staircase at the back of the cottage, Olivia entered the kitchen. "Well, aren't you a surprise?" The room was out of place and from another time entirely. Marble countertops atop painted cabinets in a gray, woodsy green. This is far, far newer. Can lights in the ceiling? She inventoried: a double oven, commercial grade refrigerator, Bosch dishwasher. Oh, what? This too? A pantry? She moved toward an open door into a darkened closet.

She flipped the switch to see shelves replete with every manner of china and serving piece any hostess could hope to have. Someone was hosting some fancy parties here! Who needs this much china for a small cottage? Cringing at the evidence of mice having scurried across a white porcelain platter, she turned and saw yet another door. She went to open it. No luck. It had a dead bolt that opened from the other side. Where would this go? "Note to self, ask Frankie," she said aloud.

Back into the kitchen proper, Olivia took a closer look at the open shelving running across two walls of the room, separated by a newer window positioned over the sink. She looked out at the expanse of pine trees all around and then cranked open the window to inhale the piney scent. If she squinted, could she make out the water and the Mackinac Bridge? More realistically, she might be able to from the roof in the dead of winter.

"So, no water view. Big deal. I'll have that aplenty while I'm waiting tables on the patio." Hearing herself say that was kind of a shock. Since when did she wait tables on a waterfront patio? Who does that? At her age? Was it unseemly for a wife of Nathan Nash to work for tips? Was it beneath her? Desperate? A break from reality? Maybe. Okay, yes. Yes, it was. But in that moment, she couldn't have been happier.

Chapter 16

The Carriage House awakened slowly to the summer season. It worked out its creaks and kinks with a staff, both front and back of the house, who were still learning their trade with every order. Computerized orders-in and computer-tabulated bills out were new to Olivia, but the napkins were still folded in the same pyramid shape, plates were served only from the left and removed from the right, and even on a slow night, a server could walk away with a little in cash tips and more tallied to the next paycheck. Olivia planned to use that found money to purchase anything she needed to set up her new household.

The world was going cashless, and her cash and her stash would be known only to her. It was almost as if by spending from her tips, she wasn't outlaying real money. It was more like Monopoly money. And she wasn't taking any money from the family budget. You could argue she was actually saving them money. Or so she reasoned as she made her way from Doud's Market to Lilac Cottage. She'd moved in her spare belongings two weeks before. The quiet retreat, dust-covered and pine-paneled from an earlier century (or two), had potential. All Lilac Cottage needed was more of the Iroquois's homemade cleanser; wallpaper removal; a few (honestly, ten) gallons of paint; fresh bedding for four beds; and two, maybe three new rugs—oh, and a reupholstered sofa and restored rocker. It wasn't too far from perfect. One day, anyway.

Olivia passed the historic Biddle House, juggling two brown paper bags stuffed with apples, berries, cheeses, a bottle of wine, and the additional cleaning supplies. She'd over-shopped given her decision to walk and forgo the bike ride to town. When her phone rang, she shifted the bags to retrieve it from her tote. Nope. Her pocket? No. The ring became more insistent and then she remembered tossing her phone into a grocery bag. She lowered a bag to the sidewalk to grab the phone before the call was lost and, instead, lost the apples balanced on top of the other bag. Letting them roll in order to retrieve the phone, Olivia could see it was Luke calling. "Luke? It's you?"

"Mom. Yeah, it's me. What are you doing?"

"Oh well, um. Just some grocery shopping. You know, putting away some groceries," she said as she darted into Market Street in pursuit of the still-rolling apples. Thankfully at just after nine o'clock, tourist traffic by foot, bike, or carriage was still light. She kneeled in the middle of the street, reaching out for the apples with her left hand while balancing the phone and paper shopping bag in her right.

"Mom? You sound out of breath. Are you okay?"

"Of course! I dropped a few things. Don't want the apples to trip up any horse… radish. Horse… radish… jar. It rolled right out of my bag. Whew. They uh, you know, horseradish jars, well really, jars in general can just get away from you. You'd be surprised," she offered, realizing again what a novice liar she was. She turned her back to the street and the remaining apples to focus on Luke. "So, honey, how are you? Are you liking it? You don't post many pix."

"Mom, I'm good. Great even. It's awesome. The campers are good kids," he said of the "kids" who were maybe three to four years younger than his advanced age, soon to be twenty-one. "Some of them have never been out of the city and never up in the trees walking on wires. It's pretty cool that I can help them get over their fear and get across. You wouldn't believe what it does for them."

"Oh, Luke, I'd love to hear more about it."

"That's why I'm calling. I only have a couple of minutes. Do you think you and Dad could come here around my birthday? Looks like I can get a couple of days off on the weekend between sessions five and six. That'd be right around my birthday. What do you think?"

What Luke couldn't have known was that Olivia would find it nearly impossible to get away from the restaurant during any of the summer yacht races, especially that weekend. "Of course," she said, because nearly impossible wouldn't keep her away from her son. "What do you have in mind?"

"I was thinking we should go to that island you were talking about. Some people here have talked about it. It'd be close to camp anyway."

"It sure would," and closer to Olivia than Luke could imagine. "But, Buddy, unless things have changed, July weekends on Mackinac are nuts. Crowded. Hot. I'm not even sure we could get a room." Her words were being drummed out by the clop-clop sound of an approaching team of horses and a man's voice, amplified, saying, "To your right is the Biddle House, home to merchants Agatha and Edward Biddle who moved here in…"

"Mom? What's *that*?" Olivia left the grocery bag on the sidewalk, put an apple over the phone's mic, and made her way inside the whitewashed cabin.

"Whoops. TV. Had it on a travel channel last night. So loud, huh?"

"Ma'am," the voice came from behind her. "Your ticket?" She covered the phone mic again.

"Mom? Are you there?"

She turned to the waiting docent in her eighteenth-century dress and mouthed an apology, gesturing with the apple in her left hand to the phone in her right, while struggling to keep the remaining bag in her arm upright.

"Luke, bad connection. I can barely hear you. Let's sort it all out by text. Can't wait. Love you so much." Click. I just hung up on my son. The realization hurt.

"So sorry about that," she offered the docent. "I actually don't have a ticket and I'm not touring. I work here. On the island, I mean." Just then the door darkened with an imposing figure in its frame.

"Nash?" It was Sean, Carriage House chef. He was holding her other grocery bag. "Did you forget this in your hurry to tour the Biddle House?" He looked at the young woman in eighteenth-century costume who was now too confused to say anything. "This lady's been known to skip lines and dip out on entrance fees. I'd kick her out."

Olivia scowled at Sean and then turned to the docent. "He's kidding." She explained that she was on an important call when the carriage driver's spiel interrupted. "I'm sorry, I ran into your open door to find quiet. I'll be back, though, for a proper tour." She took the bag from Sean and backed him out of the door.

"How did you…?"

"I was watching you. I was coming from the bank and saw your little spill in the street." He tilted his head in the direction of the island's only bank. "You got some moves there, Mrs. Nash, chasing apples. Wish you'd move that fast in the kitchen."

"Again. So funny." Embarrassed and now annoyed, she rebalanced the bags in her arms and lowered her gaze. "Excuse me, Chef. I've got to go. I have a lunch shift." She walked past him, down the wooden steps to the sidewalk.

"Mrs. Nash! You forgot one!" She turned to see an apple sailing toward her. She shifted her weight to lean left and the apple landed safely in the bag. On the strawberries.

She turned to walk away, this time without responding. "Mrs. Nash!"

"Uggh." She stopped and swiveled her shoulders. "*Yes*? I'm in a hurry. You know. Lunch?"

"Nice reflexes. You could be a decent waitress one day, even at your age. With enough practice. And a better attitude."

"Thanks." She nodded once, turned, and straightened her shoulders, starting again toward the cottage, saying in a whisper, "Yeah, okay, boy wonder chef, you can take this apple *and* my attitude and just… stuff…"

"To your right—the Biddle House," said another carriage driver on speaker to the passengers on his tour. "Constructed in the late 1700s back when the majority of the island's residents were Native Americans. It's the oldest home on the island."

Chapter 17

Olivia could still make it to her lunch shift on time. Barely. It was a little more than a mile to the restaurant by bike. Hers was a blue and cream three-speed with a basket in front and a tear on the vinyl seat. She'd gotten it for a song at the police station, just as the Star Line employee had said. She had later discovered there were other forgotten items to purchase at the local church, Ste. Anne's. When island workers left for the summer, instead of wasting time packing, some left belongings in bins or closets at the employee apartments. Security deposits were mom and dad money. Who cared? Ste. Anne's sold the castoffs for a small profit that they used to offer food and beverage to groups that met at the church: a knitting group, book clubs and Bible studies, a gathering of international island workers, and AA among them.

After she'd arrived, Olivia had picked up a yoga mat and straps, some batik-printed pillows, and a few brushed cotton sweatshirts for thirty-seven dollars. There were other items there, too. Some halter dresses with built-in shorts, good for biking or knocking around town. She might go back and have a closer look, one day, maybe, if she kept up her new routines.

She was changing and her reflection was becoming less familiar. Instead of taming her hair into a smooth, contoured bob, she gave in to the winds and let it go. It now framed her face in waves. And being outside, biking the island, and serving patio tables had lightened her hair color and coaxed out freckles dotting her nose. Her shoulders were becoming defined with the help of the trays she balanced on them, and thanks to the Community Center yoga classes, her arms were looking sculpted. She felt better too. Stronger, independent. Free, if a little guilty when she considered her newfound freedom for too long.

Olivia arrived at the restaurant and locked her bike to the out-of-sight employee bike rack. Hurrying through the employee entrance into the kitchen, she nearly collided with Mrs. B.

"Olivia Nash." The woman stood motionless as Olivia skidded to a stop in front of her. "You're just the person I need. Amanda isn't well today. We're short-staffed as it is. Would you take her section? You'll have the patio. All of it. Can you handle that?"

"Nash! Order up! Let's go!"

"Of course," Olivia replied to Mrs. B, ignoring Chef. "Did Amanda say anything more? I hope she's all right."

"Mrs. Nash!"

"I hope so. She's scheduled to work tomorrow night and we need her. Race weeks are coming up fast." On consecutive July weekends, the Port Huron to Mackinac and Chicago to Mackinac yacht races filled every available hotel room. They booked as soon as the reservation window opened. Dinner reservations were made months in advance. Sailors celebrated their long races by passing the baton to island employees who started their own races. The prize for winning the yacht races was bragging rights. That was it. But island servers received generous tips from sailors intoxicated by their accomplishment and the spirits they lifted high to toast themselves and their crew.

"Nash!" Sean's bark put an end to their discussion. "Mrs. Nash!" he shouted again a second later. She looked toward the line and back to the swinging doors that Mrs. B passed through. She was gone.

"Holy shi… shi… holy shiitake mushrooms!" she sputtered.

"Nash!"

"Cheez… its, Chef!" *I will* not *lose my cool. He's just a guy. A summer worker like me. Breathe.* Olivia spun on her heels toward the plates under the warmers.

Neither the oppressive heat nor his arrogance would make her lose it here. *I will not lose my composure. I'm bigger than that. Inhale.* "Chef. Danny," she gave a nod to the line cook just behind Sean. She inhaled. "You may have noticed that I was talking with Mrs. B, your employer and mine, when you rudely interrupted us." She slapped the stainless covers over the plates of grilled salmon salads and the Monte Cristo sandwiches and stacked them on her tray. "Besides, I heard you the first time."

"You heard me? At your age? Hearing loss, you know. Pretty common."

"You just get funnier."

"Not laughing, Nash. Salmon's getting cold. How about you get that to table five? You know, do your job?"

"On. My. Way. Chef," she said through gritted teeth. Insufferable. What was he doing working lunch anyway? As executive chef, he was way too highbrow for that. Or, he thought so. "By the way," she said over her right shoulder. "There's no grass growing under these feet. My tips would tell you that." She walked out the doors and up the four stairs to the dining room and patio beyond.

"Grass under her feet? What the hell?" said Danny, wiping the sweat from his forehead. "I don't get her. Shiitake mushrooms? Jesus!" Danny laughed. "Shiitake mushrooms, fudge, Cheez-Its." Her fake swears were becoming an amusement for the guys on the line. "She's a nut job."

"Eh, she's on her best behavior," Chef replied. "Mrs. B was here. In time you'll break her. I have faith in you." And he turned back to finish plating four more whitefish sandwiches. "I want to be there when it happens." He looked under the rack and saw no servers waiting.

"Order up! *Damn it to hell!* Where *is* everyone?"

Chapter 18

Olivia didn't get back to Lilac Cottage until five o'clock. She'd stuck around after the lunch shift to continue working the patio and serving the boozy ice cream drinks the Carriage House was known for. Fruity daiquiris of all kinds and piña coladas. They were perfect on a hot summer afternoon, but even this many years later, when a man ordered a strawberry daiquiri which the bartender topped with whipped cream and a berry, Olivia couldn't help but to have a little less respect for the guy. Really? An ice cream drink? How about a beer or martini? She'd observed long ago that guys who ordered ice cream daiquiris were never good tippers. That hadn't changed.

Once home, she stripped off her uniform and put on some shorts and an oversized Spartan T-shirt she'd picked up at Ste. Anne's orphaned items sale. She opened a Bell's Oberon and sat down at her laptop, hoping she'd find an email reply from Frankie. She'd written the day before to ask about removing the wallpaper and painting the wood panels. The cottage deserved some pampering and a little frivolity to liven up her inborn sensibility.

Thankfully, internet service on the island was surprisingly good, even at Lilac Cottage, another anachronistic feature of her new home. She scrolled through the incoming messages. There it was. Terrific. Olivia wanted Frankie's permission. Maybe she'd get it.

Dear Olivia,

Thank you for your last note. I'm so glad you've found Lilac Cottage to be a peaceful retreat from the busyness of our island in summer. I'm further delighted that you've enjoyed the quilts left in the armoire. So, you discovered the paint in the storage shed? I don't suppose it owes us anything. How long has it been there? I can't recall. Perhaps the label will give you a clue.

No matter. I think you should purchase new paint. I've come around. As much as my husband loved the tongue-and-groove paneling (and I've come to believe most men do like dark wood paneling), it's time to brighten up the place. I agree. It's time to think of the next residents of our little cottage.

There's a hardware store in St. Ignace. Webber's. Perhaps you could visit. They'll bill your purchase to our house account and they can deliver all you need to the cottage. Please purchase any and all supplies that might make the job easier.

I wonder, though, are you sure you're quite up to this? I am aware how busy island establishments become as we near race weeks. You've said you love to paint (and I admire you all the more for it), but this might prove to be too much. Should you change your mind, deciding the task too herculean, I will understand. Say nothing more. Just knowing someone loves my cottage as much as I have over so many years warms my heart.

Fondly,
Frankie

P.S. I nearly forgot. You've no doubt discovered the annex off the kitchen and the locked door that leads to it. We've three additional bedrooms, quite small, and a bathroom there. I will send you the key, via the restaurant. You're welcome to have a look. Years ago, when the island wasn't the attraction it is now, those rooms were rented. Sometimes to seasonal workers, and sometimes to transients who needed a refuge, a safe spot to rest their heads for a time. My parents became known for that. It didn't help pay the expenses but they never seemed to mind. Anyway, take care as you travel to St. Ignace. I just hope you're not overwhelmed by these projects. It seems an enormous undertaking. F.

Overwhelmed? Oh no, Frankie. Painting is soothing. Olivia loved seeing a space transformed with just a brush and a gallon of paint. And painting allowed her mind to wander. She stared at Frankie's message on the computer screen and thought about Luke and Nate.

Nate. Oh, they'd talked every few days at first. Then it was text messages every few days and a call once a week. She learned where she should go when they talked so he'd have no reason to suspect she was anywhere but Lake Ellyn. But she was far from there and getting more distant, not that she sought that. Their lives, lived in parallel now, used to intersect over Luke, the house, their friends, and their calendars. With Luke happily absorbed in his work at the camp, and Nate, overwhelmed by the merger's demands, their calendars were quite separate—not even shared on their phones any longer.

A chasm formed in their relationship. It had alarmed her at first, when their conversations had become less frequent and more superficial. Now, when she forced herself to stop and consider it, she was more alarmed that the chasm, even as it widened, was becoming familiar and not so alarming at all.

This can't be good, she thought. *This isn't what a marriage is supposed to be.* She took another drink from the bottle in her hand and resolved to call Nate. Tomorrow. Well, maybe tomorrow.

Chapter 19

Olivia awoke later than she'd expected. The rain falling on the roof of Lilac Cottage and blowing against the windows had soothed her into the deep escape of sleep. She made her way down the stairs, a warm light and the smell of coffee drawing her to the kitchen. She filled her favorite mug (of the dozen there) with its thumb handle inviting her hands to wrap themselves around its warm, full belly, and she looked out to the porch. The narrow slats of the wood floor were dotted with puddles in the uneven places.

This wasn't the right day to ferry to St. Ignace. The water would be rough and the winds cold. Instead, she decided to linger—to read a little and fuss around the cottage, watering the plants she'd picked up at a weekend market and freshening the cream pitchers, teacups, and bottles that she'd filled with flowers from the perennial beds ribboning the cottage's foundation.

Her thoughts drifted to Amanda. They often did. Amanda presented a steel exterior, cool and unaffected in conversation with servers and kitchen staff her age. Oh, she was competent and professional at her station, but she rarely engaged in small talk with fellow servers or guests. She revealed little and did her job.

That steel exterior seemed a thin veneer to Olivia. While she did her job ably, Amanda was also prone to slip away, Olivia noticed, for just a few minutes. She'd return, swigging from a ginger ale bottle that seemed always to be at hand. She recalled Amanda's light-headedness when they'd met, and she'd seen Amanda sweep a hand over her belly, like she was checking on it. She's pregnant. Of course. Olivia was beginning to recognize the signs even if the younger servers weren't. Mrs. B must have her suspicions also. Amanda was looking pale and unsteady before most of her lunch shifts. Maybe Mrs. B thought Amanda was hungover. Summer employees were known to work hard and play hard, and the dock porters were more than willing to initiate newcomers like Amanda. They were a party on wheels—on and off shift. Olivia had worked with Amanda often enough to doubt entanglements with a dock porter. Amanda wouldn't fall for their frat-boy antics. But maybe she had? Just once? Which brought Olivia full circle. How long could Amanda conceal what would soon become obvious?

That in mind, Olivia determined to dress for the wet weather and take a walk to the Island Bookstore. It might be a good time to pull a book on pregnancy. She'd called the Island Bookstore days before to ask if they might carry the pregnancy bible, *What to Expect When You're Expecting*. The clerk she'd spoken to said they did. She thanked him and said she'd stop in sometime to buy it.

When she first worked on the island, the bookstore was above Doud's, on the second floor. A dim and dusty trove of new, used, and old books, it offered an assortment of printed items. If it was still there. She conjured the memory of its keeper long ago. His name was Cliff. He was pretty old even then, she thought. But when she'd worked on the island, fifty seemed old. Practically ancient.

"Shoot," she reminded herself. "I really should check in with Nate." Taking a deep breath, she dialed his number and promptly got his voicemail message. After the beep she offered, "Hey, it's me. Just checking in. Rainy day here. Off to run a couple of errands. I hope you're managing. Oh, and hey, we've got to talk about Luke's birthday. Twenty-one! I may go see him." (Though how that would work, she wasn't sure.) "Okay, love you." Click.

Hmm… *was* it rainy in Lake Ellyn too? She hoped so. But would Nate think to check? Or care to? Doubtful. He would see that Olivia had called and save himself the time of listening to her message and just text a reply. Maybe he'd text that he missed her and would call her at the first opportunity. *That hadn't happened in a while*, Olivia thought, as she pulled on a rain jacket and lifted its hood to cover her head.

At least I tried. She sighed and stepped onto the porch, yanked the heavy door closed, and let the screen door bang shut behind her.

Although the rain had slowed, the day was gray and dreary. Olivia decided to walk into town instead of taking her bike. The walk would do her good. Clear her mind. She wandered down a back road and the Annex to walk through the Grand Hotel property and down Cadotte Avenue. From her view near the Grand, Cadotte was all but deserted. Horses pulled carriage taxis with their clear acetate wings down. The wings were meant to protect the one or two hotel guests and their luggage riding inside. A raw day like this might keep a day-tripper off the island, but the prepaid price of a night at the Grand together with its stingy cancellation policy made every guest intrepid. Hope for the best weather, drink at a bar through the worst of it.

The clip-clop of the horses was slow. Tired. The rain muffled the sound of their slog up the hill. Why hurry? Olivia passed the taxi, and gave an insider's nod to the driver clad in a rain jacket and bandana, barely protected from the occasional gust that would stir up and slap the plastic wings against the carriage frame. Olivia continued her slow, puddle-avoiding walk down the hill, moving past the maples in the wide tree lawn between the street and sidewalks. In the center of this promenade to the Grand were stately lampposts in a belle epoque style as old as the hotel itself. The flowers around their bases bent over themselves as if to protect their faces from the wind and rain. It was a dreary day all in all. One of her favorite kinds, really. Just a day to move slowly, absentmindedly, letting sadness, like rain, seep through her soul.

She missed Luke and Nate and how they defined her life. Their absence; no, it was their ability to do life so easily without her, that's what felt heavy. It erased what she'd known about herself—who she was. This break from familiar patterns and the life that had been hers was a way of consoling herself. Or so she reasoned. She was processing a transition. Grieving what was slipping from her grasp so she could free herself to accept the future. She had counseled her friends with those same words. Why wouldn't they also apply to her? This waitress stint was just a break. A sabbatical of sorts.

The guilt that buzzed around her like a no-see-um was absolved, at least for the moment, by recognizing her own sadness. Olivia let out an audible sigh. No one was near enough to notice. Sorrow, she thought, must be the seed of wisdom. She was getting wiser by the day. But she was also getting comfortable living without a plan. The uncharted was less dangerous than she'd figured. Some days it was deliciously satisfying. What did that mean? She shook her head to close her mind to all of it. Enough analysis for today. Like a tour guide at Fort Mackinac she moved herself along, "And we're walking. And we're walking."

Olivia went right at the end of the promenade to head toward the water. The gray sky seemed to press on it. A faint carbon line marked their boundaries. A few whitecaps were offshore but they weren't angry. In the distance, she saw a man straining to affix a white golf umbrella to some sort of stand. He eventually accomplished his mission. As she got closer, Olivia saw the man was wearing a tattered tweed blazer. He had a multicolored bucket hat pulled low over his ears and tortoiseshell reading glasses balanced on his nose. The stand she'd seen was a tripod.

"Greetings!" said the man at her approach. He looked at her over the rims of his glasses. "Beautiful day!" He returned his gaze to the tripod.

Olivia walked closer. "Beautiful? I'm not sure I'd go that far. Not quite yet."

"Oh, this? It's clearing up. Don't you see? A perfect day to capture the sun breaking through the clouds."

Was it his voice or his enthusiasm that seemed familiar to Olivia? She took a closer look at the setup on the tripod. It was some sort of makeshift easel. A board with holes to the left into which the man was placing brushes. A mess of paints were to the right of the brushes. The man clipped a canvas with pencil etchings to a vertical surface. "Oh. You're a painter." Well, obviously. What a stupid statement.

"Oh, *that* I'd like to be. But I suppose if one paints, and I do, then one is a painter. I'd prefer to be called an artist but painter will do for now. And it's a truthful assessment." He straightened the canvas. "As my friend and yours, the Bard of Avon, has adeptly articulated," the man cleared his throat to boom, "'To thine own self be true, and it must follow, as the night the day, one cannot then be false to any man.'"

He wriggled his nose and snuffed, and turned toward Olivia. Leveling his gaze he asked, "And you? Are you a visitor to our fine island? What brings you here?"

"Well, funny you should ask. I'm a visitor to be sure, but I also landed a summer job on the island. Somehow." She pulled the hood off her head, releasing the curls the humidity had encouraged. She pushed the damp mop off her face. "It's a long story."

"I love nothing better than a long story. The longer the better. But let's not watch paint dry. I must be about my work."

"Oh, of course! I need to be on my way. I like long stories, too, so I'm off to the bookstore to pick up a few."

"I'm afraid that won't be possible today." He kept his eyes steady on the canvas.

"Oh?"

"Well, certainly. I know the proprietor, if it's the bookstore on Main Street you're hoping to patronize."

"You know him?" she asked, but she felt she knew.

"Indeed, I do." And he jabbed his brush into some muddy brown paint. "I am he. And my bookstore is open twice weekly on Wednesday and Thursday only."

So, it was Cliff. No doubt. Who else talks like that? But did he recognize her? Not likely.

"Oh, shoot. It's Tuesday, isn't it?" She just wasn't ready to engage in a long conversation about her, her past, present, or future. None of it seemed worth opening the door to recall how she'd known him and what had become of her. Not today anyway. She needed to move along, but he kept talking. And jabbing paint onto the canvas.

"It is indeed, Tuesday. In time, I'll have this troublesome knee repaired and I'll once again climb to the rafters without strain or regret. Until that time, it's twice weekly."

"That sounds wise."

"Wise? We both know what Hemingway said about the wisdom of old men, don't we?" He turned his head and glanced at her before continuing as if she might join him in recitation. Olivia smiled and, like a pitcher on the mound, shook him off.

"'Old men do not grow wise. They grow careful.' And so I am."

"Ah, of course. I'm sorry about your knee. You really must be careful." She tiptoed around the back of the painter, Cliff, and toward town. Over her shoulder she said, "I'll stop in, or up, sometime, maybe next week, or the following, during your open hours." Oh geez. Keep walking. He doesn't seem to recognize you, thank goodness. "Happy painting!" Anonymity once given up is gone forever.

"I shall await your visit."

Olivia heard him murmur something else. Maybe something about catching up, but she needed to move along. She'd reintroduce herself some other time, when she had composed a better story about herself and her summer situation.

With the rain now barely a mist, Olivia wandered further into town and took a right toward the Star Line docks. Why not go to St. Ignace? I'm a painter, too, she figured. And a painter needs paint.

The ferry ride was quick as promised and staying below kept Olivia in her bubble of quiet thought, until she walked out of the ferry and up the dock toward State Street. A squeal, a horn, a backfire. Cars. She'd forgotten how irksome traffic noise was, even in a small town. She found the boardwalk and made her way south toward Webber's Hardware. One gift shop lured her to enter. Another drew her in. She happened upon a café. Why not? She had the time to enjoy a leisurely brunch. She even found a Sunday *New York Times* puzzle left behind on the seat beside her. Only a few squares were filled in with pencil gray. *Let's see if I can help.* She started, in ink and without hesitation. First instinct responses. If they were wrong, so be it.

An hour later, she left a thirty percent tip for the server who let her loiter in the booth. Having finished the puzzle with only two looks at the solution, and quite pleased with herself, she gathered her thoughts and set out to purchase paint on Frankie's house account.

Door bells tinkled as she pushed open the heavy blue door into Webber's. Over his shoulder a man in a red vest hollered, "I'll be right with you. Help yourself to coffee while you wait."

"Thank you. No rush. I'm here for paint and paint supplies. I'll just nose around." She wandered the aisles while the man helped his customer. Gadgets, cleaning implements, gardening tools, whatnots for every thingamajig. No one ever left a hardware store without something that was needed but never scribbled on a list. She found her way to the Benjamin Moore display and pulled the paint strip with "White Dove" on the lineup. White Dove never disappoints.

"Now, may I help you, ma'am?" She saw the man in the red vest had a name tag. His name was Tom. Tom Webber, she assumed.

"Yes, please. I'd like three, well, actually make that *four* gallons of White Dove, Satin Impervo, please. Oh, and the same amount of your best primer." At once, a man whose back had been toward her, turned.

"Nash? What are you doing with four gallons of paint?"

Startled at being recognized by someone unexpected in an unfamiliar place, she said, "Chef? What are *you* doing here?"

"I asked you first. What are you doing with all that paint?"

"It's really none of your business, you know, but to answer your question I'll be painting fourteen hundred square feet of knotty pine paneling. And window trim. A lot of it. With Benjamin Moore. My preferred medium."

"What the hell? You painting the waitresses' apartment? It's paneled in pine? I'll be damned. No wonder you came back to work as a waitress. At your age." Chef whistled and rubbed his hands together. "Employee apartment living must be pretty good these days." By this time Tom, the store clerk, likely the owner, was observing their conversation with obvious interest.

"No, Chef," in the tone of a frustrated mother to a petulant child, "first of all, I think the term 'server' is preferred to 'waitress' these days. Must be your age. Second, I'm not living with the other employees. I have a special arrangement to care for a lovely little cottage."

She turned her full attention to the clerk, dismissing Chef, but he stood still, ignoring her dismissal.

"Tom," she said, "since you heard most of our conversation, I'd like those four gallons of paint, oh, and the primer and assorted supplies, billed to the house account for Frankie. Goodness, I don't actually know her last name, but she owns Lilac Cottage. I'm doing some work there. She may have contacted you about that."

"Lilac Cottage?" Chef and Tom asked in unison.

"Oh, you know of it? Both of you? Clearly," she answered her own question. "Yes, Lilac Cottage."

"You know Frankie?" asked Chef.

"Apparently so. I'm living in her home and restoring it—a bit of it anyway." She put the paint strip on the counter. "White Dove. It's a classic, isn't it?" Tom nodded and went about his business with an ear turned toward the conversation continuing across the counter.

"So, I take it you know Frankie?" she asked Chef.

"I do. Very well." He took a step closer.

"She's charming. I love her already. But how do *you* know her?"

"Well, Mrs. Nash, that's really none of *your* business, but I've known her a good long time. Charming isn't the first word that comes to mind, though. Demanding, determined, particular, maybe. Not exactly charming."

"Hmm. I suppose it's like the law of sowing and reaping, isn't it? Charm begets charm. She's been nothing but charming and delightful to me. Like an old friend."

Chef continued his inquiry. "So, just to get this right, you're living—now—in Lilac Cottage?"

Tom was placing another paint can on the shaker, but his neck strained toward them as if to hear her response.

"Yes, so I said." A little more slowly she repeated, "I'm living at Lilac Cottage."

"I'll be damned," Chef said quietly.

"I'm sorry. You said?"

"Nothing. Nothing." He began a slow walk toward the door. He stopped. "You're sure you're painting Lilac Cottage?" He emphasized again, "Lilac Cottage?"

"Oh, I'm quite sure it's Lilac Cottage. I have a key. Several of them to be precise. And every one of them seems to unlock the front door."

"Well, let me get this straight. You're painting perfectly fine pine paneling. You know there are knots and it'll bleed. Do you know that?"

"I *do* know that, Chef. That's why I'm buying oil-based primer and the best possible acrylic paint. I know. What I *don't* know is why I have to convince you of that." She tilted her head. "Do you have a ferry to catch?"

He looked at her for a moment and smiled slightly, murmuring something under his breath. Turning back to the door, he shot over his shoulder, "Tom, I know you'll take good care of Mrs. Nash."

"Oh yeah. Of course," Tom replied. "And, Sean, I'll call you when those parts come in. It'll be a few days."

"Great. Tom, make sure Mrs. Nash agrees to delivery. I can't have her carrying paint to the docks. I need her at full strength to wait on my tables. She's a little slow as it is." He stopped again, turned, and cupped his hands around his mouth. In a loud whisper and with a wink he said, "It's her age."

Tom laughed. Olivia rolled her eyes, picked up a fuzzy roller cover, and considered throwing it at his head.

Chapter 20

Amanda had been scheduled to work a double that day, an uncharacteristically slow one. The weather system that had stalled over the upper Midwest deposited a misty gloom over the island that had lingered, uninvited. It emptied the ferries and slowed traffic to the island's eateries as well. Carriage House reservations were trimmed to the hotel's guests, while day-trippers canceled with a promise to rebook (as if that were possible) at a later date.

With the lunch crowd thin, and prep work for dinner service complete, Amanda slipped into the closet where newly pressed napkins awaited folding in the restaurant's signature style. The repetitive work kept her in a quiet trance. She was soothed by the dim light, the small space, and the feel of the smooth, starched cotton under her hands.

"Amanda."

"Shit!" She jumped. Her chair fell backward and her hand knocked the glass of ginger ale she'd been sipping on its edge. Out of the corner of her eye Amanda saw the swift hand of Mrs. B grab the glass before its contents could drench the tower of napkins just folded.

Mrs. B handed the ginger ale to Amanda, ignoring her surprised greeting. "Amanda," she said calmly for the second time. "I think you're finished here."

"Oh no, Mrs. B, I'm sorry. You scared me. That's all. I never swear in front of customers—I mean, guests." She needed this job.

Actually, she needed the housing and food it provided more.

"Amanda," for the third time, this time sounding impatient. "You haven't lost your employment at the Carriage House. In fact, your work has been above par." Mrs. B added, "for the most part." Mrs. B never offered an unqualified compliment—unless you stayed the whole season. Then you became like family, or at least a favored domestic. That's what Amanda had been told anyway. Mrs. B continued. "We've a number of cancellations for this evening and with this intermittent rain, there will be no service on the patio. You'll have the evening off."

"Oh, but… but I was planning on it." The lost income was one thing, but she didn't relish the idea of staying in the apartment with two Iroquois maids whose day work would be done and a server or two who might also be called off. Spending time with her apartment mates had no appeal. "Maybe I could just fold, or help in the kitchen, or wipe down the racks or…"

"You'll be paid your usual hourly wage, Amanda. Enjoy an evening of rest. You've been looking a bit pale of late." It seemed Mrs. B reminded herself to smile. Her thin lips morphed into a half-hearted smile that stayed south of the readers atop her nose. Mrs. B's smiles rarely reached the corners of those emerald eyes. And then she was gone.

And then she was back. "Amanda."

Amanda jumped again. "Yes, ma'am."

"As a gentle reminder, we don't '*wipe down*' anything at the Carriage House. We clean and sanitize. Hmm?" That clarified, she ghosted away.

Amanda saluted in return, grateful that the small figure hadn't come back with a final message. Well, damn. She considered her options. Her roommates in the apartment were so young. About the same age, but so young. Adolescents. Juveniles. Life that had been too easy had cocooned them. They weren't ready to fly. They hadn't fought hard enough for wings. Everything had been handed to them, and in a designer bag. Amanda had fought. She was ready to fly. But now she was trapped.

Letting out a long sigh, she resigned herself to what she needed to do next. She was smart enough to recognize what she didn't know for sure but had to find out. Google was great, almost always, except you can't dog-ear digital content. She needed a reference book she could return to as needed.

Amanda left the small folding room and took her glass to the dishwashing station in the pits. As she passed by the stainless steel service line, loosening her Iroquois-issued tie, and clocking out by the app on her phone, she hadn't realized she had company in the kitchen.

"Amanda!"

"Jesus!" she jumped and exclaimed.

"Not him. Thanks all the same." Chef was at the grill station and he'd bent down between the service line and warming shelves above to see her. "You outa here? Tell me it isn't so."

She nodded. "Sorry, Chef. Mrs. B gave me the night off. Honestly, I'd rather be here."

"Nah, make the most of it. Nights off don't come often." He turned back to the broiler. "I'll manage the princesses without you."

She made a quick exit to the left, up the stairs to the dining room bar to get him a Diet Coke. He always had one at arm's reach. She had noticed that and was happy to make sure his well never ran dry. Whatever the reason, they had developed an understanding, a rapport.

She had said little, but maybe her expressions, if someone had noticed (and apparently, he had), maybe they gave her away. She bet her expressions spoke mostly about her disdain of princesses who'd been asked to work in a place they'd never return to. Correction, they'd be happy to return out of uniform and checked in as guests in waterfront suites.

When Amanda slid the glass of Diet Coke with lime and straw across the stainless steel counter, Chef was still at the broiler. "I'm out," she said. "Good luck with the princesses." She got out of his line of sight before succumbing to a dry heave. Whitefish. She could barely stand the smell anymore. Outside the restaurant with her jacket's hood over her head, she walked up Main Street toward the bookstore she'd found a few weeks ago. It was a good day for that.

Pushing the hefty wooden door and stepping inside to let it close, she climbed the uneven stairs, worn concave from summers of *"Serving Travelers to Other Worlds Since 1975."*

"Hello? *Hello*?" The place was softly lit and smelled like pine, pipe, and coffee. "Hello?"

"Yes, yes. I'm here. Just can't get *there* easily," came a muffled voice from near the counter to her right. She looked, but no one stood there.

"Okay. I'll just look around." She walked toward a bookcase with the sign at the end of it reading: Health and Personal Wellness. "Don't hurry on account of me," she said a little louder.

Amanda wandered through the racks. Finding the book she'd been looking for, she walked toward the library table in the middle of the store and settled into one of its leather wingback chairs. She began to read. Before long, her head and the book in her hands felt heavy. The book slipped down her lap to the floor. She dozed comfortably until a voice nearby stirred her awake. She stretched and yawned.

"You've been asleep for some time." A man with a cane set an unsteady teacup and saucer on the table in front of her. "It's almost closing time."

"It is?" She looked for her phone to tell her what the shadows already had. "I'm so sorry. I just want this book." She looked around and then saw it on the floor. "Sorry about that. I'll buy it. I'm so sorry I fell asleep. I didn't mean to. It was just so warm in here." She looked at the cup of tea. "Is that for me?" She leaned in for a closer look and inhaled. "It smells so good."

"Yes. Yes, it's for you. Of course." Amanda took a small sip followed by another. The older man continued. "And that book? Someone phoned to put a hold on it. That's the second copy I've sold today. Strange that. Perhaps a virus. More likely, a fever." He chuckled softly, seeming to amuse himself. And then he handed her a book that he'd tucked under his arm. "I have another for you. He placed a hardback copy of *The Lion, the Witch and the Wardrobe* on the table near her cup.

"Oh, but I can only afford this one. But thank you anyway." She drank again from her teacup.

"Well, Daughter of Eve, it's your lucky day." Amanda gave him a side-eye at that. "I have a two-for-one sale going on today, in honor of the rain. Your total will be eight dollars and twelve cents."

She paused a moment. "Only?" The book she had come in for was twenty-four dollars, more with tax. "But even if I *could* buy two books, shouldn't you charge me for the more expensive book and then the cheaper one would be free? That's how it works. Usually."

"Well, that's not how I do it here." He looked around the darkening room with a wide grin. "How do you think I've managed this thriving empire for years and years?"

"That's really nice and sorta strange," Amanda replied.

"Or bonkers maybe?"

She nodded, finishing the aromatic tea in the floral cup. "Yeah, maybe a little."

"You know what Lewis Carroll said about that, don't you?"

"I'm sorry. Who?"

"You've never met my friend, the inimitable Lewis Carroll, creator of *Alice's Adventures in Wonderland*?"

"Oh yes, I think I saw the movie once. I was little."

"Ah yes, perhaps, then, you remember this from the film." The man straightened, cleared his throat, and recited, "You're mad, bonkers, completely off your head. But I'll tell you a secret. All the best people are." He looked at her with kindness in his eyes. "I suspect you're in a wonderland yourself." And he nodded at the book on her lap: *What to Expect When You're Expecting.*

"Oh, this? Oh, no, no. No! This isn't for me. It's for a friend. A gift. In fact, do you gift wrap here?"

"I'm sorry, I do not any longer. But now, be sure to keep this one for yourself." He tapped his forefinger on the hardback book on the table. "Don't send it off to your friend."

"This?" She picked up the book. "I think I've heard of it." She flipped through its pages with the sketches of children, beavers, a witch. "A fairy tale, isn't it? Actually, I'm not in the market for that."

"So, you're too old for fairy tales?"

"Something like that. And I don't really know any kids."

"Ah, my." He was tsk, tsking. "What is your name, my dear? I'm sorry I neglected to ask."

"Amanda."

"Amanda, a beautiful name. Derived from the Latin, *amare*, meaning love or one loved. Well then, dear Amanda, one who is lovable, indulge me as I quote the author of this fine book who wrote in its dedication…" He cleared his throat. "Ahem, 'Someday you will be old enough to start reading fairy tales again.'" He took the book from her hands and turned to the opening pages. "Ah yes, here we are." He cleared his throat again and dragged his finger across the page, "'And then you can take it down from some upper shelf, dust it, and then I hope you'll tell me what you think of it.'" He closed the book and handed it back to Amanda. "I do hope you'll tell me one day. In fact, I won't think of accepting payment until you've read it and told me what you think. If you don't like it, I won't accept any payment at all."

"Okay. Thank you. I can do that." Her lips curved into a small smile.

"You think perhaps I am bonkers?" the old man asked.

"Yeah. Maybe. A little." She smiled. "Thanks for the tea. That was really good."

"A little Earl Grey for our own gray day. I always have the kettle on. Come back when you've finished that book and tell me about it."

Amanda's eyes widened and she looked at the bigger of the two in her hands, the one about being pregnant.

"The fairy tale, my dear. The fairy tale."

Chapter 21

Olivia stood at the kitchen sink looking at the yard beyond and reviewing the conversation she'd had with the man on the boardwalk, the painter. He was the bookstore owner she'd known years ago: Cliff. (When did he become a painter anyway?) If he recognized her, he said nothing of it. But quoting Hemingway? Of course, it was him.

Oh, Cliff. She and her waitress friends had loved his quirkiness and his riffs on Shakespeare and other literature. He was routinely shocked that college-educated women from reputable schools would fail to recognize his references. "What *are* they teaching these days if not the classics?" They frequented the bookstore, together or individually, as their shifts permitted. They had all become something more than casual acquaintances. Maybe they were like fellow adventurers on a vacation trip and Cliff was their affable tour guide. Whatever. He was an odd treasure, that one, and a visit to his Island Bookstore had been a regular errand for Olivia.

There was little else but a good book for entertainment on their days off. Without TVs in employee housing and with smart phones not yet imagined, watching a show had been an impossibility and mindless scrolling didn't exist. Of course, you could watch *Somewhere in Time* that ran on Tuesdays and Thursdays in town, but once or twice was "Time" enough. Running a trail, laying out in Marquette Park, browsing a gift shop, or turning a page were the available boredom-breaking activities. Sampling fudge was another option. But when the sun and temperatures climbed high, Main Street fudge shops filled with perspiring tourists and red-faced, irritable children. All of them pressed in and around the knee walls separating fudgies from the fudge-turning employees working with paddles over marble slabs. And outside the doors? Horses and their expelled fuel. It was a muddle of sight and smell. No. Midsummer, noonday fudge wasn't appealing. A quick, very quick, dip in the cold of Lake Huron or an icy drink were better options.

After a long night at the restaurant, with wads of cash stuffed into the pockets of their uniform aprons, if it wasn't much past eleven, she and her friends would change clothes and bike to the Jockey Club to meet Cliff for a cocktail, a beer, or on colder nights, an Irish coffee. Was he always there or had they made prior plans? That was unclear. Somehow, he was with them. Often. Martha, Cheri, and PJ (if she wasn't on the sailboat with the guy she'd met while sunbathing topless on the rocks) would be pushed into a booth with Cliff. They'd regale him with descriptions of people they'd served that night, but only after scanning the room to make sure none had ended up in the same place for a nightcap. They'd laugh over mishaps that they'd managed and carefully concealed from the watchful eyes of Mrs. B.

Cliff loved the stories. He was fascinated, it seemed, by the goings on at the Carriage House. He seemed equally interested in the family that had made the Iroquois so unique. It was *the* place to be—unless you had the money to stay at the Grand. In that case, if you had serious money, you'd skip the dinner you'd already paid dearly for, leave your jacket and formal attire behind, and enjoy the hospitality and creative cuisine of the less pretentious Carriage House. You didn't have to be a guest to recognize and admire the restrained confidence of the Carriage House. The hotel and its restaurant had a reputation that was well deserved. Nothing more, nothing less. The employees knew it was top-notch. Quality. By extension, they also were quality. The Iroquois seemed to hire young, well-bred, and semi-affluent summer employees who were earning supplemental funds for college barhopping. It reminded her of her sister's rule to live by (one of many): "Never marry a man until you've saved enough money to leave him." The Iroquois didn't hire anyone who actually needed to be hired. Not back then anyway. Thinking of her own employment now, Olivia laughed. Well-bred? She was compelled to say so. Thank you, Mom and Dad. Semi-affluent? Semi, thanks to Nate. Young? That she was not. Decidedly *not* college-aged.

Now Cliff, she wondered, what had become of him? Was he still alone? Back then, when they'd meet up with him, they never thought to inquire about his marital status. He didn't wear a ring that she remembered, and he never spoke of a wife. In fact, he didn't speak of himself at all. Case in point: Who among them knew he was also a painter? He spoke mostly of books and asked about their thoughts on life. He may have been a teacher. That sounded vaguely familiar. She thought maybe history or English. Cliff did have a way of reciting lines from poems, plays, and novels that spoke to the situations they described. And, as Olivia recalled, they did go into detail on their drama du jour. All of them. At once. *We must have seemed like the essence of youth,* she thought, *wrapped up in our own stories and eager to share them, unaware that our rapt audience of one might have had stories of his own. And quite likely, more interesting ones.*

"Oh Cliff," she whispered to herself, "I'll do better this time, although your listening ear might be the tonic I really need. That and gin. And let's throw in a lime while we're at it. For old time's sake." While she was still lost in her thoughts, her phone rang. It was Nate. Why was he calling during the middle of his work day?

"Nate? Why are you calling?"

"And hello to you, too," he replied. "No worries. Everything's fine." Olivia could hear noises and chatter in the background. "Hang on. I'm walking into my office." She heard the whoomph of a closing door. "As I was saying, I missed you and I wanted to hear your voice. How *are* you?"

"Me? I'm fine. It's a gloomy day here but you know I don't mind that."

"What's the weekend looking like?"

"Why do I think you already know that answer?" Nate was a weather watcher and storm chaser wannabe. Runners often are.

"I was just thinking I might fly home this weekend."

"This weekend? You mean, Friday?" She didn't have to scan her calendar to know this weekend was out of the question. Race weekend number one.

"Yes, this weekend. Well, it'll be late Friday and I'll have to be on my way Sunday afternoon, but we'll have a full day. Maybe we can take a drive to see Luke. You could drop me at the airport on the way back or maybe I can fly out of Detroit."

"No way," she said aloud before she could stop herself. She was scheduled to work the whole weekend. They all were. *Everyone* works race weekends. Even housekeepers were pulled into the kitchen to stay ahead of the crush. The first wave was the families of sailors who set off from the start and the second wave, usually beginning on a Sunday, were the fastest finishers, the race winners among them.

"Yes, way. Really." Nate continued. "I was about to book my flight and surprise you, but then I thought better of it."

"Thank God."

"Liv, why do you say that? I thought you were doing pretty well without me."

"Oh, of course, yes, yes. I *am* doing pretty well without you. But I miss you too, Nate. I do." She thought she did anyway. Hearing his voice and the kindness in it made that feeling real. "The thing is," she paused to construct her reply—not completely dishonest, but he simply could not fly home to Lake Ellyn and discover a dusty house that no one had been living in for weeks.

"The thing is… is… well, I'm working this weekend." There. That was truthful.

"Working?"

"Yup. You know, Nina has a catering job at a remote venue, on a lake. I promised I'd help. She's desperate. I mean, desperate. Hundreds invited." Three truths and a lie. Not bad, all things considered. "But,

Nate, what about Luke's birthday? I thought we talked about that. Or at least I texted you. Twenty-one. A milestone. We can buy him his first drink."

"His first legal one." Nate corrected her.

"I think you're wrong there. He doesn't drink on campus. He signed that pledge to be a high school mentor, remember?"

"Well, if we're thanking God, let's thank him that Luke behaves more like you at that age than me." They both laughed. A quiet pause settled. When it became too long, Olivia spoke.

"So, what about it? Would that work for you?" She knew she could get time off and arrange for a weekend to meet Nate and visit their son's camp.

"Liv, I know it's Luke's birthday. And a big one. But I can't get away that weekend."

"No?" she asked weakly, disappointed for herself, and more disappointed for Luke. She wandered from the kitchen to the living room and dropped onto the drop cloth–protected sofa. She looked outside to the porch and studied the drops of rain on the spiderweb in the corner of the window.

"No chance," Nate replied. "We've got regulators coming in. They'll be swarming. Everyone's going to be at their beck and call, providing any documents, files, anything they need. It'll be a nightmare. They'll be here for weeks."

"Okay. I see." She felt tears welling up. A couple rolled onto her cheeks. She wiped them off with her sleeve, not sure why they wouldn't stop. She'd been fine until this call. Nate filled the silence.

"You know, I've been thinking of London a lot these days."

"London?" she whispered. "You have? Why?" That was a blast from the past. They'd been married over a year and both were doing well in their careers. They were making a good income and had few financial obligations. A house and hopefully a baby to fill one of its bedrooms were next on the list. When United promoted additional nonstop flights to London, Nate had said, "Let's go." When she'd asked when, he'd said "Friday." And they went.

"Why was I thinking of it?" Nate asked. "It was our first adventure and maybe the last time we did something impetuous." Nate clearly didn't know that Olivia had stumbled into impetuousness on a large scale. "Do you remember?"

"Oh, Nate, I remember." She laughed quietly and murmured, "We wasted a lot of money, didn't we?" She smiled. They'd booked a room at a quaint hotel overlooking Hyde Park, an easy walk to Buckingham Palace, Harrod's, and Westminster Abbey. They landed at dawn on a Saturday morning and took the Underground to the hotel. Far too early to check in, they walked the neighborhood and found a pub for a few pints. They made their way back to the hotel, stumbling here and there, laughing and stopping for kisses on the sidewalk. Drunk on jet lag, Guinness, and love, they'd spent the rest of the day and into the early evening in bed. Eventually they rallied and wandered out for some fish and chips and a few more pints, then returned to their room.

Nate interrupted her reminiscing. "I've never had better fish and chips."

"Is that what we were calling it? Fish and chips?" Nate laughed. Intending to hit all the highlights of the city that day and the next, they'd instead spent most of their weekend under, over, and bound up in the sheets, and in each other's arms. The Frommer's guide to London untouched. The changing of the guard unseen.

"Oh, Nate. That was so long ago." She was drawn back to the golden hour of their last night there. Wrapped in just a sheet, she'd sat on a tufted chair, looking out the window at the park below. When she looked over her left shoulder she'd found Nate studying her.

"What are you doing?" she asked.

"Looking at you. Admiring my wife. That's all." He smiled. "What's happening out there? What's got you so locked in?"

She turned back to the window. "Just watching the nannies and the mums pushing prams around the park."

"Do you think you could do that?"

"Push a pram?" Olivia looked over at him again with a smile. Nate was barely covered with the duvet, hair tousled. "I could manage to push a pram," she offered. "It's the rest of it that worries me." She turned in the chair to look at him straight on. "And you?"

"I suppose I could push a pram, a manly one. But I'm not wearing one of those baby hammocks. Not me." He shook his head. "Nope. Not ever. No."

"So you feel strongly about that. Duly noted. But seriously, Nate, can you see yourself becoming a dad?" she asked with hesitancy and hopefulness.

"Yeah, of course. You know that. But for now, I just want this. I want to stop time and keep this… this… I don't know. This picture and go back into it whenever I want. Live inside it." Nate rarely said anything so romantic or so revealing. Before she could think more of it, he added, "I'm cold. Get back here. Leave the nannies to their work. Let's make more memories of London." She climbed back into bed to be encircled by Nate's waiting arms. Had Luke been a girl they might have named her London.

"Nathan! Why haven't you answered my texts?" An exasperated voice, audible even for Olivia on her side of the line, barged into the moment they were sharing. Nathan? Olivia recognized the voice. It was *Landon* who interfered with their London. She remembered what Abby had said about Landon. Into the phone she said without thinking, "chocolate-covered spider."

"Liv, what? Spider? Hope you can kill it." Just as quickly he ended the conversation. "I'm sorry, Liv. Really. Let's plan another time. Labor Day at the least."

"Labor Day? That's practically two months away. But sure, I'll pencil you in." Sarcasm intended.

"Right. Love you." And he was gone from her, sucked up into demands of a major drug company merger and his ever-present colleague.

"Right," Olivia repeated aloud and stood, putting her phone into a back pocket and her hands to her hips. After replaying the conversation in her mind a second and then a third time, she stood for a long while looking out the window, suspended in sadness.

"Enough," she said as she changed the channel on her thoughts. The primer and paint she'd ordered had been delivered earlier that morning. They demanded her attention. "I suppose these walls won't paint themselves." She went back to prepping them. As she worked, she thought through her next note to Frankie.

Chapter 22

To: lilaccottage@gmail.com

Dear Frankie,

You've been patient, not requesting any photos of the progress I've made at Lilac Cottage. I'm attaching a few now so that you can see how much brighter the cottage is even with primer over the paneling. It's as if the cottage is showing her personality. I wonder if LC's like a girl who was dressed in sensible sportswear all her childhood when what she really wanted to wear was a tiara and pink tulle skirt.

Anyway, what I'm coming to realize is that the cottage could wear—quite well I think—a little color. Bright pastels set off by the white walls. Maybe I'm persuaded by the Iroquois. The colors there are like a garden blooming indoors. Prints, florals, geometrics but all in a compatible, color-drenched palette. It shouldn't make sense but it does. What would you think if I introduced a little color? (And I'm aware that if you sell this sweet place the colors need to be agreeable to future buyers. But, honestly, I'm growing so tired of houses showing gray and more gray.) Also, you mentioned an upholsterer off the island? In Mackinaw City? I'd love to inquire about slipcovers for a couple of chairs and pillows. May I ask? I have found a great fabric source online and could even send you samples. I'd love to coordinate that.

You asked how I'm getting along at the Carriage House. Frankly, it's the perfect escape for me. You can't serve tables of people all day and not get drawn into the dramas playing out before you. Couples in deep conversation while their children squirm through a long, ~~elegant~~ boring dinner when they'd rather be flying a kite at Windermere Point. Torture! (Until the fudge ice cream puff comes.) And couples. One couple drives up from Ann Arbor twice a month. It's their summer routine. They've started requesting my station when they dine. And another couple that I served the other night—oh boy. The husband was a taciturn, mean drunk. As the night continued and I delivered more gin martinis, he got increasingly rude. His wife would smile at me, as though apologizing for his behavior. He left a penny tip. One cent! At least I didn't go home with him. His poor wife. I'm glad I got the table and not a younger server. I don't bank on my tips the way some do.

Speaking of the other servers, I mentioned Amanda the last time I wrote, yes? She's the quiet one, the college student who I have to believe is pregnant. She talks to me—though she doesn't talk to anyone much. But I've covered for her from time to time. I'm thinking I may ask her about her situation. I can't imagine living with the other Iroquois employees while managing morning sickness. If she's pregnant. And I can't help but wonder what she plans to do, or how frightened she might be. When I met her during orientation, she told me her mother is no longer in her life and she seems to have a strong dislike of her father. Strong. She seems very much alone, in every way.

Which all leads me to this rather unusual request. Would you consider allowing me to invite Amanda to live with me here at the Cottage? I know it's a big request and I don't know that she'll agree, but I feel compelled to help. Honestly, she breaks my heart.

Heartbreak. Well, that is a subject familiar to us all, isn't it? You also asked about my son, Luke, and husband, Nate. Part of me hates to admit it—possibly a large part—but they are fine. Both of them. Thriving even. I've either done my job superbly to launch Luke and set Nate free or I was never that essential anyway. I think about that while I paint. And of course I pray for them. That much I can do from a distance. That may be the very best thing I can do. That and miss them.

I need to sign off and get ready for my dinner shift. We somehow managed through the Fourth, and race weeks are coming up fast. Everyone's a little tense. Not Mrs. B, though. Did she always have nerves of steel? Have you ever seen her laugh—like belly laugh? I'd love to see that. I've never known anyone so small who could provoke such fear and affection at the same time. She's a mystery.

With many thanks and warm wishes—
Olivia

P.S. I hope you like the photos!

Chapter 23

Before Olivia could finish knotting her uniform's tie there was a knock at the cottage door. She made her way downstairs to see an imposing figure on the other side of the Dutch door.

"Can't be. What's he doing here?" she said under her breath. With a heave she pulled the door toward her and saw Chef standing at the threshold in his usual kitchen wear.

He cleared his throat. "You work tonight, don't you?"

"I was on my way. See?" Olivia pulled the tie toward him and continued to loop its wide end into a Windsor knot. "Do you check on the whereabouts of the night's servers very often? Don't you have better things to do? Seems a little stalker-ish."

"I don't get you." He shook his head. "You're this nice mother figure to everyone in the kitchen but me. Sassy, snarky. What'd I do to you?"

"Mother figure? That might have done it." She added, lightly, "Kidding." Olivia reached behind for her purse on the table near the door. "Sorry, Chef. Can we continue this conversation on the porch?"

He took a step back to let her through.

"So, not to be rude, but why are you here?"

"Yeah, so, Amanda. She likes you," he offered.

"Hmm, Amanda. She's quiet, complicated but I do think we have a friendship. Why do you mention that? And can we keep moving?" She walked down the porch steps and to her robin's egg blue bike locked beside the front walk. Chef followed.

"So, what do you think?" he asked. She was studying her lock and aligning the numbers on their dials to release the cable. He continued. "I think she's pregnant." At this, Olivia straightened.

"I think so too," she said evenly. Quietly. "Why are you bringing this up? And why to *me*?"

"I dunno. There's something about her." Olivia's face squinched at that. A cringy thought. Chef read her expression.

"Oh, sweet Jesus, no. No! I'm not interested in her. God no. She's a child!" He wiped his hand down his face. "What kind of guy do you think I am?" and quickly, "Don't answer that."

Olivia wrapped the bike cable around the seat and apologized. "Sorry. I see how you treat her in the kitchen and how she keeps your Diet Coke coming. By the way, you might want to ease up on those. Can't be good for you."

"Thanks, Mom," he retorted. Olivia raised her eyebrows at that. "Anyway, I see how you two have a thing in the kitchen," he said. "You're kind to her. At least that's one of us."

Olivia suppressed a grin and rolled her bike down the walk. Chef followed.

"What are you getting at Chef?"

"You can call me Sean."

"Ooo… kay… *Sean*. What's your point?"

"I think she should live here with you. Frankie would go for it. I know it."

Olivia stopped at this and looked at him over the bike between them. "Chef…"

"Sean," he corrected her.

"It's got to be Chef when we're dressed like this, okay?"

"Yup. Got it. So what do you think?"

She inhaled deeply. "Actually, I was thinking the same thing. I don't think the other servers or kitchen staff know what early pregnancy looks like. I suspect Mrs. B has noticed too."

He nodded, agreeing.

"Are you thinking—like I was—that it'd be better for her to be out of employee housing? Maybe even save her a little money if she lived here with me?"

He clapped his hands together. "That's exactly what I was thinking."

She stared at him for a long moment. Gold flecks in his green eyes. Long lashes. Never noticed that before. She startled herself back to the issue at hand. "Well on this matter we see eye to eye. I just sent Frankie an email to ask if she might consider opening another bedroom in Lilac Cottage to someone who may need a place to call home. Let me hear back from Frankie and get her okay. If she's good with it, I can approach Amanda." She started again to roll the bike down the walk. Chef kept pace. She kept her hands on the bike handles and her eyes on the walk between them. "It's a good idea. Thoughtful."

"Surprised, aren't you?" Without looking up at him she smiled and nodded, admitting as much.

"Mrs. Nash, you may need to reevaluate your assessment of my character." He smacked a hand on the bike seat. "But, now, you ought to be on your way to the restaurant. Given your advanced age, it might take you a while."

She moved ahead of him, put her left foot on the pedal, and swung her right leg over the seat. She started a slow pedal. Without a look back she raised her right hand and threw him a gesture. "Oh, I'll get there long before you. *You'd* better get a move on!"

He watched her make her way down the walk and turn onto the street, then said, loudly, "I have the night off. Another thing," he shouted in her direction. "I'd like to see you out of uniform sometime… when you can call me Sean." Still louder he shouted, "And Mrs. Nash—watch your language. Flipping your boss the bird? What's gotten into you?"

Olivia heard his parting comment but didn't dare acknowledge it. When Chef yelled, "Nice ass, Mrs. Nash," she blushed and kept pedaling, hoping that no one else had heard him.

Chapter 24

Montreal, Quebec

On a late Wednesday afternoon in July, Nathan Nash laced up his shoes for a long run. He'd hoped to be booking a flight for a trip home. Instead, he'd be spending the weekend in Montreal. Struck with a homesickness he hadn't felt before, he left the hotel, his temporary home, and set out on an eight-mile course. Earbuds in, he'd listened to a podcast which distracted him for a while. When that ended, he switched to eighties rock, added a half mile to his run, and pushed his pace back to the hotel.

He looked at his watch. "An hour and twenty-two minutes. Not bad," he thought to himself as he walked to the elevator bank. He figured he'd order a pizza, grab a beer, and try to find the Cubs on the hotel TV.

"Hey, handsome." A soft southern voice came from behind him and a finger pressed the elevator up button.

"Well hello, yourself," Nate turned and replied. "Don't come too close. It was a long run and it's hot as hell out there." The doors opened and they stepped inside.

"I wouldn't think of it. I like my men to look athletic and smell freshly showered. You've exceeded my expectations in one category only."

"Thanks. I think."

"Nate, if you don't have plans tonight, I was thinking we could take in some jazz at a sweet spot I discovered and then dinner in China Town?"

He was considering the offer when the doors opened. "This is me."

"I'll come along, if you don't mind?" She walked out of the elevator without seeming to need a reply. "You've earned yourself a beer. I have too. Let me treat you to a beer from your own mini fridge." She walked with him to his room. She'd met him there before, to pick him up before work when they didn't meet up in the lobby. Most days they walked together to their offices. They would compare notes on the way in to save the time of having a formal status meeting.

Nate unlocked the door with his key card and let them both into the one-bedroom suite which was just like the others assigned to the expats on the merger team. Landon made her way to the fridge and pulled out two Molsons. Nate had grabbed a towel from the bathroom. Using it to wipe his face, he waved off the beer she offered and grabbed a water bottle from the fridge, opened it, and took a long drink.

"Needed that." He leaned against the desk in the room while Landon found the love seat and curled her legs under herself, settling comfortably on the cushioned seat. She tossed her wavy hair from her face to over her shoulder. "So, how's that darlin' wife of yours? Is she enjoying her summer of leisure?"

"She's fine. Good. And I'm not sure I'd call it a leisurely summer. She's one of the busiest people I know."

"But she doesn't work, does she?"

"What do you mean?" He took a longer drink and dropped to the wheeled desk chair opposite her.

"Well, she's been at home while you're here and your son is off to college and now at that camp. I can't imagine what she does all day."

"Like I said. She stays pretty busy. Busier than I am some days."

Landon shook her head. "That's simply not possible. I've watched you. Did she ever work?"

"She did."

"But she doesn't work now." Landon continued prosecuting her case.

"No. Not a paying job if that's what you mean."

"Bet she misses it."

"I don't think so."

"I'm not sure I could do that," Landon continued, "you know, be dependent on someone—for everything from my home to my clothes to what I do and where I go. And you, it's got to be hard for you. Do you ever resent having to provide for everyone?" She looked at him with concern.

"I guess I don't see it that way." Nate drained the last of his water.

"So, what did she do? What was her line of work? Administrative assistant? Customer service? HR?"

"Landon. You're full of questions, aren't you?" He leaned forward in his chair, opened the fridge, and, this time, pulled out a beer. "She *did* work, and she had a senior level position as a buyer for a high-end retailer. She loved it. She got her bachelor's in interior design and a master's in business."

"Really? Impressive! I wouldn't have guessed, except that you describe her as being so capable. And then?"

"And then?" He ran a hand through his hair and took another drink. He picked at the label around the neck of the bottle and peeled it off. "And then." More quietly he continued. "Do you remember the blackout that shut down the East Coast about fifteen years ago?"

Landon paused. "I think I recall that."

"That day Olivia collapsed on a New York City sidewalk." Landon's eyes widened and she put a hand to her lips. "She had a miscarriage, an ectopic pregnancy." Nate looked out the room's expansive window for a few moments, like he was retrieving a memory. "She was taken by ambulance and needed surgery. I got a call from her coworker. I found friends, and my sister-in-law, to take care of Luke. I tried to book a flight. The mess on the East Coast shut down all air travel. I had to drive and couldn't get there before, well, before all of it. We lost our baby. A girl. That's the whole story. That's all I've got." He took a longer drink.

Landon looked down at her hands and interlaced her fingers in a tight squeeze. "Oh, Nate. That's awful. I'm so sorry." She looked up at him again. In a quiet voice she continued, "So, if I may ask, no more children after that?"

"Not possible." Nate stood up and tossed the beer bottle into the trash. He took off his watch and dropped it and his phone on the desk opposite Landon. He turned toward the bathroom. "Listen, I'm not up for dinner. Thanks anyway. I'm hitting the shower. Let yourself out when you finish your beer."

"Nate, one more question… so I understand." He swung around to look at her and she continued. "You had only one child and no more to follow and you said Olivia loved her career. Why wouldn't she go back to it? I would think she'd miss her career more than ever."

"I don't think she wanted to go back."

"Don't you wonder about that now? People change. Maybe she misses it?"

"I don't think so. She's never said so." He turned all the way around to face her. He took the towel from his shoulder and wiped his face again. "Are we good here?"

"Oh, Nate." Landon shook her head slightly and pressed on. "Maybe you should ask. As I said, people change. She may miss her work and maybe you miss sharing your life with someone who understands you."

"My life? You mean my work?"

"Yes, of course. It's so much of who you are. I can't imagine living with someone who has no real sense of what I do all day, the stress I'm under, the responsibilities… all of it. I would think Olivia would want to share that with you. I would think it would strengthen your marriage." At that, Nate took a step toward her and bent to look at her, seated as she was.

"Landon," he was unblinking. "Have you ever seen someone you love shatter?"

She shook her head slowly. "I'm not sure I know what you mean."

"I mean, have you ever watched someone you love shatter into a million pieces and then realize you have no power, no ability, nothing to offer to put the pieces back together? Has that ever happened to you?"

"No." She shook her head again. "I can't say that it has." At that, Nate straightened.

"Then I can't explain Olivia to you—or our marriage." He turned from her. "Just let yourself out. I'll see you later." Nate walked into the bathroom.

Landon uncurled her legs from the love seat to stand and make her exit. When his phone lit up with an incoming call, Landon reached for it. The screen showed it was Olivia. "Your ears must have been burning," she said to the photo of Luke and Olivia on his screen. She answered and put the phone to her ear. She wasn't sure what possessed her to answer Nate's phone. Or why she knew it would be intentionally misleading and, in a way, cruel. She wanted what they had. Desperately. The more she longed for that kind of relationship, the one she hadn't claimed, the longer was the reach. She should have known better and behaved better, but, what the hell.

"Hello? Olivia? This is Landon."

"Oh Landon. Did I misdial? I don't even think I have your number."

"Oh no, darlin', you've got the right number. I've got Nate's phone. He's in the shower. We're going out to dinner tonight. Shall I walk the phone to him?" She smiled, seeming pleased with her maneuver.

There was a long silence. "Uh, no, no. That's not necessary."

"Shall I tell him you called? I'm happy to pass along the message."

"No, Landon. Thank you. We'll just talk later."

"All right. It may be a long night. Perhaps you could try him in the morning." She smiled as she offered that helpful bit of misinformation.

"Oh, is that right?"

"I think so. But, Olivia, we had such a nice talk about you. I had no idea about the career you once had and your accomplishments of the past. I am *so* impressed."

"Hmm." Olivia said nothing more for a time. "Thanks," she eventually offered. "Goodbye, Landon."

"Bye, Olivia. Have a lovely night. I'll be sure to tell Nate you called."

With that, Landon put Nate's phone down on the desk. She looked at it and then picked it up again. With a swipe of her finger, she deleted Olivia's number from the list of recent calls.

As soon as she had done it, she paused. She realized what she'd done and felt remorse. She liked Olivia. Sometimes, her better self wasn't able to restrain the actions born from her usually suppressed jealousy and sadness. Appalled at what she'd done, she put the phone down again and tapped it with two fingers. "Forgive me, Olivia. I mean you no harm."

Landon slipped out of Nate's room. She'd find time to explain, explain everything, and apologize. Later.

Chapter 25

"What?" Olivia stood by her bike, looking at the phone in her hand. On a break she had gone outside to the employee bike racks to call Nate to tell him that their conversation the other day had meant a lot to her. Instead, she got Landon. On Nate's phone. In Nate's room. While he showered. Oh God, she hoped it was Nate's room and not Landon's.

What was that all about? His call just days ago. Was Nate easing a guilty conscience? And Landon? That soft drawl sugar-coated an innuendo that cut Olivia. I don't care that Landon is an "esteemed colleague." Or that Nate's merger integration partner, the lawyer, was "savvy, smart beyond her years." All Olivia could imagine were her heels, those long legs, and her slate eyes. She let out a long sigh.

"Olivia?" It was Amanda who joined her, with what appeared to be another ginger ale in her hand. "Are you okay?" Olivia nodded and slipped her phone in the back pocket of her uniform khakis. "Hey, they're getting ready to seat a group of ten in your section. I'll back you up if I can. Sorry to cut your break short."

Olivia gave her a smile and put a hand on her forearm. "It's fine. And I'd love the help. But I want to talk to you sometime soon. I'm hoping I can help you."

Amanda gave her a quizzical look.

"Olivia!" A voice shouted out to her from inside.

"We'll talk." Olivia took a step toward the door. "Actually, I'd like to take you to lunch or dinner. Can we do that?" Amanda nodded her consent. "Great." Olivia walked toward the employee dining room, the "EDR," and the kitchen beyond. "Let's sync our schedules after race weekend."

Back in the dining room, the night proved busier than most. The first race weekend of the season was still days away, but already, the island teemed with visitors. The island didn't need discovering, but glowing reviews in food and travel publications didn't hurt. Neither did social media and newly initiated fans sharing photos and experiences. Not everyone was thrilled. Most visitors imagined a more private island experience. *For that, my friends, you have to wait—wait until late September or October when residents and long-term workers take the island back*, she thought to herself.

The dining room quieted around nine o'clock that night, and when it did, Olivia turned her attention to the assorted mindless side duties to prep for service the next day: filling and cleaning salt and pepper shakers, replenishing oil candles, napkin folding, and tending to the dining room to check off items on a job list created by an OCD mind. To be honest, the OCD mindset is what made the place hum. You don't become first in class without majoring in minor details. When the list was completed and double-checked, and when Olivia could no longer push the memory of her conversation with Landon out of her mind, she decided to take her bike and peddle herself to the Jockey Club. She'd soothe her sad heart with a cold drink, or maybe a hot Irish coffee. Maybe both.

She unlocked her bike, climbed on, and pushed off. She had to let go of the image of Landon with Nate. She wouldn't let the idea corrode her insides. And so what? A dinner? Nate was never wise to a woman's wiles. He wouldn't read anything into a dinner. It could all be innocent—on his part anyway. And a simple misunderstanding on Olivia's part. She'd straighten it out in the morning. Head on, like an adult woman in a mature, loving, and unquestionably faithful marriage. Olivia looked down at her thighs, pumping the pedals of her bike up the hill toward the Grand Hotel's clubby bar. She was wearing a server's uniform, on an island, heading to a bar by herself and intending to drink a lot, while her husband and son thought she was at home in Lake Ellyn, likely watching HGTV. "Unquestionably faithful" could be an overstatement. Or a technicality. But what the hell, Nate?

Her anger fueled her ride up Cadotte Avenue. She parked her bike and entered the dimly lit room. She slid into a booth. The Jockey Club was quiet at ten-thirty. People looking to drink this late were more inclined to go to Main Street where cheaper beer in greater quantity could be had at the Pink Pony or VI. Olivia no longer had wads of cash in her pockets like she and her fellow waitresses used to. Few paid or tipped in cash anymore, but her month-old First National Bank account was growing fat, and its companion card allowed her to indulge herself then and again with no one needing an accounting of her earnings or her spending. The server approached her table before she had looked at the menu. It didn't matter.

Olivia asked for a tall vodka tonic and a burger and fries, oh, and also onion rings. She looked around the room to see a man beckoning to someone. There were two men at a corner table, one wearing glasses. Before she could look away, the one in glasses got up and started walking toward her. Chef?

He approached her booth and stopped to stand above her. He was tall. Over six feet. "How'd it go tonight? You look a little, mmm, like it was a rough one."

"Well, that's honest if not complimentary." She pushed the hair that had fallen over her face behind her ear. "Danny had his hands full, and so did we. Just one regrettable mishap. He'll fill you in, or Mrs. B will for sure."

As though embarrassed that he hadn't been at the helm he said, "This is my last night off before race weeks." He shrugged his shoulders. "So I met a friend here."

Olivia looked around him to the table across the room. "I noticed. Is that…?"

"Cliff," they said in unison. Again, in unison, they said, "*You* know Cliff?"

"I've been here a long time, remember?" he answered. "Yes, I know Cliff. We're friends. Drinking buddies, you could say."

"I only know Cliff from one summer. Ages ago. We, well, my friends and I, would meet him here for drinks after late shifts once in a while. That was such a long time ago. I ran into him, painting on the boardwalk, then I called the store to order a book, but he didn't recognize the name. He won't remember me."

"Oh, but he does. You just proved the point." Chef corrected her. "Come on. Join us."

She protested. "No, really. I, uh…" She looked at him again. "You wear glasses?" The dark frames suited him.

"Sometimes. Not in the kitchen. Are you coming?" He picked up her water glass and motioned to her server that she'd be moving to a different table. Olivia watched him, detached for a moment. She hadn't paid such close attention when he surprised her at the cottage earlier that day, still in his chef's uniform. He looked different here, all cleaned up. Wearing an untucked button-down shirt, his hair freed from the bandanas he always wore in the kitchen, red ones that wrapped around his head to keep the sweat from his eyes. He looked… smart? Sophisticated? He looked good enough to follow. Damn you, Landon McCall. She got up to join him and Cliff.

Once seated at the table, Chef made introductions. "Cliff, you were right. Olivia, now Olivia Nash, once worked for me, well us, at the Carriage House." She reached out a hand to shake Cliff's.

"Olivia," he took her hand in his, "I recognized you the other day, during our brief encounter. Of course I remember you. Still lovely."

"Oh, gosh, Cliff. I just got off work." His attention made her self-conscious. She pushed her hair off her face again. "I'm a mess."

"Ah, Olivia, the beauty I remember and see even now radiates from within."

Chef laughed. "Cliff, you're coming on strong. She's married, or so she says, and you're old!" He gave Cliff a loving push on the shoulder.

"You are exactly the Cliff I remember." She paused and looked at Chef to emphasize her point. "And I am married." She turned her attention again to Cliff. "And while you may be older, Cliff, you're every bit as charming as you were years ago. Which makes me wonder, how is it that you two are friends?"

The two men were chuckling at that when the server approached the table with her drink. Another approached to serve her burger, fries, and onion rings.

"Lady," said Chef, "you have some appetite!"

"I don't eat like this very often but tonight I needed a little more substance. Maybe you two could help me. Have some fries."

"I might. I hate to admit it when another restaurant trumps ours, but damn, their fries are good. So's their fish sandwich." Chef took a few fries. Still chewing them, he stood. He pulled a few bills out of his pocket and threw them on the table. "Cliff, this should cover the damage. I've gotta go. I need sleep before race weeks begin."

Cliff nodded. "Til anon, my friend. Be well."

Sean returned the nod and looked again at Olivia. "Don't get carried away here. I'll need you this weekend. Can't risk having any hungover staff in my kitchen. Especially older ones—the fall risk, you know."

She shook her head in feigned exasperation as he turned for the door.

Once Chef left, Olivia and Cliff got reacquainted. They spent the better part of an hour as she ate her dinner, talking about her season on the island years ago. She skirted the question of how it was that she was waiting tables again at the Carriage House. Had he asked her, she'd have said, "It's a frivolous adventure while my boys are pursuing adventures of their own. We'll return to life as we knew it in due time." If he'd asked. He didn't. But he did ask about Chef. Yes, it was true, back in the day, she and her friends loved sharing stories with Cliff but they had never socialized with Chef. How odd, it seemed, that Chef and Cliff were friends.

Cliff asked what she remembered about Chef, from back then. "Honestly," Olivia replied, "he seemed so much older then, so we didn't think much. I know he's only five or six years older than I am, than we were, but he seemed both older and… hmm, superior. I never even saw him outside of the Carriage House. We all thought he slept there."

"I imagine he did. Some nights." Cliff continued. "Sean's told me many times that life in a kitchen is unconventional, most would think it unhealthy. Fourteen-, fifteen-hour days, he'd say. We'd run into each other late at night, closing down bars at quiet corner tables." He opened his hands between them, flipped them over to study his palms. He looked again at her. "I've always been a night owl, and Sean, well, he was a creature of the night. You probably never saw us."

She nodded. "Doubtful, not after we left you from this place anyway."

"You wouldn't have wanted to." Cliff clasped his hands together like he was about to pray. "Olivia dear, those days are passed. And thankfully so. As you and I both know, 'The companion of fools shall suffer for it.' And we both did. I am far more sensible these days, as is your Chef."

"My Chef? He's certainly not my Chef. Let's be clear: He's my boss. And while he's changed a little, he's still arrogant and hotheaded." She took a drink. "Drives me crazy."

"Does he now?" Cliff raised his wooly eyebrows.

She ignored his look and changed the subject. No more about Chef and no further details about Nate. She was in too much turmoil to share about him and Landon and the thoughts she couldn't entertain or put voice to. Not now and not here.

"Now, when will you be in to purchase the book you inquired about last week?"

"So, you did take that call. You knew that was me?"

"I didn't then, but I do now. Your voice, meeting you on the boardwalk… it all squares. Except for the book in question. I suspect you are not the intended user of said reference manual." Cliff winked at her. "Perhaps you've put it on hold for Amanda."

"*Amanda*? You know Amanda? How?"

"How? She visited the bookstore a few days ago in search of the very same title. She fell asleep at my library table and startled when I woke her, more than an hour later."

"She's been especially tired, I think," Olivia offered.

"I imagine so," he said with an expression of concerned understanding. "She is an endearing young woman. Respectful and frightened."

"Frightened? How do you figure?"

"Oh, Olivia, I've had hundreds, no, thousands of students her age in my lecture halls. Their eyes say more than they'd ever like anyone to know. If you look into their eyes, their expression, they'll tell you." He tilted his head. "She's frightened, and I'd like to help somehow. But how's an old man like me able to assist a young woman in her situation?"

"Cliff, there may be something actually." Olivia took her napkin and wiped the water rings off the table's surface. "I wonder about Amanda waiting tables, you know, as the weeks go by. I think she could use another kind of employment. Maybe a shift at the bookstore?" She looked expectantly at Cliff. "What do you think?"

"Hmm," he paused. "I think that's a capital idea. It might allow me to have additional open hours while I rest this petrifying knee of mine." Cliff tapped his right knee and then put a finger to his lips. "But, dear Olivia, let us recognize that in spite of our suspicions, we have no confirmation that Amanda is, in fact, with child. We are merely speculating, and worse, I fear, meddling. Wouldn't you think it far better to address this directly with Amanda and not in committee as we seem to be doing now?"

He was spot on. "You are absolutely right. I've diagnosed a problem and come up with a solution and Amanda has asked for neither. Cliff, you really haven't changed. You're a wise soul. Thank you." Olivia pushed out her chair and started to stand. "It's late, Cliff. I really should be on my way. Since I am so old." She rolled her eyes.

Cliff laughed and with a wave said, "Olivia, might I also suggest that you may not have diagnosed a problem, as you have put it. Perhaps what you have discovered is less of a problem for Amanda and possibly more of an opportunity, perhaps even a gift?"

Olivia took a breath before responding. "I hope so, Cliff. I'm not sure how this becomes a gift for her at her age, but we can hope so. God only knows."

Olivia moved to the bar to settle her bill. But when she pulled out her card, the bartender waved her off. "You're all good! Sean paid your tab before he left. He does that." The bartender turned to the beer taps behind her, and then looked over her right shoulder. "And he's the best tipper. Always a treat."

"Hmm, I'm sure he is," she replied, not entirely convinced.

Chapter 26

A short time later, Olivia locked her bike and climbed the stairs to Lilac Cottage. The front porch light glowed and lightning bugs were blinking, floating in and out of the perennials: astilbe, black-eyed Susans, bee balm, and cone flowers, almost all of which were in bloom.

Before unlocking the door, she slid into the porch swing, gave a push with her toes, and breathed in the fragrant summer air. It was beautiful here. As strange as it seemed, especially to her, she realized that she'd been letting go of the rope that had tethered her to the life she'd created, that *they'd* created, in Chicago. The work of holding on, a false security, wasn't as rewarding as letting go and feeling herself caught.

Luke was settled into his camp and thriving. That much was obvious in every brief communication. Ceci was still Ceci, in perpetual motion propelled by one spontaneous, zany idea after another. Just the same, and she was good.

Nate? That was a different matter. He was stressed but succeeding in his role in Montreal. She knew that. She knew success was assured. Failure was something that happened to other people. Not Nate. But satisfaction? She wasn't sure about that. Maybe that explained Landon. Maybe Landon understood something about him that she could not. Landon. The image of her brought a pain to Olivia's gut. The image of Nate with her brought another and stole her breath. Olivia brought the curtain down on those thoughts. *Not now. It's late, and I'm not rational.* Olivia willed her thoughts to the present moment and looked again around her. This view, the porch, this pace of life. This chance to breathe. It was unexpected and a little crazy. *Wrong?* Probably. But somehow it suited her. Right or wrong, she was grateful for it.

She rose from the swing and unlocked the door. Once inside, she was greeted with the smell of oil paint and a reflective glow from the walls around her. Slowly, the rooms in the cottage were transforming. The paint she'd applied, in multiple coats, brightened the space. If and when she heard back from Frankie, and with her consent, Olivia would add some color to the place—and maybe a colorful roommate, with a phoenix tattoo, and baby on the way. Yes—crazy. That's probably the best description of this escapade of hers. Without brewing her nightly chamomile tea (with a drizzle of honey), Olivia took herself to her bedroom with its view of the treetops. She shed her uniform and her unanswered questions to be picked up some other time. She slipped between the bed's crisp sheets and pulled a Lilac Cottage quilt over her body. Olivia fell asleep in the peace of knowing she was, undeniably, happy here. For now, that was enough.

When she awoke the next morning, she discovered a message from Frankie.

To: onash1017@gmail.com
July 14

Dearest Olivia,

I've been quite busy myself! I apologize for my tardy reply, which will be all too brief, I fear. To answer your questions: First, by all means! Color the walls. I've wanted to do that for so many years and have done so in many other places, but Lilac Cottage... well, I had others' preferences to satisfy there. I quite agree with you about the Iroquois. The palette there lifts one's spirits. I so agree. And I'd also add that the décor at the Grand is equally lovely. I do hope you've found time to rock on the porch there—even if you'll pay dearly for that pleasure. I suppose it keeps the uncouth away. Forgive my assessment. I suppose better said is that the porch-fee policy deters those who don't really appreciate the experience and simply want a photo to broadcast on their instant gram.

Second, and oh my, such a request. Of course, you must invite this young woman into our home. That much is plain. But what of her and her situation? That demands consideration and prayer, both of which I have undertaken since reading your last message. I believe you'll find the medical center on the island adequate to confirm pregnancy or not. But she will need more. I am acquainted with a medical practice off island that might be helpful. It's a bit of a drive to Petoskey but I imagine you have access to a car? Perhaps there is an office even closer. I recommend Dr. Samantha Ryder at North Shore Obstetrics. She is a wise woman and familiar with matters of this nature, and courses of action should that be deemed necessary. You must understand my meaning, though I regret even making mention of it. But we must deal in reality, mustn't we?

I have much to do still tonight. I had thought older age might bring a slower pace. It hasn't thus far. I continue to take my place on the carousel and hold on. I wish you the same. Hold on—especially in the upcoming weeks. You'll need a firm grip for race weeks!

Fondly and with many thanks—
Frankie

P.S. The photos are marvelous. And I agree. Our little cottage deserves a tiara.

Chapter 27

The weekend of the Bayview Mackinac Race dawned with blue skies and steady winds—at least off Windermere Point where the race would finish. More than 275 sailboats had registered for the storied race that dated back to 1925. The official start was on Saturday, but fans and family members had already started gathering on the island. By Friday afternoon, it was abuzz and the Carriage House patio filled to capacity.

As all the servers expected (they'd been forewarned and often), they'd be working doubles all weekend. That Friday Amanda had a station inside, while Olivia pulled a station on the patio. She and Amanda worked across from one another, separated only by dining room windows and glass double doors. As they passed each other, shouldering trays heavy with dishes and drinks, the two women communicated. Winks, grimaces, and other facial expressions entertained them while they served a genial and hopeful crowd. Even if you weren't a sailor, didn't know one, or had never known one, you couldn't help being swept up in their excitement.

That excitement was heightened by the risks undertaken by sailboat crews. Unspoken anxiety mixed with anticipation. The Chicago to Mackinac race was said to be more treacherous than the Bayview race. Years ago, a boat had capsized in stiff winds on Lake Michigan, and a crew member had died of head trauma. The story had been in the Chicago news. Olivia recalled hearing about it. She was reminded of that tragedy when Tricia, the restaurant's manager, told the serving staff about the incident during their prerace week, all-hands meeting. "Racing is a pastime and passion, but it's risky all the same," she said with a seriousness that compelled their attention. "And a successful finish depends on skill—and luck."

This upcoming race, though, from Port Huron north on Lake Huron to Mackinac, was thought to be safer, but not without its own hazards. Back in 1925, so they were told, a few dozen boats sailed, and only six made it to the island. Accidents and equipment failure could happen anytime on any of the Great Lakes. Tricia shared those messages in that early morning meeting so Iroquois employees could understand the emotions of the (hot, hungry, tired, excited, edgy, impatient) guests who would be filling guest rooms and tables.

"We're screwed." That was Amanda's reaction to the meeting.

Olivia nodded. "Yup. That's about the sum of it. The upside, Amanda, are the celebrations which mean drinks for everyone, champagne by the buckets, and tips that will make you glad you stuck it out." Olivia looked into Amanda's eyes. "If you start feeling unwell, or get a nervous stomach, let me know." Olivia wasn't ready to name the nausea for what it was. "I can cover for you for a while if you need a break." Amanda nodded with a slight smile. "A *short* break," added Olivia.

Lunch service was steady but not chaotic. By this point in the summer, they'd all gained speed and proficiency. Servers had mastered time-saving shortcuts by mid-July. When they took orders on their notepads, servers sketched little diagrams of large tables of eight or ten or even more. Most used their own shorthand to describe the guests: BM: bald man; FM: fat man; M: mom; RC: redhead child; BR: brat. Everyone had their own codes. These allowed them to serve all the diners accurately, with dishes and exceptions as ordered. The shorthand made it look like they'd remembered every guest and every guest's order. And they did. More or less.

Around two o'clock Olivia was still serving the patio, about to end her shift which would resume at five-thirty. The hostess, Haley, let her know that a couple had seated themselves at the far corner of the patio, "a woman and young guy, maybe her son."

"Got it. Maybe they'll just want a drink. Hopefully not an ice cream drink with its extra scooping fuss required. Spare me that." Olivia pushed through the doors and walked out into the sun, squinting as she approached the table. She saw the back of a young man who was seated to face the lake. He looked to be tall and thin, in a polo and khakis. The woman to his left was wearing a stylish straw hat that hid her profile from Olivia's view. She was steps away from the table when the woman turned her head in Olivia's direction. In an instant, the woman's mouth dropped open and she pulled the sunglasses from her face, but not before Olivia turned on her heels to rush to the dining room.

"Sheeee—ittt!" Olivia whispered and walked along the paver stone path as fast as she could without running or calling attention to her distress. *What in the world is Ceci doing here? Who is that young man? Is that Luke? God, I hope so, or my sister is just creepy. But, wait,* she counseled herself. *Not Luke. No, no. Oh my God. That's even worse!* She passed through the doors and found Amanda on the other side in the dining room manning her station. She grabbed Amanda by her tie and sputtered under her breath, "Can you come with me to the kitchen? Please? *Now*? Turns out I need a little assist."

Amanda smiled to the two-top she was standing near and told them she'd return promptly. She followed Olivia, down the stairs, through the swinging doors, and into the kitchen.

"My sister's here with my son! Shit!" At that word coming from Olivia the kitchen crew within earshot quieted.

"But oh, that's nice, isn't it? Do you want to go join them?" Amanda offered. "I can handle your station."

"No! It is not nice, and I do *not* want to join them!"

Amanda looked bewildered.

"I'm not supposed to be here! I'm in Chicago! At home!" Just then, the swinging doors blew in and with them, the woman in the straw hat.

Olivia spoke first. "Ceci, what are you doing here?"

"What am I doing here?" She stepped closer. "*What am* I *doing here*?" Ceci repeated the question for dramatic effect. The kitchen quieted further. All eyes were on the show. "What the hell are you doing in a uniform taking orders at a restaurant? Why aren't you in Montreal? Liv, what the hell is going on? Have you lost your mind?"

"Yes. Yes, I have, but we can't talk about that now. Please tell me that boy—young man—is Luke, that you don't have a boyfriend that young."

"Ew, Livy. You *have* lost your mind."

"Order up," came the voice of Chef from the line.

"That's a relief. But he didn't see me… Luke, I mean. Did he? Did you…?"

"No, he didn't see a thing. I excused myself to go to the ladies room."

"Order UP!!" came a louder voice and with it, Chef stepped out from behind the line. "Nash, what the hell?"

"That's exactly what I want to know!" shouted Ceci back at him.

"Who the hell are you? And why are you in my kitchen?" he lobbed back.

"Okay, okay." Olivia held her hands out in two directions and gestured for quiet. "Chef, meet my sister Ceci. Ceci, this is Chef."

"Nice to meet you," they said in unison and then looked at Olivia.

"What the hell, Liv!"

"Yeah, what she said."

"Excuse me for a minute. I gotta go." And a pale Amanda took her leave. The remaining three stood in the middle of the kitchen.

"Well, Chef," Olivia turned to him. "This is an unexpected visit from my sister. A big surprise."

"Oh, I'll say," Ceci retorted.

"We," and with this Olivia looked at Ceci and began to talk slowly with a series of nods as if to say, "please play along." "We are going to meet later for a drink, right Ceci? We were just making plans. Right? You're here just for the day. Right?"

"Nope, sister. All night. At Mission Point."

"Really, on race weekend?" Olivia was so impressed that Ceci could wrangle a room during race week that she forgot the issue at hand.

"Yes, race weekend… because I learned my nephew was being overlooked on his twenty-first birthday, and I simply couldn't stand for that."

Indignant, Olivia replied, "Well, his birthday isn't this weekend anyway."

"Sure. All right. I'm early, but far better than you and Nate. You told him you had some big to-do in Montreal. *Really*?"

"Really!" Chef interrupted. "Can you two do this anywhere else but my kitchen? This. Is. My. Kitchen. Order Effing UP!"

"Rude!" Olivia shouted at him and immediately regretted it. "Ceci, help me here. I can explain. Get Luke out of here and we'll meet later. Just you and me. I'll text you. Please?" She grabbed Ceci by her hands and mouthed, "I'm so sorry."

"All right, fine," she said to Olivia. "And you," she turned to Chef. "I hope you never speak that way to your paying guests."

"Only when they're IN. MY. FUCKING. KITCHEN!"

"Geez, calm down. I'm leaving already." With a look of annoyance shot back at him, she let go of Olivia's hands. "Your hair, Livvy. Honestly. You look good, whatever the hell is going on here." Ceci swept out the doors, leaving Olivia with Chef.

Olivia looked up at him, towering inches above her.

"So you're supposed to be in Montreal? Canada? Is that so?" He yanked off the bandana wrapping his head, wiped his forehead, and continued in a growl, "how about you just be here. Here. And serve your tables? You *do* work here, don't you?"

"Honestly, you… you," she shook her head, mustering restraint to guard her tongue. He was egotistical and obstreperous. And right.

"Yes! I work here. Still. Though I don't know why."

"Apparently that makes two of us." He stomped back to the line. "Order UP!"

Chapter 28

Just on time, Kelley arrived in the kitchen to relieve Olivia of her shift working the patio. "Everyone's set except the two-top by the water," Olivia relayed. "I didn't have a chance to meet them." Not exactly true, she thought. "Seems like the woman is in charge. I expect her to tip well. Let me know if she doesn't."

With a puzzled look on her face, Kelley said, "Got it. I think." The two parted and Olivia grabbed a forgotten Tigers cap from the employee dining room, determined to get to Lilac Cottage quickly and unnoticed by anyone, especially her son and her sister.

They were staying at Mission Point. Surprising. It was a pretty lakeside retreat which she was reminded of as a series of texts and photos that started pinging her phone. Olivia figured Luke was texting as he and his aunt waited for their food.

You guys - Aunt C surprised me. Showed up at camp. We're at that place mom worked. Mackinac. Cool patio for lunch. Best burger. Fudge is good too. Weddings and stuff going on. We should come back. Mom - you'd love it.

And in came photos of the ferry, the docks, the horses, the putting greens at Mission Point. And the patio at the Iroquois. *Oh, no.* Olivia tapped on that one to enlarge it. *Please, please tell me, I'm not in this shot.* She wasn't.

Olivia texted back a lighthearted reply. She began a dialog with herself as she replied: Fantastic! I hope it's as pretty as I remember it. (This morning.) The fudge! OMG, had so much of it back then. (Last weekend.) Aunt C is a sport. (A little angry and hopefully a secret keeper.) We'll go back sometime. (How's now?) When Dad's work slows down. (Never.) Love you both. xoxo

That last bit was true. Her phone stopped pinging. Nate didn't reply to Luke's texts. Maybe he would after work. She put the phone in her shirt pocket and peddled to the cottage, head down, noticing no one in particular and hoping no one noticed her. Of course, it was bound to happen and probably would happen again. Too many people from Chicago found their way to the island. She just needed a better alibi. Waiting tables for fun and kicks? Probably not. Maybe doing research to help Nina with her catering biz? Like gathering intel? Plausible, but weak.

She arrived at Lilac Cottage not ten minutes later and pulled her phone from her pocket. Sweaty and shaky now, and sitting on the top step, she texted Ceci:

Ceece. I'm sorry. Long story. Not sure I can explain it, but I'll try. Meet me at 10. Keep Luke at MP. Did you rent a bike? Probably not, knowing Ceci. She'd have hired a horse-drawn taxi. Meet me at the park by the marina. Behind the statue of Father Marquette. No quiet spots in town. It's jamming. Thanks for loving on Luke. You're a good aunt.

That bit was also true. She was a wonderful aunt, more fun and amusing than Olivia. And loads more entertaining than Nate. She dashed off the text and Ceci replied moments later with her own text: 10 sharp behind the priest. Bring booze. We'll need it.

As she settled into the cottage for a few hours' break, she considered the evening ahead. Her five-thirty shift would end at nine-thirty. She didn't have to close. That was a relief. She climbed the cottage stairs to take a shower and wash the smell of whitefish and beef out of her hair. She tried to take a nap. What a joke. Nap? With her son and sister on the island, just a few miles from her? Not a chance. Instead, she surveyed her fridge and packed a picnic for her meeting with Ceci.

She'd pick up a cold bottle of wine from Doud's on her way to the park.

Still unable to settle, she grabbed her paint supplies and started again. One more coat on the paneling up to the chair rail and she could add some color. With Frankie's go-ahead granted, she could soon add some color and a roommate, too. She considered a pale pink or maybe fuchsia on the walls as she began her work. And she steadied herself. Painting calmed her. Things transformed with the sweep of her brush, and her attention was drawn elsewhere, away from the vortex that seemed her life at the moment. Almost two hours later, she rushed to clean up her work and dress for her shift. She grabbed the picnic things she'd gathered for the truth-telling session that would happen later. She was dreading it. But as she left the cottage, her phone pinged with another text from Ceci:

And bring fudge. That son of yours inhaled ½ pound by himself. And don't worry. Love you.

At work, her worry receded. The Carriage House was too busy to allow her to fixate on her drama with drama enough in the dining room. She had the pleasure of serving sixteen—sixteen(!)—in the alcove in the "new" dining room with the great view. The host of that gathering proudly entertained his family, practically busting the buttons of his white shirt that he wore under a baby blue seersucker blazer. A gold chain tight around his neck looked like it could threaten his oxygen intake. One exceptional request after another came from him: "And we'd like the two younger ones here to split the strip steak; he likes it rare. Chloe would like it well done. She's dairy free, so you must have some substitute for sour cream? Oh, and we'd like more drinks down at the other end. The daiquiris, but, obviously, dairy-free whipped cream for Chloe. And the ceiling fan. My mother is cold. Can you turn that off?" She described him in her shorthand as SSG: seersucker guy and later changed it to PIA: pain in the ass.

He made toasts. He told jokes. He glowed with the retelling of how his sailboat once came in top five at the race. He asked for more drinks with cherries, entrees not as described "but even more exceptional," and side dishes without sauce or a different sauce, water cold but without ice, and coffee, just half-caf with almond milk. With every request, he'd look at Olivia, wink, and say, "Don't you worry. I'll take good care of you."

Eventually, Olivia presented the check folder for a whopping $1475.21 to the host, PIA. Without a look inside, he motioned her away. "Mom's taking care of this. Give it to her." Olivia moved around the table to place the folder to the right of the elderly woman with the white hair and little pocketbook. She was SSM: seersucker mom. Olivia dropped the bill with her left hand and with the coffeepot in her right hand, offered refills. She noticed that from his mom's little pocketbook came a pristine AARP credit card. The silver on the embossed numbers was as fresh as the day it was issued. A virgin credit card. SSM took her time appearing to do math in her head, tallied the tab, and signed her name carefully. Olivia overheard her say to the woman on her left, "Honey, I think that's plenty for a tip given how much we've spent here on dinner." The DFB (daughter fake boobs) agreed. As the group of sixteen made their way out of the dining room, Olivia turned the fan back on and peeked at the slip within the folder.

SSM had signed her name in a small and jagged script. She had rounded the total to a neat, if miserly, fifteen hundred dollars. Olivia had made twenty-five bucks in two hours serving a table of sixteen. The Iroquois never included a service charge, not even for large parties. Whatever. Her favorite couple, the one from Ann Arbor, would return and make up for the loss—in so many ways. She never used shorthand for them. They insisted that she know them as Susan and John. She cleared the PIA table with her favorite busser and told him there wouldn't be much to share from the tip out. He said he figured that. "The loud ones don't tip."

With the alcove returned to its four-table setup, she passed through the kitchen to the employee dining room to retrieve her backpack stowed in a locker.

"I'm glad you're here, Olivia." Olivia jumped. Mrs. B had appeared from nowhere and suddenly was at her side.

"Mrs. B, you frightened me."

"I apologize. Olivia, I have a serious matter to discuss with you." And she motioned for Olivia to follow her to the back of the room. They stopped at the EDR table farthest away from the kitchen. "Olivia, there's been some theft in the restaurant."

"Oh no." She was genuinely surprised and even more surprised that she was the recipient of such information. "But, why are you…?"

"No, dear, I'm not suggesting the perpetrator is you. Someone thinks it could be your friend. Amanda."

"Amanda?" She was in disbelief. "Who thinks that? And what could she steal? There's no cash. Not much anyway." Olivia was offended on Amanda's behalf. She wouldn't steal.

"Oh, there are things here worth stealing. Copper cups for cocktails, gold-rimmed creamers. Silver tea service. Tenderloins."

"Tenderloins? You mean meat? Amanda is stealing whole tenderloins?"

"Well, that is what has been alleged."

"Mrs. B," Olivia lowered her voice. "You know that Amanda can barely stand the look of rare beef, the smell of whitefish, or escargot. You've seen her go pale and dry heave around here. I know you've noticed." Mrs. B gave an almost imperceptible nod. Olivia stepped closer. "Why would she steal a whole tenderloin? And what in the world would she do with it? Cook it in employee housing?" She shook her head with the impossibility of it.

"Now, Olivia, I'm not convinced that Amanda is stealing, but I must talk with her about the claim. I thought it best if you were there with her when I do."

"Of course. I'd like to be there. Someone should. But this will be devastating to her, don't you think? To be accused of something… something… so ridiculous. And who is this accuser? I'd like to know that."

"I'm not at liberty to say."

"That's patently unfair," she said more vigorously than intended.

"Nonetheless," Mrs. B straightened further, rising to her full five-feet-and-not-much-more height, "we need to put the matter to rest.

I'd like to meet with her next week after the balance of our race guests have departed. I'll let her know. I simply wanted you to be aware and present when we meet."

"I guess you'll be watching her closely until then." Mrs. B set her lips and nodded. "Given that, is there any way we could delay this meeting? Amanda seems to have a lot on her mind lately, and I think she might be more fragile than we'd guess." Mrs. B took a moment to consider that. "And, actually, I've written to Frankie to see if she might move into Lilac Cottage with me. She was quick to agree with the idea, actually."

"Really? Hmm, yes, I think that could be more suitable, though unusual."

"Besides," Olivia rushed on, "you won't find anything. I don't believe she'd steal from the Carriage House. But, Mrs. B, may I ask— creamers? Why would people steal those?"

"Oh, not only those. We lose whole place settings, a piece at a time. Not as often anymore. The pit crew keeps a count for me when I ask. I know when a pattern is developing. And then I put an end to it."

"Oh, I believe that. I just can't imagine someone walking out of here with plates and a whole tenderloin in their backpack." Olivia remembered that she actually had a backpack in that very room stuffed with plates, napkins, and picnic provisions. Everything *on loan* from Lilac Cottage.

"Thank you, Olivia. We'll give it another week. That's all." Mrs. B turned away and swept through the door before Olivia could say good night.

"Yes, ma'am." She realized she'd nearly genuflected, and she wasn't even Catholic.

Chapter 29

As if getting stiffed on a table of sixteen and hearing that Amanda was being unfairly accused of theft wasn't bad enough, Luke had been blowing up Olivia's phone with messages to her and Nate and photos (so many photos!) of his time on the island. He texted about the horses, the fort, and the bikes he and Aunt C had rented. He sent photos of all the typical spots, all photo worthy.

At the fort. Guide said toys in this room where officer kids played in the 1800s sometimes move during the night when no one's there - Ghosts!

They had moved on—photos of Skull Cave, Arch Rock… dinner at Stonecliffe. Again, Ceci, how in the world did you score a table there this weekend?

Sunset over the bridge! You'd love it Mom - your kind of place.

She'd read that one at the bar, waiting for her six-top's drink order. She imagined her reply—*Don't I know it, Luke. From where you were, you and Aunt C were a quick walk to my cottage.*—*Well, not my cottage,* she mentally corrected herself. *Just the one that I call home. For now.*

The texts kept coming and Luke's excitement was so sincere that even Nate replied:

We'll get there Luke! Mom, too, when she's not busy catering parties with her friend. ☺

Was that a jab at her for not being available when *Nate* had time *this weekend* to finally come home? Nate wasn't typically passive-aggressive. Besides, he was the one busy at dinners and parties with Landon. In the shower while she was in his room?! The thought of it turned her stomach and stiffened her spine at the same time.

"Olivia? Hey," the affable bartender poked her gently with a cocktail pick. "The ice is melting."

"Mark, so sorry. I'm here. Physically, at least." She slipped her phone into her apron and picked up her tray.

"Make sure Mrs. B doesn't catch you staring at your phone. She'll take it."

"I think that's illegal, Mark."

"And you think that would stop her?"

She turned from the bar and thought of Mrs. B reading her texts—and stealing her phone. That would only seed greater doubt about Olivia and what she was doing at the Carriage House. No need for that.

The night clipped along. As expected, they served buckets of champagne, and thankfully without popping a single cork like a bullet into the chest of any guests—which had happened and surely would happen again. Olivia's tables were impatient and hangry once seated, but every one of them was completely satisfied by the time the check arrived.

Now, Olivia had to hustle to Marquette Park. Dodging bikes, horses, and overnight guests with no need to hurry to a ferry, she made it there before sunset. As far north as they were, July days were long. Olivia sat behind the statue of Father Marquette and waited for Ceci.

"Ah-ha!!!" Two hands were on her shoulders, and then they slid around her neck into a hug.

"You scared me, Ceece!"

"Just now or earlier today?" Ceci stepped around and dropped beside Olivia on the grass.

"Both." Olivia reached for the backpack to pull it closer to them, saying nothing.

"Well?"

"Well, what exactly?" Olivia replied.

"Well, how about you tell me what the hell's going on here? Start with these awful khaki pants and sensible shoes."

"These?" She looked down at her uniformed legs. "So…" she stammered a little. "Ceece, I don't know. I don't know." She dropped her head and let out a quiet sob.

"Oh, shit, Liv. Come here." She grabbed her sister in a hug—an intense one, like always. Ceci was intense in every way.

After Olivia snuffled over Ceci's shoulder, she said, "I don't exactly know where to begin." She spoke with her gaze fixed on the harbor lights beyond instead of looking at Ceci.

"How about why you're waiting tables in a tourist trap and why you're not in Montreal?" Ceci prompted.

"First, it's not a tourist trap."

Ceci snickered at that.

"Well only when the cruise ships or bus trips descend. Fair enough. But I'm not in Montreal because Nate didn't want me there."

"Didn't want you in Montreal? But he knows you're here? Or I guess he doesn't." Ceci answered her own question. "Luke thinks you're at home in Lake Ellyn, so Nate must think that too."

"That's right. They think I'm at home."

"But I thought you were having the time of your life in Montreal. Your very occasional texts said so. And, wait, you even sent photos!"

"I sent cropped photos I found on Google Images. That was easy." Olivia continued. "You're not the only one who thinks I'm in Montreal. So do Abby and Nina and our neighbors, the mailman, the lawn care company. You know, all the people."

"Just wait a sec. Back up. Nate the Great didn't want you in Montreal? How'd that go down? Before you tell me, can we open that backpack?" Ceci gestured toward it. "You promised me some booze. I need it."

Olivia opened the backpack, pulled out a sweating bottle of Pouilly-Fuissé, and handed it to Ceci while she fished out two wine glasses and Ziplocs with cheeses and fruit.

"Your taste in wine has improved, Liv. Hope you've got some fudge in there. You promised that too."

"Wouldn't forget that," Olivia assured her.

Ceci poured the wine into the glasses. After they clinked, she said, "Go on. Every detail."

Olivia took a deep breath. "When I talked to Nate before he left and proposed that I go along, you know, do the stuff you and I talked about—explore, maybe do a little cooking, just be his companion through a hard time of work—he… he said he wouldn't have any time to entertain me."

"Wait. What?" Ceci sat up straighter. "He said he couldn't *entertain* you?"

"Well, yes. Pretty much those words verbatim."

"Screw you, Nate."

"Ceci. Come on. He's still my guy."

"You know he makes me crazy sometimes."

"Yeah, that's apparent."

"So, how does he still think you're in Chicago? You must talk to him more than you do me. What about your phones? Didn't he check your location? Didn't Luke?"

"I turned my location off."

"Premeditated."

"Not exactly premeditated. We never really used that app anyway. And no one really cared where I'd be." It hurt to say that aloud. "So when I dropped Luke off, I thought I'd swing south and see you. Remember?"

"I do. And you canceled on me to get home." Ceci pulled the backpack toward her. "I def need this fudge. Go on."

"And then… and then, I dunno. I asked for a sign and got one. That's about when I bought a ticket for the ferry and put my car in long-term parking."

"You got a sign?"

"Well, kind of. It was more like advice from a mechanic."

"This makes less sense all the time, but I'm liking it. And you packed for this?"

"I did not. I've bought a new wardrobe here from boutiques on the island and the Ste. Anne's thrift shop."

"And this very nonbinary uniform. I hope it was free. That's the only way you got your money's worth."

Olivia pushed Ceci. She fell back on her left side and they both laughed. "Hey, I, we—all the servers—we look professional."

"Yeah, that tie you were wearing. Awesome. Professional. But I did notice your hair, your color. And, if I may say so, you've lost a little weight. You look years younger. Nonbinary, but young."

"Ceci, really."

"Okay, so back to this situation. Why not tell Nate and Luke? It's weird, not at all like you, but, what the hell? If anyone could, you could make it sound rational."

"I guess I'm not ready for that."

"And furthermore, why not me? Why didn't you tell me, your only sister? You know I love a good adventure."

"Well, it's a little more involved than that. I've met some people."

Ceci interrupted. "That chef. I knew it! He's a looker."

"No! Not 'that chef.' He's my boss. And he's, I don't know—off-limits. Sort of a pain, arrogant. And Ceci, you forget. I'm married."

"Oh yeah. How could I forget? This is what marriage looks like—living a secret life in a theme park."

"It is *not* a theme park."

"But is it a marriage?"

"Ceece, that sounds so… so dramatic and damning. It's complicated."

"I'd say so."

"Like I said, I've met some people. A college girl. I'm pretty sure she's pregnant and alone. And I have this cottage I'm restoring—just the décor. It's not mine. I'm just living there, rent free. And, Cliff, the bookstore owner. He's a dear and I think he's lonely and might need help if his knee gets any worse."

"Shit, Olivia. You've set up shop here. Are you going around rescuing people and serving drinks on the side? Like a nonprofit? Church lady, this is a lot. Even for you." She shook her head. "I need more wine." Ceci refilled Olivia's glass and her own. "And fudge." She took the knife and cut off a sizable hunk. "Continue. Like when do you let your family know? When do you go home?"

"I don't have an answer for either of those." Olivia paused for a long while. "You know, for the first time in forever, I don't have a plan. My life isn't dictated by someone else's schedule. I'm just taking every day one at a time. I feel like I can breathe. I have run away, that's true. And I do feel some shame. But if I'm being completely honest, it feels good most days, breathing, being free."

"As it should. I mean, shouldn't breathing be a good thing?"

Olivia changed the subject. "And there's Landon."

"Who?"

"Landon, Nate's colleague."

"Oh, her. I remember." She bit into more fudge, a different flavor this time. "This sounds like something I'm going to kill Nate for."

"Ceece, I trust Nate. You should too."

"And…"

"And…" Olivia shot back.

"And, should you trust that Landon woman?" Ceci continued. "I don't trust her and I've never even met her."

"That's not the point. If I can trust Nate, she doesn't matter." They sat in silence for a moment and listened to the horns from the day's last ferries leaving the docks and the clip-clop of horses pulling their carriages on Main Street.

"But," Olivia went on, quietly, dreading Ceci's response, "she did answer Nate's phone when I called the other day. She said he was in the shower."

"WHAT?" Ceci dropped the fudge into her lap.

"I know. Unusual."

"Unusual unless you're having an affair. Liv, sissy, you've got to wake up. Something is going very wrong here."

"No. Stop Ceece. I'm trying not to think that. The worst."

"How soon can you get to Montreal?"

"Nope. Not going there unless I'm invited. I haven't been invited."

"Sorry," she shook her head. "I'm no marriage expert. I know— obviously. But all the same, aren't you supposed to fight for this thing?

Go up there. Set the boundaries."

"Hmm. We did that once. Years ago. You were there, Ceece." She looked down and spun the rings on the finger of her left hand. "I'm not fighting that way. I need to let it play out. I trust Nate."

"All right. I'll accept that only because I love you. But I don't like it one bit. Not one bit. Let me have that on the record."

They sat quietly for a moment, both absorbing what Olivia had said.

"I don't want to talk about Nate the Great anymore. It won't make me love him more." Ceci took another bite of fudge. "This is too good," she said, looking at what remained in her hand.

They sat in silence again.

"So, change of subject." Ceci lightened the mood. "Tell me more about this house of yours and I'll tell you about me."

For the next half hour, they talked about Lilac Cottage and Ceci's work and weekend adventures. Olivia asked again about Luke. "Tell me more, everything he told you. Seems like he's loving it. Do you agree? I miss him so much."

Ceci gave Olivia all the details she could recall and recounted their day on the island.

"This secrecy, Liv. I get it, I think. It sounds almost understandable until I think about Luke. You're asking me to lie to him. I'll be with him all day tomorrow and I'm supposed to act like I know nothing about this? Nothing at all?"

"Well…" Olivia began.

"I know where you're going and don't. Don't say that. I may not always be on top of your life and everything that's happening, but he is my only nephew. I love him like a son. I hate the idea of lying to him. You know, all day today I had to listen to him say, 'Mom would love that we're here. I wish she was too.'"

That's what hurt Olivia the most. She dropped her head. "Please. Just for a little longer, Ceece. I'll go to him—at camp. I'll tell him what's going on."

Not knowing what else to do, Olivia pulled out the cash tips she'd stuffed in her pocket. Almost two hundred dollars. Race week tippers were generous, and unlike most diners, they often left cash. "Give this to Luke," she said. "Tell him it's from you. Hit some shops tomorrow and let him pick out some things he might like. Sweatshirt, more fudge, anything at all. Whatever he wants."

"Okay, I've got you," she said, sounding resigned, but bound to her promise.

Ceci took the cash and told her sister what she had planned for the next day: brunch, a little shopping, probably more fudge, and then catching a noon ferry.

The sisters parted shortly after.

"Ceece, your hugs," Olivia coughed. "They're strangling."

"That's my love language. Strangling. You know that."

Olivia heard from Ceci the next day. Her text read: Gave Lukers the money. He bought more fudge. Spent the rest on you. He wanted to surprise you with stuff he knew you'd love.

Chapter 30

With regret, Amanda had left the scene that had erupted between Olivia and her sister. But she couldn't very well throw up in the kitchen. That would be gross. She managed to get herself into the employee bathroom just in time. She did what she had to and, after, splashed water on her face. She allowed herself a few minutes to sit on the toilet and cool down. The kitchen at the Carriage House was in the basement of the hotel. She'd been told that the air conditioning was a recent addition, and that she wouldn't have wanted to experience what it was like before the A/C. In those days, Olivia had said servers were only women and they were required to wear panty hose under their black uniform dresses with white collars, white aprons, and white French maid headbands. Whose idea was that anyway? A French maid? Whose sick fantasy was that? Anyway, Olivia told her they wore panty hose, the uniform, and nothing else. Bras were too hot. Panties were restrictive. Sweat just dripped down between their boobs to their stomachs. And what? In the old days, they were practically naked under those black dresses but nowadays, tattoos are forbidden? Someone has that messed up.

Amanda stood to look at herself in the mirror, in her button-down shirt and tie. She looked okay. What was unseen was her phoenix tattoo. And her cardinal tattoo. And a baby, or something like that. Amanda had known she was pregnant for about a week. Actually, it was the day before she got the book from the Island Bookstore. She had figured she was, but she had held out hope that she was just adjusting to the island and the smells. That pee stick was the only thing positive in her life, and it wasn't good news. But what could she do? Her mom hadn't wanted her. She'd heard that enough. Still, Amanda was the proof that while she might have been unwanted, at least she was given a chance. It wasn't looking like a good bet.

She opened the door and immediately jumped back. "Mrs. B! I'm so sorry. Do you need the bathroom? This one?"

Mrs. B raised her brows over the glasses perched, per usual, on her nose. And though Mrs. B was so small, Amanda always felt she was looking down on her. "No Amanda, I do not use the employee facilities. Thank you." Mrs. B stepped back to allow Amanda to step forward.

"Dear," she continued.

Dear? Is she on something?

"Dear, I am aware that you haven't been well lately. Hmm?" She raised her eyebrows again. They often said more than words spoken by the diminutive matriarch.

"Uh, yeah, well my stomach has been off lately. It's the smells. But, I mean, not the food here. No, not the Carriage House food. It's good enough to eat. I mean, so much better than that." Her words tumbled and stumbled. Mrs. B interrupted.

"Yes. Like you, we're all quite proud of our reputation for fine cuisine. Amanda, given your… hmm, weak stomach, I'd like you to take tonight off. No protests. You'll make plenty of money on other shifts in the upcoming weeks."

Amanda nodded.

"Take the night off and then early next week, please speak to Olivia. She has a proposal for you that I'd like you to consider. And she has another matter I asked her to discuss with you."

Mrs. B must have been aware how Olivia had created relationships with the other servers. She remembered stuff about them. Always checked in. Covered for them. Listened to them. Made jokes with them. Olivia had become like a room mother to some of them. The servers anyway. The line cooks, especially Danny, didn't seem to like her. Maybe they thought she was a plant sent by Mrs. B. Well… maybe she was? Now there's a thought.

"So, Amanda." The woman interrupted Amanda's thoughts. "You'll meet with Olivia? I imagine she'll approach you."

"Oh sure. We get along fine. I'll talk to her. And about this whatever you said… proposal? Can I ask what it's about?"

"I think you'll find it helpful. It's nothing to worry about." It looked like Mrs. B was about to say something more and then stopped herself. "That's all, Amanda. Thank you."

"Okay, sure," she said to Mrs. B's back.

Amanda didn't see Olivia the rest of that lunch shift. Kelley had shown up early and taken over for her. Amanda wrapped up early herself and headed into the island's interior to employee housing. She decided to shower, find something to eat, and go to the bookstore. She'd read the book Cliff had given her and she was ready to report back—and find another book.

The store wasn't open regularly. She'd noticed that. Cliff said his knee made it harder to get around. Unloading inventory with the bending and lifting hurt, and his knee would swell up afterward. Not to mention climbing the stairs to his store and then up another floor to his apartment. She always walked by just to check and to talk to him. He had a way of making her feel comfortable. And he brought her tea in china teacups, of all things.

If it was open and she had an hour or more, she'd take a book to the library table and her favorite chair and read. She could work her way through a book in a couple of days if she wasn't working doubles. She didn't even have to buy the books. She was careful not to break the spine or dog-ear a page.

The store was open that afternoon, probably because of race weeks, she figured. Amanda pushed open the heavy door and heard the familiar tinkling bells and voices on the floor above where the shop did its business. Once she climbed the stairs, she saw shoppers engrossed in the stacks of books on tables, and others with their heads turned sideways to read titles on the spines of shelved books. Several were milling around the stationery goods placed here and there around the store. A burning candle offered up the aroma of cedar and tobacco.

It was a cool and quiet retreat from the noise and chaos of race week. Music played from speakers around the room. She knew it was classical and if Cliff were standing in front of her, he'd quiz her on the composer. "Knox College students should know these pieces. They better your concentration and steady your soul." He'd already said that to her a time or two. And he'd add, "Now you do know how to pronounce 'Mozart,' don't you? It's 'Moat-zart,' and don't let anyone suggest otherwise." As though that mattered. She hated to admit it, but she liked the music and sometimes listened to a "Best of Beethoven" playlist. A long time ago she took piano lessons. She once dreamed of having a piano herself and playing every day, but her dad laughed when she told him. He took her hands and said, "These fingers will never touch anything like that. They're dirty. All that stupid foraging with your grandmother. They're trash." He gripped her hands in his own until she cried out in pain, and then he shoved them away and left. That time. She forced the thoughts from her mind.

Not seeing Cliff anywhere, Amanda grabbed a bestseller from the table near the counter and made her way to the table and wingback chair that had become hers. So comfortable and so drowsy, she didn't notice when shadows fell over the table and the store emptied of customers.

Sometime later, a light touch on her shoulder and the smell of a sweet something awakened her. Cliff greeted her while putting a teacup in front of her.

"Cliff," she said sleepily, "how do you do that without spilling? With your knee. Do you know our trick? At the restaurant?"

"What trick is that?"

Cliff dropped into the chair at the end of the table with a slight grimace. Amanda mirrored it, in sympathy, and went on to explain how to balance cups or glasses on a tray. "You have to look into the distance, to the table you are going to. If you look down, all the liquid just splashes out, all over." She continued. "The key is to look ahead, to where you're going, not at what you're balancing on the tray."

"Amanda, by George, you've given yourself a bit of wise advice there." He clapped his hands softly in delight. "Look to the future. Staring too long at the present leads to, well what would it be? A mess?"

"A shit tip. That's what."

"I suppose that too. Let's say an unfortunate mess."

Amanda took a sip of tea. "What's this? It's not Earl Grey."

"No. I've decided to expand your palate, Amanda dear. You are drinking rooibos tea, from the fermented leaves of the *Aspalathus linearis* shrub, native to South Africa."

"Okay, wow. It's really good. Sweet."

"It is that. It is also chock-full of antioxidants. And no caffeine." She took another sip. Cliff continued. "It also suppresses morning sickness."

Amanda spit out the tea. "Sorry. What?"

"I read it's an excellent concoction for expectant mothers." Cliff pulled a handkerchief from his pocket and leaned toward her and whispered, "if you happen to know one."

Amanda began shaking her head no and then, looking at Cliff's concerned and kind face, she stilled and began to move her chin up and down, slowly. Tears spilled from her brown eyes. "Cliff, I'm pregnant."

"I know," he offered quietly. "And what wonderful news that is, Amanda." He patted her hand gently. "Not expected news, perhaps, but wonderful all the same."

"No, Cliff. You don't get it. It's messed up." She looked at the bookshelves behind him, avoiding his face and the tender expression in his eyes. "I don't know how to do this."

"I don't suppose any woman does. Not the first time."

"But I'm in college. I'm not married. I don't want a kid. I never even had a dog. Or a hamster." She snapped her gaze back to him. "And why would it be a good thing?"

"Dearest Amanda, for many years I had been in residence with hundreds, nay, thousands of young people. I was a professor long ago. I had the opportunity to teach a few young women in your condition. A privilege it was."

"A professor? Where?"

"A small college. We'll talk more about that one day. For today, let's talk about you and keeping that tray balanced. Let's look ahead. I have a proposition for you."

Amanda began to feel better the longer they talked. It was a relief that someone else knew she was pregnant and didn't hate her for it. Or think she was a total screwup. Cliff told her that he and Olivia both had an idea that she was "with child" and might need a more suitable form of employment.

"Wait, you know Olivia? The one I work with?"

"The very same."

"And she knows too?" She dropped her chin and exhaled with a sigh.

"Oh now, Amanda. Don't look so forlorn. I think Olivia holds you in very high regard and with great affection."

"But she knows? How? I haven't told anyone until you."

"I can't be sure, but I suspect a woman who has been with child herself detects these things."

"That doesn't explain how you knew. So early. Unless you had a baby once." She let a small smile escape her.

"Can't say that I have. And my powers of deduction aren't so well formed. But the two of you were seeking the very same book on pregnancy. She seemed, how should I say, too experienced to be interested in that particular reference guide. And you denied personal interest in it with such fervor. You confirmed my suspicions."

"Is she gonna tell Mrs. B?" She looked panicked. "I really need my job."

"No, I don't believe she will. I knew Olivia when she was about your age. We've just begun to rekindle our friendship. You can trust her."

"Why do you think that? That had to be a long time ago. When you knew her."

Cliff drew his right hand over his jawline and chin. "Amanda, over many years I've observed that someone's character is very much like a fingerprint. It is unique to a person and it takes something quite extraordinary to change it. At least in my experience."

"Hmm, maybe." She thought about it some more. "That means I won't end up any better."

"Better than?"

"Better than who I am now. Better than her. My mother. She had me and then she left. Drugs, I dunno. No one ever told me much. Just that she had me and bolted."

"And now, as you are, do you understand the fear she might have had?"

"I dunno. Not sure." She took another sip of tea and placed the cup back on the saucer. "She left. She still sucked as a mother. So anyway, what's your idea? The proposition. Kinda weird. Mrs. B said she has something like that too. With Olivia."

"Yes, yes. I am aware. But let's begin here." Cliff reached into his shirt's breast pocket and pulled out a small calendar and laid it flat on the table between them. He turned to the month of July.

Amanda pulled her chair closer to take a closer look at the pocket calendar. "What is all this? It's in code."

Cliff shared his system for marking store open days. Book deliveries expected. His appointments. The two pages were filled with color and writing in tiny letters that he said held all the information he needed to run the shop.

"Cliff, you know they make computers and software for this kind of stuff. And phones. Your phone could do this." She pulled the calendar even closer to take another look and shook her head. "Sorry, but this…" She pushed the booklet back to him. "This gives me a headache."

"There you have it! Amanda, that's exactly what I am suggesting. What if I trained you? You could continue our open hours here at the Island Bookstore while I rest my knee. At least until I have that surgery and perhaps for a recovery period afterward."

Amanda sat up straighter upon hearing the idea. "Here? Work here?" She looked around and then back at Cliff. "Here?"

"Yes, here. That's exactly what I mean."

Amanda smiled. At once, her bright expression washed away with a wave of realization. "No. I can't. I can't." She shrugged her shoulders. "The Iroquois provides housing and meals. If I quit, that would stop." She looked at her hands in fists on her lap. "I'm sorry, Cliff. I can't."

"Ah. That's the only impediment? We may have a solution for that too, Amanda. Olivia is currently tending a cottage on the island. You knew that?" Amanda nodded that she did.

"You will discuss the matter with her, but I believe she is securing the consent of the cottage's owner for you to find accommodations there."

"You mean I would live in that cottage with Olivia?"

"That's the idea as Olivia conveyed it to me."

"Huh." She looked beyond Cliff and wondered, out loud, "Do you really think you could?"

"Could what?"

"Train me? To run a bookstore?"

"I do think so! You have an obvious appreciation for books and learning. You've already noted how I could be helped by modernizing my system here. It has worked well for many years, but I might be helped by some technological advances."

Amanda looked down at his calendar booklet on the table and back at Cliff. "You think?" They both laughed.

"It's getting late, young one. Let's just leave it that you'll speak to Olivia. Later we'll set up some time to talk about this bookselling operation." Cliff rested both hands on the table and pushed himself upward to stand.

"Wow, yes. I'm… I'm so surprised. Um, thank you." She stood and reached out an unsteady hand to shake his. He took it and gently covered it with his other hand.

"Thank you, Cliff. I don't think anyone has ever done anything like this for me. You know, believed in me. You *and* Olivia."

"Is that so?"

Amanda nodded. He kept hold of her hand. She didn't mind.

"Amanda, have you read *To Kill a Mockingbird*? Surely, they haven't dispensed with that classic."

"Oh, yeah. In high school. It's one of my favorites."

"Perhaps you remember the words of the judge—in the courtroom. He said, 'People generally see what they look for, and hear what they listen for.' Do you recall that?"

She nodded again. "Vaguely."

"I see potential in you, Amanda. A strong mind and a good heart. In time, you'll see the same." She squirmed a little at the suggestion, unaccustomed to such kind words. "Now," he continued, "I have a question for you. A delicate one."

"Oh. Do I have to answer it?"

Cliff shook his head slowly and he looked at the girl standing before him with a smile in his eyes. "Certainly not. My question, Amanda, is this. Does the father of your child know that he is going to be a parent? Have you told him?"

Amanda pulled her hand away from his suddenly and bent toward the table to pick up the book she'd left there. "There's no one to tell, Cliff. That's the honest-to-God truth."

Looking at the book in her hand, she changed the subject. "Can I take this one? I'll be careful. I'll bring it back when I'm done. Tomorrow." Amanda reached for the teacup and saucer and said, "I'll put this on the counter for now, but soon I'll be washing this and any other stuff. We should wash the floors, polish the tables and stuff, too. I can do all of that." She walked away with the book under her arm and teacup in her right hand and moved toward the stairs. "You won't be sorry, Cliff. I promise."

Chapter 31

Wednesdays used to be quiet on the island. Olivia could count on that midweek oasis between extended-weekend visits and early-weekend getaways. Though Wednesdays proved to be almost as busy as the weekends, breakfast during the midweek, especially before seven o'clock, was a peaceful retreat at the Water's Edge Café, the best breakfast spot on the island, serving up omelets and lake views.

Already tucked into a booth with a mug in one hand and pen in the other, Olivia was interrupted by a small voice, almost a whisper.

"Hey."

She looked up to see Amanda, wearing an oversized hoodie over yoga tights, a backpack hanging off one shoulder. "Amanda!" She sounded surprised and smiled at the girl. "Good morning." Olivia dropped her pen and pushed the crossword aside. "You're up early. I didn't think kids your age knew about this place, or that it opened so early. Join me?"

"Yeah, sure. Thanks." She slid into the booth opposite Olivia. "Early is right. You know what's weird about that?" Olivia shook her head. "Yeah, well, on my way here I saw Chef and Cliff coming out of the church together."

"Ste. Anne's?"

"Yeah. The white one across the street. A few other people were coming out too. Do people go to church on Wednesdays this early in the morning?"

Olivia shrugged her shoulders. "I wouldn't know but I also wouldn't have expected Chef to darken the doors of a church." They both had a quiet laugh at that.

"I'm just glad I'm not Catholic. I'd be in big trouble."

"Why do you say that?" Before Amanda could answer, the server came by and began to pour coffee into the mug she held in her other hand.

Amanda waved her off. "Oh, no! Not for me, thanks. I'll take tea. Chamomile if you have it." She gestured for the server to wait a minute while she scanned the laminated menu that had been left on the table. "I'll have the Mighty Mac breakfast with sausage. Oh, and bacon, too." The server made a note and said she'd be back.

"Hungry," Olivia remarked.

"Yeah, some days." She stretched out her hands on the table. A tiny cross was tattooed on her ring finger. "So, I know you know."

"Know? Know what?"

"About me being…" She spoke more quietly and drew her hands back into fists. "…pregnant and all. Cliff knows. He told me you figured it out too."

"Hmm, yeah. I had a pretty good idea. I've been there, you know." She crooked her head. "Not at your age, though. How are you managing?"

"Oh, fine, I guess. I'm just trying to forget about it and work."

Olivia nodded. "Bet that's not easy. To forget."

"Yeah. Work helps. I need the job and the housing. I've got to figure out what I'm gonna do." She dropped her head and moved a hand to her belly. "About this… situation."

The server dropped off a teapot and teabag and Amanda busied herself with it while Olivia continued their conversation.

"Amanda, does anyone else know? Like your dad…?"

Amanda shook her head. "God, no. Absolutely not."

"The father?"

"No."

"A relative?"

"Don't have any."

"None? An aunt? A grandma?"

Amanda smiled a little at that. "I had a grandma. Her name was Gertrude but we called her Trudy." She looked at her mug and added a little more sugar. "She died after I went to college." She stirred her tea.

"How about a family friend?"

"Nope."

"None? None at all?"

"No one I can think of."

Olivia took a breath. "Well, you're wrong there. You have me. And it sounds like you have Cliff."

Amanda looked up at Olivia through the bangs that hung over her dark eyebrows. "Yeah. He said you two have an idea. He said I could work at the bookstore. And that I might be able to live with you." She looked down at her mug again as if waiting for the bad news that the idea was preposterous and Olivia was about to tell her so.

"That's exactly right. I'd like you to live at Lilac Cottage."

Amanda lifted her chin and looked at her. "For real?"

"For real." Their breakfasts were delivered and the two spent the half hour talking through the details of moving her belongings—not many according to Amanda—and whether she could request reduced hours at the Carriage House so she could also keep open hours at the bookstore, or if she'd have to quit outright.

"I expect Mrs. B will ask that you work through Chicago-Mackinac race week. I'm sure Cliff would like to keep the store open then too. Maybe I can help here and there."

Amanda was dragging the last of her pancakes through syrup left on the plate when Olivia said, "You need to see a doctor, Amanda. An ob-gyn. I don't suppose you have one, a gynecologist, I mean."

"Nope."

"So you've never been to one? Ever?"

"No. Never needed to."

"Hmm. Well, you have a need for one now. The woman who owns Lilac Cottage…"

"Wait." She dropped her fork. "She knows? You told her?"

"She does. I had to get her permission to offer you a place to stay, right?"

Amanda nodded and picked up her fork again.

"Anyway, she gave me the name of an ob-gyn off island and I happen to have a car in the ferry lot to get us there. What if I see about making an appointment for you?"

"Like you were my mom or something?"

"At least to inquire about how we might start. Would that be all right?"

"I guess." She put her paper napkin on her plate and pushed it away. "You know, I usually do stuff on my own. I mean, I got into college by myself and I get good grades. I got a job here and figured that out too." She looked at her lap and back at Olivia. "I'm not a screwup."

"Oh, Amanda, I apologize if I've offended you. I care about you. I remember being pregnant at a much older age with every support and advantage. You are so capable. I see that every day. But maybe having a little support, a friend like me, might help?"

Amanda paused as if weighing Olivia's sincerity. She nodded and continued, "So, I don't have insurance. Just the crappy stuff they give you at Knox if you're in school there. I don't have anything else."

"Let's not worry about that for now. We'll sort that out. Why don't you just gather your things in the apartment and get ready to find your favorite spot to read at the sweetest little cottage you've ever seen. Maybe you'll like the porch swing like I do, or the sunny window seat that I'm getting ready to recover. You'll have your own room, of course."

"I will?"

"Sure you will. You can choose which one. And you can help me pick out the color we'll paint it too—once race weeks are behind us."

Amanda sat in silence, looking out the window, as a boat pushed off from the dock. She turned her attention back to Olivia. "Can I get this?" She put a hand on the check that the server had left on the table. "I want to say thanks."

"You just did." Olivia slipped the check out from under Amanda's hand. "Come on, let's get out of here."

They parted ways and Olivia went home to call the ob-gyn's office. She got a few appointment options and quickly texted Amanda to settle on a time. Fortunately, though Dr. Ryder delivered babies out of Petoskey, she also had office hours one day a week in St. Ignace. On Wednesdays.

Olivia texted Amanda: This is quick, but Dr. Ryder can see you today at 3:00. A cancellation. Meet at the ferry at 1:45. Shepler's. Work for you?

A thumbs-up was the reply. When Olivia suggested she bring her ID and any insurance information she had, Amanda sent another thumbs-up. *Well*, she thought, *Amanda must not be too overwhelmed by all of this, her first gynecology appointment.* Not like Olivia was anyway. She talked herself through it. Pretend you're a friend, a concerned confidante. No, that's not right. Maybe an aunt. Yes, an aunt. Better.

Olivia did a rough calculation in her head. Without knowing how far along Amanda was, Olivia guessed she would deliver after the first of the year. Maybe February. If she delivered. Olivia had already searched and determined that abortion was a legal procedure for an adult at any time during pregnancy in the state of Michigan. That was a legitimate possibility for a young woman like Amanda, though the idea felt heavy on Olivia, remembering the pain that lingers after losing a baby—a baby so wanted. But Amanda's was a different story. At least, it seemed different.

She wished she could talk to someone about all of it. Nate. He'd be the one. He always saw straight through to a logical answer. He could wipe away the fog of emotion to reveal what made most sense, the rational course of action. She could use that now. Without the benefit of his clear thinking, she conjured up what he might say (after he exploded, quietly, on the inside, at the fact that she was a runaway wife). He'd probably say that this was beyond her capacity, or her place, to solve. As though there was a solution. *Is there a solution to a* baby *and whether or not to have one?* She had to rely on her own judgment. *I mean, Nate's not here, right? This is up to me. To help.* All she knew to do was to take the next right step. And the one after that.

The time passed, too slowly for Olivia, and after one o'clock, the two women met on the docks. Olivia had already bought two tickets and she handed one to her companion. Amanda was wearing a jeans jacket, and underneath, a blue sundress, tight across the bust and flowing beyond her rib cage. She wore white tennis shoes which made her look even younger than she was.

"You look adorable." Amanda's facial expression in response told Olivia that was not the look Amanda was going for. Adorable is good when you're ten, less so when you're twenty and pregnant.

They followed other passengers onto the ferry and climbed the stairs to the top deck since the temperature was mild and the sun was showing in and out of wispy clouds. Having no interest in talking above the noise of the engine, they sat quietly and let the spray blow against them. As they docked and the engine quieted, Olivia slipped her hand atop Amanda's where it rested on her lap. "This is going to be okay." Amanda gave a reluctant nod.

Olivia had studied the way to the doctor's office. She wanted the trip to seem as normal as an errand to the grocery store. "It's about a mile from here. I figured we could hoof it. Yeah?"

Amanda agreed and they had a quiet walk to the medical building. "Amanda," said Olivia, "I can go with you into the examination room or I can stay in the waiting room. Whatever you want. I want this to be easy for you. Comfortable."

"Comfortable?" Amanda gave her such a look of disbelief that they both smiled.

"Okay, this isn't going to be comfortable. But you call the shots. I'll be with you or not. Whatever you want."

"With me is good." Olivia nodded without giving away her relief.

After a twenty-minute wait in the outer office, a nurse led them into the examination room. She weighed Amanda and took her vitals and then they waited some more, both in chairs by the door.

The door opened and in walked a tall woman, long blonde hair pulled back by a wide barrette at her nape. She wore large tortoiseshell glasses that made her blue eyes look oversized for her delicate facial features.

"Amanda," she moved forward with a hand extended. "Thank you for coming to see me. I'm so glad to meet you." Her sincerity seemed genuine. "And you must be Amanda's friend."

"Yes, Olivia. Olivia Nash."

Dr. Ryder dropped onto the wheeled stool and with her heels moved herself opposite the two women. "I understand you're pregnant, Amanda. That's wonderful news, at least for most women. To get right to it, I noted that you are unmarried and young so I expect this might be a time of uncertainty and probably some confusion too." She raised her eyebrows over the wide rims of her glasses. Amanda nodded.

"Given that, let's just start with some basic information, some questions that will guide us." Pushing off with her thick-soled tennis shoes, she wheeled herself to the computer station to their right. She clarified what was already uploaded and then typed in additional detail.

"Amanda, your last name here is…"

"Rojas. R-O-J-A-S," Amanda said.

"Ah. There was a typo here. Glad we caught it. And you live in…"

"Knox College."

"Knox? Great school. But that's not your permanent address, right?"

"I guess not." And she went on to say that she would live with her father for one more year. "And that's all." She relayed that he was a farmworker, mostly seasonal, on various Michigan farms. "Nothing steady. No insurance," she added. The doctor nodded.

Having completed some additional information, Dr. Sam (she asked that they call her that) continued. "So, Amanda, can you tell me how long you've been sexually active?"

"I'm not. Or maybe I don't know what you mean," Amanda replied.

"Well, given that you're pregnant, for how long have you been sexually active?"

"I wasn't active." That comment hung in the air. The buzz of the lights above them seemed especially loud.

Dr. Sam spun all the way around on her stool and looked at Amanda, eye to eye. "Amanda, what are…?"

"I wasn't active. I was passive."

Dr. Sam pushed off her heels and wheeled inches closer. "Amanda, are you saying what I think you are?" Silence.

Olivia found herself sitting more upright, trying to breathe.

"Can you tell me more?" The doctor tried again.

"I can tell you what I know. What I think I know." She took a big breath. "I was at a party. Last week of classes. I had one more exam. I knew I'd pass it. Well, better than pass it. I studied all the time." She looked at Dr. Sam. "My scholarship, and all." She looked back down at her lap and fussed with the watch wristband as she told them more. There had been a party at a campus house. She'd been invited by a guy she thought was a good guy. A guy who'd taken interest in her.

"Micah was that guy that everyone liked, and I thought he liked me. A little. We have the same major, so we had a couple of seminars together. He asked me that day in the English house, after our last seminar, to come to the party. So, I went. I'd never done that before, not to a house and not by myself." Amanda wrapped her arms around herself and talked to her feet.

"I danced with him once and two other guys. One guy got me a drink. We danced a little more. I don't know what happened after that. I woke up in a room on a sofa. A gross sofa." She spoke more quickly now as if to spill it all in one breath. "It was really late. No one was in the room and I left. I was bleeding a little, you know. There." She took a breath and looked up at them.

"That's what happened. I took my exam. I packed up later and left. That's all."

Olivia instinctively put her arm around Amanda. "Oh honey. Oh my God. That was, that is—so awful."

"Amanda, you were raped." The doctor was direct but not unkind. "Is that correct?"

"I don't know. I guess? I shouldn't have been there. I shouldn't have had that drink. I didn't recognize the guy and I know about roofies and stuff. Stupid. So stupid."

"No. I won't allow you to say that about yourself, Amanda." The doctor continued. "You were likely drugged and then you were raped. That is not your fault. Not any of it. Not one moment of it." Dr. Sam waited for Amanda to raise her gaze. Her blue eyes bore into Amanda's brown. "Do you understand?"

"I think so."

"Amanda, I am so sorry. You've been traumatized and somehow kept this to yourself. I'm gathering from what you said that you didn't go to the Knox Health Center or to a doctor to report this?"

"No. I couldn't. I couldn't miss my exam. I showered and took it. After, I went back to the apartment and slept. When I woke up, I packed. I just wanted to forget about it. Forever."

The women beside and in front of her stayed silent and nodded their understanding.

"And now I can't forget."

"Amanda, there are a few things that can happen here. You can still file a report, with the college."

"No!" Amanda shook off the suggestion. "No way. And who would I even say?"

"The young man… Micah?" Dr. Sam asked.

"No, I don't even think it was his house. I don't think he'd do that to me. And if he did," she shook her head, shaking free tears that dropped from her cheeks to her hands, "I don't want to know."

"Okay, that's fine but you will still have recourse in the future, should you choose it."

"Okay."

Olivia gave the girl's shoulders a light squeeze before dropping her arm, and Dr. Sam continued.

"Amanda, because of my profession I'm aware of research studies on rape-related pregnancy. It happens more often than you might think. And most women—or girls in some cases—don't know about it for weeks, sometimes into their second trimester. I also know that about a third of women keep the baby and about half decide to terminate their pregnancy." The doctor continued and Amanda took in the information, looking at Dr. Sam and then dropping her head to study her shoes again.

"And miscarriages can happen in the first twelve weeks. As many as eleven percent of pregnancies."

"Should I want that? Can I make that happen?" She looked up to the ceiling tiles.

"Neither of us can answer that for you. Should you decide to terminate, sooner would be better."

"But it's not like it's the baby's fault." Amanda lowered her gaze to look at the doctor.

"No, it isn't," Dr. Sam replied.

Amanda looked at Olivia. "What should I do?"

"Oh, Amanda, that's not for me to say. But whatever you decide, I'll stand by you."

"There is another option, Amanda." Dr. Sam continued. "You could carry the baby to term and offer the baby for adoption to a couple who would consider her—or him—a gift. The best gift ever."

Amanda sat still. "But I don't have to decide that now, right?"

"No, you don't, though I would suggest you talk with someone you trust. Your parents?"

Amanda shook her head. "No, and I just have one. And I can't. Not…" She looked like she was forming a response. None was forthcoming. "Just no."

"Okay, or an adult you trust. Or, I can refer you to a counselor with experience in these cases."

"I have Olivia." She turned her head and looked at the woman to her left and said softly, "Right?"

Olivia put her hand over the girl's. "You do. All the way."

Chapter 32

The ferry ride home was a relief. The passengers, the engine noise, the wind, it all quelled the turmoil Olivia felt and assumed Amanda did too. No, she didn't feel any motion sickness when Olivia asked her, but the girl seemed a little shell-shocked by what she had told them, the confirmation of her pregnancy, the pelvic exam, and blood work. Dr. Sam was competent and kind. Even so, the events of the appointment proved what had been suspected (and wished away, Amanda had confessed) in a way that a drugstore test couldn't. Amanda wasn't unwell because of heat, snails, fudge, or horse manure. This baby. It was real.

Amanda planned to move to the cottage tomorrow. She would tell her two trusted fellow servers that night. Carley and Allie might be surprised but they would offer their support. Amanda had said she was sure of that.

Olivia had her own growing predicament that was becoming harder to hide, now that Ceci knew about Olivia's summer escape. And the predicament was harder to walk away from, more so now with her pledge to Amanda. Luke would think she'd gotten herself into a strange situation, but not entirely surprising either, knowing his mom. He knew his mom was a soft touch when it came to helping people. Nate would think it was typical and outrageous. A step too far. Way over the line this time.

So instead of dealing with any of it, Olivia dashed off a text to Nate and Luke—the usual inane, partially true updates she'd been sending: stores packed today; lovely weather; workout was good; haircut; bills, etc. None of it interesting to anyone, including Olivia. She hated the duplicity, but it wasn't the right time to reveal her shadow adventure.

She did take a moment to write a note to Frankie. She thanked her for the referral to Dr. Ryder and told her how grateful Amanda was for the chance to stay at Lilac Cottage. Once that was done, she remembered that Amanda had asked her who Frankie was. What was her last name? Olivia had admitted that she wasn't sure. Frankie was just an old friend of Mrs. Branagan.

Out of curiosity, she opened her laptop and Googled the Lilac Cottage address and the name "Frankie." None of the real estate sites had anything but an old photo of the cottage barely visible through the high hedgerow that ringed it. Some had a supposed valuation and a high one at that. The only owner of the property she could find, which wasn't entirely clear, was a trust, M. F. Davidson Trust. *Well*, she thought, *that might explain Frankie. Maybe her middle name was Frances.* Satisfied with that partial information and a little ashamed to have been sleuthing on sweet Frankie, Olivia stepped away from her computer. She put on a bathing suit and a sundress, packed a towel, a few nibbles, and a water bottle and set off for that inlet she had found years ago. Back then, it was a quiet place between Mission Point and Arch Rock, hidden from the road. A screen of trees and bushes blocked the view of any onlookers who might be riding their bikes or out for a run around the island. She'd never seen another person when she'd waded into the water there, years ago, on the hottest of evenings, to rinse away the day. Today that rinse was sorely needed. It was a day to let go of, to let it float for a time and hope that a few answers might somehow materialize.

Olivia parked her bike, dropped her bag, and pulled off her cover-up. The inlet hadn't changed over all those years. She entered the water carefully since the lake's bottom was made of smooth rocks and not soft sand. And though the water could be shockingly cold earlier in the season, on some of the hottest summer days in July when the winds and the currents were favorable, the water was temperate—at least for twenty minutes. That evening was such a night.

Lying back in the water, toes to the sky, she watched the sinking sun paint the clouds. Olivia suspended thoughts about the commitment she'd made to Amanda, and those she'd made to Frankie, and the others she'd made to her husband and son. She just let the water lift her and the sky above capture her thoughts. She didn't notice the plopping sounds around her until something dropped in the water by her shoulder and splashed her face.

"Hey," a voice called out. "Those waters are cold. You don't want to stay out there too long!" Olivia went from totally relaxed to tense and alert. She dropped her feet and spun to look at the shore, at once recognizing Chef's imposing figure. And while she couldn't see his face because of the shadows of the trees, she knew he'd be smirking. *What's he doing here?*

"Are you following me?" she spoke loudly. "I could report you, you know."

"No, I am not following you. I just happened to see you ride by on my run. I thought I should turn around and follow you in case you got yourself into some trouble."

"Trouble? Here?" She looked around at the serene setting.

"Distress," he clarified.

"Well, as you can see, I am in no distress. See?" She stood up out of the water and started to the shore.

"Oh yeah." His eyes widened, and quickly he dropped his head.

She continued, pretending not to notice and more eager to have her towel. "I was having a perfectly fine time by myself. Alone. Until you scared me. Why aren't you in the restaurant anyway?"

"I manage to take a night off once in a while. I already told you that, before, at the Jockey Club." Olivia continued a careful walk over the rocky lake floor toward him and her towel.

"I would think you'd have better things to do on your nights off than to creep on me."

"Creeping? I'm just looking out after you. You're not as young as you used to be." He added, "But you still look pretty good." He eyed her with a smile and walked closer with her towel that he'd picked up from her belongings.

She regretted again that she'd bought a two-piece swimsuit covering only essential parts of her body. There wasn't much else to choose from and the clerk helping her thought she looked "on fire." Now, a regrettable purchase. Olivia was close enough to snatch her towel from his hands. Almost. She reached out for it. Leaning forward, she lost her footing. Olivia grabbed the towel Chef was holding above their heads and fell into him at the same time.

"Damn it."

"Whoa. Listen to you." He laughed while he steadied her and wrapped the towel around her shoulders. "Honestly, I wasn't creeping. The waters can be really cold for people not used to it. One slip, and…" He gestured to her as if to remind her of what had just happened, "It can be dangerous. Really. Not kidding."

Olivia shivered a little which only proved his point. "Well, then, thank you. I appreciate your concern. Not necessary," she added. "You know I have lived here before. I know my way around."

Chef changed the subject. "So, you like the water?" He offered her his arm to walk with her back to her bike and backpack.

"I do. Why would someone be here if they didn't?" She turned back to see the water beyond and looked up to see the clouds. "I love it. Especially on a night like this." She turned back and smiled at him. "It's magical."

"Couldn't agree more. You know, I have an easier way for you to enjoy all this."

"Oh, really? Something short of getting me fired so I can spend all my days here, on the shore?"

"Mrs. B wouldn't fire you. Not now. You're like the mom to the kids on the waitstaff. You've actually given her a break."

"Not that she needs one," Olivia volunteered.

"No. She is a force of nature. But speaking of that. Nature, I mean. I keep my boat on the island. One of the few that dock at the marina for the season. Why don't you come out with me? We'll go under the bridge if it's calm enough and around the island."

"You have a boat here?"

He nodded, having just made that clear. "Yup, just said as much. She's a Chris-Craft. 1962. Possibly the love of my life."

"Huh." The information was unexpected.

"Huh what?"

"Just, huh. You don't seem like a boater."

"Based on…?"

"Well, based on… never mind. That sounds nice, a boat ride. But I can't see when that could happen."

"After the Chicago race. Early August—which is only a week and a little more away. I like to go out in the late afternoon and drop anchor. Stay awhile. There's nothing like being out there when a freighter ghosts by. So huge and still so quiet. And the sunsets. Blow your mind."

"I bet." She was actually trying to imagine spending the better part of an evening with him. It didn't seem safe or practical or necessarily honoring to Nate. It wasn't something she'd ever do.

"Yes, that sounds great. I can pack dinner for us." And there was that voice. The one that sounded like her but said things she didn't recognize.

"I'll look at the schedule and get us an evening off together." She nodded her agreement. *This could be fun. And also a bad idea.*

Chef interrupted her. "I'm gonna finish my run. It's a beautiful night. Are you okay from here? To get back to the cottage?"

"Of course I am." She said it with an edge and quickly realized Chef was offering his genuine concern. "Yes, I'll be fine. Truly."

"All right then," and he started for the road. He turned back as if to say something and then thought better of it."

"What?"

"Nothing. I guess I didn't peg you as the bikini type." With that, he walked away.

"Oh geez," Olivia muttered. She'd order a sensible swimsuit from Amazon tomorrow.

Chapter 33

Montreal, Quebec

Nathan Nash sat at the InterContinental bar, the Sarah B, near Old Montreal. He habitually retreated there after long days advocating SpiraVecta's interests in the Canadian pharma acquisition. While he was typically a beer guy, he'd grown to like the Gregory James pinot, a US import. (Sorry, France.) With a plate of pommes frites before him, and his iPad streaming the Cubs game, he could almost imagine he was back in the States, in a Chicago bar. Not exactly home, but closer.

It had been a day, all right. Only Wednesday, it felt every bit a week, the way all of them had recently. A week that didn't end on Friday. Weekends had shrunk to a day long, just Sundays. More often, he gave himself only Sunday evenings. It sucked. He glanced at the game from time to time, swirled his wine in the goblet, and stared at the collection of bottles on the lighted shelves beyond the bar counter. It sucked, but the only way out of this assignment was through it. He had to persevere even though the finish line kept moving and seemed less attainable by the day. And worse, even when the merger closed, the award for the finish was losing its luster. At best, it was seeming more like a consolation prize.

"Well, hello," came a voice to his right with the thunk of a wallet on the bar beside him.

Nate turned his head slowly to view the person who dropped onto the stool next to his. Landon. He didn't have it in him to play her cat and mouse game. He knew he was the mouse, but it was never clear what she wanted from him. They were both on SV's Team US, trying to collaborate with their Canadian counterparts who didn't appreciate being acquired. Landon's sweet southern drawl softened her directives to them. Only upon reflection would the Canadians realize that they'd agreed to something almost impossible to implement in the time allowed. She extracted what she wanted from them with her charm. No wonder she'd been sent to be the legal complement to his communications mission.

"I said, 'hello, handsome.'"

"I heard you. I'm just tired."

"I'm not sure I've ever heard that tone of voice from you. What's the trouble?"

"Apparently you missed the memo."

"Which was…?"

"The memo with my next assignment. The message I have to spin." Landon got the bartender's attention and ordered a dirty martini.

"Go on," she prompted him.

"Merger expenses have piled up so fast that we've got to suspend the trials for the Alzheimer's drug."

"Memistin? No way."

"The same. You might not know the extent of it, but trials have been successful, and the FDA was on board. We were creating launch strategies and campaigns to doctors, patients, influencers. And now, we're stopped. No more funding for the foreseeable future." He took his voice lower to sound official. "We must maintain shareholder value. We can't continue to fund an uncertain endeavor just now when analysts and investors are expecting a demonstrable return from this merger." He took a drink. "No money on a drug that could extend lives. Gotta pay for an international marriage of unequal partners."

"Nate, c'mon. You know how the system works as well as anyone. R&D has to be funded somehow. No one wins if we can't raise capital."

"Yada, yada. All of that. I get it. But we're so close to a breakthrough and FDA approval." He sighed. "It's a horrific disease." He shook his head as though shaking painful images from his mind. "Instead of forwarding a cure or at least a treatment, we're buying a competitor to enlarge our footprint and our coffers. For what? To what end? I got into pharma for the good it does, not to make the wealthy wealthier."

"Wow. I didn't take you for a socialist."

Nate gave Landon a sour look.

"Besides," she continued. "There are other ways, other sources of funding. The NIH for example."

He raised an eyebrow at that. "Really? Like government-funded research is going to find something in my lifetime or yours? And, by the way, *not* a socialist."

"All right. Redirect. This isn't cheering you up at all. How's home? How's that darlin' wife of yours?"

"And that's gonna cheer me up?"

"Well, I assumed so. Is she painting like she said she would?"

"Painting? Painting what?"

"You don't remember? The night I came to dinner. Olivia said she might be refreshing the color on the walls of that dollhouse of a home you have."

"Oh yeah. I remember that. Vaguely. I remember home. Vaguely." He looked at Landon. "I miss them. Liv and Luke." He sighed. "You wouldn't know how much."

His confession silenced her. He looked down at his iPad to check on the score. Landon took a sip from the martini that had been delivered to her.

"Nate, I uh, I think you're right. I don't know how much you miss them. But that doesn't mean I can't imagine it." After a quiet moment, she continued. "I'm not heartless. Or all business, you know. I miss people… and home too."

"Yeah?" He turned his head to look at her. "You never mention anyone. Ever, come to think of it. Who are you missing? Why haven't you told me?"

"I haven't told you because you haven't asked."

"Fair enough. I'm asking now. Who do you miss?"

"You."

Nate's mouth dropped open for a nanosecond. "Huh?"

"Not *you*, exactly, but who you represent. A smart, aggressive, accomplished, and sexy guy."

"Hey, hey, now. Easy." He backed away from her a little.

"I wasn't finished." She held up a hand. "Relax. A guy who loves his wife. I miss that, or I must have missed that."

"What do you mean, 'you must have missed that'?"

"It's not happening for me. Marriage and family." It sounded like a confession. "Once I came close, a long time ago. But that's over."

"It's over? Are you sure?"

"Oh, I'm sure. He's happily married to his partner, Anthony."

"Ahh." Without knowing how to reply, Nate took another drink of his wine. "You didn't know?"

"Obviously not."

"No clue? Not at all?"

"Listen, not all men who love fashion, food, and décor are gay." She laughed a little at that. "How was I to know? I was young. I thought it was the real deal." She looked down at her drink and swirled its contents. "It was real for me, at least."

"So, no one after him? You had to have been in other relationships. I mean, look at you."

"Look at me? I'm forty-two and single. I've had other dates, but it was never the same. You know, you give your heart to someone only to realize you've totally misjudged. I was so wrong. And worse, I was probably a cover for what he really wanted. Or needed."

Nate nodded as she went on.

"I'm a competitor."

Nate raised his eyebrows and smirked at her statement of self-awareness.

"I see that look, Nate. It's that obvious? But, really, how do I compete against a guy?"

"I don't think you compete for someone's love. It happens or it doesn't—the initial spark. Then you tend it. Like a fire."

"So that's all, huh? You make it sound so simple."

"Simple, or it used to be. But not easy. There's a difference."

"I think the problem is I can't trust anyone. You know?" She looked at his uneaten fries. "May I?"

"You may." Nate stole a glance at the iPad.

Landon continued. "I've come to realize over time that the ones I'm really attracted to are already married and in love with their wives."

"Yes!" Nate yelled.

"Sorry?" She looked stunned.

"Home run!"

"You've been watching a baseball game the whole time I've been pouring my heart out to you?"

"No. Not the whole time. Sorry. It's just, you know. The Cubs."

"Yeah, that makes it official. You're off my list."

"List of?" Nate asked.

"Potentials. I'm a Braves fan." She smiled, a sad, resigned sort of smile and took another sip of her drink. She gestured for the bartender to bring her check. "You were off the list a while ago which is why I owe you an apology."

"An apology for what?"

"Thinking you were my type, and… well, never mind." She thought of telling him about her conversation with Olivia. She couldn't bring herself to. Instead she admitted, "Something else I should tell you. And I will. Another time."

"Well, if your type is a happily married man—like you said—I am your type. Just not your guy. And I think your strategy needs an overhaul."

"Oh?"

"Targeting married men is… come on, Landon. That's a problem. You know that."

"Yeah. I suppose I do." She let go a long sigh.

"And that's the game."

"It's not a game, Nate. I never meant it to be. I was being honest with you."

"No, Landon." Nate tilted his head toward the device on the bar top. "Cubs won the game. It's over."

"Nate, truer words were never spoken." She drained the last of her martini and set the glass down. She left twenty dollars on the bar top and looked at Nate a moment longer before she waved a hand, like a motion of surrender.

"Good night. See you tomorrow." She walked out of the bar and into the hotel proper.

She left him there without sharing what she really wanted, her secret. She wanted to be a mother. *Oh*, she thought, *Nate and dozens of others would laugh*. Landon McCall—a mother? The privileged, competitive sophisticate. Landon, wanting baby spittle on the shoulders of her cashmere sweaters? A baby to keep her from galas on Saturday nights? A toddler to tear apart her tastefully designed home in its shades of cream and taupe? As though a child's cozy coupe car would fit that décor. Imagine a distractable middle schooler in her care. Would Landon McCall work on a book report with a ten-year-old in perpetual motion? What about a moody teenager? A rebellious fifteen-year-old? What if she was asked to raise a boy? Landon McCall? Mother of a boy dropping dirty socks, pretzel crumbs, and trial F bombs through her elegant home. Not a chance. They'd all think that.

But she never pictured that—what others might. She imagined walks in the park. Milk shakes. Play-Doh. Christmas mornings. Board books, blanket forts, and thunderstorms. Boy or girl. It wouldn't matter. She'd been raised by strong women. Her mom and her aunts and Grandmother McCall. They held the family together and showed her what mattered. She wanted to carry on their legacy—not her dad's. Landon was successful, and celebrated, but she was climbing a ladder that was taking her to a place she didn't aspire to be. Climbing down the ladder wasn't possible. Not now. Besides, she didn't want off the ladder exactly. She wanted a more meaningful reason to stay on it. She wanted to be a mom but there didn't seem to be a path to that or anyone to ask her if she'd like the title. Where was HR when you needed them?

Some other time she might tell Nate. He was someone who might understand. Saying it out loud might be helpful, even if her dream couldn't materialize.

Chapter 34

Olivia had texted to tell Amanda she'd meet her at her apartment. She'd reserved a dock porter to bike Amanda's belongings from her assigned housing, inland, to Lilac Cottage.

When Olivia arrived, Amanda was already outside, straddling her bike, bearing an oversized duffle bag on her like a backpack. A purse and a smaller bag were in the bike basket. So was a little stuffed lion.

"Morning, Amanda! The dock porter should be here soon."

"Oh, he was here."

"Really? And gone?" Olivia looked around the area quickly. "Did you tell him how to get to the cottage?"

"No, I sent him away. Didn't need him."

Olivia gave her a questioning look.

"This is all I have."

"Really?" In the years of moving Luke in and out of college dorms, a pretty streamlined packer himself, she had never known someone his age with so few belongings. "The lion is cute," Olivia offered.

"Oh, yeah." Amanda fluffed his mane with her hand. "Cliff gave him to me. Said he was good. Not safe, but good. From the book he gave me. I could use some good."

"I agree. Good for Cliff—and you. So, then, let's go. Follow me."

They set off on their bikes, eventually making their way down to Market Street, avoiding Main Street which was already mobbed owing to the start of race week. It was hot, humid, and sunny. When they arrived at Lilac Cottage, Olivia insisted on taking the duffle bag off Amanda's back to carry it inside.

"Amanda, this weighs a ton. What do you have in here? Bricks?"

"Books," she corrected her. "Mostly. I borrow them from Cliff."

"Well, let's get them and you inside where it's a little cooler."

Olivia dropped the bag, opened the screen door, and unlocked the Dutch door beyond. She pushed it open and motioned for Amanda to go inside. Amanda stepped on the threshold and stopped.

Olivia stood behind her, waiting. "Amanda, go on in," she prodded. They both moved into the room. Olivia dropped the heavy bag and Amanda stood motionless again.

"Amanda? Are you okay? Need to sit down?"

"No," she replied. "Just looking." After a time she added, "There's a piano."

"Oh, and don't I know it. I keep working around it. It's a beast."

Olivia watched her move toward it. Amanda slid onto the bench and placed her hands on the keys with barely a touch.

"Do you play?"

"Maybe. I might. It's been so long. I used to—at the center I went to and sometimes at church, when my grandma took me. This lady, Marilyn." She shook her head. "Her hands were so small and wrinkly, but they were steady." Amanda stared at the empty music stand above the keys, entranced. "She used to let me turn the pages when she played. I was little, but I watched her, and I started seeing patterns of her hands, the keys, and the music. She gave me butterscotch candy every time I helped her." She looked at her own hands and then dropped them to her lap. "I always wanted a piano. And here it is."

She turned to look at Olivia. "Do you think I could play it? Sometime?"

"Yes, of course. Anytime you want. We'll see if there's music in the bench seat. Or we'll order you some through Cliff."

A smile broke over Amanda's face. It was the first time Olivia had seen a lightness about her.

"Amanda, see… this must be some sort of sign. You being here. It was meant to be. I think Frankie will be thrilled the piano's being played. Bet it's out of tune, though."

"That's okay. So am I." They both smiled at that.

"Come on. Let's have you pick out your room and then get a cold drink. We'll need to be at the restaurant soon enough."

Amanda chose her room quickly. It was the formerly Pepto pink room, upstairs. Olivia had just finished covering walls and ceiling with a crisp white paint. The room had a view through the trees and overlooked the garden, now fully in bloom. Centered in the room was a cast iron bed frame painted white. One of the cottage's vintage quilts covered it and graced the wood floor on three sides. Though faded from use and sun, on each quilt square, the pattern looked like sails. Eyelet curtains framed the windows, fluttering in and out with the lake breeze. Opposite the bed sat an old desk, also painted white. A trifold mirror was positioned on top of it.

"It's so girly."

"You should have seen it in all its Pepto pink."

Amanda gave her a look.

"Pepto Bismol? Think Pink Pony."

"Oh, right."

"I toned it down. A lot. Is it too girly for you?" Amanda never gave a girly-girl vibe, despite the dress she'd worn to meet Dr. Sam. Ruffles didn't seem her style. She was more likely to wear a black belt. "I can repaint in a different color. Any one you like."

"No. It's all good. I like it." She said nothing for a long while. Her face showed no expression, which was typical, but it unnerved Olivia just now. Did she? Why would she want to live with a woman twice her age in a house that seemed more museum than home—although that was changing.

"Okay, well," Olivia filled the silence. "The bathroom is out the door and to the right. We'll be sharing it if you don't mind."

Amanda shook her head no. Apparently that wouldn't be a problem. "Can I lie down?"

"Oh, yes. Sure." Olivia backed out of the room and closed the door. She opened it quickly again and saw Amanda's profile and her fingertips running over the quilt. Amanda jumped a little at the unexpected intrusion.

"Just wanted to tell you, if you're not up, I'll give you a knock an hour before our shift. Okay? Oh, and I'll make a sandwich for you and leave it in the fridge. Whenever you're hungry. Help yourself. And drinks are in the fridge. I actually baked some cookies to send to Luke. A few extra are in the Tupperware on the counter. I can iron your shirt if you'd like me to. No problem." Why did she always talk so much when silence could simply be met with silence? "Okay. All right, then. Good. Everything fine?" Because sometimes you blather into the awkward silence like you beat a dead horse—to the same avail.

Without turning toward Olivia, the girl gave a nod. "Yup."

Olivia crept down the stairs not wanting to disturb the quiet that— this time—didn't bother her at all. It soothed her. She figured she had about an hour to cut in the sea glass paint color she'd chosen for the dining room. The ceilings weren't terribly high so she could move around the room, taking a chair with her and climbing up and down, covering an arm's length at a time. When she was nearly done, she sat for a moment. Her phone lit up. It was Luke.

Before she could say hello he spoke. "Mom. Hi, it's me. Have you talked to Dad?"

"We spoke a few days ago. What's going on?"

"He just sounds, I dunno, not like him. Bummed or something. I just thought you'd know."

"Luke, I don't, but I'll check in with him. You know, we're both disappointed we can't be with you on your big day to buy your first drink. Maybe he's missing you and home. I know I am."

"Missing me or missing home?"

"Both," she said without thinking. Luke was quiet and at once, Olivia realized what she'd said. It startled her. "You know, I miss home without you and Dad. It's not the same. That's what I meant."

"Okay, sure. Just thought you'd know about Dad or want to know anyway."

His overdeveloped sense of responsibility was on full display and Olivia spent a few minutes in their conversation establishing normalcy. She asked about the care package she had sent ahead of his birthday.

"Yeah! I meant to text you. Thanks for the cookies. They were awesome. How'd you get that peanut butter fudge? I loved that stuff. Where'd you find it?"

"Oh easy. Online ordering, like I do most of my shopping." She lied. Getting the fudge was even easier than that. His other gifts actually did come from online orders. And thanks to flat-rate boxes, no postmark gave away her location.

"That was nice. All of it was great. Thanks."

"Of course, honey. Hey, and I'll be there the twenty-eighth of August to pack you up for school, right? Dad too. And I'm making plans to come earlier too, just to see you." How she was going to do that was still unclear. A few days off? Leave Amanda to care for the cottage? The drive wasn't a problem at only two and a half, three hours tops. She really should have found a way sooner.

"Yeah so…"

"So, do you have plans for your birthday? It's a big one!"

"Nothing solid. Plus I'll be working. But they always do something for birthdays. I'm sure it'll be good." He paused. "So you haven't seen Dad yet? I thought you were going." She could hear worry in his voice.

"Oh, we were planning on it. Dad was actually going to fly home, but only for a day and a half. I was already committed to a catering gig for Nina. It just didn't make sense. But I'm planning to visit over Labor Day once you're settled back at school. You'll already have a few days of classes under your belt! And how smart was it to put your stuff in campus storage? For once, move-in will be a breeze."

"Suuuupppp!!!" he shouted, but not into the phone. "Sorry, Mom, gotta go."

"Yeah, I can tell." She chuckled. "Love you, honey."

"Me too. Bye." And just that fast he was gone.

She took the phone from her ear, hung her head, and ran a hand through her hair. "Oh God, what am I doing?"

"Olivia?"

She'd forgotten the housemate who had walked into the dining room without a sound. Her head popped up to look at her. "Amanda. Hi. Did I wake you?"

"No, no. I slept for a long time. The bed is amazing." She rubbed her hands down her pant legs. "Are you sorry?"

"Sorry? About?"

"I heard you say something. Just now. If this is too much, I can go back to the apartment. Really, I can."

Olivia rose from her chair, dropped her phone on the table, and moved toward Amanda. She put her hands on Amanda's shoulders. "Absolutely not. This is not too much. What is too much is that my son thinks I'm in Chicago. He's only three hours away and I haven't seen him in over a month."

"Luke? He was here with your sister, right?"

She dropped her hands and motioned her through to the kitchen. "Now that you mention it, yes. I have seen him. He just hasn't seen me. Not here. Which makes it worse."

"Yeah. Kelley served them. You know, after your sister busted into the kitchen." Her eyes widened. "That was crazy. Kelley said she was hilarious, and that your son, Luke, was nice. She thought he was cute." Amanda looked a little embarrassed having shared that. "You know Kelley."

"Oh, Kelley. Of course she would see him that way. He's my buddy— just taller, and I guess better looking these days." What mother ever looks at her grown son without seeing the sweet and awkward sixth grader he once was. "And Ceci? Well, everyone thinks Ceci is hilarious. And that *is* the problem. It only encourages her." Olivia sighed as she opened the refrigerator door. "How about that sandwich? I'll grab something later from the EDR. Gotta get ready for our shift."

Amanda took the sandwich from Olivia's outstretched hand. "So, you're sure?"

"About?"

"About me living here?"

"Oh that?" Olivia gave her a smile. "More than sure. You belong here as much as I do." She tilted her head. "Which, honestly, isn't saying much. But it's all we've got right now. So let's take it." She winked and brushed a strand of thick dark hair off Amanda's shoulder. "Now eat!"

While Olivia was suiting up in her "nonbinary" uniform (*thank you, Ceci, I now have even less confidence than before*) and pulling her curling hair back in a bandana headband, she checked her email and found a message from Frankie.

Dear Olivia,

By now our young guest, Amanda, may have moved into Lilac Cottage. Yes? I do hope she settles in comfortably. Has she had any interest in meeting with Dr. Ryder? Samantha is a young doctor, I recognize, but I have known her parents for years and Samantha has always been a standout, in every way. Further, I expect she could be quite compassionate given Amanda's circumstances.

The purpose of my message is to give you greater latitude and resources for your continuing restoration of Lilac Cottage. The photos you sent yesterday of the built-in shelves, painted fresh white with the display of my china collection and books (classics, all of them, and a few first editions among those) strikes just the right note. And the woven shades you installed (bamboo matchstick?) marry the vintage sensibilities of the cottage with a contemporary expression beautifully. That much established, please expect Mrs. Branagan to give you eight gift cards, $500 each, to continue your work. Do contact the upholsterer as you'd suggested and order what you think best from the sources you mentioned. Décor, additional furnishings, and the like. Note, delivery is surprisingly fast from Amazon and UPS. It's horse-powered but expedient.

Also, you have discovered the piano? I smile as I type that. There is no hiding it, is there? I meant to mention this earlier... please have it tuned if you play. Ask Charlie, the Carriage House pianist. You will have met him, certainly by now. I'm told he has an eye for design and architecture. Don't hesitate to consult with him if you'd like an opinion on your choices. You might ask Mary too. She has exquisite taste, though I expect she is as busy as a one-handed paperhanger at this point in the season!

I must be off.

Yours fondly,
Frankie

Mary? Mary Branagan? No one I know calls her Mary. They wouldn't dare. I'll just stick with Mrs. B. But, what? A four thousand dollar decorating allowance!? That means more than paint for sure. A few rugs, a sofa, and drapery. And the piano? Kind of strange that would come to mind just as Amanda found it. She looked around her room. Wonder if there are cameras here. No, she assured herself. Frankie doesn't seem to have that kind of tech sophistication, nor a bent for suspicion. Four thousand dollars!? She could make this sweet cottage sing with that sum. It offered so much as it was.

The vote of confidence and funding to outsource some of her ideas gave her a little boost as Olivia and her housemate peddled through the crowd on their way to the Carriage House. The temperatures were rising with the scores of visitors coming off the ferries to witness the biggest and last race of the season.

"If we can manage through this, Amanda, we're golden."

"Golden? I hope you mean richer. I need the money."

"I know," Olivia replied. She thought again about Amanda's situation which brought her both sadness and greater resolve.

"You know," she continued once they reached the bike racks at the restaurant, "you'll need to meet with Mrs. B to tell her about your job opportunity at the bookstore. I think she'll take the idea pretty well, especially if you can work weekend nights. If you're feeling up to it."

They edged their way from the bike racks to continue a more private conversation on the plan. "I'll go with you. In fact, Mrs. B wanted to meet with both of us once race weekend was behind us. Has she mentioned that to you?"

"She did. But why? Kind of freaks me out."

"Don't worry. I told her that I'd asked Frankie if you could move into Lilac Cottage with me. That's the most of it. And there have been some shenanigans going on in the restaurant. I think she wants your take on them."

"Me? Why me?" Amanda's face had a look of despair mixed with fear.

Olivia put a hand on Amanda's back to move her toward the employee entrance. "I don't exactly know. But I'll be there and even though Mrs. B seems scary…"

"You mean bitchy."

"No, I mean exacting and demanding."

Amanda exhaled with a harrumph.

Olivia continued. "She's a woman with a big heart. I think she hides it to keep an upper hand."

"Yeah, well, if you say so. She's really good at hiding it. She could be a spy."

"Oh, but she is. Didn't you know?"

Chapter 35

They'd been gathered for the same kind of all-hands meeting they'd had a week earlier before the Bayview Mackinac Race. This time they were reminded that the Chicago to Mackinac race, the Mac, would attract sailors from around the world. It wasn't exactly America's Cup but it was the oldest freshwater distance race in the world. (However, Bayview Mackinac sailors were typically quick to point out *their* race was the oldest *continuously running* race. Your tips were better if you knew the distinction.) Both ran about three hundred miles over fresh water. To the uninitiated that sounded tame compared to saltwater races. Anyone living near the Great Lakes would argue otherwise. And anyone sailing north to Mackinac Island would tell you that Lake Michigan was just an inland ocean. It was no gentle lake, not always. It could be angry and unforgiving. One year, Olivia was told, winds were clocked at seventy-five miles per hour.

This year, the conditions for the sailors were perfect, fair winds and following seas. Everyone expected finishes in record times. Roy Disney was the record holder with a magical time under twenty-four hours. Sailors on a multihull yacht managed an even quicker finish one year. Everyone was in a good mood and ready to celebrate. That mood carried over to the waitstaff and kitchen crew at the Carriage House. But a good mood didn't mean it would be an effortless weekend. Chicago race weekend usually proved to be a madhouse, and this year, it seemed like it might get mad sooner than usual.

Lunch and dinner shifts went smoothly enough Friday and Saturday, but the conditions that made for record finishes on Sunday caused the island's population to swell that day with the usual weekend tourists converging with sailors and their families ready to celebrate a race that everyone—*everyone*—said would be "one for the books." This confluence of visitors wasn't like an oil and water meeting. More like fudge meets diesel fuel. There were meltdowns and blowups as wait times for dinner grew longer and longer at every island eatery.

Olivia was never sure why the Carriage House decided to serve prime rib on race weekend Sundays. It's not as though sailors were without food and water for a week. It was more like twenty-four to thirty hours. Even so, meat and potatoes and copious amounts of bubbly and booze were the orders of the day. Literally. Prime rib and au jus simply meant "prime rib and oh shit" while serving the meat slices drenched in the hot, savory liquid. Olivia warned Amanda accordingly.

It was reassuring that Amanda had settled into Lilac Cottage by Sunday and seemed well rested. As if that were enough. Caffeine coupled with Advil and humor were essential, though some hosts and servers may have upped that ante to include Red Bull. All of that was off the table for Amanda. Instead, Olivia encouraged her with reminders of the financial reward to come.

"You hang in there," she said, looking into Amanda's eyes. "And I've got you. Whatever you need. We'll work as a team, right?" Amanda could fool most of the Carriage House employees, but Olivia had noticed the tic over Amanda's right brow when things got intense, and the color that drained from her face when nausea set in. "I've got you," she repeated.

Good thing. The hostess assigned the women stations at the windows, next to each other. When they looked at the reservations for their stations, Olivia and Amanda noted two prominent names in Amanda's station. Her head shot up and her brow twitched as she mouthed to Olivia, "Branagan and Mosher." The Moshers were the owners of the Grand Hotel. These uber stewards of island hospitality dined together regularly, alternating host restaurants, and often on Sundays.

"Shit," Amanda breathed that into Olivia's ear as they walked toward their stations for the night. Olivia stopped her and put a steadying hand on her shoulder. "Hey, Mrs. B picked the table and you as the server. She has control over everything. She wouldn't have chosen a lesser server to wait on the Moshers." Amanda shrugged off the idea.

"And Amanda, remember, this isn't brain surgery. It's meat on a platter." As soon as those words were out of her mouth Olivia remembered Amanda's occasional involuntary reactions to rare meats (and likely the thought of brain surgery). "Forget I said that. You're a pro. You'll do fine."

The early diners were excited and cordial and not yet sauced up enough to order free-flowing Dom. Tips were appropriate but not yet alcohol-infused generous. That was coming—usually after pregaming on the docks or the Pony. Promptly at seven-thirty, Haley led the Moshers to the window four-top where Mrs. B was already seated. Mr. Mosher greeted Mrs. B and helped his wife into her chair. Haley handed them their menus (as if that was necessary) and introduced them to Amanda, already at attention.

"Lovely," said Mrs. B. "Let's start with champagne. Amanda, a bottle of the Clicquot please." Olivia overheard the request and caught Amanda's expression just as she was serving her two-top. She followed Amanda to the bar and caught her elbow to steady her. "You've got this. You've done wine service dozens of times."

"I've never served a two-hundred-and-fifty-dollar bottle!"

"Oh, come on, that's retail. You know Mrs. B wouldn't pay that!" Olivia laughed and tried to make Amanda do the same. Nothing doing. "Okay, I've got a minute. Let's do this." They gathered the napkins, one to diaper the bottle and another to cover it once in the bucket. Amanda asked Mark for three champagne glasses, "For Mrs. B and the Moshers." Wise to that message, Mark held the stemware to the light to spot any smudges. Seeing none, he polished them all the same.

Olivia draped the cork-bottomed bar tray with a napkin and stood the three flutes on it. Olivia had taken the bottle from Mark after she'd secured the silver bucket and filled it with water and ice.

Olivia suggested that Amanda diaper the bottle.

"Guess I gotta learn how to do this, huh?" she whispered to Olivia and Olivia grinned.

"I'll follow you with the ice bucket and then you're on your own. Remember, present the bottle, unscrew the cage, and cover it with a napkin before you release. Turn the bottle, not the cork. Right?" Olivia nodded and expected Amanda to nod in return. All she got was "I think so."

"No, you *know* so. Muscle memory. You'll be fine. It's just like serving expensive Kool-Aid to grown-up kids."

Amanda looked at her, exasperated. "You're such a weirdo sometimes."

Olivia gave her a gentle push. "Go."

With the flutes balanced on the tray in her left hand and champagne bottle in her right, she approached the table. Olivia set the bucket and its stand to Mrs. B's right, since she was the hostess. As she walked away, Olivia overheard some pleasantries being exchanged. Amanda's voice sounded steady. Olivia had just enough time to get to the bar and turn to watch. What unfolded, and shouldn't have, was the napkin meant to contain the cage and cork exploding with the pressure of the bottle's CO_2, suddenly released. The napkin slipped off the cork. The cork sailed to the brick wall above the heads of Mrs. B and the Moshers. It bounced off the brick at a high speed and back toward Amanda. Still holding the bottle in her left hand, she reached her right hand high to catch the ricocheting cork. In a voice loud enough for the surrounding tables and even Olivia at the bar to hear, she said, "Shiiii—take mushrooms tonight with the prime rib." Cork in hand, she turned her attention to the table. "Anyone?" Somewhere along the way, Amanda had picked up Olivia's fake swear vocabulary.

"Damn, what a catch!" Mr. Mosher was laughing. Mrs. Mosher looked thoroughly amused. Mrs. B's face was impassive above her nose, but around her mouth it looked like she'd sewn her lips tight so not to bust out in laughter. Amanda opened her hand to reveal the caught cork and politely, just as trained, asked if anyone would like to keep it. Kind Mr. Mosher said he'd love to have it. He remarked that it might be worth a lot one day when Amanda earned a Gold Glove.

Everyone returned to their conversations and Amanda began to pour champagne into their glasses with an unsteady hand. Satisfied, Olivia pulled herself away to collect the salads for another table. In the kitchen, already word had traveled that Amanda had nearly taken out Mr. Mosher's left eye. Not true, of course, but everyone in the kitchen was howling at Sydney who was embellishing the near catastrophe.

"That's not entirely right everyone." Olivia tried to quiet the cackling crew. "You should have seen her grab that cork. I guarantee you that's worth a big bill slipped under Mr. Mosher's plate." Olivia moved through the door and up the steps to the dining room, passing Amanda on her way.

"Damn it. I screwed up. I knew I would."

"Stop. I think Mr. Mosher was charmed. Really, forget about it." Olivia grinned at Amanda and thought she'd convinced her. It was no big deal. The two of them and their fellow servers, bussers, and bartenders continued their business uneventfully for the next hour or so. The evening was frenetic at times, to be sure, but Charlie at the piano was playing melody after melody that seemed to soothe everyone. Champagne, cocktails, and prime rib, not to mention the sun that had kissed sailors and their fans, lulled Carriage House guests into an amiable somnolence.

Near sunset, a table of eight was seated in Amanda's section. Olivia helped her take orders since she had a moment to help. One bulbous guest asked for the end cut of the prime rib. "Tell me, Amanda honey, you've got to have it. I was dreaming of an end cut as we crossed the finish. I'm a winner and a starving man." (Doubtful. He might have been a winner but he bore no resemblance to a starving man or one who'd ever missed a meal.) Amanda assured him pleasantly enough that if there was an end cut to be had, she'd fight for it. Olivia was impressed that Amanda played the game so well and had learned how to have fun with the guests—if they were the teasing type like this guy was.

Once appetizers and salads were served, Olivia and Amanda were back in the kitchen. It was bumping. The dining room may have quieted but the kitchen was still clanging, producing a steady stream of Carriage House specials for a ravenous crowd. Luckily for Mr. Bulbous, there was one end cut left. Only one. Amanda was stationed at the line, her tray resting on the rails waiting for her orders as Danny, now expediting, handed them to her. He used a towel to wipe any stray drop or misplaced garnish that might detract from the dish's presentation. Plate after plate, for her eight-top and for the four-top nearby, Amanda took what had been handed to her and placed a silver cover on each plate in its turn, and stacked them atop one another on the large oval tray.

Finally, the end cut of prime rib, resting in a sea of au jus, was placed on top of a stack of three covered plates. Its shape was too large for a silver cover so the dish was uncovered and needed to be served quickly to retain its temperature. Bending low to anchor the tray to her right shoulder, to later shift it to her left, Amanda began to rise. It was an impressive feat to handle twelve plated dinners at a time. Sympathetic servers behind her watched, holding their breath. Olivia held hers as Amanda rose to her full height.

A breath later, the end cut started rocking. It tipped off its perch. The plate slid back toward Amanda, depositing hot au jus down her shirt. The end cut followed and rolled down her chest, off the stainless line rails, and onto the floor.

"Ooowww," Amanda mouthed. She was too shocked to swear but not everyone was stunned to silence.

"God damn it, you fucking beaner whore!" Danny screamed into Amanda's face.

Immediately, Olivia stepped in front of Amanda and grabbed Danny's cheeks in her right hand using it like a claw, just like she had when Luke was nine and shot her a loathsome term. (Never to be repeated.) Danny was older, taller, and just as ignorant. While the other servers had taken Amanda's tray from her, Olivia locked eyes with Danny. "Danny, don't… you… ever… *ever*… speak to this young woman with such utterly uncouth, offensive, and inappropriate language again." She gripped his cheeks tighter. Tears formed in his eyes, and he squirmed beneath her grip. "Danny, do you understand me? *Do you?*"

"Okay, Okay." Chef pulled her hand off Danny and shooed him back to the line. He roared at everyone who had been stunned motionless. "Where's the goddamn meat? Get me the meat!" At that Allie scrambled under the line and crawled out again with the end cut, holding it high in the air like a found treasure. Chef grabbed it with tongs and tossed it under the broiler.

Looking at Amanda, Chef barked, "Get her a clean shirt. Now!" At that Olivia loosened Amanda's tie and started unbuttoning her shirt. The female servers and Mia at the salad station formed a circle around the two women, taking Amanda's shirt from her and drying her chest and back with dining room napkins. With Amanda's impressive phoenix art on her back now on full display, the attendants paused momentarily in awe. And then they remembered what had just poured down Amanda's chest, her skin pink from the hot juice that had washed over her. Was Amanda okay? Was she burned? Did it hurt? They asked but didn't stop for an answer. Ever stoic, Amanda wouldn't have answered anyway. Olivia handed them her shirt and they gave her the wet napkins in a trade.

Moments later, with the speed of an Indy race pit stop, Amanda was dressed in Olivia's shirt and tie with a stack of plates settled on a tray which now rested securely on her shoulder. Following her was Sydney, carrying the end cut of beef out on a plate positioned on its own tray like it was a crown jewel from the House of Windsor. (And one that had never toppled unceremoniously and later been charred in flames to kill wayward bacteria. That had never happened. Not at all. At least from all appearances.)

With au jus–soaked napkins like a halter top covering her essentials, Olivia turned for the EDR to retrieve the spare shirt she always kept in a locker.

"Mrs. B!" Damn, that woman was stealthy.

"Olivia, dear, you look… mmm, underdressed."

Dear? That's a surprise. "Mrs. B, yes, you could say that." The color was rising in her cheeks. "Did you see or maybe hear…?"

"Oh, indeed. I had an earful." Her timing was uncanny. "I'm sorry to say." Did she add that line just to land an appropriate degree of shame?

Olivia gave a repentant nod of acknowledgment while keeping a grip on the napkins, her back exposed to the cooks, Mia the salad girl, the pits, and any servers who were still at the line. "I should probably go and, you know…"

"Oh, I think so. We don't approach our tables shirtless, do we?" *Was she restraining a smile?* Mrs. B's facial expression was eternally inscrutable, at least to her staff. On occasion when it did reveal emotion, that was quickly whisked away like a crumb brushed off a neatly set table. But still, her eyes were laughing. Weren't they? No. Olivia was simply traumatized. That had to explain it.

"Olivia, I'd like to meet with you and Amanda tomorrow morning, in my office. Nine o'clock?"

"Yes, ma'am." Olivia bowed. *What? Why did I bow?* She backed away from Mrs. B so not to expose herself any further.

"Tomorrow then? You'll tell Amanda?"

"Yes, of course. Of course."

Mrs. B turned to leave and then she turned back to face Olivia.

"Well done, by the way. Our guests had no idea chaos was reigning in the kitchen."

"Oh." Olivia, still clutching napkins to her chest, could conjure no suitable reply. "No problem. I'm good at chaos."

"So it appears. It also appears you have no fear at reprimanding a man half your age and half again your size." Olivia's eyebrows shot up at the compliment. *It was a compliment, wasn't it?*

"Good night, Olivia."

"Good night." She bowed. *Oh my gosh, I have* got *to stop doing that.*

Chapter 36

Olivia had been assigned to close. The balance of the servers, including Amanda, had left. Olivia wondered how the girl was processing what had happened earlier. The misfired cork was a charming mishap viewed from the eyes of an older adult and parent. Olivia believed the Moshers and even Mrs. B (in her heart of hearts) would have seen it that way.

The kitchen episode was different. Not different because of the end cut rolling off the plate. That was inconsequential. Embarrassing, but inconsequential. Danny's viciousness is what concerned Olivia. The slur he hissed at Amanda was part of it, but only part. It was his stare and the delivery of the slur that disturbed her. It was menacing. But why? What could Amanda have done to make herself the target of such viciousness? Amanda largely kept to herself. Over the past weeks, she had befriended most of the servers who'd come to know her as a calm and closed-mouth teammate. Chef seemed to admire her poise and self-assurance.

Her beauty was undeniable, but Amanda never put it on display. Quite the opposite. She rarely wore makeup which would only enhance her dark eyes, her perfectly brown complexion, and her full lips. Her silken black hair was always bound in a wide barrette at the base of her neck or in a single braid down her back. The Carriage House uniforms did little to define a server as male or female, and yet, it took very little imagination to see that Amanda was a shapely young woman—whose shape was going to become motherly in the coming months. The aprons they wore disguised that. For now.

Suspicious of Danny and his intentions toward Amanda, Olivia determined to watch him more closely. He shot off his mouth routinely. Most of what he said was pretty funny and Olivia would laugh in spite of herself. He'd catch her laughing and say something like, "See, you're not so innocent, Miss Olivia. I know you'll be cussing like the rest of us soon. I'll teach you how." To which she would reply, "Okay, Danny. Maybe you can make me a vocabulary list. Or flash cards."

Tomorrow's meeting with Mrs. B. How would Amanda respond to that? Would Mrs. B fire her? Maybe fire both of them? Amanda would survive the financial consequences of that. Like the rest of the servers, she'd made a tidy sum during race weeks, and Olivia had regularly added a few twenties to the pile of cash tips that Amanda left carelessly on the living room credenza where she also dropped her uniform tie. Beyond that, Amanda had already secured a new job, helping Cliff manage the bookstore as he prepared for the knee surgery he'd have when he closed the shop at the end of the season. Financially, she'd be fine.

But emotionally? That response was even more uncertain because Olivia had never found the right time to tell her about her conversation with Mrs. B, the recent theft that Mrs. B told her about, and the unnamed person who'd accused Amanda of it. The accusation could destroy what little confidence Amanda possessed. Even in the short time they'd lived together, Olivia could see that Amanda's poise was a practiced act to conceal her insecurity. The accusation would shake her. Regardless, Olivia was certain that Amanda was no thief. She knew it the way she knew that Mrs. B was deeply kind. Oh sure, like Amanda, she disguised it well. She did so in the same way Amanda hid her vulnerability. However, Mrs. B's kindness and Amanda's vulnerability shone like light around a locked door. No one could enter the room beyond, not without permission, but there was no hiding the glow that escaped the doorframe, try as they might. There was more behind that door than either would concede.

Olivia moved around the restaurant floor quietly, carrying those thoughts. She extinguished the candles on the tables each in its turn, only after she was satisfied each table was properly set for the next day. Her reflection in the windows disappeared as she moved from table to table. It was a mundane process like the one that had become habitual at home. Unnoticed and therefore unimportant. Who really cares if the kitchen island gleams before the pendant lights blink out? No one notices. But here, the simple act of setting a table was stage setting for some of the most significant of human experiences—race finishes toasted, birthdays and anniversaries celebrated, proposals accepted (sometimes on the patio before dessert was served)—and the laughter and revelry of family, together, away from the mainland frenzy across the Straits and beyond. So simple. Just a dinner at a restaurant, or another breakfast served at a diner or a kitchen island. The act repeated so many times that its being habitual made less of its importance: habitual, unnoticed, and seemingly unimportant—like taking one breath after another.

She recalled something from the Bible that a friend had shared with her long ago. Something like, "Do not despise the day of small things for God takes joy in seeing the work begin." The days of small things felt far behind her. They were the days that defined who she was, why she got up in the morning, and what the day, and those that followed, would hold. In Chicago, those days were ending. But here, at the Carriage House, the small things happened daily—for a season, until the season ended. Then they began again, anew. For decades in the past and decades to come, this hotel and its restaurant had been and would continue to be a haven prepared for people to pause, just long enough to realize the world on its axis spins fast. You've got to travel right to the center to find a still point and, once there, mark it. The horses, the fudge, and the exquisite cuisine were well-worn, trustworthy paths to that still point.

Enough, Olivia thought. She finished with the last table. The dining rooms were finally asleep and low lights of the patio beyond were reflected in slow waves that rose and kissed the decking. She stood still for a while and imagined what her family was doing at the same moment. Luke was probably kicking back after a long day of encouraging kids across a rope bridge. No big deal, he'd tell them. Except it was. For an awkward eleven-year-old, a walk across a (seemingly) rickety bridge suspended twenty feet above ground could teach them that some risks are worth taking. What seemed insubstantial could carry their weight. One step in front of the other was all it would take to arrive safely at the next platform.

And Nate? They'd established a comfortable cadence of texting a couple of times a week. They didn't talk by phone—they couldn't quite establish a schedule for that. Nate's days ended, or at least paused, for dinner at six-thirty. By that time, she was in the thick of her work (and he was still believing she was living life in Central Time). Never mind that Nate thought she'd become especially busy in his absence, every night. It was yoga three times a week (which was new and true, though less frequently), and Nina's catering business was blowing up as she promoted charcuterie boards and themed happy hours, personalized and delivered for a small fee. Such a help to a hostess or a thoughtful surprise. Lake Ellyn and surrounds had gone for it in a big way. (She intended to drop the idea on Nina and execute with her when she got back to Chicagoland.) Being none the wiser, Nate was impressed with Nina's vision. So, they didn't talk much. Honestly, it was a little uncomfortable. Their conversations felt staccato when, given their long marriage, they should have been legato, smooth and easy. They sounded more like two people stepping on each other's lines, with lots of "Sorry, I got interrupted. What were you saying?" or "Bad connection, so many angry drivers (ferry horn in the background). I'll try you again tomorrow." Without saying as much, they'd settled for an occasional text message, and that was satisfactory. "Not ideal," she acknowledged to herself and sighed. "It'll have to do for now."

At once, Olivia became aware of movement behind her. A swishing sound followed by the sound of a zipper. She turned slowly to acclimate to the faint light from the small eye-level windows in the kitchen doors.

The light was just enough to make out a figure moving behind the bar.

"Mark?" she called out. "Is that you? Need some light back there?" She approached the bar, careful not to trip in the dark. Surely it was Mark. She stopped short when she realized her error.

"Danny? Is that you?" She took a few steps closer and saw the Detroit Lions hat he always wore and a backpack in one of his hands.

He choked a little, clearing his throat. "Yeah, it's me."

"Danny, what are you doing back there?"

"Just getting brandy for tomorrow's special. But that's really none of your business. I do this all the time." He turned his back to her and she could hear a zipper sealing the backpack. "If your work is done here, you should leave." The surprise she'd heard in his voice now sounded like contempt with a splash of arrogance.

"Really? Chef doesn't do that himself? Pull brandy out of inventory, to track it?" Her seemingly innocent question was intended to reveal more. "You know," she pressed, "Mark inventories the bar every night."

"Yeah, of course I know that. I've got what I need."

She came closer, standing near the hinged bar counter, now raised to allow his exit from the bar through the kitchen beyond.

"You should leave, Olivia."

Now he was making her angry. Again. "Oh, I'm planning on it. I only have a few more things to do. Let me walk you out the door. After you leave the brandy in the kitchen."

They were now a few feet from one another. She was close enough to see light reflected in Danny's dark eyes. Close enough to see a bottle in his hand and likely another in his bulging backpack. Close enough to smell alcohol on his breath. "Danny, *you* should leave. Now."

He turned, dropped the hinged bar counter behind him, and walked through the doors to the kitchen. He left a bottle of brandy on the salad prep station on his way out. As she followed Danny, she noticed Chef crouched near the floor, polishing the stainless steel of the serving counter, the one that had been splashed with au jus hours before.

Without saying a word to Chef, Olivia kept walking behind Danny as if throwing him out of the kitchen with her stare alone. When the screen door of the EDR had thwacked shut, she reentered the kitchen to drop her cleaning towel into the laundry.

Chef stood as she walked by. "What was that about? I sent Danny home an hour ago."

"Honestly, I don't know what just happened—with him. Let me sleep on it. I'm too tired right now." She dropped the towel and walked back again through the kitchen without a look at the celebrated chef still cleaning the line like a scullery maid. The work was beneath him. Olivia had seen him do these tasks before, unable to trust the work to others. Or maybe taking pleasure in it? Whichever. It impressed her, but not tonight. She was tired—too tired to think about Danny, or Amanda, or an unplanned pregnancy, purported theft, and especially a marriage feeling more like a mirage. Too tired.

"Goodnight, Chef," she said without a look at him as she passed by. Almost out of sight, Olivia stopped and turned. "Chef, are you serving a special tomorrow that calls for brandy?"

"Brandy?" His back was still turned to her.

"Yeah, brandy."

"Nope." And he kept on task.

"Ah, damn." Olivia walked through the room to the door, murmuring, "Danny, what's with you, anyway?"

Chapter 37

Olivia climbed on her bike in her stupor. She went right at Main Street to go toward town, when going left would have taken her to Lilac Cottage more quickly. She peddled slowly, her front tire moving in a meandering zigzag as she looked at people strolling the storefront sidewalks. None seemed to have a reason to hurry. She rode through shallow puddles to hear the splash and the hiss of her tires over the rain-dampened pavement. A summer storm had barreled through town, leaving in its wake an easy breeze that lifted and then released flower baskets hanging from chains on sidewalk light poles. Horse tails swayed, helped by the same breeze. The hoofed laborers, on late duty waiting for passengers, seemed soothed by the night air, a respite from July heat. The island was taking a breath.

Olivia continued on her way toward the marina, intending to sit on a bench there and reckon with what had just happened and imagine what was yet to be. At the corner, she looked up and saw light through the windows above Doud's where Cliff must have been working, maybe painting. He had said the pace of the summer season kept him from his canvases. When he couldn't stand it any longer, he would paint at night. All night sometimes. He'd recreate the views along the shore from images held safe in his memory. Sights he knew and loved deeply. She had only seen one of his pieces so far, and that one still in progress. One day, she'd ask to see his portfolio.

Olivia continued, eventually stopping at the docks to look at the sliver of moon dangled above the ruffled waters. Boats were resting also, bobbing in their slips. She thought of Cliff, of him at his canvases. If only she were more like him, knowing how to capture what had once been so familiar and fleetingly beautiful. That life, or that part of it, had slipped by. There was no stopping it. No asking it to hold still while she sketched the image on canvas. No, life, or at least the best of it, demanded your full attention. Even pausing to take a photo risked having the moment get up and leave. All too aware of its own worth to obey orders and sit still, the moment argues, "Don't make me pose or wait on your device. Capture me in the secret place that admits no intrusion or decay." She had never learned to do that. Not fully. Not like Cliff.

She scolded herself. "I'm thinking like a sad, old woman." She had enjoyed those moments. She had. Or at least she'd tried. It was natural that Luke's childhood should come to an end. That was always the plan. And it was normal to be wistful at its passing.

"All right." She stopped herself. No more looking back and no time right now to play out the possibilities of her future. Right now, she had a housemate. A young woman. Correction: a young *pregnant* woman, who seemed to accept the condition as though it were a virus that might pass. Olivia's future was beside the point. At least for now. It was Amanda who needed a friend. Or did she need a mother? Would she want one? If she did, Olivia was available to take on a new client.

Nate would hate that.

Wouldn't he?

Did it matter?

She had agency. Olivia could make decisions that involved them and their marriage too. He had, right? He had made decisions unilaterally. He had hardly considered her wishes to be with him in Montreal. If it was acceptable for him to leave their home without her, trusting that she'd be just fine, well then, so be it. Being fine meant being true to herself. She was being true to herself. Or maybe not? Does living with a new identity hidden from Luke and Nate, only known to Ceci, count as being true or terribly untrue? Would Nate accept the ambiguity?

No. She knew better. Nate would not roll with this. Her only hope was that he loved her and knew her well enough to understand how she might have ended up here: here, in this place, in these relationships, with responsibilities to people he'd never met.

"It's a toss-up at best," she whispered.

She moved off her mark, pushed up onto her bike seat, and made her way back across Market and up Cadotte, peddling in rhythm with the clip-clop of horses taxiing guests to the Grand. With so little moonlight, the old hotel shone against the velvet sky like a jewel. Its illuminated porch beckoned guests to enter its world, one that suspended time. It was perhaps clever or en vogue to disparage the Grand, but that cynicism hardly mattered to the guests who loved it, or to the Grand itself. Mock it. Think it too expensive, trite, or clichéd. Whatever. The Grand had nothing to prove. It was breathtaking. Olivia regarded it with a long, appraising look, slowed as she was on her ascent up the hill. The climb (or was it the Grand itself?) compelled her to walk her bike and pay her proper respects as she passed by. In minutes, she was back on her bike and moving downhill again. Soon she was back at Lilac Cottage.

She locked her bike and crept up the stairs to the porch. "Hey," came a quiet voice from the porch swing.

Olivia jerked at the unexpected greeting. "Whoa! You got me! I thought you'd have been asleep by now."

"I was. I tried. It was no use." Amanda was wrapped in a quilt, moving the swing inches back and forth with one foot on the floorboards. She scooted slightly to one side, making room for Olivia to join her, coming short of actually inviting her.

Olivia sat and let Amanda move the swing and the conversation.

"So, I'll get fired tomorrow." It was a statement, not a question. An owl hooted, "oooo… hoo, hoo, hoo," as if to say, "Oh yeah, fired and then some." Olivia let the swing's momentum carry them for a while.

"Well, possibly."

"I probably got you fired, too."

"Oh? I wouldn't be so sure in either case. You did nothing wrong. I, on the other hand, might have."

Amanda replied into the darkness. "It doesn't matter. This is what happens with me. I'm bad luck. I mess stuff up for people."

"Is that so?" Olivia let another owl have its say before she continued. "I think we mess up stuff for each other. That's what we do. People. In general."

"I know you're trying to be nice, but that's not what I mean. I'm trouble."

"You're not trouble, Amanda. Where did you get that idea?"

"Where? From everyone, like my dad. It would have been better for him if I was never born. That's what he says. My mom would have stayed if it wasn't for me. And my grandma wouldn't have died. I'm the reason. That's what he says."

Instinctively, Olivia reached an arm over Amanda, stiff in her stoicism. The girl didn't flinch. After a few moments she softened and dropped her head onto Olivia's shoulder.

"Amanda, that cannot be true. It's weak and it's mean. It sounds to me like the bitterness of a man who can't take responsibility for his life."

Amanda groaned in response.

"And I can tell you that your mother had to have been in the grip of something absolutely overwhelming to think of you, her baby, as anything but the greatest gift she'd ever been given."

"And that's why she left? I don't think so. That makes zero sense."

"Well, I'm a mom and I think it does. I don't know anyone who's held their baby without feeling an avalanche of love mixed with awe and terror. You know, the fear of doing something wrong that would hurt that helpless life in your arms. I'm guessing you can understand how she might have been afraid."

"Yeah. I guess so." After a time of silence, Amanda whispered, "I'm afraid too."

And after a few more moments Olivia whispered back, "I know." She put a light kiss on the top of the girl's head. The cicadas and the crickets and a far-off owl were the only witnesses to the promise Olivia made to the girl. None of them, including Olivia, knew how she intended to keep it: "I'm not leaving you, Amanda. I don't know what to expect—and neither do you, I realize, but we'll find a way. Together. For as long as you need me."

The next morning, Olivia was up early and she readied herself quietly. She wanted to talk with Mrs. B before Amanda arrived for their meeting in her office. She wanted to tell Mrs. B about Danny and what she'd seen last night. If only she could track her down. She was here, there, everywhere, and nowhere. The woman had to have body doubles. One would appear when least expected but none could be summoned upon request. She needed to catch her. This was important for Amanda and the restaurant. She was on a mission.

Before she left, Olivia penned a quick note to Amanda suggesting she meet her at the hotel, outside Mrs. B's office. She left the note on the piano which had become their communications hub. In the time Amanda had been there, she'd already developed a habit of sitting at the piano to practice a familiar piece and then try a new one every day. She played timidly, like she was afraid to make a mistake, but she made few of those. It all sounded melodic to Olivia and soothing to paint by on the few quiet afternoons and evenings they'd had together.

Olivia had packed an overnight bag which she tried to stuff into her bike basket. Some of it fit. Some of it spilled over the bike's basket like a belt cinching an oversized belly. She was no dock porter, that was for sure. So preoccupied with the effort, she almost missed that Amanda's bike was gone. Already. "Up so early," she remarked to herself.

"Oh, Luke." She nearly forgot. Gotta text him. The week before, they'd made plans for her to visit that afternoon. She would spend the night at the camp's guest lodge. Still on for today? Can't wait to see you. Hopefully, she'd be able to catch a noon ferry to arrive at camp before dinner. Ceci's counsel had convinced her. Was it counsel or a threat? Either way, Ceci was right. She needed to tell her son where she'd been all summer. No big deal. Just a summer job on Mackinac Island. You know, waiting tables. Nothing she hadn't been doing for the last twenty-four years, give or take. Granted, this time for a paycheck and tips.

The fudge she would add to her overnight bag might make amends for any betrayal he'd feel. In truth, her temporary home base hadn't impacted him at all. Nothing had changed for him aside from a canceled twenty-first birthday celebration, the one canceled because Nate couldn't *possibly* get away. And Luke seemed happy to celebrate with fellow interns and staffers at camp. He'd texted and sent them photos. Best Birthday EVER. Even later into the summer, Nate was unable to commit to even a day or two to see Luke on the job, up in the treetops. Fudge might help dull that pain, or at least lull him into a temporary sugar coma.

Or… not so fast. She was reminded by a flashback: When Luke would go to the free throw line during his high school basketball games, he'd loosen up, bending and straightening, bouncing the ball, bending and bouncing again. He'd turn his head, appearing to cast a casual glance at the home stands. He wanted to know that they were there. Kids want to be seen and noticed by parents who raise them. "Do you see me? Are you watching me?" *Back then, we always were. Back then.*

She stood over her bike, phone in hand, scanning her new emails. Maybe Nate had sent a note instead of a text. He hadn't. But there was a message from Frankie. Oh, she'd begun to love communications from her. Each one was a comfort, or an encouragement. In a way, Olivia had found a parent who was watching and applauding her progress at Lilac Cottage. And, better, she had found a confidante. Olivia could share her concerns about Amanda with Frankie. In their correspondence, Olivia worked out the options available to Amanda and what might result. The idea of Amanda working at the bookshop delighted Frankie. No better place for Amanda, she concurred. Largely by reputation (because Frankie said she hadn't seen Cliff in a long,

long while), she knew him to be a good man and a generous employer who would treat Amanda well.

What about private pay for Dr. Sam until the future for Amanda and her pregnancy became clear? Of course, that was a wonderful idea to pursue. Maybe there would be discounts afforded her or perhaps another form of help? Perhaps pro bono services to extend to Amanda? Frankie was quick to agree: *Dr. Sam is that sort of doctor. One with a heart as expansive as her intellect.*

With Frankie, she talked herself in and out of guidance to offer Amanda without fear of judgment. Frankie gave no prescription for care, and she offered no rigid opinion on Amanda's situation or how Olivia might counsel her. What Frankie offered, in email after formal email, was unflagging support.

To any nascent idea that Olivia might float, Frankie would reply with a comment like: *You are quite right and very wise. You will arrive at the most helpful and loving course of action for dear Amanda even if that isn't yet clear to you. I have faith in you. The way will become clear.*

Never quite sure how Frankie could have arrived at such a high opinion of Olivia with no face-to-face knowledge of her, Olivia nonetheless accepted the support. Actually, she depended on it. Frankie's encouragement sustained her when it seemed no one was watching her take her next shot, or cared that she was at the line.

Chapter 38

Olivia peddled her blue and cream cruiser toward the Iroquois. The bike had become a comfortable extension of herself. Sliding onto its seat and coasting off was second nature, like slipping on and, later, kicking off a pair of flip-flops. Now *this* morning, she thought, was one to savor. Uncharacteristically cool, it teased September mornings to come. The air was crisp and the sky clear. The streets that had been rain soaked the night before were clean. No taxi residue this early in the day. Day-trippers off the first ferry window-shopped on Main Street, waiting for a store, any store, to open so they could buy the sweatshirt they hadn't expected to need, the one they wouldn't need by midday.

Olivia wedged the bike's front tire into the steel rack and went through the screen door into the employee dining room, and beyond into the kitchen. It was already bright and buzzing. Apron-clad staff were cleaning and prepping produce for the day's fare. "Salad girls" scheduled on the early shift were slicing fruit for hotel guest breakfasts. Olivia looked around and inhaled. The coffee brewing in multiple pots smelled rich and smoky. A lemony scent from freshly baked blueberry muffins mingled with that aroma, and together they were like incense filling the sacred space of the Carriage House kitchen. The only sweeter fragrance she could recall was the scent of onions, celery, butter, and sage being sauteed early on a Thanksgiving morning. If you could capture that scent, and that feeling, in a candle, you could make serious money.

She grabbed a mug from the random assortment, poured herself a cup of coffee, and pulled a day-old muffin from the basket of those saved for staff. (They were every bit as good a day later.) Munching on it, Olivia stood unnoticed, and watched for a time. The hustle-bustle of the kitchen shouldn't have calmed her nerves. It was a busy place. Even so, watching it put her mind at ease. Sometimes, back home, when life became too big, she would tie an apron around her waist, throw a cotton towel over her shoulder, and get to work. She'd slice and dice, make a pot of soup, or a nut bread, and scrub her sink to shining. Eventually, and without meds, her muscles would relax and her jaw would unclench. Her fretful thoughts would skim the surface of her troubles without pulling her under. She managed through many of life's worries and heartaches with an apron tied around her waist.

"Olivia." She jumped at hearing her name from behind her.

She turned to the voice. "Mrs. B! Perfect. I was hoping to have a word with you—before our meeting." Suddenly sure she'd committed a breach of Iroquois etiquette, Olivia added, "And how are you this morning?"

"I'm quite well. Thank you very much, Olivia." Mrs. B punctuated her reply with a quick smile. The smile saw its shadow and vanished. "I'm afraid I haven't a moment to spare this morning before our meeting. Nine o'clock. My office. Hmm?" She often ended her statements with "hmm?" as a more pleasant way to say, "and that's an order." Staff understood them to mean the same thing.

She continued, throwing Olivia off balance, "You needn't worry, neither of you. I'm aware of a number of behaviors and circumstances that have brought us to this point. My only interest is in helping Amanda. I once had a similar struggle."

She took a step from Olivia and repeated, "Nine o'clock. Hmm?"

"Yes, ma'am."

With that, the small woman ghost-glided through the kitchen to the service entrance and into the hotel proper. Kitchen workers had taken note of her presence and silenced their conversations and eighties rock. When she was out of sight and earshot, they turned up the music again.

Olivia stood stunned. *Huh? Similar struggles? With a guy like Danny? With accusations? With pregnancy? What did she mean?* Of course, she could never ask Mrs. B what she'd meant. That would be like asking Queen Elizabeth to spill the tea and explain herself. No one would do that. Still, what?

With twenty minutes to fill and eager for distraction, Olivia took her coffee mug and made the rounds, chatting with staff at their stations. There weren't that many of them after all, and fewer in the kitchen this early. The full team of forty could clean, plan, prep, cook, set, seat, pour, and serve a hundred guests at twenty-four tables in two dining rooms and do it all again, twice more, and serve a patio too, day after day all summer. No wonder that by August, with race weeks a memory, the team that remained (because some had dropped out, predictably), the stalwarts were practiced, facile, and friendly. Together, they had sweated the heat of race weeks and grimaced with each other when guests were temperamental. They shared frustration-meets-elation when Chef wrote "86" on the white board and yelled out "eighty-six the cioppino." The seafood-loving guest who'd just ordered the special would be disappointed, sometimes angry, but the dish had been a hit. Chef was pleased, and the mood in the kitchen was playful. The night was a success. It was a feeling to relish, and, in its way, addictive—like putting on a performance for an appreciative audience. The footlights of Broadway and the warming lamps on the service line weren't so different for the staff who starred in the nightly Carriage House show.

By five minutes to nine, Olivia had wandered from the comfort of the kitchen into the hotel's nerve center. She found Amanda waiting outside the closed door of Mrs. B's office. She was dressed in a chambray shirt and flouncy skirt. Her long legs looked even longer under her short skirt. She had on her white tennis shoes. Her arms hugged her middle and her right foot was tapping, likely expending her nervous energy.

Olivia had been pushing the boundaries of physical, motherly affection and had been finding no resistance, so she approached Amanda and placed an arm over her shoulder. With a squeeze she whispered in the girl's ear, "It's okay. Don't worry. How long have you been here anyway?"

"A while. I got up early to have breakfast at the Café. I was starving and I didn't want to wake you up."

"I didn't hear a peep. I'm sorry I didn't notice you were gone. Was it good?"

"Always," the girl answered. "But it was weird too. I saw Cliff with Chef again."

"Oh?" Olivia raised her brows. "Is that weird?"

"Well, Cliff was walking pretty slow. He was using a cane and they came out of Ste. Anne's Church again. You know, like I saw them that one time. There were other people too."

"You don't think they're going to services, you know, Catholic mass?"

"Um, nooo. Do *you*?"

Just then a voice came from behind them. (*Why was she always coming from behind?*) "Here you are. Let's go in, shall we?" Olivia and Amanda separated to allow Mrs. B to open the door to her well-appointed office. They followed her inside. Two chairs opposite a desk were upholstered in bright chintzes to match the Iroquois décor. A thick glass top rested on a Kelly green base with bamboo-looking embellishments. On the glass desktop was a single folder. The glass top could hide no clutter, but, obviously, there was never clutter to hide. Not in this office. Under the lake-facing window was a sideboard like the one in the Carriage House dining room. A Carriage House tray, napkin-lined per standard, had been placed on top. On the tray were cups and saucers, two silver pots, and the stem of a blue hydrangea in a crystal bud vase. A cream pitcher and sugar bowl were nestled beside. Someone had gotten the memo to deliver coffee service for this meeting. Mrs. B walked toward the tray.

"Would either of you care for coffee?" She turned a small, manicured hand toward them, the reflexive gesture of a natural hostess. Neither of them accepted.

"Please sit. Make yourselves comfortable." Carefully, she poured coffee into the hotel's signature floral cup and took it on a saucer to her desk with neither shake nor spill. She sat softly down and crossed her ankles like a socialite hosting a charity luncheon and not a seventy-five-year-old business owner about to fire an employee. Or two.

Mrs. B took a sip of her coffee. Placing the cup back in the saucer, she drew her hands to her chest and clasped them together as if in prayer. Directing her emerald cat eyes to Amanda she began. "Amanda, I suppose you know why I've asked you here. Why I asked both of you here." She glanced at Olivia.

"Yeah, I guess so. I'm… you're, well, I'm not going to be working here anymore. Is that it?"

Mrs. B didn't respond immediately.

As though no news always meant bad news, Amanda began to stand. "I thought so."

"Amanda, sit," Mrs. B said abruptly, but not unkindly. "Sit. Please." Amanda dropped back into her seat. She dropped her head too and Olivia noticed a tear splash on one of her legs. She would not embarrass Amanda by pushing a tissue into her hand.

Mrs. B continued. "Amanda, I don't suppose you would know that I had recently discovered theft in the restaurant. Petty at first, a missing paring knife or copper mule mug. I thought perhaps we were misplacing items early in the season. It became a bit more frequent *and* more expensive. I don't suppose you were aware of that?"

Amanda lifted her head, tears visible on her cheeks. She used the heels of her hands to wipe them away. "No, Mrs. B, no. I didn't know that." She paused. "You think I was stealing things." It wasn't a question.

Mrs. B continued her prosecution. "Amanda, the theft became increasingly troubling and bold. We were losing full bottles of alcohol and entire tenderloins of beef." Amanda's face twisted at that. The phrase "tenderloins of beef" seemed to bother her. "You wouldn't have been aware of that."

"No, Mrs. B. Just looking at raw meat makes me—and I don't drink." She corrected herself, "Anymore."

"Yes, of course." Mrs. B took another sip from her cup, uncrossed and recrossed her ankles. In navy flats with gold buckles, she was ever comfortably chic. "Amanda, given your unfamiliarity with the pattern of theft I became aware of, I don't suppose you'd know of anyone who might accuse you of the acts?"

Olivia stiffened. She gripped the chair arms to stop herself from grabbing Amanda's hand and taking control of the conversation.

"Um, I don't know," Amanda said. "I don't know why someone would do that. I'm pretty much friends with everyone here."

"Oh, and I can vouch for that." Olivia stood. "Mrs. B, you've seen how hard Amanda works. She's so professional and she has gotten any number of us out of jams when service has gone sideways. She's always there to help, but she never calls attention to herself." Olivia looked at Amanda and back to Mrs. B. "You have to have noticed that yourself."

"Thank you, Olivia. That'll do."

Silenced, she sat again.

In her same steady manner, Mrs. B continued. "Amanda, would you have known that I installed a camera in the walk-in refrigerator?"

The girl shook her head no.

"So, you wouldn't have known that the camera recorded your visits to the walk-in?"

"I'm sorry. Sorry to interrupt…" Olivia couldn't help herself. "Is that legal? Without informing anyone? That doesn't seem—"

"It is very legal, Olivia. This establishment is mine and so is the refrigerator and its contents. All the contents. Those who accept employment here do so with the understanding that the tools I make available in the performance of their duties are the exclusive property of the Iroquois Hotel and its Carriage House restaurant. And, as I said before, mine. In answer to your question, Olivia, the installation of the security camera was a regrettable necessity and quite within the boundaries of the law. Thank you."

Dismissed, Olivia sat silent. Mrs. B pressed on. "Amanda, the camera provided me with footage of you in the walk-in."

"Oh, yeah. Yes, I mean." She nodded. "But I can explain. I was so hot sometimes, you know… because…" She looked down at her lap and then up at Mrs. B through her bangs. "I felt like I was going to puke. Like, a lot. I couldn't just abandon my tables or, you know, throw up on them, so I'd go in there to cool off. That's all. I couldn't do that in the kitchen. Or at my station. I wouldn't do that. You know, puke."

Mrs. B had blinked at each utterance of the word "puke." She cleared her throat, like she was suppressing a gag. Clearing it one more time, she looked at Amanda. "Yes, well. May I get to the point?"

"Yes, please, ma'am. That would help."

"Last week, upon reviewing film, I saw something disturbing. You weren't alone in the walk-in."

Olivia slid to the edge of her chair. "Oh now, just wait. There is no possible way Amanda was conspiring with someone in the walk-in refrigerator. That is simply preposterous!"

"Olivia," Mrs. B lowered her voice, "would you help yourself to a cup of coffee? Decaf perhaps." Mrs. B took a paper, a photo, from the folder on her desk and handed it to Amanda. "Amanda, dear, this is Danny in the walk-in, near you. Am I right?"

Amanda took the photo from Mrs. B's outstretched hand and nodded. She lifted her gaze to Mrs. B as she returned the photo to her hand.

"There are other photos." At this, Olivia, who'd made her way to the sideboard to pour the suggested cup of coffee, dropped the teaspoon into her cup. It bounced from cup to tray, splashing its contents and making a clattering noise. She turned, jaw dropped.

"Amanda, the other photos suggest to me that Danny was somehow threatening you." She was shuffling and scanning the other papers from the folder. More photos. "Your expression, even from a distance, shows fear. One photo seems to show you cowering, covering your head as though you were about to be hit. Amanda, has Danny been harassing you? Did he assault you?"

Mrs. B had finally landed the plane. Olivia was relieved and horrified at the same time. She left the coffee cup and its mess where it was, took three steps toward Amanda and stood beside her. "Amanda? Has Danny harassed you?"

She nodded. "He asked me out. A while ago. I said I didn't want to, couldn't. And it's like I offended him. He doesn't like me."

Mrs. B picked up the questioning. "Did he assault you?"

"No," she shook her head. "No. He didn't. Really. *Really,*" she emphasized. "And I don't want to cause any trouble. I don't need enemies right now."

Mrs. B leaned forward in her chair to look into Amanda's downcast eyes. Having caught them, Mrs. B raised her chin as though to raise Amanda's gaze with them. Neither of them blinked. "Dear, can I trust that you are telling me the truth? If Danny has assaulted you, I must know. I have already witnessed myself that he has committed theft."

"You have?" Olivia burst out. She stepped toward the desk. "Then why hasn't he been fired? Days ago? Why make Amanda go through all this? That's, that's just… cruel."

"I had no intention of being cruel. I simply wanted to hear from Amanda to confirm what I believed to be true." She paused again. With her eyes alone she invited Olivia to take her seat. "Amanda, I admire your strength in keeping this to yourself, but you must ask for help when you need it. Do you understand what I'm saying?"

"Yeah, I think so." She hung her head again and kicked her feet back and forth, just slightly, like a child being disciplined. "I guess I do."

"But I don't." Olivia interrupted. "I'm sorry, Mrs. B, can you explain to me why Amanda is being put through this and Danny is still working here? You said yourself that you have proof he's stealing. Last night I caught him behind the bar. He said he was getting brandy for Chef's special. I think I caught him before he got away with it. I was going to tell Chef this morning."

"Olivia, I appreciate your concern for Amanda and your protection of her. And, no, I won't explain myself. I have no need to." She was controlled, even-tempered. "I will only say that despite this evidence," she glanced down at the photos in her hands and sighed, "not everything is as it appears. Of course, I believe what Amanda has told me—told us. And I deeply, *deeply* regret Danny's actions, but firing him is not what I have in mind. I want to ensure Amanda's safety and well-being. And I will. As for Danny, the restaurant can survive his petty theft. Which will stop today," she added. "Danny, on the other hand, may not survive the loss of his employment here. There is more to this story that I cannot share with either of you. But I mean no harm to you, Amanda, or to you, Olivia."

That was simply a kind lead-in to soften the blow that followed.

"And yes, as you suspected, your employment at the Carriage House has ended."

Chapter 39

Montreal, Quebec

"Just looking at you depresses me." Landon dropped her tray on the café table beside Nate and sat down.

"Well, hello to you, too." Nate looked at his coworker who'd stabbed a fork at her salad. "And if I were depressed, that wouldn't have helped, by the way."

"Nob krying ah hep," she said, her mouth full of greens. It was uncharacteristic for the well-bred sophisticate that she was. "Sabing the obious." She swallowed. And then took a drink from the glass on her tray. "Really, that dour expression. Keep it up, and it could be a career limiter."

"Do I care? A severance package is sounding pretty good right now." He took a long drink from the can in his hand.

"Hush now," she sounded again like her southern belle self. "The walls have ears. Tell me—quietly—what's with you?"

"I'm tired. That's all. Simple as that."

"Really? It looks more complicated. Tell me what's going on." She sounded like the true friend she'd become since she and Nate had brokered an understanding. Since then, she'd shared further that the single men she met online were cads, sometimes out-and-out lechers. Married men with mortgages and dogs seemed safer. They came preprogrammed. But Nate wasn't that man. Moreover, in her failed flirtations with Nate, she eventually realized that she didn't really want a fully baked, happily married man. She wanted a role in training up a happily married man, even though her prospects were slim and getting slimmer. Working twelve-hour days, six days a week in Canada—"good gracious"—was not an ideal place for an Atlanta-born peach to lure a gentleman, especially since the man in her current orbit, Nate, had reframed her goals. She was grateful for that. And grateful to call him a friend. One day she might tell him her secret dream that went beyond finding a partner. One day, maybe, she could tell him she wanted to be a mom. That simple. But not today.

They ate in comfortable silence. She took the last bite of her salad and pushed the tray to the center of the table. "Lord, I'm full as a tick." She reached into her purse and discreetly reapplied her lipstick. That accomplished, she looked at Nate. "All right, then. What's going on?"

"Not much. I just wish I wasn't here." He offered nothing more. He sat, expressionless.

"I hope that wasn't meant to be existential."

Nate smiled. "No." He ran his right hand through his close-cut hair. "I should be in Michigan today, visiting Luke. Surprising Olivia."

"Ahh. I see." She waited for him to go on.

"Last week, Luke told me that Olivia was driving there for a visit. He asked if I could fly in. See him and surprise his mom."

"Fly in? To the middle-of-God-forsaken, nowhere Michigan?"

"No, to Traverse City and then, you know, rent a car to get to the camp. A family reunion."

"Ahh. But you're not doing that. Not today." She was trying to sort it all out.

"Nope. Too much happening this week. The news drops Friday." He looked at her accusingly. "You know that. Investors are going to want more answers than we can give. And I don't even know all the answers anyway. I'm just… I was hoping…"

"Yeah, yeah, I get it. I'm sorry. You miss her." She stated what was becoming obvious.

"Yup. I miss them."

"So that was a great idea, the surprise visit. Good for Luke. He must get that from Olivia."

"Meaning?"

"You don't exactly exude 'surprise-my-wife' vibes. In the weeks we've worked together, I haven't seen a sentimental side to you—over Olivia, I mean."

"No, I don't know what you mean. Sentimental? How so?"

"Well, for example, when we've been out at dinner and I've pulled you into a store, I've never been aware of you choosing something for her. A gift. You know, a bauble."

"A bobble?" He gave her a blank expression.

Landon sighed with exasperation. "Mercy. I see your struggle. Not a bobblehead, Nate. I mean a B-A-U-B-L-E bauble. A whatnot. A thingamajig."

"Okay. No. I don't do that. I don't know what she'd like."

"That's beside the point. It wouldn't matter."

He looked bewildered. She flipped her amber hair off her left shoulder, swung it around to her right shoulder, and leaned in.

"Nate, what's her favorite flower?"

"I'm not sure. Pink?"

"Who's your florist?"

"My florist? FTD I guess. Does that count?"

She shook her head. "No. Shame on you. Let's continue. What's her favorite scent, the perfume she wears?"

"Ahh… Okay, it's… like… glass, round, and a gold something on top. Umm…"

"Nate, really. This is embarrassing. These are essentials. Don't you see?" She continued. "Cotton or cashmere?"

He snapped back. "What?"

"You heard me. Cotton or cashmere? Her favorite kind of sweater. Silver or gold? Diamonds or gemstones? Hoops or studs?"

"Stop." He pushed back from the table, leaning back into his chair. He dropped his hands to his thighs. "Got it. Most of the time, when gifts are involved, I get her pajamas, soft ones… books… gift cards. Aprons. She loves that kind of stuff. She always says so."

"Nate!" She slapped her hands on the table. "Those are gifts for your elderly mother!" And then, "Bless her heart. But that is not how you romance your wife."

"Romance my wife? Why would I do that? We're married." He smiled at that, like he recognized his error and wanted to see Landon's reaction.

"Lord, have mercy. Were you raised by a pack of wolves?"

"No. Swedes." He paused. "We're not overly dramatic."

"Or romantic. We've established that." She sighed again. Louder this time. "Nate, you have got to step it up. I can help you, but I'll need your full cooperation." She paused. "And your credit card."

"What makes you an expert? Landon, we've talked about this. You're, um, you know, not married. And I know that's not what you'd hoped for, but still, how can you know this stuff?"

"Just because I'm unmarried doesn't mean I don't know what a functioning marriage looks like."

"We're functioning."

"Are you sure? You're not wooing."

"Wooing." He repeated the word like it was new to him.

"Listen, Nate, I once dated a man who, on a Friday morning, delivered to my office an airline ticket with instructions to meet him at Hartsfield midday."

"Pretty presumptuous. What if you couldn't make it?"

"Hang on, mister. Said gentleman met me at the airport and he flew us to DC to have dinner at a sweet little spot on the Potomac and a walk through the monuments lit up at night. Nate, *that* is what I call wooing."

"Oh sure." He took a hand to his chin and swept it down the stubble there. "What'd he want in return?"

"Nathan, you are entirely too cynical. And I'm not that kind of girl. At least I wasn't then. I was home by midnight. It was a dream of a date."

"Impressive. So, what happened to him?"

She tilted her head, looking for a suitable reply. "Let's say he was attracted to me for my law degree and career, and possibly my daddy's money and connections. In the end, he was looking for a different kind of woman. One who could master his mother's sweet potato pie recipe and produce Sanford Lewis Hawthorne the third to be raised by a proper nanny. That wasn't me. Not then anyway."

Nate nodded, like that sounded right knowing Landon.

"I've got another for you. One gentleman I dated arranged for private dance lessons for us. I once said, quite casually, that I had always wanted to waltz. You know, to learn how. He surprised me with lessons."

Nate shook his head. "Not happening. Not ever."

"Oh Nate, where's your imagination?"

"Well, where's your dance partner?"

"Lovely man. Truly. But he insisted on leading. Oh, and I would have loved that, but he didn't know how. Not how I wanted to be led. But he was sweet. And besides…"

"And, besides," he added, "you were still hung up on…"

"Yes, him. I sure was. But back to you." She clapped her hands, indicating the change of topic. "Olivia would fly here in a moment's notice to spend even an evening with you if she only knew you missed her."

"Yeah well, I don't know about that. She's got a full life back in Chicago, and some new catering thing she's been texting about. She's busy."

"Nate, you have too little confidence in my understanding of relationships. Let's put it this way. You are not living with a fraternity brother. You are living with a woman. Have you forgotten?"

"Landon, I'm living alone in a lousy hotel suite with a noisy refrigerator and crappy bed."

"And you might keep living like that if you don't get it together. Trust me on this, Nathan Nash. I admire you. I care for you. Enough so that I want the very best for you." She put a finger, its nail tip neatly painted white, on his shoulder. "You, my friend, are not meant to be a divorcé. It's not in you."

She dropped her hand. "And if I recall correctly, you are the one who told me that once you find the right person, once that spark happens, you have to tend the fire. Remember?"

"I said that?"

"Mister, you did indeed." She stopped and looked at Nate as though she'd had a revelation. "Nate, you do want this, right? I mean, you love Olivia, and it seems to me you miss her terribly. Am I right?"

"Yeah. I think so. We're just, I don't know. Out of step. We're not connecting. We never talk."

"Is that her fault or yours?"

"Honestly? I'm not sure. I just wonder if things are changing."

"Changing? Of course they are, you goose. They're always changing. The woman you married isn't Olivia anymore."

He shot her a look.

"I mean, she isn't the *same* Olivia. She's all the Olivias you've lived with and loved for… how many years?"

Nate paused to consider. "Mmm, twenty-three? No, I think twenty-four. Pretty sure. Yeah. In November."

"I guarantee you she's a different woman than she was twenty-three or twenty-four years ago." She looked at him with gentle scorn. "You need to get that number down. With authority. Anyway, Nate, if you want to find out who she is now, you'd better get busy."

Nate's lips were drawn tight. He lowered his chin and took a hand to his brow. He nodded slowly like he was coming around to Landon's point of view.

She didn't hesitate. "Let's find you a respectable Chicago florist. There must be one. And you need to get cozy with them. A good one will know how long you've been married. Spare you a whole lot of grief."

She pushed her chair away from the table and stood. She gave him a last look. "Honestly, Nate. I love you. But for a smart man…" She picked up her tray and turned, tsk, tsking on her way.

Chapter 40

Mrs. B hadn't dismissed Amanda and Olivia with the news of their firing and nothing else. She had continued, "As I said, you're both fired from your roles as Carriage House servers but there is more, isn't there?" She looked at Olivia and then her green eyes rested on Amanda. "Olivia has told me that you've established a fast friendship with Cliff at the bookshop. Is that so?"

"Um, yes. We are friends and I said I could help him when I wasn't scheduled here. Was that a bad thing? I didn't know."

"Of course not, Amanda. That's just fine. Olivia tells me you might be a great help to him. And perhaps he needs your help more than ever." She quickly added, "I wouldn't know, mind you. I haven't visited the Island Bookstore in years." She swiveled in her chair and turned her head toward the window. "Not with the library only steps away." The library, clad in robin's egg blue paint, was in view just across Windermere Point. "And Cliff is a good man. We once," she stopped, staring out the window. "We were…" She seemed to be searching for words that might be riding the waves. She began again. "We were childhood friends."

She looked back at Amanda. "Anyway, it seems you've found suitable employment. And I don't suspect Danny frequents the bookstore. Do you?" She raised an eyebrow. Olivia caught it, but Amanda didn't seem to.

"Oh, I've never seen him there. Never."

"And I don't believe you shall. Now, Olivia, I am relieving you from serving duties with something else in mind. Frankie has told me about your progress at Lilac Cottage."

"She has? Really?"

"Yes, and I've seen the photos." Before Olivia could respond, Mrs. B continued. "As we enter the season's final months, we have vacancies—few of them, granted, but we have ones here and there. I am always renovating and redecorating our rooms. Perhaps you're aware?"

Both women nodded because, of course, the Iroquois was always in process. They knew the building and its rooms required continuous attention to look perpetually serene and effortlessly beautiful.

"Yes, well. Olivia, reliable painters are a rare commodity. You seem quite skilled. You also possess an eye for color and décor. I'd like to hire you to refresh our rooms and public spaces as the opportunities arise. That is, when we have a vacancy or when our guest list is light. Paint out scuffs, touch up nicks. Repaint a room when needed. I'll pay triple your hourly rate and require half as much of your time here. And no nights. Is that agreeable?"

Olivia felt compelled to accept the offer like she owed Mrs. B something. "Sure, I think so. Yes, that would be interesting. A little strange maybe…"

"Well, then, it's settled. Do speak with Cindy and she'll discuss payroll matters with you and provide you with your schedule for next week." To seal the deal she added, "Hmm?"

"Okay, sure…" How was Olivia supposed to refuse? It seemed predetermined, or like it was being forced on her. The woman in her Talbots petites and Gucci belt held Olivia in a full nelson. She was pinned. But, even so, the offer wasn't a bad one, at least until she would go back home. Whenever that would be.

"Well then, these matters are settled. Thank you both." The featherweight excused them with the tilt of her white head toward the door.

Having been excused, the women made their way through the kitchen, toward the bike racks outside. They walked by the swinging door to the dining room, left open this early in the day. Amanda said only loud enough for Olivia to hear, "So long beauty. I won't be back until I can sit at one of those tables as a paying guest."

Olivia put her arm around Amanda's shoulders.

"Like that will ever happen."

"Oh, you're wrong there." She gave Amanda's shoulders a squeeze. "If that's what you really want. It'll happen one day. Trust me."

Amanda waited for Olivia as she retrieved her duffle bag from a locker. Together, they walked to the bike racks. Olivia would be leaving her bike there and heading to the docks for the ferry, but only before buying three pounds of fudge on her way. For her part, Amanda was planning to spend the day with Cliff, learning the payment system, how to close out the day's sales and, hopefully, giving Cliff some help with software and shortcuts, the ones already in his system that could help him organize his days. Her time at the Carriage House had shown her some tricks on recording sales and calculating taxes owed. When she had been assigned to close, she had studied Mark and Tricia settling each day's take—what was electronically posted and the cash that would be stowed overnight in the safe. She helped them here and there, and they had remarked once to Olivia that Amanda was a quick study. Cliff would benefit from her newly acquired skills.

"Okay, then," Olivia put a hand on Amanda's arm. "You'll be okay with Cliff, right?"

Amanda nodded she would.

"And you'll be okay at Lilac Cottage without me?"

"Like will I throw a big party that the police," she paused for effect, "*on horseback*, will have to bust up?" She smiled.

"Not exactly that, but if you want to go there, sure." Olivia relaxed hearing a lightness in her teasing. "I'll be back tomorrow night." She dropped her hand and continued. "Amanda, can I ask you a question—about Danny?"

"I guess so. Sure."

"Remember when we met? And when we talked, the first time?" Amanda nodded that she did.

"You told me that you did self-defense training. You know, that martial art."

"Jiu-jitsu," Amanda helped her.

"Yes, that. Having that training, why didn't you back Danny away from you?" Olivia waited.

"I said he didn't assault me." She looked down and kicked away some stones on the path.

"I know you said that, but I guess I'm not totally convinced. Did you think about," Olivia's voice softened, "you know, fighting back?"

"No." She shook her head and then looked at Olivia. "I think he was drunk. I don't fight drunk guys. They don't fight fair. I learned that the hard way."

Olivia took one of Amanda's hands and gave it a squeeze. "You are remarkable."

Amanda shook her head to deny that.

"You are. I'm older and I know what remarkable looks like. Hmm?" She employed Mrs. B's technique for suggesting there would be no further argument.

"And then, dear, remarkable Amanda, we'll need to talk about these next weeks. You know, another visit with Dr. Sam and how you're feeling about the future." She smiled gently at the girl. "I can't really understand how big this must feel for you, but I think the sooner you can imagine your future—the very best scenario you can imagine— the sooner you can make plans to walk into it."

Amanda returned a squeeze to Olivia's hand and moved her chin up and down. "I know. I don't want to think about it. It's… it's just hard."

"That's why we imagine the best and walk toward it, one step at a time. Just one after the other. You know what they say about eating an elephant?"

"Not really. And that sounds disgusting." She made a face, one that had become familiar to Olivia. "I should go." Amanda heaved her bike from the hold of the rack and settled on its seat. She'd already left the subject of her pregnancy. "I'm actually excited. Working in a bookstore. I never thought about that."

"All right then, go! We'll talk about eating elephants another time." Amanda started a slow peddle. Olivia spoke to the departing figure. "And you have my number. Text me if you need me. Anything!"

"Okay, okay," and waved the back of her hand to Olivia. She turned her head and over her shoulder called, "I'll be good. Promise. Maybe I'll practice piano." She seemed to know that would please Olivia.

Olivia watched her go and offered a silent prayer for her and the baby. She moved to the walk, heading toward the docks, bag over her shoulder and purse strapped across her chest.

"Hey!" A hand gripped her shoulder. She turned.

"Wha… Chef? You scared me!"

"Are you leaving? Where to?"

"I am. I'm not sure I need to tell you, but I'm going off island to see my son."

Chef moved them both off to the right and into an alley that cut between the water and Main Street. "Your son? The one that was here with your sister? The woman who barreled into my kitchen?"

"The same. And she didn't exactly barrel."

"Oh, yeah, she did."

"We can debate that later. I need three pounds of fudge and the next ferry. Are we done here?"

"Not yet." His hair was wavy, and his eyes looked especially green. His gaze softened as he looked at her. "I just needed to know how you are. And Amanda."

"Thank you. That's kind of you. I think Amanda is fine. Why?"

"Mrs. B told me that you had a meeting in her office. That you wouldn't be—well, really, that Amanda wouldn't be back." He looked a little distraught at having said that. "I care about her. That's all. I wanted to make sure she was okay."

Olivia nodded and softened. "She'll be fine. I think. I wonder if Mrs. B told you that she'll be working with Cliff at the bookstore?"

His eyes widened. "Cliff? Really? He's the best. You know that. He hadn't told me."

"Yeah well." *Awkward pause*, she thought. "I need to get to that ferry."

"But," he stopped her, "Cliff told me about Amanda. Her, well, situation."

"Did he? I'm not surprised. Not sorry he told you either."

"I already liked her. Now I'll worry about her."

"You will? Truly?"

"Yeah, Olivia." He paused. "I'm not a dick." She winced a little. He tried again. "I'm not a jerk."

"Right. I'm discovering that. A few people have mentioned so."

"And you believed them?"

"Maybe. I'm beginning to." She winked and tucked strands of wind-tossed hair behind her ear. They stood looking at each other. She didn't know where to take the conversation next. And she had a ferry to catch.

"So…" she began. She shifted her weight. The bag was feeling heavy. He must have noticed.

He took it from her shoulder without asking. It seemed natural. "Listen, I know about your new arrangement with Mrs. B."

"Oh, do you?"

"Yeah, but what I wanted you to know is that I'm sorry." He moved the bag over his shoulder and shoved his hands in his pockets. "Really. I'm sorry."

His eyes, very green, she noticed again, bore into hers. It was a little unsettling. And then she remembered. "Sorry? About?"

"About Danny. I should have been on him. I'm responsible for him. Or I feel responsible for him. In a way."

"What do you mean?"

He opened his mouth in reply but the horn of a departing ferry muffled his words. He waited to try again. A few bicyclers went behind them, ringing their bells and laughing at the sound.

He exhaled and continued. "I'll tell you more sometime. His story.

I'm offering help, but he says he doesn't need it. It's complicated."

"Mrs. B said as much to me. Well, my interest is Amanda. I just want him away from her."

"Sure, of course." He shook his head and looked frustrated. "It's not what you think about him. I'll tell you sometime."

"Okay then." She tilted her head toward the ferry docks. "I need to be on my way."

"I'll walk you."

"That's not necessary but thank you." She reached for her bag, but he turned her shoulder gently.

"No, I've got it." When Olivia protested, he lowered his chin and his voice. "Would you just let me?"

She held up a hand. "Okay, sure. I have to stop at Murdick's and pick up some fudge."

"Yeah, great. I'm always up for some fudge. Can't get enough of the stuff." Olivia doubted that. Her expression showed it.

"Okay. Not always, I admit. Sounds good today though."

"All right then. Come on." She resigned herself to the shared outing. The idea wasn't altogether awful.

They set off toward the center of town, him carrying her overstuffed bag and Olivia on a mission to buy some fudge. If you didn't know either of them, you'd think they were a typical couple, returning to the ferry after an overnight on the island.

"What'd you put in here anyway? Wine bottles? Horseshoes? Bricks?" He swung the bag to his opposite shoulder.

"Hey now, look here Chef—"

"Sean," he interrupted. "We're not at the Carriage House."

"Okay, *Sean*," she laughed. "You asked for this. In fact, you insisted." She elbowed the arm where the bag was tucked.

He smiled. "You're right. I don't mind." They kept walking. A horn blasted again. Olivia thought she heard him add, "In fact, I kind of like it."

Chapter 41

Olivia boarded the eleven o'clock ferry. Three pounds of fudge had been procured and stowed in an inconspicuous bag, as though she'd ordered it for delivery to Lake Ellyn and was driving it to Luke. She had plans to tell Luke about her summer assignment on the island. She could imagine doing that, but she hadn't worked out the rest of it. Would Luke text Nate in shock: *Did you know that mom was working on Mackinac Island?!?* Could she ask Luke to keep that bit quiet until she figured out how to tell Nate? Should she tell Luke about Amanda? Could he understand a girl his age pregnant by way of rape? How would he process that? And what about the quirky bookstore owner that she was beginning to see as a father figure—well, not exactly that. More of an uncle. A wise one with a kind heart and wry sense of humor. Would Luke come to love the guy like she had?

It all seemed too soon, too much to expect from Luke. Coming clean now seemed a terrible idea, despite what Ceci had asked of her. It was far easier for Ceci to hold this secret than it was for Olivia to share it. Secret. Was it? Not exactly. It's not as though she'd inconvenienced anyone. She'd been over her rationalizations many times before, and they still made sense. And really, why ruin a visit with Luke? If he was happy, that was all that mattered. No one was hurt by her change in location. In fact, her location was irrelevant. If that wasn't a soul-sucking revelation, what was? It was, nonetheless, true.

The ferry's horn made her jump. Again. Olivia had been so lost in her thoughts she'd not even taken in the view, port to port. The captain slowed the engine to snug the boat next to the docks where island goers were already lined up for embarking. Yesterday Olivia had called to request retrieval of her car from its stay in long-term parking. She waited fifteen minutes to be reunited with her SUV. Sliding into the leather seat she realized that the vehicle was cavernous, and strange feeling. She closed the door, turned the key, and instead of feeling summer winds and hearing waterfront noises, a radio ad assailed her. She turned it off, and with a parting look at the docks, she registered her sense of melancholy. If this was to have been her final goodbye it would have been… complicated? No, more like incomplete. Maybe a kind of defeat. She wasn't ready to leave. Not yet—not for good. Over the growl of the engine she decided. "Let's consider this a midterm break and enjoy Luke, just him and me. Us and three hundred high school kids."

Eventually, Olivia tuned into an audiobook on her way to the camp. The time passed quickly, absorbed as she was in someone else's life and dilemmas. Hers was straightforward by comparison. No Nazis. No imminent threat of invasion. No war orphans. Well, actually, she might have an orphan on her hands. But that's not for now, she reminded herself, as she silenced the book to concentrate on navigating through the tree-canopied road. Still treacherous. Like she'd said to Luke when she'd dropped him off, "How *do* they get buses through here?"

Then, as before, the camp opened up in front of her. This time, there were kids everywhere. She scanned the scene left to right. Kids in bright colors, bathing suits, shorts and in groups of four and more. Some were crossing the large field from the enormous swimming pool heading toward the lake. Others kicked soccer balls and some chased frisbees while still others were keeping a ball aloft on volleyball courts. It was humming. She lowered the windows to take in the sights and the sounds. For all its busyness, it looked peaceful, like a page out of a Richard Scarry book, the ones Luke had loved as a boy.

She jumped at the sound of hoots and hollers above her. Then she caught sight of a boy in red shorts, high in the sky, tethered to some sort of harness. He sailed over her car and down the hill, finally splashing into the lake. "So, it looks like I've arrived. Hope I don't have to do that." Olivia eased her car around the bend and into a parking spot in front of the camp's offices.

Once inside, Olivia was greeted warmly by the camp director, Josh, and later given a guest name tag and escorted to the lodge where she'd spend the night. Luke was already on the ropes course, but he'd be called off when the camp assembled for dinner in an hour, leaving her time to freshen. She texted Luke to say she'd find her way to the guest tables in the dining hall. He replied with three hearts—uncharacteristically—and: can't wait. He added: if I don't text back it's bc we don't let kids have cell phones so we don't. FYI.

Recognizing her "guest" name tag, staff ushered her into the dining hall, through the buzz of hungry kids waiting outside, swarming around the doors. She was led to a table in a huge space reverberating with music and laughter. College kids, or so it appeared, stood on chairs at tables, one at every table. They began clapping to the music. They had to be leaders, she figured. At a voice saying, "Ready. Open the doors," the music changed and the leaders on chairs started cheering, dancing, and singing as kids rushed into the room to find their place. The younger kids, campers, were high-fived and slapped on the back. Before long, the whole room seemed to be moving to the downbeat of the welcoming song. She caught a glimpse of Luke doing a choreographed handshake with a few younger campers. She blinked back tears. *Get a grip, girl. We haven't even started.*

She was grateful to break away from watching Luke (and feeling bowled over) when everyone sat down. The cheers went up again when someone over the sound system yelled, "Let's hear it for your work crew!" At this, other kids, young-looking like high school kids themselves, came out in a line with trays on their shoulders, just like Olivia had been doing all summer at the restaurant. Here, the guests were cheering and tapping the tables with their hands and silverware to the beat of a song, repeating "my hands go up, down, up, down."

New to Olivia, everyone under the age of twenty-two seemed to know it. Luke had not prepared her for this. Incredible. She had a vision of the uber sophisticated Carriage House guests being served to this beat instead of smooth jazz and laughed to herself. This was going to be… she could hear Luke's voice in her head. It was going to be "EPIC."

Their table's server was Austin from Cincinnati. He served their table and another. He was running. And kept running. More potatoes, more purple drink, more chicken, followed by a drum roll for the "big cookie." A crazy skit began from the stage at the far end of the room and then a guy dropped down from the ceiling suspended by a harness and rope. Once out of it, he decked a guy dressed like a banana meant to be his nemesis. For anyone with ADHD tendencies, this was a circus that could summon hyper-focused attention. It kept her attention anyway. Just as quickly, the skit ended and kids rushed out of their chairs, leaving behind plates, napkins, glasses, and all the flotsam of teenage diners.

"I'm not sure what just happened," she said to a fellow guest who looked equally befuddled. Out of habit, she started organizing dishes left on the table until a hug that grabbed her from behind.

She turned. "Luke! This is incredible! I didn't know."

"Right! I know! How do you explain this?" He took the plates from her hands and set them on the table. "Austin will get those."

"Doesn't he have to go to the room with us and the other kids?"

"Nope," Luke explained. "He stays here with the other servers and the crew in the pits to clean up and set the tables for tomorrow's breakfast."

She scanned the room. "How many kids are here?"

"Hmm, this week we have about three hundred and eighty."

She looked again around the room, imagining the work. "Geez, that's what we do at the restaurant on a busy night."

"Sorry?"

"Ha!" She laughed—awkwardly. "Just remembering when I worked at a restaurant. This takes me back." She hugged him again. "I just hope the tips are good." She winked at him.

"Mom, no tips."

"I know. Kidding. But I hope they are paid something."

"Nope. They work for a month, unpaid."

"Truly? Nothing?"

"Nope," he answered again. "You know I get a small stipend for the summer, but these guys don't get anything. And they pay their way here."

"So, free stuff in the camp store?" She'd passed it on her way to the dining hall.

"Nope." He put an arm around the small of her back. "Let's go to the club room. It'll be starting soon."

She looked for Austin to thank him, but he and his team must have been in the kitchen.

"Come on, Mom. You can thank Austin tomorrow."

As Luke moved her along to the doors Olivia noticed how tan he'd become. He seemed taller too and sure of himself. Then she noticed a handheld radio on his belt loop.

"Luke," she pointed to it. "What's this?"

"My tattoo?" He looked at the underside of his arm.

"Oh, hadn't noticed that actually. A tattoo? Huh. There it is."

"I'm twenty-one now. That was the deal, right?"

"Absolutely." She was resigned to it and pointed again at the radio on his belt.

"Summer staff have these on us all the time. It's how we notify everyone on the team. You know, a hurt camper, an approaching storm, delays in the program. That kind of stuff." As soon as he'd explained, someone called out his name over the radio and asked him to go to the booth.

"Roger that." He looked at Olivia and gave her a quick hug. "Gotta go. Head that way—follow the kids." He pointed toward another building with columns and a porch and more rocking chairs. "Club starts in about ten minutes. I'll find you later. Oh, there are chairs inside, at the back of the room, for old people. Don't let the kids sit there."

"Okay…" and he turned from her. "Not insulted," in case he wondered. Luke was too far from her to have heard.

Again, Olivia was noticed by someone on staff who led her into the club room. She found one of several theater chairs in the back and pulled out her phone to send a quick text to Amanda:

Hey! How are you? Great here. Amazing. How was the store? Busy?

Her phone lit up almost immediately with a reply: Awesome. Learning lots, teaching Cliff too. He's so funny. Late dinner with him and Chef. They're buds.

Olivia replied: Wow. Feeling okay?

Good. Normal.

Olivia supposed "normal" meant "like I'm not pregnant."

The music came on in a blast and seconds later, sets of double doors flew open and the throngs of kids that had been in the dining room now ran down the steps to take places as close to the stage as they could. As suddenly as the kids surged into the room, at the signal, they settled on their seats and a speaker came out on stage. For the cacophony that had begun the night, the room was inconceivably hushed. For the next twenty minutes, the speaker drew them in, telling a story from the Bible deftly related to the kids and their lives. And hers.

The speaker's message followed her as she left the room on the heels of the hundreds of kids who filed out in front of her. She walked the winding road up the hill to the adult guest lodge convinced the message had been for her. And for Amanda. She could explain all this craziness to Luke, and eventually to Nate. Luke would totally get it. Nate? She had hope that he would.

When she arrived at the lodge, she brewed a cup of tea, wandered to the porch, and settled into a rocking chair. A distance below and to her left were the dining hall and club room. In front of her were the lake and the pool beyond it. Light posts dotted the expanse and string lights hung over the beachfront at the lake. As she looked, the camp went dark, startling her. Her phone pinged.

This is for you mom. And three hundred kids. Every week after that talk.

The sky lit up with fireworks bursting over the lake. She heard echoes of kids applauding and sounding their oohs and ahhs. The colors climbed and sizzled in front of her. It seemed nonstop. After an exploding finale the grounds went dark again and became silent. Heat lightning in the distance illuminated faraway hills. The camp lights came back on and her phone lit up again.

Sorry mom. Storms coming. Need to secure some stuff. You okay?

All good here. Thanks for the show. c u in the am? She got a thumbs-up in reply.

After a torrential downpour later that night, made all the more melodic by the lodge's metal roof, Olivia followed the schedule (left in her room with a camp coffee mug filled with chocolates) and walked down the hill with other guests. The same happy chaos greeted them as they entered from the back of the room. Leaders on chairs, and music thumping a welcome to campers pouring in, but showing less energy than they had the night before. She spotted Luke in the crowd once and not again as the room settled to eat breakfast.

"Mom, Mom!"

"Oh, honey, sorry. I didn't hear you over all this. You should be deaf by now." She gave him a hug and broad smile.

"Almost. But, Mom, I can't take the morning off to show you around. I'm sorry. Hannah has a fever. And Ben only just got here."

"So, you have to show him the ropes? Huh?" She grinned.

Luke rolled his eyes. But he was still smiling. "Come and see us on the ropes course. I'll be able to talk between groups in their turn."

"Will do." That settled, he rejoined the throng now headed out the doors.

She'd resolved that morning to have a heart-to-heart with Luke, but now it might not happen. Or at least, not in the way she'd imagined. Later in the morning, she walked to the ropes course where Luke was working—harnessing, clipping, triple-checking the clipping, and later cajoling reluctant campers through the course. It was hot. He looked tired. It occurred to her that Luke was spending all he had to help these kids. Some looked more like city kids, boys in oversized sweats who might be more comfortable on a basketball court. Others, the girls she saw, seemed self-conscious in full-face makeup, looking around not so casually to see which boys were noticing them. Twenty feet in the air on a four-by-four-foot platform, their fear looked every bit the same. This course was a great equalizer. And, she saw for herself, an aerial foundation for compassion and encouragement.

When Luke left the course for a break she wrapped him in a full-on hug, absorbing some of his perspiration on her hands and shirt front. "Well done, Luke. Really, truly amazing."

"Mom, I'm gross!"

She stepped back. "Huh, that's not at all what I see." And she hugged him again.

"Hey, Mom, okay." He pulled away. "I'm stuck here all day. Sorry." His upturned palms were like a plea for forgiveness. "The rain pushed all the events back. We have to get other groups up here today—all day."

"Oh yeah, Luke honey, that's fine. I got to see everything I wanted to. You, mostly."

He grinned and bobbed his head like he was dodging her sentimentality.

"I brought you some stuff. Can I drop it in your dorm before I take off?"

"Oh yeah, perfect. I kinda thought you'd bring me some cookies or something. I got you some stuff too."

"You did?"

"Yeah. There's a bag on the big table in the lobby. It has your name on it." He pointed in the direction of the staff housing. "Through there. You'll see the dorm names. You're okay? Really, Mom?" Always taking her emotional temperature.

"I'm good! I'll get my stuff together and drive the back road to the dorms. I'll swap bags with you. Can't believe you got me stuff! From where?" she asked, but she already knew.

"I'm not saying." He looked so pleased with himself she almost couldn't stand it. She fought the urge to grab him, drag him to her car, and drive away. She took a breath instead. Like a punch in the gut. Leaving him was never easy.

Luke gave her another hug, this time not seeming to mind the wet impression it left on her. She didn't mind. When she made it to the dorm to leave his care package, she found a shopping bag on a center table labeled with her name. In it, fudge. (More fudge.) And a Mackinac Island sweatshirt in surprisingly good taste. A Christmas ornament and a Carriage House coffee mug. There was a handwritten note in the mug. In his scraggly print he'd written, *"Let's go here sometime. All of us. Love, Luke."*

"Oh, Luke." Olivia gathered up his gifts to her, relieved the dorm was empty of staffers. This camp—it released too much of her emotion.

She started the drive back to Mackinaw City, deciding to meander a bit. She thought she'd find some pillows and décor for the cottage. Lake-themed, but classy. That proved to be harder than she thought, so it was late when she returned to the docks to stow her car. This time, unlike the first, the trunk was full.

As she waited with the others for the next ferry her phone pinged with an incoming call. She should have sent it to voicemail, but when she saw it was Nina, she couldn't resist.

"Nina! Hi!"

"Liv? Hey! I've missed you so much!"

"I've missed *you*!"

"I'm glad I found you."

"Why? Is something wrong?"

"Not wrong, just kind of strange. So Mr. Lowe tracked me down through the business. I would have thought he'd have your number. But, anyway, he called because flowers were delivered to you and when you weren't there, and hadn't been there in weeks, he walked over to explain that. The delivery guy left them with the Lowes. He wondered when you'd be back. So, I'm here. Outside your house."

"Oh gosh," was all Olivia could muster. "Flowers?"

"He didn't seem to know you were in Montreal."

"Yeah, well, with Betsy being so sick—how is she by the way?

She's such a love."

"She was there, with him, a little unsteady but she looked good. Oh, and he said they have Tupperware to return to you."

Nina continued. "But, see, when they tried to tell the guy you hadn't been home in a while, the delivery guy insisted. So apparently, they opened the card. Just in case there was a mistake. The flowers were from Nate. They are spectacular. Enormous. There must be some reason…"

"Nate? Really? That's so nice." A reflexive reply.

"Yeah, nice. But. Liv, aren't you with him?" She sounded confused. "Why would he send flowers to you in Lake Ellyn?"

"Hmm… right." She regrouped. "You are so right, Nina. The florist obviously confused the billing address with our hotel address. In Montreal. Where I am. You know, staying with Nate. All summer." Did that sound convincing? Probably not, but she carried on. "Nina, can you read the card to me?"

"Sure. Hang on." She paused, for too long.

"Nina?"

"Yeah, I'm here. It's romantic. I think."

"Okay, I'm ready," and impatient because the ferry would be pulling in and leaving soon.

"It says, and it's handwritten so I'm not sure exactly, but I'm pretty sure it says, 'All I think about is Landon and I can't stop smiling. Love – your Nate'."

"Oh. That's what it said? Exactly?"

"I don't know Liv, maybe it's an 'o' so that it's London but it looks a lot like an 'a,' which means it's *Landon*." Nina was silent for a few beats and then added, "Isn't she the one? The tall… spider… coworker?"

"How funny!" Olivia's voice cracked a little. "What a mix-up! Nina, you're the best. How about you keep the flowers or give them back to the Lowes and I'll talk with Nate. We'll figure out what happened from our end. Bet I get another beautiful vase of flowers." She forced a laugh. "Gotta go, my friend. Thank you so much! Love you." She hung up on Nina just before the ferry *Huron* pulled in with a loud bellow.

For the love of God, Nate! Was it Landon or London? Never had the words, spelled so similarly, meant something so different. If they were meant for Landon, why would he have sent them to Lake Ellyn? If they were meant for her, why now? And London? Maybe. Weeks ago, they'd reminisced about that. But "*your* Nate"? Since when? He never talked like that. Not ever.

If they were meant for her, Nate would be expecting her thanks and probably had been waiting all day. If they were meant for Landon— sent to their home address? But if they *were* meant for Landon, then what? The worst. My friends were right. Ceci, too. I'm such a fool.

She stayed with the thought she was a fool through the ferry ride and her return to Lilac Cottage. The dock porter was well tipped for going ahead of her to unload her mainland purchases. She had time to pull herself together before she'd see Amanda who didn't need more drama in her life. Besides which, when Nate called, if he called, he'd ask her if she loved the flowers, and the drama would be over. Problem solved.

When she arrived, a little out of breath, Olivia was happy to step foot on her porch. No, not *her* porch, but, still, it felt like home. She heard the piano and Amanda playing with confidence. So beautiful. She stood for a moment, listening, and looked through the screen door to notice something new over the fireplace.

Without interrupting Amanda, Olivia walked through the door and straight to the painting of a blonde woman. In pearls. Amanda stopped playing and Olivia looked over her left shoulder. "Amanda, this is exquisite. Where on earth…?"

"Um," Amanda replied and someone in the corner coughed. She turned all the way around to see Cliff sitting on the overstuffed chair beyond Amanda with his leg resting on the ottoman.

"Cliff! I didn't expect to see you. Are you all right?" She moved quickly to him and Amanda got up from the bench and went to her side.

"Olivia, this was all my idea. I can explain. This is how it happened, yesterday, when you were gone."

Chapter 42

The night before, across the state from where Olivia was with Luke, Amanda noticed her phone light up. It was Olivia, checking on her.

"Was that…?" one of her dinner guests asked.

"Yup, Olivia." She put the phone back on the dining table at Lilac Cottage and looked at Chef to her left and Cliff to her right. "She didn't really say, but I bet she's happy to be with her son. Kelley thought he was cute. When he came to the Carriage House and she was the server. But no one was supposed to know it was him."

"Kelley!" Chef boomed. "That girl. She's boy crazy."

"And how have you determined this, my friend?" the older man asked.

"'Cause they're all boy crazy. Alex in the pits is apparently hot." Chef tore off another bite of crusty bread with his teeth.

Amanda blanched. "Eww. Not Alex. Just no." She changed the subject. "So, what do you call this again? It's really good. I mean, solid."

"Chicken marsala. Pretty basic."

"Basically pretty good."

"I second that!" The older man grimaced a bit.

"I like the mushrooms," she continued. "So, have you ever used morel mushrooms? Like in a stew?"

"Morel mushrooms? Yeah, they're expensive. Hard to come by, too. Why? And how do you know about them?"

"Mmm," she was chewing. "My grandma Trudy and I used to hunt for them on her farm. In the woods. We foraged."

"Young woman," Cliff interjected. "This is some bit of news. Foraging on a family farm?"

"Yeah, mushrooms, lavender, wild bergamot. It makes the best tea. You would have loved it, Cliff. We have some here at the cottage. Olivia calls it bee balm. Same thing." She shrugged her shoulders confidently.

"Well, this is a surprise." Cliff watched her.

Chef paused too. "You have a farm? You never mentioned it."

"Used to." She tore off another piece of bread, dunked it into some olive oil, and chewed while she talked. She studied the candle on the table and spoke. "It's another thing my dad ruined. He sold it when she died. He said the money was for me. For my college. He just wanted me to take the blame or feel guilty. I loved her so much." She shook her head a little, remembering. "But I think he spent the money and now we—I mean he—lives in a crap apartment. I'm never going back there. Not ever."

The men seemed surprised by her story and unsure how to respond.

Cliff repositioned himself and was about to speak when he grimaced and let out a stifled moan.

"Cliff, are you okay?" She pushed her chair away from the table. "Let me get more ice." Though he waved her off, Amanda took the bag from Cliff's knee, which was elevated on an ottoman and walked into the kitchen. She hadn't told Olivia that she was actually hosting a dinner at Lilac Cottage for the three of them. Not that it was planned. Not at all. It was too long a story to text.

She lingered and reviewed the day's events and what she might tell Olivia (and what she'd keep to herself) when Olivia got back to the island. She remembered it this way:

Earlier that afternoon, when Cliff went down on his bad knee and couldn't get up, she panicked. She didn't want to move him and cause him more pain, so she took Cliff's phone and texted Chef. It didn't take long for him to come up to the bookstore. He had a few days off, he said. Anyway, they got Cliff up into a chair and raised his right leg on another chair. Amanda found his knee brace behind the counter.

"Cliff, you should have been wearing this." *I gave him the business*, she recalled.

He was chill about the whole thing. And still weird. But lovable. He quoted his favorite, the guy who wrote the Narnia book. "God whispers in our pleasures and shouts when it hurts. It's how he gets our attention." Something like that. Cliff was always quoting some author. How did he know so many? Had to be all the books. He'd told her he was a professor. And he probably had a photographic memory. But for a pretty smart guy, he still needed her for technology. For real.

Once Chef had arrived, Cliff asked her to climb the flight of stairs to his living quarters and look around for a cardigan and his ice pack. No problem. She was happy to do it. She wanted to see what was up there anyway. Sometimes when she couldn't sleep, when she first came to the island, she'd leave her room in the staff apartments and ride her bike to the marina. She'd pass by Doud's Market. The bookstore was on the building's second floor and there was a third floor above that. The lights there were almost always on—shining out from big windows on every side. She had wondered what was going on up there. Once Cliff had told her he lived up there and painted there. He said that was his other true love.

As close as she had become to Cliff, she still couldn't ask to see where he lived, there above the bookstore. But she was dying to see it all the same. She imagined it being like a huge ballroom with wooden floors and tall ceilings and maybe a little plate with a burner where he cooked his food. And maybe an old sink, rusted out but with paintbrushes all around it, drying. She imagined it smelling like pine and paint, pretty much like Lilac Cottage. It might be a mess. Except Cliff was pretty neat in the store. She'd held those thoughts as she climbed and counted sixteen stairs, carpeted in a ruby red pattern. Fancy. She got to the top and stood, hands on her hips, and caught her breath.

"Oh my gosh, Cliff. This… *this*??" She took three steps in, lifted her chin to the ceiling, and turned in a small circle. The ceiling seemed like it was as high as the roof. Wood beams and wood slats in between were painted white. All of them. She walked over old wood floors covered in more thick, patterned rugs toward the big windows. The glass in rectangular panes rose from her kneecaps to far above her head. In front of those windows were books in piles—neat piles, but piles and piles. The west windows were letting in late-day sunbeams that made waves in a painting, the one sitting on a big easel, glow. "Oh my gosh," she whispered again.

Above the easel, on the walls between the windows were paintings. Rows of them from shoulder height and higher. They were brilliant in thick paint sweeping across their canvases. Most were framed in rough wood frames. Some had smooth black frames. Others were just canvases. And then against the walls… "Shit, Cliff, you never said." Against the walls were large canvases. They were upright and leaning on the brick walls behind them. It looked like they were almost finished. Or maybe they were as finished as he wanted them to be.

"Cliff, you were holding out on me." Sure, the store had some framed pictures but they were only initialed. She didn't know if they were his. But they looked like these. She got closer to study them. "RAC" in tiny letters at the right corners was all that identified them—just like the ones in the store. A few, they seemed older from what she could tell, were signed "Clifton." Hmm. Clifton. So stuffy. Maybe he liked Cliff better. She did anyway.

"I gotta hurry," she'd reminded herself. She walked by a tufted velvet sofa and floor lamps, then passed by an enormous kitchen table. Was it an old door? Like a church door? It had thick glass over it to make it smooth. Crazy but cool. There was a full kitchen with red pots and a big teakettle on the stove. He had tins and tins with patterns and colors stacked around the counters. They were tea tins. Well, that makes sense. She walked to the refrigerator and opened the freezer door. Ice and an ice cream carton and some fudge were taking very little space inside. Finding the ice pack was easy. She grabbed it and went through a door to a room beyond. It was his bedroom. So clean and neat, and a little surprising. She took a visual sweep and then spotted a cardigan lying over a chair in the corner. That's when she saw it. "Whoa!" She stepped back because it was looking at her.

Above the chair, opposite the bed, was a framed painting of a lady. Not the whole lady, just from her bare shoulders up. Amanda stepped forward for a better look. "Who are *you*?" she asked. "You're beautiful." The girl was looking at Amanda over her shoulder. Her blonde hair fell in waves over her bare back. No earrings. But pearls. Only pearls. She was looking at Amanda with her slanty green eyes like she was laughing. Her mouth wasn't open in a laugh, but her eyes were definitely laughing, or maybe teasing. "I feel like I know you," she said to the girl. "Kinda creepy." She looked away to grab the cardigan and glanced back at the girl one last time. "See ya. You're really gorgeous, you know." And she ran through the door across the floor and down sixteen stairs to Cliff and Chef who were waiting below.

Cliff was still seated in her favorite chair at the long oak table. Chef was seeing a few remaining customers down the bookshop stairs and out the door. Amanda delivered the sweater and ice pack to Cliff as Chef came back up the stairs to join them.

"Closed for the day." He looked at Cliff and added, "Maybe longer, huh?"

"Quite possibly." He turned his attention to Amanda. "Thank you, Amanda. You've gone above and beyond the call and I shall compensate you generously to express my gratitude."

Chef spoke up. "He means he'll pay you extra for hunting down his favorite cardigan."

"You know about his cardigan?" That fact struck her as odd. She handed the sweater to Cliff and bent to put the ice pack, gently, on his knee.

"Yeah, well, when you spend enough time together, like we have, you know these things."

She stood again and a new idea came to her. "You mean, are you? I mean, are you…?" She motioned with her hands, moving them apart and clasping them again. "You're like, together?" That kind of creeped her out and she was sure her face wasn't hiding it.

Cliff and Chef looked at each other for a long moment, realizing what Amanda was imagining, and they started laughing. Chef threw his head back and cackled. Cliff's eyes watered.

"I'm sorry. Is that funny?" She was trying to get them to be serious. "I mean, I've seen you together. A lot. It would be okay, you know. I'd be cool with it."

"Oh, Amanda dear," the older man took a breath and looked at Chef. "No. I love this man. We're, well, we're friends of Bill."

"Bill? You mean?" Eww, this was going from bad to worse. "You're like a…" She hesitated, "a threesome?"

This time Chef lost it. He spit out his gum and began heaving and snorting in laughter.

She stood still watching them, feeling more offended as their laughter kept rolling, slowing, and then rolling. "Look, I'm not sure this is funny. Is it?"

"Ooo, ooo," Cliff took a handkerchief from his pocket and wiped his eyes. Chef picked up his gum and looked at it like he might reclaim it. Amanda grabbed a napkin from the table and shoved it toward him. He dropped the wad in the center of it and she said "eww" another time.

This time Chef gave it a try. "Amanda, this is serious. Really." He looked at Cliff and they both got the giggles again. And they kept giggling.

"Okay, if you're just going to make fun of me, I'm going to go close out the register."

Chef held her back. "Don't go."

"Yes. Sit, dear one. We have something to share with you."

She walked around the table and kicked out a chair and plopped down, not happily.

"Amanda, when I said we were friends of Bill, I was saying something far more significant, at least for the two of us and many, many others."

"Okay…" She was still unsure.

"Sean and I are both in a club. One that's changed our lives. When someone is a 'friend of Bill' it means that person is a member of

Alcoholics Anonymous. That's how Sean, here, and I became such good friends."

"More than that," Chef added. "Cliff is my sponsor. I owe him my life."

Cliff tried to stop him there.

"Okay, I owe him my sobriety at the very least."

Amanda said nothing as she considered the data points. She looked at Chef. "So is that why you always drink Diet Coke—with lime?"

"Oh yeah."

"Like obsessively and nonstop?"

"It's hard to give up a compulsion to drink without replacing it with another compulsion. You wouldn't know."

"I might." She turned her attention to Cliff. "And is that why I see you together? I've seen you sometimes coming out of Ste. Anne's. Olivia thought maybe you were both good Catholics."

For some reason that threw the men into more convulsive laughter.

"I'm sorry, Amanda." Chef got himself together. "No one's ever accused me of that."

"Nor me," laughed Cliff.

"Ste. Anne's has meetings every morning at six-thirty for anyone on the island, residents, summer workers, or guests. Cliffy and I go often."

"Cliffy?" Seemed weird for a guy to call another guy that, honestly.

"Yeah. Cliffy. He's my buddy. Actually, more than that. I could have lost my job and my career. Or more. Cliff found me when I was at my lowest."

"We don't always realize when we need help," Cliff went on. "Not until we get to the end of ourselves."

"I wish I'd gotten there faster. I wasted a lot of time."

"Does Olivia know?" she interrupted.

Chef answered. "I don't think she does. No reason for her to know, or suspect."

"So I shouldn't say anything?"

Cliff answered this time. "It's not a secret. Nothing we're ashamed of, but why not let us tell her—at some point." He looked at her for her consent. She agreed with a nod of her head.

"I'm kinda surprised. Not in a bad way. I wish my dad was like you. He drinks. A lot. Like all the time. I hate it."

Cliff reached across the table, grimacing as he shifted his knee and grabbed one of her hands. "Oh, young one, I am sorry. I see your pain. If only we recognized there are no private sins." He patted her hand. "Your father may not realize the power alcohol has over him or that he is powerless to control its hold on him." He kept looking at her, his bushy eyebrows over sparkly blue eyes. "Admitting our powerlessness is what restores our control. It's a paradox."

She nodded. Okay, that was pretty serious. "So what do we do now?" And, seeing Cliff's cardigan, she remembered what brought her to the table in the first place.

"Cliff, your house. I mean your loft or whatever. It's, well, it's amazing. I mean, all those paintings. You should sell them. Like here. But, wow, sixteen steps. I counted." She glanced over the table at his elevated leg. "Not good."

"Yeah, about that, Cliff." Chef joined her. "There's no way you're going up and down those stairs. Not for a while anyway."

"Could he stay with you?" she looked at Chef.

They both smiled at that. Cliff waited for him to explain.

"Probably not. Amanda, my housing situation is," he paused, "unstable. I have a boat docked in the marina. Most of the time I sleep there. Sometimes, I take a room at the Yacht Club and other times I'm on Cliff's sofa. And, if the Iroquois has a vacancy and it's been a tough night I sleep there."

"Well, that sucks."

"It works for me." Chef seemed somehow insulted.

"I mean, it sucks for Cliff. He can stay with me."

"Stay with you?" Cliff asked. "Where?"

"Lilac Cottage."

Both of them frowned and Cliff shook his head a little. She answered their silence. "Well, do either of you have a better idea? The cottage has two bedrooms on the first floor and a whole bathroom. Olivia just finished painting them. You can stay there. I know she'd want that."

She said that with conviction.

"You do?" Chef asked.

"I do. But she's not here now. She's at Luke's camp. She said cell service is horrible. Besides, we can't just leave Cliff here."

"Are you always this bossy?"

She responded to Chef's question. "When there's a problem and I know the answer, I can be bossy. So yeah."

"She does have a point," Cliff asserted.

Chef agreed. "Okay, then. As the lady has ordered. We should round up some of your things. I'll call a taxi to get us all across the island to the cottage. Amanda, really, shouldn't you try to text Olivia first?" Cliff nodded like that was a good idea.

"No. I know her. She'd totally want this. She adopts people. She told me that once."

"Then I shall be adopted and gratefully so. I look forward to the surgeon's magic that will restore full use of my knee. Until then, as the poet has said, 'The burden is light that is shared by love.'"

"Cliff, geez." She rolled her eyes.

"Cliffy! Love? Really? What poet this time?"

"The Roman poet Ovid."

"Too bad he's not here to get you down these stairs, on a horse-drawn taxi, and up the stairs to a cottage. How about *we* decide whether the burden is light?" Chef reached out a hand to squeeze Cliff's shoulder. "Amanda, what do you say we pack a bag for ole Cliffy here. I have a pretty good idea of what he'd like."

"Okay." She looked at him as she stood from the table. "Cliff, could we take some of your paintings too? They're incredible. I bet Olivia would love them for the cottage."

"Really?" He considered it for a short time. "If you think so. Of course. A capital idea. Let's put my work to good use. Take what you like." Amanda started to follow Chef. "And Amanda," Cliff called to her, "do you feel up to managing this enterprise while I convalesce? Are you willing?"

"If you think I can. I'd love it." And she would. Like really. "But you'll be close to your phone? In case I get stuck? I don't want to blow it."

"Of course, I will be close at hand with no worries about your ability to handle our little bookshop. We've already established that you are, well, rather bossy, haven't we?"

"Yes, Cliffy," she said with teasing emphasis. She had a job to do and an old guy, a silly one, to take care of. That was good enough. For as long as it lasted.

Chapter 43

The following night, when Olivia returned to the island and discovered Amanda had welcomed a new housemate, she had to agree. Amanda gave her a stripped-down version of events, withholding a few details, like Cliff and Chef's relationship to one another and AA.

"Well of course you did exactly the right thing. Both of you. Knowing Frankie the way I'm starting to, she would think it a wise idea too." She stopped to consider. "Cliff, do you know Frankie?"

"I once did. Haven't seen her in years."

"I think she'd be fine with this arrangement. I mean, she said her grandparents used to take in strays all the time." She stopped. "Not that you're a stray, Cliff." She walked around the living room into the adjoining dining room, stepping closer and bending low to look at a few paintings leaning against the wall where they might be hung. "And these pieces. I mean, Cliff—this is you? They are phenomenal." She stood in front of them. "How could Frankie resist this? It's like a gallery in here."

While she continued looking around, entranced, there was a knock on the doorjamb. The screen door swung wide, then slammed shut.

"Chef," they said, practically in unison.

"It's a little late, Chef."

He corrected Olivia. "It's Sean. And welcome back, by the way."

"Sean, it's still a little late."

"I know. You have to come with me."

"Who?" asked Amanda.

"Where?" asked Olivia.

"Both of you. You've got to come with me." He turned to Cliff, seated in the chair. "Cliffy, you'll have to stay here. You okay with that? The skies have something for us tonight."

"Ohh, do they now?" The older man seemed to understand. "Aurora, daughter of the dawn, with rosy luster o'er the lawn."

Amanda rolled her eyes, a grin betraying her exasperation. "Whatever that was."

"That was Homer, young lady! They don't teach that anymore either?"

"Anyway," Amanda looked back at Chef, "I'm wiped. Maybe another time."

"If there is one." He pressed. "Are you sure?"

"I'm sure. Take Olivia though."

"Or not." Olivia said to the watching three.

"Oh, come on. You won't be sorry. Trust me." He put a hand out. Slowly, she dropped her hand in his. "Come on, we need to hustle."

"Hustle where?"

"The golf course at the Grand. No more questions, okay?"

She agreed and they left, screen door slamming again. They moved down the stairs and around to the cottage's backyard.

"It's dark. Like really dark."

"Well, yeah, that's why I've got your hand. Just hang on." He led them through grassy yards to Annex Road, behind the Grand and beyond.

"Are we there yet? And, besides, what's the hurry?"

"Almost there," he answered impatiently, pulling her through a field and leading her to a small bridge over a stream. "Watch your step here," he cautioned. Once over the bridge he led her to the middle of a patch of low-cut grass. "This is it."

"*What* is it?" She saw nothing but a black sky and crystal stars flickering in it. Beautiful. And nothing new.

"The second hole. Now lie down."

"That's it. Nope. Not doing that." She looked at him, or as much of him as she could make out in the dark. She put her hands on her hips. "Is this a joke?"

Without answering he turned her around by her shoulders and told her to look up. "Now keep watching." After a few moments the sky started changing, lighting up. "C'mon, sit. If you want to. *I'm* lying down." He dropped down. "Welcome to the show."

She sunk down beside him, and lay down, eyes fixed on the sky.

"Ohh. Wow. I've never…"

The sky was moving—dancing—glowing in transparent colors of green, purple, and pink. Like someone was sweeping the sky with paint over a black canvas. It kept moving, in and out, arcs of purple and green swelling in the sky and then retreating only to release another color wave. It was like music, only in color.

Neither spoke for a long time. Sean reached for Olivia's hand and gave it a squeeze and let go. After a time, the colors dissipated like they'd been swept away for another night. The stars held their places waiting for applause, but there would be no encore. Not tonight.

Sean sat up and leaned on his elbow, looking at her. "Well?"

"Well. Indeed," she whispered. "Sorry I doubted you." She couldn't really see his expression, dark as it was, and she hoped he wasn't seeing hers. They stayed that way for a time and then he leaned toward her. Just as quickly, he pulled back and pushed himself up from the ground. He reached for her hands to pull her up. "Time to get you home to your housemates. It's late."

She stood and brushed herself off. "Sean," she started. "Were you ever married?"

"I was. A long time ago, probably when you last worked here. Why?"

"Just curious. I don't think any of us knew or would have guessed. Not back then. You were kind of a pain."

"Hey now, easy. Yeah, you might not have guessed. Running a kitchen isn't a good backdrop for marriage. Long days, weekends, stress. She left. I couldn't blame her."

"And you never…?"

"Nope." He dropped the subject. "Let's go." Sean grabbed her hand and they reversed course. When they got back to the cottage, they lingered at the bottom of the steps. "You know, tomorrow should be just as beautiful as tonight." He looked up. "With a sky like this, the water will be perfect." He looked back at her. "Come out with me."

She said nothing, considering the invitation.

"I'll need to get dinner service going but I can be at the marina around seven. How about seven-thirty?"

I probably shouldn't, she thought. *Not a great idea. But it's just a boat ride.* "Well, okay. Yes. Let's." *What could it hurt? I mean, Nate. Really? What about those flowers?* She had figured what his answer would be. "So, can I bring dinner?"

"I'm the chef here. What if you get the wine instead? I'll make dinner." Words she'd never heard out of Nate.

"Who's manning the kitchen tomorrow? Or, come to think of it, any night when you're off?" It occurred to her that she hadn't known how the restaurant ran in his absence. He was almost always there.

"Danny's in charge."

"Danny?" She had no love for Danny.

"Let's talk about him tomorrow. He's got so much freaking talent. More than I ever had at that age. He knows plants, herbs native to the island. The stuff he's made and suggested for the menu—amazing. You wait. He's gonna be somebody."

"Hmm. I'll have to take your word for that." She moved to the first step toward the door and turned back toward him. It brought her eye to eye with Sean. "Okay, then." She repeated, "okay, then."

He was slow to move. "Wear that swimsuit I saw you in? You know, before."

That woke her up. Embarrassed, she turned away. "Maybe. See you tomorrow, Sean." She couldn't look back at him. She knew she'd text him tomorrow and cancel. Being out on a boat with him was a bad idea.

Chapter 44

Sean was already on the boat when Olivia approached the dock at seven-thirty, wine and assorted cheeses and crackers in a canvas bag slung over her arm. The boat ride that had struck her as a bad idea the night before seemed less so as the day wore on with no word from Nate. By five o'clock, it seemed a pretty good idea after all.

Sean looked like he'd already been at work. Whether owing to the late-day heat or a run-in with a dock hose, Sean's cotton crewneck stuck to him like a runner's compression shirt. Olivia stopped and watched him working on deck just long enough to feel guilty. And long enough to be caught gaping.

"Have you ever seen anything like it?"

And there it was. That's the guy—and the ego from long ago.

"Yes, ma'am. She's a Chris-Craft Roamer. 1962. Bought her five years ago, from a guy in Minnesota. He bought her in the eighties from a guy who'd made it big in Motown and then had to sell his toys when he outlived his royalty checks." He reached out a hand. "C'mon. Let me help you. You won't believe the mahogany in the cabin."

His right hand grasped her elbow and his left hand reached out to take hold of her canvas bag and steady her as she stepped aboard. For a moment, they stood eye to eye and she saw again how his green eyes glinted with gold, softened with black lashes. Confirmed: This was a bad idea. But here they were.

Once aboard he showed off his prize. The Roamer had been a luxury powerboat in its day, first of its kind made of fiberglass. Owned only by the wealthy, or thanks to the Chris-Craft installment plan, anyone who wanted to look like it. The boat was trimmed in mahogany, teak, and brass.

"I've never had the guts to figure out whether I have spent as many hours enjoying her as I have working on her. But I guess if I enjoy it, it's not really work, right?" He tugged the last of the lines from the dock's cleats and, with a foot, pushed them away from the dock before raising the fenders. Leaving her at the back while he went to the helm, Sean pulled back the throttle to ease the boat out of the marina and Haldimand Bay. Not long after, they were out in the Straits. They rounded the east side of the island for a bit and circled back near Round Island lighthouse (it looked even more like a schoolhouse up close). Finally satisfied with the boat's position, he cut the engine and came back to sit with her.

He uncorked the perspiring wine bottle while she pulled wine glasses from the bag. He filled her glass and then his with Diet Coke he had nearby.

"I'm sorry. You don't like the wine?"

"Well, I am the boat driver. It's helpful if I stay sober."

"You do drink a lot of Diet Coke."

"I do. And that's how I stay sober. That and AA. And Cliff."

"What? Really?" A few random scenes from her memory were coming together to paint a clearer picture. "So, you and Cliff…"

"Yup, both of us. He's my sponsor."

"Oh. That's well, incredible. I never knew."

"Amanda knows. We told her the other night. When you were with your son. She didn't tell you?"

"No, she said nothing of it."

He took another drink. "So she didn't tell you that she thought ole Cliffy and I were an item?"

She nearly spit out her wine.

"What's so funny about that? He's a great guy. And I'm a catch."

"Oh, are you?"

"So I've been told. Not so much when I first met Cliff. He saved me."

"Hmm." She inhaled the warm breeze that was playing with her shirttails and smiled with her exhale.

"And the name *'Patience'*? Is that related to AA? It's not exactly the first word I'd associate with you."

"Really? Not what you would have guessed? Instead, maybe 'Impatience'? 'Inflamed'? Or, something obvious, like, hmm… 'Meathead'?"

"No, stop." Yeah, he could be funny. "On the other hand, you may have a point."

"I admit I spent a little time thinking of better names. Then it felt like a sign. I bought her about the same time I started praying for patience." He took another drink. "So I kept the name."

"Really? More surprises." She took the hair tie from around her wrist and pulled back the flyaway hair from her face. "I just find it hard to believe that a guy who seems to thrive on the chaos of a kitchen could really enjoy quiet like this—for long periods of time. I can't see you sitting still. Or praying. That's news." She shrugged an apology.

"I see that. Running a restaurant, all that adrenaline. It can make you a jerk. Or a drunk. Both. But I crave quiet." He looked into the distance.

"It's not like I wanted to run a kitchen. I didn't want to be 'the boy wonder chef' or whatever it was they called me. I just wanted the food and the experience to be perfect. Perfect," he said for emphasis. "Pretty soon that meant running the operation—at least in the back of the house. It wasn't an ego trip. And I like to think it helped keep the place in the family. I tell myself that anyway."

"So, this crazy season of nonstop hospitality. Year after year. You're telling me it's not your thing?"

"Oh, I like to be near the buzz of other people. I do. Just not at the center of it. You know when guests ask if they can speak to the chef? Usually to thank me? I hate that. Honestly, I'm an introvert. I like to be alone. I love to nap in sunbeams. A little jazz to snore by, and I'm a happy guy. I don't need more."

When she asked how it was that he loved jazz, but worked to Metallica and Iron Maiden, he brushed it off. "I let the young guys pick the music. I don't really hear it anyway." He said he focused with the kitchen sounds as his soundtrack: knives on cutting boards, stainless steel bowls in the pits, voices of the waitstaff, dining room door opening and closing. That activity set his pace. He said he could predict the tally on the night's service by kitchen noise alone, without needing the POS ticket count.

"Well then," she said, raising her chin to acknowledge the sun pulling away from the puff of a cloud overhead, "you now have a setting sunbeam." She sat forward in the lounge chair he'd positioned on the deck. One for her and one for him. Draining her glass, she focused on her phone and then put it on his chest.

"Call up some music to your liking if you don't like this playlist, a favorite of mine." He was already reclining comfortably, legs stretched out in front. "Snore to this while I find my way around the galley and serve up the dinner you brought for us. Thank you for that, by the way." He settled deeper into his chair and pulled his cap down over his eyes.

She stood and stretched her arms over her head.

"I like being alone with you, Mrs. Nash."

She bent over to lift his cap enough to see his eyes. He opened his eyes to look at her. "I like being with you also, and, just as you said, I am *Mrs.* Nash."

"Yup. So you say." And he closed his eyes again.

Sometime after they ate, he took *Patience* under the Mackinac Bridge, and they had a quick dip. It wasn't always possible, he'd said. Some boats would leave St. Ignace in the morning and later in the day, the winds, the currents, and too small a boat made the return trip impossible.

This evening was different, calm and quiet with temperatures still in the eighties. The sun was melting in the western sky, which glowed pink and peach like the silky inside of a shell. As it sank below the bridge, it became time to head back. Olivia needed an early start on the back rooms at Lilac Cottage. She wanted it ready for any buyers that Frankie might be sending by, though the thought of someone else living there made her a little sad. Impractically so. It wasn't hers and she knew it. But still, it had come to feel like home, and she loved it more every day.

They didn't talk much as they made their way back to the marina. By the time he guided *Patience* into her slip and secured the lines to the dock cleats, the sky was charcoal gray and the breezes had cooled. When Sean looked over at her, Olivia was shivering.

"You need a hot shower."

"And I expect to have one as soon as I get home."

"You don't have to wait that long. There are showers below the clubhouse. He pointed to the Yacht Club across the street. They're not used very often, since most guests prefer to shower in their rooms. And they're kind of rustic. But nothing feels better after a day on the water."

"All right. I suppose." She was unsure. "I'd rather not bike home like this. A hot shower and dry clothes sound better. Are you sure it's okay?"

"It's fine. Really. No big deal." Sean helped her from the boat. He grabbed her tote bag and threw it over his shoulder. He led them to the tandem showers in the dimly lit underbelly of the clubhouse. When she said it was a little creepy, he assured her that he would inspect the shower stalls to make sure there was nothing there to worry about. The Yacht Club kept the space clean and stocked with an assortment of toiletries and thick white towels for its members. Sean wasn't an active member per se, but tradition assured that owners and chefs of local eateries and clubs had reciprocal privileges around the island. He'd picked up the tab for the Yacht Club's manager a time or two—or ten—before.

Sean pushed open the heavy door and led her inside. There were two deep shower stalls inside. Opposite their three-quarter doors was a wooden bench with hooks and shelves above serving as the showers' lockers. "You can shower in your swimsuit or change. Whatever. There are hooks on the wall." He handed Olivia her bag, then reached into the stall farthest from the door to turn on the water and let it warm to a comfortable temperature. He stepped back through, took two towels from shelves above them, and handed her one.

"You're okay? It's a little dark in there, but the water is warm by now. I promise, you won't meet any spiders or snakes nesting in there."

"Oh! Seriously? I wasn't imagining that. Until now. Thanks a lot." Sean nudged Olivia toward the shower stall.

"Go. Before the warm water runs out of steam—so to speak."

"What if somebody else comes by? Not sure I'm completely comfortable in here. I think I'll shower with my suit on."

"You're fine," he assured her. "If it makes you feel better, I'll stand here and make sure no one surprises you. Seriously. I've never seen another person here when I'm showering. They'd rather be in their room upstairs."

Reluctantly, but shivering, Olivia dropped her bag, slipped off the skirt she wore as a cover-up, and walked through the stall door. She let the water fall on her hand to test its temperature, then stepped closer. The white noise of the water and its warm, gentle touch on her chilled skin relaxed her. She had forgotten her fears, and everything else for that matter. Until she remembered soap. Where was that?

"Chef, I mean, Sean? Are you still there? I, uh, think I forgot the soap. Sean?"

"Hang on. I'll get it."

Olivia stepped away from the shower's stream to wait for the handoff. A short while later there was a tap on the stall door and his bare feet below it. Shivering now, she pushed the door open. He had clearly abandoned his post to shower in the stall beside hers. His skin was dappled with water drops. He had been showering in his black compression shorts. No swimsuit.

Embarrassed that her gaze had left his face to make certain she had, in fact, noticed he was no longer wearing swim trunks, she reached for the soap in his hand. She'd started to pull the door closed when he put his hand on her wrist and stepped inside. Closing the door behind him, Sean stepped closer and inched her back until they were under the shower's stream. He ran his hands from the crown of her head to her neck. Cradling her face, jawline to cheeks, he tilted her head slightly upward and brushed a light kiss on her lips and then pulled her closer, enfolding her in his arms.

Olivia didn't object. She accepted the feeling of his muscled arms around her back and the weight of his head resting on her own. And his breathing. Deep but getting faster. She ought to push him away. When she pulled back to look at him, his eyes were already on her. He seemed to be studying her with eyes that smiled.

"I think…" and whether he or she moved first she couldn't recall. All she knew was his lips on hers and her responding in a way she hadn't with Nate in such a long time. Nate. *My husband.* Repulsed, not by Sean's kiss, but by herself, she pushed him back into the shower stall door.

"I can't do this," she managed.

"Actually, I think you can. You're pretty good at it." He lifted her chin and leaned down to give her another kiss.

"Stop. Really. Sean. I can't do this." She turned off the water and looked around for her towel. Sean stepped back, toward the three-quarter door, and handed her a towel, taking the one he'd thrown over the door for himself.

"Why? Why stop?" he asked.

"*Why*? For one, I'm married. You know that. Sean, I'm married." She said it a second time just to remind herself. Olivia buried her face in the white cotton towel.

"Really? Well, you sure as hell don't look married. Or act like it." She stopped toweling off and glared at him.

He whisked the towel over his hair and face and continued. "Looks to me like you were left by an idiot husband who doesn't know what he's missing."

"Thank you, I think. But he didn't leave me."

"Really?"

"Again with the really. Yes, really. I came here on my own volition.

And he's not an idiot." She tried to squeeze by him but that only brought her closer to him. "I'm leaving."

Sean reached behind his back, opening the shower stall door all the way to let her pass. He began to help her gather her things. She threw the towel at his chest and picked up the skirt she'd tossed on the bench. She teetered on one foot in her hurry to slip it on, nearly falling into him. It looked like he was trying not to laugh, which only fueled her anger. But, still, she was having a hard time getting the damn skirt on.

He put his hands on her shoulders to steady her and continued. "So, let me get this straight. Your husband leaves you for a six-month assignment and doesn't invite you to come with him. Hell, doesn't *insist* you come with him. He doesn't ask you to visit. He doesn't even know you're here, does he?"

"Four months."

"Okay, four months. But he still doesn't know you're here, does he?"

"He knows." By now she was rifling around her bag, trying to find the flats she'd worn to pedal here. "He knows."

"He knows you're a goddamn waitress? And a painter? At the Iroquois. He knows *that*?"

"So, no. Not that. But he knows I'm at home or he thinks I am. Doing catering and stuff."

Sean finally took the bag out of her hands and dumped all its contents on the wood planks between them. He pulled the shoes out of the mix, one at a time. "Olivia. Whether you're here or at home, he's gone. He left."

"What the… Sean, you know… just." She'd slipped into her flats. "Just…" She shook off her anger and focused on stuffing the emptied bag. She did that with conviction.

"What? Just what? Go ahead," he goaded her. "Go ahead. Say what you're thinking. Say it. Say it, Olivia."

Olivia stuffed the last of her belongings into her bag, stood, and looked up at him. She took a breath as she rose to her full height and said with care, "F you, Sean."

"Well look at you. And she *almost* swears too. You know what? I still like you. In fact, I like you more. I'm not some dumbass who believes my wife is waiting for me in an empty house. A perfect wife in a perfect house. Empty all the same. You know, I'd want a wife who can get angry and say 'fuck you' when I deserve it. You should say it more often. Makes you real."

She stood motionless, waiting for the next blow. "Are you finished, Mr. Psychobabble?"

Silence and humidity hung in the air.

"Thank you for your pithy summary of my marriage. That easy, huh? That easy to understand? You didn't do so well at it yourself. Okay, then. You want more?" Olivia took a deep breath. "Fuck you. Just like that? Is that how you like it?" She tossed her bag over her shoulder and started toward the exit.

"That's how you do it. I'm telling you, you're good at it. And other things, too." He took a step toward her.

She turned and held up her hands to back him up. "Not funny. Not in the least." Compelled by her decency, she added, "Thank you for today. *Earlier* today. You were… it was… nice." She felt all the more guilty knowing she invited this. Walked right into it. Even encouraged it. "And I shouldn't let this happen. Ever again. My fault."

"Olivia, admit it. Feels good to cuss me out, right? To be honest. Real."

She shook her head. "I'm leaving." Olivia walked through the door. She knew it was wrong, getting so close to him but… *nope, not going there. Cannot. Will not.*

"And I'm just saying he's an asshole," Sean called out. "He doesn't know how lucky he is."

The door closed between them.

Chapter 45

It was well past ten and dark when Olivia arrived at Lilac Cottage, still bothered by what had happened with Sean and what hadn't yet happened with Nate. Those stupid flowers. The boat, the shower. What was happening? Her life looked nothing like the safe, predictable one she'd left in June.

Olivia slipped quietly through the screen door, hoping to be unnoticed, only to find Cliff sitting in the chair by the fireplace, working over his phone.

"Cliff, you're up?" She looked around. "And Amanda too?"

"Yes, I've been waiting for you. Anxiously. I was texting you. Several times." He raised himself to stand, leaning on his cane. "I don't know where Amanda is and I'm worried."

"Worried? Why?"

Cliff walked toward the piano and picked up a piece of paper. "Because of this." He held out a paper—a letter—that Olivia scanned.

"This is from the college." She read further. "There must have been a mix-up." She looked up at Cliff and back again at the letter. "She's overdue on her tuition and hasn't responded to their requests. Knox is going to rescind her scholarship?" She looked again at Cliff. "That can't be, can it?"

"I'm afraid it's possible. When she left, she said something about her father, mismanaging her payments and awards."

"But didn't the college send emails or try to call her?"

"Apparently not, or perhaps they called her father. Anyway, when she left, after we'd talked, she said all of it was her fault. For everything."

"She's upset, understandably." She looked one more time at the letter and back at Cliff. "But this—we can fix this."

"My dear, that's what she said when she left. 'I will fix it. Finally.' It seemed most ominous to me, Olivia, now that I reflect on our conversation before she pulled that letter from her back pocket, dropped it there, on the piano, and left."

"What do you mean? Go on."

"To start, she asked me about Arch Rock. It seemed such a casual question. Like any tourist." He looked at his feet and back at her. "I regaled her with the usual lore. She asked me if anyone had ever fallen from it and I relayed that, in fact, four years ago, a man had fallen to his death."

"Oh Cliff, no."

He had tears in his eyes. "It was a level conversation. I slipped into my professor's manner, I suppose. Of course, I had no idea about that letter and its contents at the time."

"So, are you thinking…?"

"I don't know what to think. She also asked about Mackinac's Native Americans, those living in the Village. I told her about Lila Paquette and her people." Lila, he'd told her, was still a matriarch and almost like a medicine woman. Renowned on the island. "I told her that Lila had a tonic for just about anything—all from plant life on Mackinac, just like her ancestors had. She has a cure for every ailment it seems."

"A cure. Including one for pregnancy? Is that what you're thinking?"

"I didn't imagine that at the time, but now… I don't know. Foolish man that I am." He looked anguished. "I don't know."

Olivia's phone pinged. "This could be her." She pulled her phone from her bag. It wasn't Amanda. It was Sean in a series of texts:

There's not much left of the season. Let's not end like this. friends only. Preceded by:

Truly sorry. Never again. Give you my word.

Which, as she scrolled, had been preceded by the initial text:

I'm sorry. I got carried away. Crossed a line. Got it.

Without responding to his apologetic pleas, Olivia texted back: I need help. Amanda got bad news from Knox. We're worried. Bike to Arch Rock and look for her? Going to Village now.

"Cliff, where would I find Lila?"

"Her home is near the general store, just beyond." He shook his head and looked to the ceiling. "Ask at the store. Someone will show you."

"It's too late for that. It's gotta be closed."

"Ask anyone. Knock on a door. They'll know."

Olivia left and biked toward Cadotte and beyond toward the general store. Thankfully, as she entered the Village, there were kids still out shooting hoops under a lighted makeshift court. She asked where she could find Lila and they all pointed to the same house. "The one with the white fence." She pedaled the half block to the house and leaned her bike against the fence at the edge of the yard. As she approached the porch, she made out a small red glow. A cigarette.

"What are you doing here?" She knew the voice.

"Danny? Is that you?" She walked closer to see if she'd guessed correctly.

"Yup."

"What are you doing here?" She walked to the bottom of the stairs.

"Me? This is my grandma's house. I live here."

"Oh. I didn't know." She recovered from her surprise. "I'm looking for Amanda. I don't suppose she's here."

Answering her own question, she turned away.

"She's here. Inside, with my grandma." Just then Amanda came to the door and walked onto the porch.

"Oh, thank God." Olivia rushed to her and wrapped Amanda in her arms.

"Olivia, whoa. Easy." She held something out to Olivia. "Look at this."

In the dim light, Olivia wasn't sure what she was looking at, but it seemed important to Amanda.

"It's a dream catcher. Lila gave it to me." That's when she stepped aside to reveal a small woman behind her. "This is Lila." Amanda made the introduction like Olivia was meeting royalty. Absolutely erect at about five-foot-two, with black hair, graced with gray strands, pulled back from her face. Her smile caused Olivia to still. Even in the faint glow of the porch light, it radiated a warmth that climbed to her brown eyes.

"Olivia, blessings."

"Miss Lila, so nice to meet you and thank you. Thank you." Her arm was still wrapped around Amanda's back. "We were so worried." She leaned in toward the girl. "Amanda, thank God you're here."

"I'm fine," she replied. "Well, I wasn't. I came here and Lila, well, she helped me."

"You must come back to see me, Amanda. Anytime. I'd enjoy your company."

A cough interrupted their conversation. "Excuse me." Danny made his way around them and stepped into the house. The screen door banged behind him.

"My Danny. Don't mind him. He's finding his way."

"Let's go, Olivia. I need to talk to you." Amanda led her off the porch, waving to Lila. "I will be back. Thank you. Thank you, Lila, so much."

The women went to Olivia's bike. "Where's your bike? Did you walk here?" asked Olivia.

"I did. Actually, I ran."

"We do need to talk, Amanda. You scared Cliff. Both of us." She remembered and pulled out her phone. "And Chef." She texted him quickly that she'd found Amanda. All was well. She turned back to Amanda. "Come with me. We'll find a bench over there, on the playground."

Once they'd settled, Olivia started. "What happened? Amanda, tell me everything."

The story was largely what Cliff had shared. Her dad had betrayed her. Again. "Screwed" was the word she used. He had not remitted tuition for the fall term. The money was hers per the will, to be saved for her college education upon the sale of her grandmother's farm. He must have spent it. "No surprise," she'd said.

She confessed she'd spent time with Cliff asking about Arch Rock, asking about island plants. And nightshade, in particular.

"Nightshade? What is it?"

"It's not good. Poisonous. It's called belladonna. It kinda looks like honeysuckle, but not. It's dangerous. Deadly if you eat it."

"Amanda. This is terrible, scary, what you're telling me."

"I know," she shook her head. "I wasn't really thinking I'd do something, but I wanted to know my options. All of them. You know?"

"Those are some extreme options. There are others. Better ones."

"I know. Once I started to look for Lila—in the Village—I think I knew that." Amanda went on to describe finding Lila, discovering Danny there, and then spending more than an hour in the woman's home.

"She had a picture of Jesus over the fireplace."

"She did?"

"Oh, yeah, I think so. He had a crown around his head, like in paintings. And there were wounds on his hands, but he wasn't pale and sad-looking. He was brown and wearing knee-high moccasins and beads and a cross. Lila said he was called 'Ojibwe Christ.'" She told Olivia more about Lila and the island people. Most were Ojibwe or Ottawa and French and English too. She had descended from the Bear Clan. "She's like a minister and a healer, sort of.

"So, I asked her about Arch Rock and if it was true that someone died there. She said it was the worst kind of tragedy. Her people believe that Arch Rock is where the 'Great Creator blew the breath of life into the earth.' That's why someone dying there is the worst kind of sadness."

"I'd never heard that before, about Arch Rock. That's beautiful. And tragic."

"When I asked her about nightshade, she stopped me. Right there. Stopped me. She said she knew I was carrying life. In me." She shook her head. "Freaked me out. I don't know how she knew, but she did."

Olivia was just as surprised. "What else did she say?"

"She just talked about life and how they believe it's all sacred, but she looked at me and said I looked young and might be afraid. She knew that, too."

"Hmm, I like her more and more."

"So we talked some more. She reminded me a little of my grandma. I didn't expect that. And then she gave me this." She handed Olivia the small hoop with its woven string, beads, and feathers. Olivia held it in front of them to study it while Amanda explained. "It's called a dream catcher. There's some story about the spider woman who protects children. She can't reach everyone all at once, so the mothers and grandmothers make these." She ran a finger through the feathers that were hanging from the hoop. "It catches all the bad dreams and there, in the center," she pointed to it, "that's where the good dreams come in. Only good dreams and good thoughts can come through."

"I like that." They both studied it a little longer.

"You hang it over a baby's crib."

"Ahh, I see." Olivia paused and a few moments passed. "So, are you thinking about that now? A baby's crib?"

"I'm not sure. I think so. Maybe? I mean, what am I supposed to do?" She dropped a hand to her belly.

Olivia handed the dream catcher back and put an arm around Amanda's shoulders. "Oh, honey, I wish I could answer that for you." They sat in silence for a while.

"You know, I lost a baby once. A long time ago. She'd be about sixteen right now."

"Oh." She turned her head to look at Olivia. "I'm sorry."

"Yeah, me too. Even now. That's the thing. Once you have something living inside you, something that could be someone, when that dies… it's hard to explain. But the loss and the grief, they follow you. Usually you can keep the sadness away but it doesn't leave. It lives with you." She pulled Amanda closer. "I cannot make this decision for you, but I don't want you to live with the sadness like I have. Or any of the guilt."

"Guilt? Why would you have guilt?"

"I have guilt over the work I did, the pace I kept. I don't know if that would have made a difference. The doctors said not. No way. But I always feel I did something wrong—to harm the baby. I think Nate might think that too."

"Did he say that?"

"Oh no. And I can't ask. We don't talk about those things. But that's why I focused on Luke, and on Nate. Like it was my job, and what was expected of me after we lost the baby. That worked until it ended."

"What happened then?" Amanda asked in a quiet voice.

After a long pause Olivia answered, "And then I ended up here."

Olivia shifted and turned toward Amanda. "Now, about you. I will support you. Whatever decision you make. I just want you to know that you have a choice. Real options. Options we can talk about. And we can help you. Nate and I. Okay?" She gave the girl one last squeeze and then pulled her arm away. Patting Amanda's knee, she said, "Let's get you home."

Chapter 46

Days later, gathered there at Lilac Cottage, Amanda, Cliff, and Sean sat around the table in the dining room with muraled walls partly finished in color, the rest sketched in pencil. Having cleared the air through a series of texts, and a face-to-face conversation, Olivia and Sean had reestablished a friendship at a safer distance and in the company of others.

"Mrs. Nash, this pasta of yours is pretty good. Better than fair. I might have let the brown butter go a little further. Crisp the sage a little more."

"What? Pretty good? It's spectacular!" interrupted Cliff. "I haven't had something like this since Sorrento, easily a decade ago."

"Sorrento?" Amanda looked at Cliff as she threw a piece of crusty bread at Chef, which he caught. "Seriously, Chef. You can be such a jerk. Lovable, but a jerk sometimes."

Sean threw it back. "I just don't want her gunning for my job. I'd have to work under Cliff-o here, painting daisies or daffodils or whatever the hell he's painting on these walls."

They looked at the mural Cliff had been painting on the walls, depicting the island's transformation from spring to fall. Cliff answered, "You're fired already. Daffodils don't bloom in June. You know better than that."

"All right. Stop, all of you." Olivia tried to give a stern look at everyone, then threw a piece of bread at Sean's head.

Before he could return fire, Olivia was up and into the kitchen. Amanda followed a few moments later, pasta platter in hand, and almost ran into Olivia with head down, hands on her hips.

"Olivia? Are you okay?"

Olivia lifted her head. "I'm fine." She looked toward the dining room and said, "I used to have this."

"This? In there?"

Olivia nodded.

"You mean you had a pregnant college student, an old man with a bum knee, and a chef, big-headed as hell?"

Olivia raised an eyebrow.

"Kidding. He's not that bad. Sometimes. But still he can be a real… you had *this*?"

"Not this exactly. But I had the dinners. The chaos. And laughter. I had that."

"When you had your son and husband." A quiet settled around them. "I bet you miss them."

"I think so. Well, yes, *of course* I miss them. They were everything to me. The reason I got out of bed every morning. But now, it's been weeks without them, and sure, I miss them, but I think I miss who I was when I was with them. Taking care of them. You know?" Amanda shook her head no. Of course, she couldn't understand. Not this side of motherhood.

Amanda took a step closer. "All I know is that Luke and Nate were pretty lucky to have you. And maybe they don't need you now the way I do—the way we do. Maybe you were sent to us." She looked at her belly, a bulge barely visible on her slight frame. "You know, for now. Not forever. Just for now."

"Olivia!" Sean called from the other room. Before Olivia and Amanda could move, Sean rushed into the kitchen, his phone in his outstretched hand. "It's for you."

Olivia took his phone and said an uncertain hello.

"Livy, it's me."

"Ceci, how, why in the world are you calling me on Sean's…"

"No time for that. I got his number from the restaurant. Why don't you ever answer your phone? Really, Liv! Anyway, there's been an accident. It's Luke. They couldn't find you. They called Nate. He called me. He thought you were at an event, catering. And I told him he was right. You've got to go. Get off that damn island."

"Ceci, stop. Slow down."

Cliff, with his cane, joined them in the kitchen. Amanda, overhearing the word "accident," reached for Olivia's hand.

"Tell me what you know."

"Luke was in a car accident. It rolled. He was with someone. They think he was driving. He was drunk."

"That's not possible, Ceci. That can't be," she said, shaking her head. "He's at camp, no car. He doesn't drink."

"No time for that now. He's at a trauma center in Traverse City. Munson. I'm on my way. I'll get there before you and before Nate, too. I was on my way home from Petoskey when Nate called." After another breath, she continued. "This is where it falls apart, Liv. I don't know what you're going to tell them. But you better figure it out." The call ended and Olivia stood motionless.

"Luke's been in an accident. He's been taken to a hospital in Traverse City. I have to get there. I don't know how." Olivia put a hand to her mouth and stood, unmoving, just shaking her head. It wasn't possible. Was it?

Sean took his phone from her hand. "Give me a few minutes to make some calls. I'll get you there." Sean was already punching in numbers as he walked out of the kitchen, through the living room, and onto the porch.

The door slammed, snuffing out the evening's magic.

Amanda cleared the table. Cliff hobbled to the living room and sat, head bowed. Olivia fished her phone out of her purse slung over the kitchen door's handle. She'd missed three calls from Nate and five from Ceci. And there were texts.

Where are you? from Nate.

Call me! from Ceci.

Mrs. Nash, please call camp at this number. Immediately. That text felt like a knife to her heart.

Oh my God, what have I done? And then her rational self took over: *Stop it. Even if you were in Chicago, you couldn't have prevented this. You can get there faster from here. Go. Now.*

She left the kitchen with her phone and walked toward Sean who was coming in from the porch.

He put an arm out to pull her to himself. "Amanda, would you get Olivia's purse. She'll need her ID. Grab her a jacket or sweater too." He moved Olivia from his chest and turned her to face him. His hands gripped her shoulders, and he looked her in the eye. In a steady, even voice he said, "The Moshers keep a plane here when they're on the island. We're in luck. They're here and my aunt is calling in a favor."

Cliff's head lifted at that. Olivia looked at Sean without understanding.

"We're flying to Traverse City, but first we've got to bike to the airport. Are your shoes okay for that?"

"Yes," she said, looking down at her red sneakers, "but, I don't understand."

"You don't have to. I'll be with you. I'll explain later."

Amanda rushed forward and handed Olivia's purse and sweatshirt to Sean.

"Jake's meeting us. He's a pilot and a friend. Come on, let's go." Taking Olivia by the hand, he led her to the bikes at the bottom of the stairs. In a stupor, Olivia settled on her bike and followed him.

Chapter 47

Olivia said nothing on the flight to Traverse City. Lost in her thoughts and prayers, she let Sean explain what he knew to his friend, Jake. An Uber met them at the airport. A short time later, they entered the Munson Medical Center. When they were led back into the emergency department, Olivia saw dozens of kids in the waiting room. Silent. Silent and watching them pass. A white-coated woman walked toward them.

"Mrs. Nash? Mr. Nash? I'm Dr. Woodhouse."

"Yes. No. *Yes*, I'm Mrs. Nash. He's Chef. Sean. Sean Branagan. He's only a friend." Olivia glanced at him. "A good friend." Looking back to the doctor, she croaked, "Where's Luke? Is he? Is he…?"

"He's going to be okay." She put a hand on Olivia's shaking forearm. "They both are." She started walking them back to a curtained bay. "We'll move them to a room eventually. The CT scan didn't show any internal bleeding, but he had a severed artery and has lost a lot of blood. Thankfully his friend Ben found it and applied pressure until help came. We've ordered a transfusion but wanted your permission to begin that."

Arriving in front of the bay, Dr. Woodhouse swept the curtain aside and Olivia rushed forward.

Three steps in, she looked at the sleeping boy in the bed. "This isn't him." In a loud whisper she added, "This isn't Luke."

"But Mrs. Nash, there is an ID." The doctor stepped to the counter opposite the bed and handed her the license. "This was in his wallet. In his jeans' pocket."

"This is his license but this boy, he isn't Luke. Where is my son? Where is he?"

Dr. Woodhouse paused, then pulled Olivia by the arm, speaking quietly, "This can happen in accidents. Sometimes identities are confused." She stopped their group of three at the next bay and opened the curtain to a dim room.

"Luke! Oh, God, Luke." She rushed to the bed and put a light hand to his head. She kissed his brow. "Oh Luke." Her tears were falling on his face.

"Mom? Mom. Stop. I'm okay. I'm okay," he repeated in a groggy-sounding voice. She pulled back enough to look at him. A bruise was starting to show around one swollen eye.

"Mrs. Nash," Dr. Woodhouse approached the bed. "Obviously this is Luke. Ben was in the car with him. So, Luke," she looked at him. "You were the driver?"

"I was. I had… I mean Ben had too much to drink. I gave him my license so he could get a beer. Some guys at the bar… they started buying and I don't know." He raised a hand, grimaced, and wiped the tears that were forming in the corners. "He had too much. I had one. Only one and I was okay. I swear. I was okay enough to drive. A truck crossed the line. I saw it. I tried. I tried. I don't know what happened. We rolled, I think. After, I found Ben. There was blood." At this, he broke into a sob. "So much blood. Is he? Is he alive?"

"Luke, yes, Ben is alive," the doctor answered. "He's lost a lot of blood, but he'll be fine."

"I tried to stop it, but I was so tired. I was so tired. I don't remember." He went still, tears streaming down his face.

"Luke," the doctor continued. "You need to rest. We've stabilized your right arm. We'll cast it if needed once we have another look. You've got stitches on your thigh, and a few other places where you were cut by glass."

He shrugged. "I don't feel anything."

"Not yet, but you will," she continued. "For now, rest. You're not going anywhere. Sometime later the police will want to hear what happened, but, for now, sleep. You've been through a lot. And you saved your friend's life. That's enough for one night." Dr. Woodhouse looked at Olivia and Sean and motioned them to the doorway.

Outside the bay, in front of a long counter that was the hub, Olivia asked about the driver of the truck. "Is he here? Is he all right? Was there anyone else?"

Dr. Woodhouse drew her lips in a thin line before she answered. "Just a driver. I shouldn't say, but I imagine he'll be charged with a DUI. He's not in great shape. No seat belt, but he'll recover."

Olivia nodded and closed her eyes. Sean put his arm over her shoulders. Dr. Woodhouse invited them to the waiting area where she said there were some semi-comfortable chairs. "At this hour, you may just want to stay." Olivia looked at the clock on the wall, digital numbers in red. It glowed 3:45 a.m. "At six or so I expect the police will be in for a report. I'm sorry. For all of you."

Chapter 48

Olivia and Sean moved toward the packed waiting room. In every chair, on semicircular sofas, even on the floor were summer-tanned teenagers in sweatshirts and jeans, sleeping, reading, or talking quietly. They grew quiet when Olivia and Sean entered the room. A man moved toward her. Olivia recognized the camp director.

"Josh, hello," she reached her hand to meet his. "I'm so sorry. So, so sorry. Thank you for being here. Are these…?" she looked right and left, around the room.

"They are. Camp's empty right now. They've been here all night. Holding vigil. Playing euchre."

"But the campers. Who's with them?"

"We've got a few days' break. Changeover. The next group comes in day after tomorrow."

"Of course. Luke told me. I remember now."

Josh looked at Sean. "Mr. Nash? I'm sorry to meet you in these circumstances."

"Nice to meet you," Sean gripped Josh's hand in his. "I'm not Nate Nash. My name is Sean. I'm just the means of transportation."

"He's a friend. A good friend," corrected Olivia. "My husband will be here later, and my sister, too." Olivia scanned the room. "In fact, I'm surprised she's not here, somewhere."

"If her name's Ceci she's been here for hours, hanging out with the kids. She just left. She said she was going to hunt down some food. Bagels and coffee. Or M&M's and beef jerky, depending."

"That's her. That's my sister, Ceci."

"We don't know much of anything," said Josh. "Ben's parents aren't here yet. The kids are worried. Is he…? Is Luke all right?"

Olivia nodded. "He is. Luke's banged up. Possibly a broken arm, some stitches, a few bruises. The worst of it is I think he's heartsick and embarrassed and worried about Ben most of all."

"I'm sure of that."

"The doctor said Ben has lost a lot of blood, but otherwise he's okay too. Thank God. She's waiting on his parents to arrive to do anything more." Olivia told him there'd been another driver. A driver who'd crossed the center line and hit their car.

Josh told them about the bar they'd been to before the accident. "Nice owners. Good people. It's pretty typical for summer staff to wander in between camp weeks. Games are on every TV. They serve great bar food. Some locals consider it a challenge to get these kids to drink. Most kids can handle saying no." He clearly had no ill will toward the bar or its usual customers. "A lot of the time they'll actually pick up the tab. For burgers and fries, and the occasional beer."

They talked a few more minutes. Olivia asked about the car, whose it was and what she could do to make amends. Josh told her not to worry about that now. "It's only a car and hardly important." Josh asked if he could give Luke and Ben's friends an update and Olivia agreed.

"When Luke's awake again, I'll tell him you're all here."

"Mrs. Nash?" someone called from the registration desk. "Would this be a good time to get some information?"

They thanked Josh. Olivia and Sean walked toward the desk and the woman led them to an office beyond the desk. Olivia took a seat inside and Sean excused himself and said he'd wait just outside the door.

By the time the paperwork was completed, and Olivia stepped out of the office, Ceci appeared with carafes of coffee in cardboard dispensers, and bags and bags of what must have been donuts, bagels, pastries, and everything needed to serve it. She must have found a twenty-four-hour truck stop because she looked like a one-woman breakfast buffet. The kids took the goods from Ceci, and Olivia moved toward her. She walked into Ceci's waiting arms, crumbling in her embrace.

"Oh Ceece. Thank you. I've made such a mess of things."

"Stop. Just stop," Ceci whispered into her ear. "You haven't done anything. You couldn't have prevented this accident. Not from Chicago or Montreal or anywhere else." She pulled away to look at Olivia. "Shit happens and sometimes miracles do, too."

Just then Sean approached.

"You brought your chef? Surprising. Cheeky."

"No, Ceece, it's not like that. He brought me here. By private plane."

He put a hand on Olivia's back. "Hate to interrupt you two, but Dr. Woodhouse said Luke wants to see you—and his aunt."

The sisters started toward the ED doors. Olivia stopped, turned back, and motioned to Sean. "Well, come on. Come with us."

The trio entered Luke's room quietly. Dr. Woodhouse left them. Luke opened his eyes. "Did I fall asleep?"

"You did. Sleep all you want, Bud. We're not going anywhere."

"Aunt C, hi." He lifted a left hand in a weak wave.

"Hey Lukers. You did some good work. I hear you helped saved your friend's life."

"Aunt Ceci, no. He shouldn't—we shouldn't have been there. It's my fault. All my fault."

"Luke, stop," Olivia interrupted. "Don't do this to yourself. Shit happens." His eyes widened. Ceci approved. Sean had his back to Luke's bed, looking at his phone.

"Dad?"

Sean turned around.

"Not Dad," Luke said. "Sorry, are you…?" And then, "Who are you?"

"I'm Sean. Your mom works with, I mean, we're friends. I'm her chauffeur."

"Cool." Had he been more alert, he might not have accepted that so easily. Just then, Nate walked into the room with Landon following steps behind.

"Luke! Thank God." He rushed to the bed, leaned over the rail, and kissed his son's head. Pulling back a little, he took a breath. "Luke. You scared me, scared us. Scared the hell out of all of us." Nate stood up fully and looked around the room. He saw Olivia, moved around the bed toward her, and hugged her. He saw Ceci. "Ceci, thank you."

Nate looked at Sean. "And you are?"

Sean put out his hand, "I'm Sean. Sean Branagan, chef at the Iroquois." Nate took that news like it was no surprise at all. Olivia felt a little relief.

"Liv, where's your car? I didn't see it. How'd you get here so fast?"

"I flew. Well, Sean flew us, I mean, actually Jake. Sean's friend. Jake's a pilot."

"From Chicago? From a catering thing? I'm not following." Nate looked tired. His typically starched button-down shirt was rumpled. His face was shadowed with beard stubble and his hair looked like he'd run his fingers through it a few dozen times.

"Actually, it *is* a catering gig sort of, on Mackinac Island."

"Mackinac Island. Michigan?"

"Yes, Nate, that's… uh, yes, that's right. I've been working there."

"Excuse me, working *where*?" He looked confused.

"Here, I mean there. The island."

"On Mackinac Island? In Michigan?" he asked for a second time. "Working? For how long?"

Olivia squinted and pursed her lips, summoning a reply. "For… um…" Silent, everyone awaited her reply. "Well, let me see." Her eyes shot up to the ceiling. "Actually, gosh, since June."

"I'm sorry. Did you say *June*?"

She nodded.

"So, you've been on Mackinac Island, in Michigan, since June." He said it matter-of-factly, like a statement. A ludicrous statement to her ears, but still a statement.

"Yes, I have. I guess that's right." She nodded again. "Yes, since June. Wow, time flies, doesn't it?"

"*Living* there? On Mackinac Island." He spoke in a louder voice.

Olivia pointed to the door. "Can we continue…?"

She looked at their son in his bed, but Nate continued.

"Living with *this guy*? Holy *shit*, Olivia." He shook his head like he was coming out of a dream. He ran his hand through his hair. Again.

"No, I am most definitely *not* living with *this guy*. We're coworkers."

"You work together. Catering?" Still louder.

"Please, Nate, keep your voice down." Olivia shook her head no. "No, not so much. We work at the *restaurant*. He's the chef. I wait tables. Well, not now but I used to. Can we talk about this later? It's kind of a long story." Olivia started wringing her hands.

At that, Ceci jumped in. Nate must have gotten under her skin just enough. "May I point out the other elephant? Nate, who's with *you*?"

Landon stepped out from behind Sean where she'd been hidden from view.

"Me?" she offered quietly. Landon looked like she hadn't lost a minute of sleep. Lipstick in place. Hair pulled back and tied with a silk scarf. Fresh as the dawn. Her arms were wrapped around her waist. Everyone turned their heads to look at her. She gave a small wave with a manicured hand.

"Nate, it appears you have a coworker who travels with you, too." Ceci had a way of speaking truth at inconvenient times. "This is *far* more than I *ever* expected from the two of you."

"For the love of God, Ceci." Nate shook his head in disgust. "Yes, this is Landon McCall. We're colleagues. Friends. She got us here. On her jet."

"Daddy's jet, actually," Landon corrected and then shrugged. "Privilege can be helpful in emergencies."

Everyone was still for a moment. Olivia and Ceci looked at Landon. Nate looked at Sean, and Sean and Landon looked at each other. And the monitor on Luke's IV poll punctuated the silence: Beep. Beep. Buzz. Beep.

"Um, I'm kinda hungry." Luke broke up the standoff.

"I've got you, Luke." Ceci moved to the door. "I wrangled a full breakfast buffet for everyone camped out in the waiting room. I'll get you a platter. Hospital food is horrible and served cold. Which only makes it worse, right?" She looked at the adults gathered around Luke's bed. "Am I right?" They nodded in agreement.

"Aunt C? What do you mean 'everyone'?"

Ceci stepped closer. "I wasn't a fan of this cultish camp you were working at—unpaid, I might add—but these friends of yours, they seem pretty great. And they seem to like you *a lot*. You and your friend. There must be thirty of them out there."

"They're here? Now?"

"The nurses said they've been here all night."

Luke dropped his head. He looked overwhelmed.

"Pardon me," a nurse pulled back the curtain that had encircled them. "Well, there's a lot of you. Could you all move to the waiting area? I need to change an IV bag and we'll be taking this young man to have a closer look at that arm."

With a chorus of "yes, of course, certainly," the group moved toward the door.

One voice, Ceci, could be heard to say, "Follow me. I'm serving breakfast this morning."

"Mom, can you stay?" Not that she had any intention of leaving. Nate was hanging by the door, unsure whether to stay or go.

"Give us a minute, Nate." She patted the hospital bed near Luke's hip. "May I?"

Luke moved inches off center and she perched on the bed while the nurse went about her work. "Oh, honey. Thank God you're okay. And Ben too. You'll both be okay, fine. And the other guy too."

"Mom, you're living on Mackinac Island? Like this whole time?"

A weak "yes" was all she could muster.

"Why didn't you tell me?"

"Luke, I didn't know I was going to be there. I was going to tell you when I visited, but I just couldn't. I didn't want you to worry about Dad and me." When he didn't respond, she continued. "Luke, I think I was afraid to be at home without you and without your dad."

"Afraid? Like someone would break in?"

"No, no. Not that. More like afraid to be in a place where you weren't. Where your dad wasn't. You know?" He nodded that he did, but she suspected he didn't know. He couldn't.

"But Dad didn't know either?" He was getting his facts straight.

"No, and that's something we'll talk about. Luke, we'll be okay. Your dad and I… we need a little time to find our footing. Do you understand?"

He nodded that he did, but again, how could he? Instead, he offered, "It's okay, Mom. I'm glad you're here."

"Listen, when you're discharged, why don't we go back to Mackinac together? Your assignment is up in about a week anyway. I'll take you back to campus afterward. What do you say?"

"That sounds nice, but I really want to go back to camp. I don't want to miss the last session and our last days together. If they'll let me, after this."

"Oh, I think they'll let you. And after that?"

"Then I think Evan and I can drive back to State. I can get my stuff out of storage."

"Without me? Or one of us to take you? To help?"

"Mom," he scolded gently. "I'm a senior, remember? I got this." He brightened a little more. "But maybe take Dad with you. Go back there and show him the stuff me and Aunt C did. Bet he'd like it. It'd be good for you guys. Right? Time… together."

"Yeah, honey. Maybe."

Nate walked back into the room and went to the opposite side of Luke's bed. He brushed the hair off Luke's forehead, leaned in, and kissed him there.

"Luke, I've never been so scared." He reached for Olivia and took her hand. It felt familiar. "Well, there was one other time."

"We're ready for you, Luke." The nurse interrupted. Another nurse approached the bed and lifted the brake levers. "We'll have him back in no time."

Nate and Olivia stepped back and the nurses wheeled the bed, and

Luke, out of the room. They stood there, silent, looking at each other across the space where Luke had been. Nate took a step toward her, all the invitation she needed. Olivia was in his arms, smelled his familiar smell, and remembered that place where her head would rest on his shoulder. They breathed together, in synchrony, like they hadn't in so long.

Olivia pulled back. "You too?" She reached out a hand and wiped his tears with her fingertips.

"Yeah, I guess. So, this is what it feels like when you lose your family. Or close enough."

"Nate, Luke is going to be fine. Maybe a broken bone but that's it."

He nodded and looked at her. "But what about you? I don't know whether I'm angry or crushed. Liv, what the hell? What's going on?"

"With me? Nate, it's not just me. It's you too. What's going on with you? And Landon?"

"Landon? She's a friend. A good one. She's been trying to coach me. To pay attention—more. The flowers?"

"Oh, the flowers. So they were meant for me after all?"

"What do you mean by that?"

"The card read, 'thinking of Landon and smiling.'"

"Landon? It said London. *London.* Liv, are you out of your mind?"

He ran his hand through his hair. He did that when he was frustrated. "I *knew* I should have stuck with 'love, Nate.'" He exhaled and then seemed to have another realization. "But you weren't there to get them, were you?"

"Ah, well, correct. I wasn't. Dick Lowe called Nina and then Nina called me." She felt guilty then. "She sent a photo. They were gorgeous." She reached for his hand. "Thank you. Really."

He gave her a look like he might smile. "So, what do we do now? I've got to…"

"Get back to Montreal."

He nodded.

"I figured. No surprise there."

"Liv, it's not great. I'm not loving it, and I don't like what's happening there."

"Or here."

"No, not that either, honestly." He looked so beaten down, not the hopeful, funny, energetic guy she'd known.

Olivia reached for and hugged him again. "We'll be okay," she whispered. "I have a lot to tell you, Nate. Most of all… that I can't go back. Not to Lake Ellyn."

He pulled away from her at that.

"Not yet anyway."

While they stood there waiting for Luke to return, they chatted, awkwardly. There wasn't time to go into detail, so in broad strokes and carefully, she told Nate about the island, and about Cliff and Amanda, the restaurant, and the cottage she was living in.

"Nate, this hasn't cost us anything. In fact, I've banked forty-seven hundred dollars."

"And twenty-five cents?" So he'd kept his sense of humor. Somewhere, it was there.

"No." She allowed a smile.

"So, really. What now?" he said.

"So now you go back to Montreal and merge a couple of drug companies. Keep working on a cure for Alzheimer's." She sounded like a coach in the locker room at half time. "As for me, I'll go back to the sweetest little cottage you ever saw and get her ready for sale—while caring for a bookstore owner, my old friend, as he heals."

"And that guy, the chef?"

"There is nothing to say about him. We're friends. Like you and Landon, I assume." That seemed adequate if incomplete. "More importantly, I have to go back to help Amanda with whatever comes next."

She answered the question he would likely ask next.

"She's twenty and pregnant. Nate, I—*we*—can't let Amanda walk through pregnancy and into motherhood alone. I signed us up for that without talking to you. That was wrong of me, but not unforgivable, I hope. I have to be there for her."

"We have to, you mean." His expression was inscrutable.

"Ideally, yes, but, I understand if you're not—"

"Excuse us, patient and his good news coming through." In came the nurse with Luke who was out of bed and sitting in a wheelchair. Luke filled them in.

"The radiologist said I'm clear. No damage done, well, except for…" He raised his right arm and showed a black brace that wrapped from forearm to fingers.

The nurse continued, "He'll need to have that reexamined in four weeks. That will be spelled out on his discharge papers. He can come back here…"

"Or I could do it on campus?"

"Yes, you could if that's okay with your parents."

"Well, I'm twenty-one now so—" They all smiled at that. Yup, twenty-one and still completely reliant on his parents for every dime supporting his legal independence. But sure.

"Okay, Luke, that probably works for us." Olivia looked to Nate and he nodded his assent.

Ceci entered the room and stood next to Luke.

"Did I hear that this young man is sprung? I'd like to take him back to camp, if that's okay with you two, maybe stay a couple of days." She tousled Luke's hair. "Your friends were telling me about it. I hear the store is well stocked. I think I should check it out. I am a shopper, after all."

Eventually, and after Luke had given a recounting of the accident to a police officer, the group left the ED treatment area where they met the large group of camp workers in the waiting room. Olivia and Nate spoke briefly with Ben's parents, both kind and understanding, expressing gratitude for Luke and regret for the driver who'd caused the accident. Less than an hour later, the waiting room cleared.

Landon had arranged with the pilot of her father's company plane to make a stop at the Mackinac airport.

"It's on the way, really. We do little stops all the time." As though everyone there knew what it was like to have a private jet at your disposal. Still, it was helpful. Jake, who'd brought Sean and Olivia to Traverse City, was not on call for a return leg home.

The flight was about forty minutes long, ample length for small talk but not much more, especially for passengers more than happy to skirt complicated conversations. Had Ceci been with them Nate would have broken out in a cold sweat. In fairness, so would Olivia.

About an hour later, when Olivia and Sean returned to Lilac Cottage, she stopped him at the porch steps. "Thank you. I will never forget what you did for me. For Luke. Not ever."

"Well, sure. You're welcome." He kicked the stones near the steps like a boy would. "You need to check on Cliffy and Amanda. I need to check on the kitchen and Danny. Make sure he followed through on his promise to me."

"Of course." She was about to hug him when she remembered their agreement. Maybe just this one time. The last time. She lunged at him and wrapped her arms around his shoulders. "Really, thank you."

"Mrs. Nash, I'd do just about anything for you."

Embarrassed now, she tried to reestablish their new normal. "Well then. How about dinner? Cliff and Amanda would want that. Maybe later in the week? Boundaries in place?"

He'd apologized several times already and said a few other times that Olivia, Amanda, and Cliff had become, well, like family. "A strange one, but a family."

She couldn't disagree.

Because she hadn't slept at all the night before, Olivia retreated to her room and fell into a deep sleep. When she awakened, the shadows in her room told her it was late afternoon. She wandered downstairs where Cliff worked on the dining room mural. Amanda, he told her, "was posting record sales and asked to keep the bookstore open an additional two hours. What a find she is, Olivia!"

Olivia agreed. She brewed a cup of tea, grabbed a light blanket, and made her way to the porch.

While sipping her tea and replaying what had happened hours before, a voice from the stairs below interrupted her thoughts.

"Miss Olivia, is that you?"

"It is." *Was that? Sounded like…* "Danny?"

A young man climbed the stairs and stopped awkwardly, turning toward her, his hands behind his back. "Yup. It's me. Danny."

Olivia set down her mug, pushed off the blanket, and stood. "This is a surprise. Can I help you?"

"Um, yeah. Is Amanda here?"

"No, not just now. May I give her a message?"

"No, just give her these." He pulled a bouquet of flowers from behind his back. "They're from my *nookomis*, I mean, grandma. These are from her. For Amanda." He pushed them toward Olivia.

"They're lovely." Olivia took the bouquet of wildflowers and greenery. "Thank you. How kind of Lila. Is she well?"

"Yes, she's fine. Great."

Olivia sniffed the flowers and looked up again at Danny, who'd not moved from his mark. "And something else, too."

"Danny, would you like to sit down?"

"No, ma'am. So, what I want to say… to you… to Amanda is, I'm sorry."

"Sorry?" She shook her head, not understanding. "For?"

"For so much. All of it. You see, I'm back now. Back on track," he clarified. "Sixteen days sober. Chef… he told me you knew. You know, about AA." He looked at his feet, seeming uncomfortable with his admission.

"He did mention that he wanted to help you, Danny. I didn't know the rest. He also said that you have enormous talent. You could be a chef one day yourself. A great one."

He flashed a grin that faded as quickly as it appeared. "Yeah, well, I don't know about that. When the restaurant closes, and the tourists are gone, there's not much here for me. I think that's why I started. Drinking, I mean."

"And you've never left the island in the offseason? To take another job?"

"Nope. Can't do that. My grandmother, she relies on me. And I've got nowhere to go."

"I see."

A long silence fell between them. This was a different Danny than the one she'd known of late.

"I want to, though." He interrupted her thoughts. "You know, go to culinary school, learn. One day maybe." He rose up on his toes and rocked back again to his heels. "So, that's it. Would you tell Amanda I'm sorry? And maybe explain? Everything?"

"Of course. Maybe one day you'll tell her yourself."

"Maybe."

He turned, stepping off the porch to the steps, and stopped. "Miss Olivia?" He looked back at her.

"Yes."

"I'm not so bad. It would mean a lot to me if you thought so, too."

She moved toward him.

"Seeing this Danny, the one before me, I don't think you're bad. Just the opposite. You're honest. And humble. And on a path toward something big. Maybe bigger than you can imagine right now."

"Aww, shii… take mushrooms, Miss Olivia." He smiled broadly and hung his head, teasing her like he had many times before in the kitchen—before what she now understood had been his relapse.

"Well, son of a biscuit, Danny. There's that sense of humor of yours. Don't lose that."

"I won't. Promise." He took two stairs at a time to land on the stoop below.

"Danny," she called after him, and he turned back.

"Keep going. I hope you become chef de cuisine one day. Maybe at the Carriage House."

He laughed. "Okay. Now you sound like *you've* been drinking. If I do, would you wait tables?"

Olivia smiled at the impossibility of that, waiting tables. He waved and walked toward the trees, in the direction of the Village.

Olivia inhaled the scent of the flowers again and whispered, "Go get 'em, Danny."

Chapter 49

The dinner arranged after Luke's accident was followed by others in early September, which had arrived with all its charms. The island staged its finale in the weeks after Labor Day. Warm, sunny days showcased leaves pulsating in yellow, red, and orange. The water reflected the saturated blue of the skies in ripples to the shore.

Sunsets came earlier and the nights grew cool, even mitten-worthy cold, but the island didn't doze off into winter hibernation. Hardly. Freighter traffic seemed heavier in September as if the vessels were hurrying to deliver their loads before the shipping lanes froze. The smallest animals on Mackinac seemed frenzied to stow their hauls, and the largest, the island's horses, became fewer as teams of them departed via ferry transport to their winter homes. What had slowed was the flow of tourists. The deep discounts at Main Street shops attested to that. Most tourists came on the weekends. The rest of the time the island was owned again by its residents and employees who hung on to the end. Autumn on Mackinac sparkled with bursts of energy matched by slow, peaceful nights for those living there and lucky ones able to stay on until the season was in the books.

After Luke's accident, Olivia spoke with Nate more regularly. At first, three times a week. She told him more about the cottage and her part-time painting gig at the Iroquois. She told him about Frankie and how the Lilac Cottage's owner sometimes felt like a mother to her. Strange, that. She'd been with Amanda back to Dr. Sam. While she could still decide differently (though that window was closing), Amanda had thought she might carry the baby to term. The trauma of how she became pregnant was off-limits. For now. Amanda didn't want to deal with that. Not now, she'd said. But adoption was a real possibility and college, well, that also was back on the table.

She told Nate about the dinner they'd had in the cottage after Amanda had frightened them, days before Luke's accident. Remembering it, she told Nate that Cliff said he had an apology to offer.

"Indeed I do," he'd said. "Amanda, you need not worry about tuition for your final year."

"Oh, but, it could be only a semester. I have enough credits, I think. I could graduate early in December. And then, probably, have the baby. Or maybe even wait a year."

After a moment, it seemed to dawn on her.

"Cliff, what? Why wouldn't I worry?"

"Young lady, you've mentioned having a seminar or two in your major, English, have you not?"

"Well yeah, a few in the house."

"Yes! Exactly. The house—the Clifton House for English Studies?"

"Yes…" She was thinking about that. "Clifton?"

"Hmm, precisely so. Named for me, I'm embarrassed to say."

"For *you*?" Amanda and Olivia asked in unison.

"Indeed. I was a long-tenured professor there, before retirement. My family and other donors endowed the house and a professorship."

"But, Cliff… are you?" Amanda asked.

"Well, I am called Cliff. My given name is Reginald Augustus Clifton. A mouthful. I prefer just 'Cliff.'"

"Reginald Augustus?" she spat out. "Reginald Augustus? What kind of name is that? No wonder you like Cliff. But wait, wait a minute."

She got up and moved around the cottage, looking at paintings in various places. "So all of these old ones, the ones signed RAC. These *are* all you."

"They are."

"And you taught at Knox?" She'd walked to him and stood over him. "You never told me."

"Or me," Olivia added.

"Why?" Amanda had looked hurt that he would have withheld that from her, especially with her running the bookstore.

Cliff said he feared the nature of their friendship might change if Amanda knew he was so closely connected to Knox College. But now, that connection was helpful. He could assure her that scholarship or not, the Clifton resources would be available to her, as much as she should require.

"Oh, and something else fun to report, Nate," Olivia said. Weeks earlier, Amanda had come up with an idea for Cliff, a way for him to use his skills and pass time until his knee surgery. And what an idea. Frankie had thought so too. Cliff was painting a mural on the dining room walls, one that swept from lilac season on the left wall, around to the summer season with hollyhocks and other perennials painted in full bloom on the back wall. The mural wrapped into the fall season with the right wall painted in the colors of the island in autumn. He hadn't finished it, but he would before long.

Luke had made it back to campus. His arm had healed, his bruises faded. He'd had four weeks of classes already and was doing well. He seemed satisfied that his mom and dad would be returning to Lake Ellyn, and life would continue as it always had been. For him, anyway.

It was a lot of news to share and digest, especially at first. Nate had mostly listened. He'd asked a few clarifying questions but commented on little. Was he reading emails while he listened? Maybe. She wasn't entirely sure.

For Nate's part, the merger had become increasingly complex with certain large-block shareholders organizing to oppose it. The annual meeting was approaching in mid-October which added more stress than ever. Because of that meeting, she thought (and on occasion doubted) their calls had become less frequent. She wondered again about Landon. She hadn't been able to ask Nate about the conversation she'd had earlier in the summer with Landon. While he was in the shower. But then she'd had an encounter in a shower that she was unwilling to talk about. Sometime. If they worked all this out. Sometime. Or not. Was there anything to be gained by that?

She had posed the question to Frankie because her counsel had become so valuable. Their correspondence, unlike her conversations with Nate, had become frequent and more candid—maybe because time was running out. The season's close was at hand. Frankie had no answer to this particular question.

Instead, once, she'd asked Olivia if she remembered the butterflies she'd felt when she first met and fell for Nate. In her antiquated language, Frankie wrote about the butterfly feelings she'd had for her first love and, later, for her husband, Jack. She'd written how other urgencies and preoccupations had created a separateness in their lives, tearing at the small holes in the net meant to keep the butterfly feelings. *Those feelings of first love are at risk of escaping the net if the holes get larger. Tend the net,* she'd written. *Those feelings, once gone, won't return easily. Tend the net, Dear.*

Oh Frankie, I'm trying. It's hard when your husband is so far away and maybe too far to return in the way he once had. To what they once had.

Aside from that sadness which she was usually able to shelve for another day, Olivia enjoyed the easier pace and long, late dinners with Amanda and Cliff, and sometimes Sean, when they finished their days' work. They had deeper conversations maybe because they were aware that their time together was coming to a close.

Amanda seemed increasingly curious about Cliff and his past. What about the woman in the painting? The one on the mantel? Amanda had asked once, but he offered no answer. At one dinner, she tried again. Looking again at the teasing woman on the canvas, she asked Cliff if he'd ever married. No, he had not. She tried again. "But Cliff, have you ever been in love?" She took a bite of her dinner. Her appetite had been growing along with her belly.

He seemed to consider her question and finally, in Cliff-style, answered. "Oh Amanda, 'the book of love is long and boring, and written so long ago. Full of flowers and heart-shaped boxes and things we're all too young to know.'"

"Cliff, you're *so* weird sometimes." She swallowed and shook her head.

"That was Peter Gabriel, by the way. Not a poet. Genesis, if you're familiar."

Amanda threw her head back in exaggerated frustration. "The Bible! Whatever. But hang on…" She looked at him with eyes wide in sudden realization. "Cliff, for real. Were you ever in love?" She looked again at the painting.

He paused a moment, seeming to study the wood grain on the table as his hand moved over it. He raised his head. "I was. Once. Long ago. Amanda," he spoke only to her, but Olivia and Sean were hanging on his every word, "there are so many kinds of love and characters to fall in love with. I meet them all the time. Here, on this island. And in my bookstore. You, for example." He looked around the table, "And you. And you. You're all characters I've come to love." His gaze settled on her again. "Amanda, the best love of all isn't necessarily romantic love."

"But her? Did you love *her*?" Amanda looked at the painting and waited for more, but Cliff wasn't forthcoming.

"I think you're not telling." Amanda shrugged. "That's cool. I just wondered." She got up and took her plate and his into the kitchen.

He did continue, eventually, after Amanda was out of earshot.

Only Olivia and Sean heard him say, "Some loves you don't find twice."

Chapter 50

The first week of October Frankie emailed Olivia to say a party had contacted her with interest in the cottage. She had shared a few photos which had heightened the prospective buyer's eagerness to see it. Frankie suggested a date for a walk-through, the following Sunday at two-thirty. Could Olivia arrange that and be there? Frankie hoped Olivia might be available to answer questions on recent changes in its décor.

Frankie would plan to be there too. *It is high time to see, in person, your handiwork restoring Lilac Cottage to her former glory.* Parenthetically she added, *And to price her fairly. We're not giving Lilac Cottage away, are we?*

That threw Olivia into high gear for the next week, cleaning, touching up paint where needed, organizing the kitchen shelves to display cottage pretties, carefully curated. Clutter's a deal killer. Cliff continued on his dining room mural. He had just turned the corner to the third and final wall, now painting in a palette of brilliant fall colors.

That Sunday, Olivia took a break from hand-washing the floors. She walked to the dining room and stood a few feet behind Cliff for a long while. "This is captivating. I'm in awe."

He lifted his readers from his nose and looked over his shoulder. "It's been a joy for me. A delight. I couldn't sit around all day awaiting my knee surgery. This is a most pleasant distraction." He replaced his glasses and turned back to his work. "Your appreciation is my fuel."

"I expect to keep your tank full. Your gift is extraordinary. And to think you taught literature and not art."

"Same thing," he said to the wall, his nose inches from it. "Just a different way to paint a picture."

"I suppose. So, back to these floors. Two-thirty will be here fast. And, Cliff, of course you'll stay." It was a statement, not a question.

"I won't make it far if I have to run." He chuckled. "I'll be here and out of the way. I won't interfere with a potential sale, though it does sadden me a bit. I've always loved this cottage."

She'd been halfway across the living room when she heard that. "I'm sorry, Cliff, did you say you've always loved this cottage? How's that?"

"Oh, my dear, for one, if you've lived on the island for as many summers as I have, you become familiar with its charming homes."

"Is that all?" She wasn't convinced.

He seemed focused on his brushstrokes. "I suppose I could share that I'd spent some time here eons ago when I was a much younger man."

He couldn't see Olivia's eyebrows, raised at that. Still working, he tilted his head to the right, in the direction of the fireplace, and the painting of the woman hanging above. "Her too. She belongs here." He kept at his work. "Let's not watch paint dry. We both have work to do."

Lecture over. Class dismissed. But what did he mean by *that*?

They continued their work. Olivia had everything polished and sparkling by two o'clock when she received a text from Sean: Frankie asked me to text you that she and the buyer are going to be late. Six o'clock.

She texted back: Six? That's late. And why are you texting for Frankie? She received no reply. He must have been in the midst of dinner service prep. Six? So late. Amanda will be back by then from the bookstore. The setting sun would cast the cottage in shadows. *Not ideal*, she thought, annoyed. *But it's not my call. I'm just the caretaker.*

She heard nothing more from Sean the rest of the afternoon. Cliff tidied his workspace and Olivia made soup and brownies so the cottage smelled like a home. For someone else. She welcomed Amanda when she came through the door after the store's five-thirty close. "Hang your jacket and keep your room clean, for now, please. The buyer was delayed. Should be here soon."

Olivia was still in the kitchen when she heard Sean talking to Cliff. And another, familiar voice. She moved to the living room. "Sean…" The voice. That voice. "Mrs. B?" She looked from Sean to Cliff, who'd just extended a hand to the small woman. She looked again. "Mrs. B," she repeated.

"Yes, dear. Good evening. Call me Frankie."

"Mrs. B, I'm sorry. You said?"

"Olivia. I am Frankie." She clarified. "Mary Frances Davidson. Until I married when I became Mary Frances Davidson Branagan."

Olivia recognized that name. Read it. Where? It came to her. "The M. F. Davidson Trust that owns this place? Lilac Cottage?" She looked around her, trying to make sense of it.

"That's correct."

"And I've been writing to you. And you to me, all summer. *You're* Frankie." She was trying to recollect all that she'd shared with Frankie—Mrs. B. Oh, no. All the things. About Nate and Luke. Amanda. Cliff and Chef.

"But wait," Olivia turned to Chef. "You knew. You knew and you didn't tell me." She then looked at Cliff, "And you knew. You knew. Why…??"

Mrs. B, aka Frankie, interrupted her.

"I'm afraid the blame is all mine. I asked that Sean keep my identity from you. I didn't want the work relationship between you and me, nor the friendship between you and Frankie, to be changed, or sullied. It seemed far less complicated to me."

"Less complicated?" Olivia was still in shock seeing this matriarch in her cottage which was actually *her* cottage.

Mrs. B, Frankie, continued. "Of course, things became quite a bit more tenuous when you opened the doors to Amanda and, later, to Cliff, which, by the way, was precisely the right thing to do."

There was a knock on the doorframe.

"Ah, our buyer." Mrs. B—Frankie—started toward the door.

Nate Nash walked through it and into the living room, apologizing. "Delayed flight out of Canada…" Olivia looked at him and the others in the room, clearly confused.

"Nate? What? I'm, well, my head is spinning." She sat on the piano bench.

Chef barked an order. "Get her some water."

Amanda fled the room.

"There's someone coming, Nate," she continued unsteadily, eyeing the four people now studying her. "A buyer for the cottage. You're not…"

"I am," he confirmed. "I'm the buyer. Or I'd like to be."

"Oh, sure." This sounded so preposterous it was almost full-circle logical.

"You told me about Frankie, and after I made a few calls to a real estate agency, it wasn't hard to find her and meet Mrs. Branagan." He put a gentle, affectionate hand to her back, something Olivia would never have done to Mrs. B even though she might have thrown her arms around Frankie. All of a sudden, another picture came to mind.

"Nate, you biked here? From the docks? You rented a bike?" That seemed as ridiculous as everything else.

"Yeah. You never forget. The thing is, Liv," he wrung his hands together, "I have to catch the next ferry. I've got to get back to the airport in Sault Ste. Marie. It was the fastest way here, but I have to be on the earliest flight back. Shareholder meeting Tuesday. I didn't expect the flight delay. I would have been here so much earlier. I wanted to take you to dinner."

He turned his attention to Mrs. B. "I'm delighted to meet you and so sorry I can't stay for a tour. Or to talk about the sale of the cottage."

While he made his apology, she surveyed the room. Chef was giving Nate a side-eye and standing taller than usual. Cliff was studying Mrs. B, and Mrs. B, or Frankie, was listening to Nate, but looking around at all the work done in Lilac Cottage. She walked over to the fireplace and looked up at that painting.

Oh, Olivia thought. *Oh, of course. I see it now.*

Amanda broke into the scene with a glass of water in her hand. She held it out to Olivia while noticing Frankie at the painting. She looked back, wiped the hand on her pant leg, and raised it to shake Nate's hand. "Hi. I'm Amanda."

Nate took her hand in his. "I'm Nate. Nice to meet you."

She looked at Olivia. "Maybe he wants to see the porch. It's a good place. You know, to talk."

The suggestion shook Olivia from her paralysis. Paralysis by surprise. Nate reached for her hand to help her from the piano bench to the porch door. Once outside, the cool air further awakened Olivia to the absurdity she'd left inside—an absurdity that followed her.

"What are you doing here? We didn't talk about this. Why wouldn't you…?"

He interrupted. "I'm buying this for you."

"This?" She looked around. "Lilac Cottage?"

"If you want it."

"If I want it? Nate, it's a cottage, a house. On an island. It's expensive."

"I know. We can do it."

"If I want it?" she repeated.

"Yeah, I want to buy it. Or I want us to buy it. For you. For us."

He was using his hands to explain what his words were failing to do. Obviously. "Olivia, look—this is me, wooing you."

"Wooing me?" She moved to the swing and sat.

"Yes. Would you just let me?" He sat next to her.

"I don't understand. This. Any of this."

"I know. I didn't expect you to." He reached for her hands, clenched in her lap. "Liv, we need a restart."

"Buying a cottage. That's your solution? I don't know, Nate. So much has changed."

"Yeah, I know. That's it. And I get it now. You see, I love all the Olivias."

It dawned on her. "Nate, you've been drinking."

"No. Of course not. Listen, what I mean is… I loved the Olivia I met in college, and the one I married, and the one who gave us kids. Yeah, that's right, Luke and the baby we lost. That *we* lost. Both of us. And I don't know *this* Olivia. This one in front of me. But I'd like to, if you'll let me. If you still want to know me."

"This is… I can't even find words. It's sweet and lovely and strange. Not what I expected. You were so angry. I understand why, but you were so… so remote. And then cold. I never expected this."

"I know, I know." He lifted her hands to kiss the back of them. "I'm sorry. It's been a lot. The merger, being away. A lot."

"Nate, I've made promises here to people I love. I don't expect you to understand or accept that. I don't. But you were so far away."

He took a deep breath and paused, like he was remembering what he'd seen inside. "Okay. We can talk about those. Those promises. Will you think about it? Liv, let's rethink our life. All of it."

He stood, looked at his watch and back down at her. "I feel terrible about this. I do. But I have to leave. I've got to catch that last ferry. Have to. I hate to leave you here. I didn't even see this cottage you've been restoring. But Liv," he gave her a pleading look, "I'm ready to make some changes, but for now I have to be there."

He seemed so sincere. She stood and met his gaze. "Okay," her voice communicated her skepticism. "You need to be there and I need to be *here*. For a while. Cliff. And Amanda…"

"I know." Like he knew an answer to a classroom question, he continued, "and there's that thousand-dollar bonus—the one you get if you stay until the season ends. Right?" He smiled, trying to elicit the same from her. "See, I do listen."

It'd been a long while since she'd been the center of his attention. But surely he knew the bonus wasn't keeping her there. And a cottage. How could that be the answer to what kept them apart? If only it were that simple.

"I really have to go." He took her face in his hands and gave her a kiss, slow and light. Almost polite. He took her by the hand and led her down the stairs with him toward his rented bike. Together, they walked down the walk, the bike between them. "We'll figure this out, Liv. All of it." He leaned the bike on his legs and stretched over it to wrap his arms around her in an appropriately awkward hug.

Sean had come down the steps as Nate pulled away from his wife. He approached without a sound and stood still beside her. Nate mounted the bike, a little unsteadily. He looked over his shoulder, "I'll be back."

With Olivia, Sean watched Nate regain his balance, teetering a little as he began to peddle away from them. "I'm not sure he'll make it to the ferry let alone back to this cottage."

Olivia elbowed him. "Not nice."

Sean watched with her and then whispered, "You know, I'll be here if he doesn't come back."

Olivia stood, still waving though Nate hadn't looked back. When he was out of sight, she dropped her hand and stepped in front of Sean. She took his hands in hers and looked into his eyes. "Thank you. I…" She started to say more and stopped. She squeezed his hands and let them drop.

Turning, she walked away from him. Back to Lilac Cottage, to the people she loved there, and to Mrs. B, now known as Frankie, the person she wanted to know better. Very little seemed certain but for one thing. The season hadn't ended. Not for them. And not for her.

Acknowledgments

When the Season Ends is a work of fiction, truly. However, the novel centers on the Hotel Iroquois and the Carriage House based on a season I spent waiting tables there. Just one season and so long ago. But some places linger in your memories and call you back, as my memories did.

You may recognize the likeness of beloved Islanders and Island establishments. While this novel has been created from my imagination, it has been inspired by Cliff Olson, the first owner of the very real Island Bookstore. He was a listener and became a mentor to me and several other waitresses. The novel was further and foremost inspired by the McIntire family. That summer—until the season ended—I had the blessing of knowing Mr. and Mrs. Mac, Aaron, Mary K., and the employee family (Cindy, Mark, Chef Jim) who *were* the Iroquois. My respect for them and my gratitude to them is profound. The McIntire family taught me the best of what I practice in the art and heart of hospitality. This novel is a tribute to them.

My thanks continue to Jeff who never stopped urging me to "write the book!" That I completed it owes to his encouragement and love. My life is rich because of you, Jeff. Likewise, to Matt and Haley, and their spouses, Jessica and Eric (and grandbaby boys on their way), I understand the heartache of ending a season of motherhood because you have been such a joy to me.

My lifelong cheerleader and sister, Ceci—I mean Chris Schultz.

You make me laugh! And sometimes you make my hands sweat. Everyone should be loved with such loyalty.

To Ron and Janet Windahl, my in-laws and fan base of two, thank you. Jannie was my first reader and her corrections, as a former English teacher, were invaluable.

To my first Friday writers group, or Lila's Writers, my thanks are endless. To Gail Hartman, who painstakingly and kindly noted errors, and Susan McElwain who is as wise as she is smart, your contributions were significant and I am grateful. Leslie McGinnis, Joan Ziska, Jeanne Cherney, and Amy Heath, accept my thanks and love. Lila McGinnis, I hear your voice as I write. I thank God for your generous heart, your whimsy, and your limitless optimism.

My GW friends with whom I've traveled through life and decades of getaways: Betsy Voegele, Cheryl Osborne, PJ Martin, Kim Martin, Cindy Cash, Anne Kerka, and Mary Ellen Voiers—you are sisters of my heart.

And to so many cheerleaders along my way: Libby and Eric Peterson; Terry Swenson, who gave me my first writing assignment; Jody Dreyer, my princess partner who allowed me to take a ride with her on her first book; Jeff Graham who gently chastised me saying, "You have to finish. The characters in your story deserve a chance to live outside your head"; Cleveland Clinic's Dr. Peter Rose and nurses Valerie, Deb, Danielle, and Barb who added chapters to my life; and to dear friends from Young Life and Bay Presbyterian Church, thank you.

Sharon Hegarty, thank you for your reality checks and enthusiasm, and for loving Ceci/Chrissy so well.

Heartfelt thanks to Tamara Tomac, long-time manager of The Island Bookstore, and to Mary Jane Barnwell, its co-owner. Your encouragement was the green light for me to continue this project. Thanks also to the Museum of Ojibwa Culture in St. Ignace for your time and helpful insights.

Noel Skiba, how was it that you considered this a worthwhile adventure? Your artistry is mind-boggling and your talents, a gift from God.

And a final thanks to my Mission Point Press team: Jen Wahi, Misha Neidorfler, Zinzi Robles, Darlene Short, Deirdre Wait, Julie Hazlett, Terese DiMercurio, and Alja Kooistra, what a dream team of female skill, kindness, and encouragement!

"The boundary lines for me have fallen in pleasant places" and they have wrapped all of you within my circle. That is the goodness of God.

About the Author

Stacy Windahl is a graduate of Kenyon College and Baldwin Wallace University with degrees in economics and business administration. She studied gracious hospitality for a season on Mackinac Island. No degree was conferred. Instead, she received a lifelong love of the island.

For twenty-five years, Stacy has been a marketing communications writer for both nonprofit and for-profit organizations. She coauthored a book on the magic of working for The Walt Disney Company from the experience of C-suite executive, Jody Dreyer (*Beyond the Castle: A Guide to Discovering Your Happily Ever After* [Zondervan, 2017]).

Stacy enjoys entertaining, travel (she studied economics and theology for a year in St. Andrews, Scotland), a hot cup of coffee, and a good story, believing every person has a story worth telling.

She, her husband, Jeff, and dog, Winnie, live in her hometown of Bay Village, Ohio, on the Lake Erie shore. Their son and daughter, their spouses, and recent additions to the family make their homes in the Cleveland area as well.

Follow Stacy on Instagram at @stacywindahl or on stacywindahl.com.

About the Cover Illustrator

Noel Skiba is an award-winning impressionistic painter and instructor, and fourth-generation artist. Born and raised in Alpena, Michigan, she began painting at age two. She visited Mackinac Island as a five-year-old Girl Scout and fell in love. Even then, she knew she would find her home on the island.

Noel has won numerous awards, including the Lilac Festival Poster Award (five times), Celebration at the Grand Art Award, Harbor Springs Arts Festival Poster Award, Key West Schooners Wharf Best of Show, Rockford Art in the Park Best of Show, and numerous others. She has also created art for the Murdick's Fudge seasonal and holiday boxes.

Noel's work can be seen in the Ford Presidential Museum and the Michigan House of Representatives. She paints live at the Kentucky Derby and at US monuments. She has traveled the world over from Paris to Mexico and Guatemala to Norway, inspired by God's gifts and capturing moments in time with her paintbrush.

You can catch Noel painting in her waterfront studio and gallery or on location around Mackinac Island, northern Michigan, or in the Florida Keys as she travels with her husband, Tom Kingman, a horseman, trainer, and carpenter. Her son, Paul, raised on the island, is also an artist and travels to the island often with his wife, Jess.

Learn more about Noel and see her work at noelskiba.com.

Scan for
When the Season Ends
Playlist

When the Season Ends
Playlist

1. "Both Sides Now" by Emilia Jones
2. "Breathe Again" by Sara Bareilles
3. "Photograph / Clair de Lune" by Cody Fry
4. "It's Only Life" by Kate Voegele
5. "Sailboat" by Cody Fry, Ben Rector
6. "The Ballad of Donnie Gene" by The Arcadian Wild
7. "Braver Still" (Acoustic) by JJ Heller
8. "In My Life" by The Beatles
9. "Hers" by The Arcadian Wild
10. "Grow as We Go" (feat. Sara Bareilles) by Ben Platt
11. "And So It Goes" by University of London Chamber Choir
12. "Be Okay" (feat. Ellie Holcomb) by Lauren Daigle
13. "Heart in Hand Overture" by Christy Nockels
14. "Girl of My Dreams" by Brandon Heath
15. "I Choose You" by The SteelDrivers
16. "I'm Gonna Be (500 Miles)" by JJ Heller
17. "Remembrance" by YoungMin You
18. "I Am Always Gonna Love You" by Jon McLaughlin
19. "Forever Like That" by Ben Rector
20. "You and I" by Jon McLaughlin
21. "The Best Thing" by Paper Planes
22. "Autumn's Song" by Stephen Day
23. "The Book of Love" by The New Standards
24. "The Luckiest" by Ben Folds
25. "Too Good to Not Believe" by YoungMin You